"PRECIOSA, YOU STRUGGLE AS THOUGH YOU WERE A VIRGIN."

Catherine tried to free herself, too frightened to speak. A strange expression came over Valdivia's face.

"You are too lovely a prize for a debaucher like Don Luis. If you strike out at him he will deal with you harshly. God forgive me, what I am about to do is for both our sakes."

The last words ripped in a soft whisper from his throat as he swept her into his powerful arms. Catherine knew her struggle was futile. Rigid with fear, she looked up into his face, acknowledging his bold handsomeness even as her mind screamed out against what was about to happen. Already she could feel the fire of his body, hear his breathing quicken. He held her as if she were a toy, one hand clamped across her mouth to still her voice. And he was smiling.

"There are worse fates," he whispered.

CAPTAIN'S PLEASURE

by

Mary Ruth Myers

FAWCETT GOLD MEDAL • NEW YORK

For Mother,
a lady of wisdom and courage,
and Daddy,
who rode in the cavalry,
much love and thanks

CAPTAIN'S PLEASURE

Copyright © 1981 Mary Ruth Myers

Published by Fawcett Gold Medal Books, a unit of CBS Publications, the Consumer Publishing Division of CBS Inc.

ISBN: 0-449-14399-6

Printed in the United States of America

First Fawcett Gold Medal printing: April 1981

10   9   8   7   6   5   4   3   2   1

1.

On the deck of the caravelle Catherine Bautista de Caño faced her adversaries, anger flashing in her blue-green eyes.

That she looked on white-haired Don Francisco Berruguete as an adversary no doubt marked her as a sinner. He would soon be among the most respected men in Lima. Still she was furious. His chastisement over finding her on deck unchaperoned had spoiled the most exciting morning of her life, the landing in this strange new land—Peru. Surely he knew that from the time they left Spain, just before Twelfthnight, 1544, both her dueña and her serving girl had been too indisposed to leave their beds.

"As for me, I would lock my daughter in her room had she so little regard for her family's honor!" he thundered.

Catherine stood her ground. In her veins ran the blood of a father who had laid seige to Granada with the Catholic Monarchs.

"Three months is a long time at sea," she said.

"For all of us," piped Don Francisco's daughter Elvira, virtue written on the wax perfection of her saintlike face.

Cáspitas! thought Catherine. The devil take them both. Muffled in the cape which covered her from hair to shoes she looked discreet as any nun. Nothing showed beneath it, not the glossy coil of her black hair nor her dainty waist nor her brocade dress supported by a farthingale and torturous leather corset. Even the white ruff at her throat was hidden. Why, for all the knowledge of the people that she passed she could stand beneath her cape quite naked!

"Perhaps since you're here to bear me company you'll not begrudge me a few breaths more," said Catherine, vexed past prudence. Drawing together brows too slim for fashionable beauty, she turned her oval face toward the sea.

Nearby her on the rail she heard a quiet chuckle. She had forgotten Diego Berruguete, Elvira's brother. Now she flushed to find his gaze fixed on her lips. His face always held an idle languor which, though it cast some question on the firmness of his character, gave him a charm not present in the other Berruguetes.

5

"There, you see? The breach of manners is ours more than Doña Catherine's," he said.

His sister joined them at the rail, letting slip a cloak identical to Catherine's to reveal the costly net of pearls which covered her hair. Although she was only sixteen and three years younger than Catherine she spoke with the conviction of a titled dowager.

"But surely you feel we have a responsibility in coming here?" she suggested to Catherine. "They say the rabble of Peru behave like ruffians. We must set an example by our dignity, don't you agree?"

Her words brought a flicker of smile to Catherine's mouth. From her father, an aged gentleman of Seville, Catherine had learned both dice and cards. When his eyesight failed she had read him books not suited for a lady, including the scandalous *Celestina* with which she had eased his final days, now twelve months past. Would Elvira Berruguete consider those skills deserving of example?

"I assure you, Doña Elvira, I try always to preserve my dignity," she said, resisting laughter.

Aware of mockery, Elvira tossed her head. Her small dark eyes met Catherine's with intense dislike.

"They say Leonor García was one to laugh at convention. That's why her family sent her here to wed a soldier."

Catherine hated lectures and she hated gossip.

"Doña Leonor's family needed money," she replied, emphasizing the doña title which Elvira had so pointedly omitted. She pitied women like Leonor García. What choice had they if their families chose to lend a distinguished name to a man whose New World gold would benefit their families?

"I would enter a convent before I would marry a soldier," sniffed Elvira.

"They both sound equally awful."

Tired of this quarrel Catherine turned to leave, but Don Francisco's smooth words intercepted her.

"I would say, señorita, that you require a husband to teach you manners. Your father failed, it seems. You are very willful."

At criticism of her father Catherine's small, exquisite chin went up. As a woman she was not allowed to answer such rebukes. Instead she met Don Francisco's gaze quite levelly, a tactic she'd found maddening to men, conveying as it did lack of submission.

"And now may I retire?" she asked.

Don Francisco bowed. "As you will, señorita. But I intend to speak to your brother about this matter. It is absurd that he should allow you to fill the role of housekeeper when there are men of means and background in need of wives."

A cold chill settled on Catherine's breast. Only her father's loneliness and her own cajoling had kept her unattached. It had seemed fool's luck that her brother, five years in Peru, had sent for her on their father's death, affording her escape from betrothal to a gouty widower and the prospect of continuing as mistress of herself, exactly as she had been all her life.

"My son will see you to your quarters," said Don Francisco, finally satisfied.

For the first time in her life Catherine knew fear—fear of authority. Her pride forbade her showing it. With a smile she didn't feel she took the arm Diego offered.

"You would be well advised to seek my father's favor," he said as they crossed the deck to narrow stairs. "Your fire is enchanting but he does not like being crossed."

Catherine realized her temper had led her to act unwisely. Don Francisco held an awesome power; his cousin was a member of the Royal Audencia, the powerful court of judges which was soon to arrive with Peru's first viceroy.

"Of course you have an intercessor if you like," said Diego, pausing at the door to her cabin and taking her hand.

From behind long lashes she studied him, the engaging lack of graveness in his face, his yellow silk doublet, his handsome looks.

"Oh? At what price?" she asked lightly.

He laughed his delight.

"One you would not mind paying, I assure you, señorita."

"Really? Will you become a monk then?"

"Yes—and hear your confessions."

Before she could stop him he raised her finger tips to his lips and kissed them. Catherine snatched them away, more startled than offended by this behavior.

"I think, Don Diego, I am better off without an intercessor like you!"

Although she tried to sound severe she could not keep amusement from her voice as she whisked into her cabin.

The port of Callao loomed near when Catherine returned to deck accompanied by her dueña, Doña Teresa, and Ana, a frail little maid. From this harbor sailed ships often bearing as much as eight hundred thousand ducats, treasure from a land that made Spain the envy of all Europe. With growing excitement Catherine watched the activity of barefoot seamen as they ran back and forth preparing ropes and sails.

"Stop fingering your beads," commanded Doña Teresa as Ana for the third time in as many minutes reached toward her rosary. "Your quaking makes a mockery of prayer."

Ana, at fifteen as small and timid as a child, replied in a whisper. "I saw an Indian once—in the square. He—he wore no shirt. . . ."

Catherine smiled at her. "There are no Indians in the city," she said. "Or those who live there will be christian and wear christian clothes."

Ana, fearing Doña Teresa, held her tears.

I have never seen her smile, thought Catherine. Grave as an owl, she is. How have I come here to this foreign place with the women I least favored of my father's household?

She knew the answer of course. Doña Teresa was a relative and thus her dueña, though they were less than fond of one another. Luisa, Catherine's own beloved maid, had had a sweetheart in Seville. So had María. Doña Teresa's woman Isabella had been too old to travel and others had said flatly that they wouldn't come, so here they were with only little Ana to serve them, and her atremble at every shadow.

Catherine sighed. Poor girl. She hoped that Ana would survive, she seemed so young. And then she fell to wondering about what sort of friend she would find in her sister-in-law, Juan's wife.

It had come as a surprise to learn that Juan was married. He was eighteen years Catherine's senior and seven years had passed since he had left Seville. She remembered him as quick to laugh, bored by serious conversation and, her father said, too fond of wine and gaming. He had never written her until the letter begging her to join him, saying he now had a large *encomienda* from the crown as well as a young wife who would welcome Catherine's advice on running a household.

A commotion on the ship diverted her thoughts. The poor beasts on board, five horses and a mule, had long ago caught scent of land, whinnying and tossing heads in their impatience. Now a magnificent white mare of the Andalusian breed reared on hind legs, scattering the nearby seamen as she pawed the air.

"*Qué caballo!* What a horse!" exclaimed Diego Berruguete as a rope snapped and the mare went free. His sister on his arm, he took a place at Catherine's side. They watched the seamen hurry back to fling a new rope on the white mare's neck. Once more the most precious of cargoes was secure.

A shout went up as the ship touched shore, from the travelers and the crowd awaiting them. There were men in the short capes and puffed breeches which gold-rich Spain had made the fashion of all christendom; there were soldiers with the sunlight bouncing from their armored breastplates; there were tradesmen and a solitary woman, saucy with her black hair tumbling to her shoulders and her arm around a soldier.

"Peru!" breathed Catherine.

In vain she tried to spot her brother. Not far away on board, the soon-to-be-wed Doña Leonor García searched the crowd with the pallor of one about to go before the Inquisition. Doña Teresa looked relieved. Ana clung to the rail as if to her last support.

Lightfooted in spite of the wide and swaying hoops beneath her skirt, Catherine ran down the gangplank. How many Spanish women had set foot on this soil ahead of her? Fifty? One hundred? And behind her, never to be seen again, were friends who would pass their whole lives going to daily Mass and growing fat with babies, bending over needlework to fill the rest of their hours.

A man pushed forward through the crowd. *"Hermanita!"* he cried hoarsely. *"Hermanita!* Little sister!"

Two arms fell heavily around her. The smell of sour wine engulfed her. Catherine drew back dreading—and yet knowing in her heart—that this was Juan.

She stared at him in shock. The narrow jaw, the coaxing eyes, were as familiar now as if she'd seen them only yesterday. Yet she had never seen him in this state, so drunken that he must lean on her. Her singing spirits of a moment earlier now disappeared like smoke.

Juan spun her with a feverish glee and her cloak fell back, exposing hair and dress. Lurching from his own exuberance he made a sweeping gesture.

"See, Don Luis. Did I not tell you she was lovely?"

Disgusted at the spectacle he was causing, Catherine raised her head. A pace or two away a fortyish-looking gentleman stood watching them, touching the point of a finely kept beard. He was tall and elegant of figure, with his left eyebrow set slightly higher than its neighbor. The movement of his

9

eyes told Catherine that he had been examining the small-ness of her waist.

Her anger with her brother touched her cheeks. "Your state disgraces us," she said, her voice kept low.

Juan laughed again, delirious. "Your arrival, sister, is cause for celebration." He took a loose-limbed step. "Come, let me present Don Luis de Alvarado, a member of the Cabildo. I have taxed his friendship to furnish a cart for you and your ladies."

She heard with surprise. Juan was befriended by a member of the Cabildo—the powerful city council.

"It is an honor, señorita," Luis de Alvarado said. His voice was as silken as his suit. He took her hand. For the second time in as many moments Catherine felt the urge to pull away. It was not that Don Luis's touch was icy or that he, like Juan, reeked of drink. Still something in him made Catherine shiver. And though he smiled with perfection, his eyes were as soulless and unfeeling as a dagger's edge.

"You are kind," she said, perhaps too hastily. She took the arm Luis de Alvarado offered and they started through the crowd.

Confusion reigned all around them: Families reuniting; the bought bride Leonor García standing with downcast eyes before a man with grizzled hair and saber-scarred cheek; a handful of friars welcoming a brother; cargo coming off the ship on brawny backs; impassioned barter. Trying not to frown, Catherine gathered each scene to her. She would never have seen this in Seville, she reminded herself. She did not regret her journey. Juan would sober, this would pass. Her fingers touched the silver rosary at her waist.

Her thoughts had made her lag behind. Ana and Doña Teresa already stood by the two-wheeled cart in which they would ride. Ana was clutching her rough woolen cape around her, white-faced. It wasn't the cart which frightened her, it was the sight of a stocky, brown-skinned man holding the mule which pulled it. He was an Indian.

"You see, Ana?" Catherine said. "He's dressed exactly like any man of Spain."

"And keeps a better pace without need of flogging," Don Luis said blandly. "Allow me to hand you in, Doña Catherine."

Even Doña Teresa might not have noticed anything unseemly in his actions, but Catherine felt the heaviness of his fingers as he lifted her. They slid along the stiff curve of her corset, lingering. His eyes, cool and narrowed, were shaded with pleasure and seemed to challenge her.

At first, as he set her in the cart and turned to help her dueña, she was too stunned to think. Save for a kiss or two on the fingers no man had ever touched her before. That Don Luis would take this liberty was unthinkable.

"Juan—a word," she said, struggling to keep confusion from her voice. Instinct told her one did not simply denounce a man like Don Luis. Shaking, she leaned over the side of the cart to speak to Juan, who had heaved himself upon a horse and now came toward her.

"Juan, you must be the one to help us down when we arrive," she whispered, her eyes imploring. "Do you understand? I think Don Luis is—not the gentleman his station should make him."

Juan hooked a playful finger through her hair and pulled a tendril free to lie against her cheek.

"No man is, little sister, a truth I'm sure you failed to learn from our doting father."

She watched in distress as he rode ahead, nothing more than amusement in his expression. Then, with a lurch, the cart moved forward.

For Catherine the world was turning upside down. Much the same had happened when her father, the only parent she had ever known, had died. Then well-meaning relatives had begun at once to plan matches for her, giving every thought to her physical well-being, none to her deeper needs and griefs. Had that marked the end of loving protection? The end of innocence? Her brother's attitude shocked her. Catherine suddenly realized that she was on her own. What irony that she had come across the world to see it!

She would have Juan's shelter now, even his defense against any major slight, but who would ever again take her welfare to heart as her father had done? The answer was a hollow one as the cart she rode in bumped along.

In the road ahead a horseman thundered toward them, raising dust. He wore a soldier's garb, a steel cuirass and fluted helmet, and scarlet breeches hugged his thighs. Powerful thighs, thought Catherine, her notice caught first by the color of the breeches and then by the size of the great bay stallion beneath him. The horseman passed them, then wheeled and reared his animal. His bold eyes swept over Catherine, brimming with contempt.

"Well, Juan Bautista, I see you pay your debts," he called

in loud, untutored tones. "Tell me, did you also play at dice on your mother's grave?"

He gave a low salute to Catherine and with a movement of his knees sent the horse beneath him leaping forward toward the ship.

Catherine's mouth was slack. A man would have been called out for slanders such as that—in Seville. Perhaps it was true that the soldiers of Peru were little better than outlaws. Was such behavior tolerated here? She shot a look at her companions.

Luis de Alvarado's eyes had narrowed and Juan was pale.

"How dare the upstart bastard—and in public!" Juan exclaimed.

Don Luis's laugh was cool and unperturbed. "You'll do well to be less sensitive, Bautista. A man should not spell out his name unless he means to own it. Would you cross swords with Valdivia?" He spurred ahead.

His comments puzzled Catherine. She watched color flooding back to her brother's cheeks.

"Hold your tongue," he snapped as she started to speak.

"But that man—"

Now Juan forced a laugh. "A soldier, born without a father, a nobody. Perhaps that's why he's such a pet of Gonzalo Pizarro. They are a boorish lot, *hermanita*. If we're lucky the viceroy will see them all in irons."

They rode in silence for a time, following the Rimac River past vineyards and great plantings of vegetables not known in Spain. From the first lurch of the cart the young maid Ana had stood looking backward, as though as long as she could glimpse the sea she would remain linked to her homeland. Now she suddenly pointed to something in the road behind them.

"Look, señorita!" she exclaimed.

At first Catherine was unable to make out anything. Then she saw them. Kicking up a fine gray cloud the soldier named Valdivia was returning at full gallop. Tethered to his saddle was a rope and at the end of it, so fine and fleet footed next to the enormous bay that she appeared some apparition dancing just above the ground, raced the white mare from the caravelle.

"What the devil is he doing with an animal like that?" frowned Juan, turning in his saddle.

"Receiving it for some dark-skinned Indian wench of Pizarro's," suggested Luis de Alvarado, dropping back to join them. One corner of his mouth gave a scornful twitch. Touching the point of his beard he let his eyes play over Catherine.

She pretended to ignore him. In time Valdivia, in his scarlet breeches, thundered past without a look. The mixture of crudeness and strength displayed in his sunburnt physique created a frightening whirlpool of sensation inside her, intriguing, and yet almost repelling. She turned her attention quickly to Doña Teresa who was brushing at the dust now settling on her cloak.

By midday they arrived in Lima, scarcely nine years old and already boasting handsome stone houses with turrets and terraces. Its broad, straight streets were in such contrast to the twisting alleys of her home that Catherine found herself not breathing as she stared at them. A new place. And soon she would meet her sister-in-law, an Englishwoman, Juan had confessed with discomfort. He appeared to be growing nervous.

The cart which carried her rattled through the high doors of a shuttered house and stopped in the courtyard. Juan, surly in the soberness which had overtaken him on the ride, threw his reins to a stableboy.

"Pour wine," he said to Catherine. "Don Luis will show you the way. Doña Teresa, see the luggage to your rooms and I will find my wife."

Catherine's protest died in her throat. Juan was already disappearing up the stairs, her earlier request that he hand them down on their arrival unheeded.

"You," she said to a nearby servant, who was startled into action by her firmness. "An arm for my ladies and me, if you please."

Don Luis, in the act of dismounting, looked at her. A thin smile touched his lips.

"Doña Teresa, the luggage will wait. Come and refresh yourself first," Catherine said as the servant swung her down onto the warm bricks of the courtyard.

Every breath drawn by an unmarried woman of decent name was drawn in the presence of her dueña. Only when with her father, or in the privacy of her bedchamber, dared a lady dispense with such convention. Though the need for a breath of air had prompted Catherine to risk such impropriety a few times on the ship, she knew her brother should not now order Doña Teresa to tasks which left her unchaperoned.

Doña Teresa spoke in a tone revealing the dislike she felt

for her charge. "You are not mistress in this house. I will do as your brother instructed."

Aware her dueña should not abandon her, with Don Luis watching her, Catherine drew herself together with confused determination. She didn't understand why this was happening. She was hurt by the dueña's words. Had she ever mistreated Doña Teresa? Had she ever been less than a sister to Juan? Why had Juan's wife not been waiting to meet them?

"To the right, señorita," murmured Don Luis.

Squaring slender shoulders she climbed the staircase to her right, weary in every bone. An open gallery ran on three sides of the courtyard. She paused by a railing and waited.

Don Luis stepped past her.

"Shall I take your cloak, Doña Catherine?"

She could not plead the house was chill, nor did she wish to seem a coward. She nodded slightly. He took it from her shoulders and gestured toward an oaken door.

Slowly Catherine entered the room. Uneasily she catalogued its furnishings. Four tables, benches, shelves bearing goblets. She spun, her eyes flashing.

"What kind of room is this?" she demanded.

Don Luis's thin lips wore a smile. He came toward her, close enough that she was forced to tilt her head to speak to him. Catherine realized that he wanted her to back away, to show that she was frightened.

"A gaming room, Doña Catherine. Did Juan not tell you? He draws a fine clientele."

"A . . . gaming room?"

No gentleman of property would keep a public place. Her brother's claims of owning an *encomienda,* land and Indians, must be lies.

Don Luis stripped off his velvet cape, his asymmetric gaze fixed on the outlines of her body. She smelled the spices which preserved his clothes. He tossed the cape onto a bench.

"Unfortunately," he said, "your brother's luck runs bad of late. A year ago he lost a sum to me which he could not afford to loose. To gain it back he bet this building. And when he lost it in a tumble of the dice, do you know the last thing that he wagered, Doña Catherine? You."

2

Catherine screamed the words again.

"I will not gamble with strange men! I will not be Luis de Alvarado's mistress!"

The balconied room was filled with Ana's sobbing. It was a soft sound, as diffused as the sunlight which stole its way through the grill at the bedchamber window. The maid bent over trunks, unpacking, venturing no glance at the room's other occupant.

Catherine stood at the center of the room. Her palms were pressed together at her waist. Her cheeks were bright with wounded dignity. Juan, her brother, walked to and fro, one hand clapped to the back of his neck, cursing the headache he had from the morning's wine. They had been like this for an hour.

"Have you lost all sense of decency?" demanded Catherine. "I refuse to pay the price of your bad luck at gaming, Juan. No judge would force me to."

Her brother laughed.

"It's hardly the sort of matter one puts before a judge, *hermanita*. Even if it were, there's not a one in town whom Don Luis could not control. He holds more power than any man in Lima, save possibly the archbishop. Cross him and we both might lose our heads. Please him and we might receive a sizable *encomienda*."

This turn to talk of land grants snapped Catherine's patience.

"Oh, so it's for more than gambling debts that I'm to become his whore!"

From a bench at the side of the room Juan's wife said lazily, "Dear me, I'm told a lady doesn't even know the meaning of that word."

"Shut up," said Juan across his shoulder.

The Englishwoman, blond and pale, did not obey. The bodice of her dress lay open to a shocking depth. Her name was Rose.

"I told you it would never work," she purred. "A Spanish girl raised night and day to think of nothing but her honor. Listen how she howls!"

Catherine listened with disdain. Was it for future children of this woman that she had, in her precious luggage space, carefully packed a doll across all those thousands of miles of sea?

"*Hermanita*, listen," Juan coaxed. "Never in the five years I have known him has Don Luis had a lady of pleasure, or even an Indian, though their women are comely enough and ever willing. They say his wife in Valladolid has fragile health. If you would but have a little patience you might be the second. He would dress you in rubies and pearls."

"His wife!" breathed Catherine. "He has a wife in Spain? It's an adulteress you mean to make me then!"

A blow to the side of her head sent Catherine onto the floor. Behind her Ana gasped. Juan stood above her, his fists slowly opening and closing. Gradually a look she could not read replaced the anger in his face.

"Forgive me, *hermanita*," he said in measured tones. "Your lack of prudence goads a man to rashness. It's a failing we share, perhaps. Our father's blood, or some betrayal of it. Come. Give me your hand."

He helped her to her feet. In silence Catherine dusted at her skirts. Juan eyed her shrewdly.

"I could force you to obey me, *hermanita*. But though you no doubt think I have no conscience left, you've pricked it. I have no quarrel with you; I'm merely desperate to be free of my debt to Don Luis. If I help you win your freedom will you do what I require?"

In less than half a day Catherine had learned a bitter lesson. Good name, family, social conventions did not insure survival. She could trust in nothing but her own wits—and, knowing as much, she no longer felt a great responsibility to deal openly with anyone.

"What is that?" she inquired warily.

Juan spread his hands to show the smallness of what he was asking.

"I have seen how you could charm our father, playing at once the lady and the teasing, flirting woman skilled at dice. No man could resist you. I ask only that you use that charm tonight—for me, at the tables. The sight of those small white hands holding cards with knowledge, of your mouth curving up as you win, will drive men mad. They will spend a fortune betting and drinking. Encourage them, *hermanita*, and in this single night we can put our hands on sufficient gold to buy your freedom from Don Luis."

Rose, toying with a pendant which lay on her bare neck, sat upright with a gasp.

"And then what?" Catherine asked.

"When there is sufficient money you may return to Spain—or remain, as you choose."

"And if Don Luis refuses?"

Juan hesitated. He darted a look at his wife. A smile spread slowly across his features.

"Then you will escape, I promise you. We will ride together to Trujillo, unless the rounding of your body into womanhood has spoiled your horsemanship."

Catherine's sister-in-law was on her feet, her features showing already the start of opposition.

"You have taken leave of your senses!" she cried. "This was never the plan."

"In a single night you can raise the money to pay your debt?" asked Catherine.

Juan's eyes narrowed.

"Our father left you a handsome dowry, I've no doubt. The two together should suffice."

He did not press. After a moment Catherine capitulated. The thought of money in her hands assumed a small importance next to every scrap of pride and honor she possessed. Crossing to her luggage, she raised a trunk lid and slid her fingers into a leather pocket. Inside were three bank drafts redeemable for gold. As her fingers touched them a new drive for survival fired her. Removing but two of the bank drafts she held them out wordlessly.

Juan snatched them from her. "Not quite as generous as I'd imagined," he said, frowning.

Contempt flickered in Catherine's eyes. "Perhaps Papá thought you would provide for me."

Twitching her chin with his finger her brother laughed.

"You are a very witch, Catherine *reina*. You will be splendid at the gaming tables. Come, Rose, put the pout from your face and we'll leave my sister to recover from her journey."

Only when the arched door had closed behind them did the rigid girl, with her back to Ana, put a hand to the sore spot on her cheek and allow herself the luxury of tears.

As the last glow of daylight waned Catherine sent for a pitcher of wine. She was frightened. Her father's name, his honor, everything she valued and which her brother had trampled rested on the outcome of this evening. She would not jeopardize it with failing nerves. If Juan's business tonight was good it might buy her a few days' safety. In the event he did not make good his promise, which she thought quite likely, she would then have time to cash the remaining money draft hidden in her luggage and buy a passage back to Spain.

"The green brocade," Catherine said to Ana, setting down her wine cup. Flinging aside her dressing gown she began her toilette with unusual determination.

Her small waist had no need of the corset Ana fastened around it. The stiff leather was only a foundation for the dress which went on top of it, padding her hips, pinching high, soft breasts, giving her an hourglass shape. In the mirror Catherine studied the white skin of her shoulders, the blue veins raised in flesh forced into unnatural contours beneath lace and ribbons. The thought of any man reaching beneath that lace was inconceivable to her.

A fine opposition trembled in her throat. As long as she owned her flesh she owned herself. A man's touch meant submission, loss of privacy, the end of something she could not quite name.

Over her petticoats went the wide-bottomed farthingale and finally her three skirts, each one shorter than the last. The rich color of her dress had the strange effect of intensifying both the blueness and the greenness of her eyes until they were jewels, blazing in the whiteness of her skin.

"Oh, señorita!" whispered Ana. "You are more beautiful than a princess! Surely I am blessed to serve you."

With tears which were half gratitude and half vexation at such innocence, Catherine hugged her. Then, in a voice which shook, she said, "I think no jewelry but my earrings, Ana. Will you do my hair?"

Her fingers still lamentably inexperienced, Ana combed the shining black hair before her into a coil. It was not an elaborate style, but practical with the fluted neck ruffs now in fashion, and on Catherine it revealed magnificent high cheeks and ears carved of ivory. Ana set a caul of gold threads on her handiwork and stepped back to admire.

The door flew open, admitting Rose and Juan.

"Well, well!" he said. "It seems I have undervalued my sister's beauty. But here, *hermana,* dress for men." He stepped past his wife and with his finger loosened wisps of hair at Catherine's temples. Resting his arms on her shoulders he looked into her eyes with a mixture of gravity and teasing. "It is fortunate there's blood between us, Catherine. Other-

18

wise I would not be bound by the code of morals which our father has led you to believe so widely held."

Rose, hearing all, gave a twitch of her skirts. Her eyes were mere slits. Her small mouth had an unpleasant set.

"As you're ready we will make our entrance," said Juan, straightening. With elaborate formality he offered his arm to Catherine. "Rose, go ahead of us. Doña Teresa of course will follow."

He grinned at the humor in that and Catherine, for a brief beat of her heart, could not help owning it with a slight smile of her own.

By the time they stepped out onto the gallery, Rose in her pink dress had disappeared. It was evident where. Across the courtyard, on another arm of the gallery, light spilled from the gaming room which Catherine had seen that morning. The leaping glow of candles made the edges of the night dance drunkenly. Male voices washed toward her, accompanied by the thump of wine cups onto tables. Moving slowly forward on her brother's arm, Catherine was more nervous than she had ever been in her life.

Then they were in the doorway. Entering the room in a daze Catherine heard the sudden hush of voices, felt eyes straining at her. Fire burned in her cheeks. She could not bring her gaze up from the shimmering green of her skirt.

"Gentlemen, my sister," Juan announced.

He pressed her arm. Slowly Catherine raised her eyes to a roomful of male faces, curious, speculative, delighted. She forced a smile. Conversation erupted all around her.

As if some terrible ordeal had passed her vision cleared. She saw the room, men playing cards at two tables, dice at a third, Rose and a servant circulating with pitchers of wine. Yet the strangeness of the surroundings made it hard for her to concentrate. She was aware of only three men. Don Luis, at a card game, watched her with a cold possessiveness which turned to desire even as she shivered before it. By the empty fireplace the soldier Valdivia lounged in his red breeches, the cuirass gone from his white linen shirt and a goblet in his hand. And at a fourth table, at which no game was now underway, sat a young man with golden hair and a gentle face.

Valdivia's dark eyes followed Catherine as she crossed the room, and then they jumped with active loathing to Don Luis. The soldier knew about Juan's debt, she realized suddenly. That was the reason for the insults he'd let fly that morning.

And if he knew, how many more? Had it been before a crowd like this that Juan had wagered her on a fall of the dice?

Perhaps it was instinct which told her the weak animal quickly becomes the prey of the strong. Flinging back her head she once more smiled at the men around her, and this time she knew the smile was incandescent. Valdivia drank deeply from his goblet.

The young man with the golden beard sprang to his feet. He was fine looking, his well-formed features saved from too much handsomeness only by the grave set of his mouth. His suit of dark plum silk suggested a moneyed background.

"Señorita, I have just been reading about a lovely maiden of Seville," he said with a gesture of the book of poems in his hand. "Was it written of you?"

There was in his words no hint of mockery, nothing but a frank praise of her beauty. Touched by his gallantry Catherine drew a breath.

"I've never known a poet, señor, but I know the poems well. The reading of them occupied my hours happily on our crossing. They are jewels, are they not?"

She saw surprise come to his eyes. Then, as their gazes met, a curious warmth flowed through her, as surely as if he'd reached a hand out to catch hers. She felt less nervous.

"*Hermana,* allow me to present you to Alonzo Sanchez," said Juan with tolerant amusement. "And to his excellency the Marquis de Zurbarán."

The marquis, stoop shouldered with silky white hair and a very long chin, rose and motioned Catherine toward the only true chair in the room, fussing as attentively as the nurse-maid who had catered to Catherine's every whim long years before.

"Your rogue of a brother tells us you can hold a hand of cards, señorita. Shall I run him through for slander, or will you give us a demonstration?"

His watery eyes of faded brown were so plainly excited by anticipation of her skills that Catherine could not help laughing.

"I will gladly play a hand against you, my lord marquis. But will you take the chance?"

In answer the marquis set out a formidable stack of coins. Juan, looking satisfied, placed an equal number at Catherine's side. She was aware of voices lowering in the room, knew men were watching them.

"And you, Don Alonzo," said the marquis to the young man

with the book of poems. "Will you play too or are you only gathering vignettes for the history you're writing?"

"I'll join with pleasure," Alonzo replied. With a smile to Catherine he added a stack of gold to those on the table.

Catherine was growing calm. She reveled in her ability at gaming. She would not have chosen this role, which diminished her reputation as a lady, but as it was forced on her she meant to profit by it. She intended to win the sum required to buy her freedom from Don Luis. One twentieth of every winning hand tonight would go to Juan.

By now half a dozen men had come to stand with Juan around the table, Catherine dealt the cards. The first hand went to her, and Bernál, Marquis de Zurbarán, laughed his delight. Two more men took seats on the benches. The piles of golden *escudos* were larger than before, and again Catherine won. The next time she saw luck did not go with her and wisely bet but a small amount, which fell to Alonzo Sanchez.

From the murmurs around her she knew she was meeting with approval. The men who were not playing themselves now began to make bets on the outcome of each hand.

"You have an enviable skill, my dear," said the velvet voice of Don Luis, who moved to stand behind her.

Catherine recoiled, unable to help herself. She felt the impulse to fold her cards together away from his gaze. On a bench by the nearby wall Doña Teresa stared straight ahead, her expression showing neither concern nor disapproval.

"Thank you, señor," Catherine said in her coldest tones. "I wonder, would you be so kind as to move? You block my light."

There was a laugh from Rodrigo de Valdivia who, from his spot by the fireplace, looked on with complete disdain. Catherine struggled to include him in her anger, but instead the corners of her mouth curved up. He was despicably unawed by authority, it seemed, and at that moment, as that authority was embodied in Don Luis, she could not fault him. Don Luis had moved away.

For a time thereafter she almost enjoyed herself. The awesome sums of money being wagered on the table were doubly dazzling as she had never before played for money. A goblet of wine had been placed near her arm but she did not touch it. Let Juan, who was now drinking thirstily, play the fool when he was gambling. She could not afford to.

Rose, her sister-in-law, moved back and forth about the room with a rustle of skirts, leaning brazenly down to rest an arm on this man's shoulder and then another's, deporting herself, thought Catherine, like any tavern wench. The men who watched the card game chatted. About the viceroy, newly arrived at Tumbez, who was moving toward the capital overland. About the news that he was freeing Indians at every stop. About the rumors that he carried orders from King Carlos the Fifth to reclaim lands held by any man who had taken sides in the recent bloody rivalry between the Pizarros and another faction.

There was great excitement and hinted resentment, for nearly every man in Lima stood to lose his lands if that were true. And if the viceroy was freeing Indians, how would they work those lands?

At length Catherine found she was tiring. The day had been a warm one and the room was stuffy. It took great effort to concentrate on the square boards in her hand. A moment later, at the end of a game, Alonzo Sanchez threw down his cards.

"Gentlemen, the room is over-heated," he said. "Señorita Bautista is not accustomed to long hours of gaming as we are. We must allow her and her dueña to take some air."

Standing, he offered his arm to Catherine. It was only as he moved that she realized he was lame. Doña Teresa, almost a part of the furniture in her black dress, rose and walked behind them.

"You're very kind," said Catherine as they stepped out onto the gallery.

Alonzo relinquished her arm and leaned against the rail which overlooked the courtyard

"It's pleasure, not kindness, to see to the comfort of the most beauful woman in Peru."

Catherine blushed. Though she had not been without her suitors she had never been addressed with such earnest sincerity, or by a man she found as pleasing as this one. Quiet, well-bred, something of a scholar—those were the qualities which she admired most. Nor did he seem lacking in courage. There was a thin scar which she took to be a sword mark near his hairline.

"You flatter me, Señor Sanchez," she said simply.

Alonzo shook his head.

"I only speak the truth. Do you come here betrothed?"

Her breath caught.

"No."

22

All the color drained from her voice. The word sounded strange. He did not seem to notice.

"Then I will inform your brother I intend to pay court."

She tried to shake her head and could not.

"I—"

"Does the night air agree with you, Doña Catherine? There are those who claim it is ill advised."

Don Luis spoke from the door. He wore a black silk suit shot through with threads of silver. It glimmered in the moonlight as he came toward them.

"Catherine," repeated Alonzo, scarcely heeding him. "An English name?"

"My mother long ago served in the court of the true queen of England. The English call her Catherine instead of Catalina—when they speak of her at all, poor woman."

She had tensed at the sight of Don Luis and the way his eyes were fixed upon her. He moved like some stalking predator. But she was not his prey. Juan was doing well tonight.

"Perhaps the lady would like some fruit punch," he suggested with a lift of his always arched eyebrow.

Alonzo's jaw firmed but he made a little bow.

"Of course." With a faintly uneven gait he stepped inside.

Now very close to Catherine, Don Luis was opening his mouth to speak when a voice from the darkness asked with biting laziness:

"Tell me, Don Luis, is it the custom in Castile to have lame men as your cup bearers?"

Catherine whirled, startled by the presence of someone else on the gallery. Rodrigo de Valdivia leaned against the wall. His face was hidden. Only the broad set of his shoulders and the thick waves of his hair were discernible from surrounding shadows. His white linen shirt with its flat collar seemed to challenge the splendid attire of Don Luis.

"It is no business of yours, Valdivia," the latter said.

"Ah, but I try always to improve myself by observing the manners of my betters."

The sound of sarcasm was unmistakable. Catherine saw the hand of the man beside her dart toward his sword and then fall away. Observing the movement, Valdivia smiled. His teeth flashed white and strong. He himself moved not a muscle.

"The viceroy will set you some lessons, I promise," purred Don Luis.

Catherine gathered her skirts in her hands and hurried toward the open door to the gaming room, not even pausing to note if her dueña followed. The tension between the two men on the gallery was obvious. She welcomed the opportunity it had offered for escape.

"Doña Catherine."

She stiffened at the sound of Valdivia's voice. He had turned into the room on her very heels and now stood beside her. His brazen use of her name was an irritant for which she knew no comeback.

"Señor?"

He did not speak until, reluctantly, she looked at him. The top of her head came to his beard, which was squared off, contrary to the current fashion. His face was burnt as dark as any Moor's. There was a reckless, unruly look about him but as his dark eyes mocked her she realized, with shock, that the soldier was attractive. Not only handsome, with his boldly chiseled face and raven hair, but something more—something frightening which left her feeling weak and nerveless.

"I admit, señorita, that you give a fair accounting of yourself at cards," he said. "But I have seen other women do so before you. Their luck, I notice, improves as the men who are dazzled by their charms drink more than is prudent, while the ladies themselves do nothing to dull their wits."

"Oh? And what are you suggesting? That I have won tonight unfairly? That I copy my brother in drinking?"

Her words sounded breathless. From the corner of her eyes she saw Doña Teresa clasp her hands, entirely impassive. Don Luis had also come into the room and was listening with intense impatience.

Valdivia flashed his teeth again, a smile which must have won many a tavern maid, Catherine thought.

"Not at all, señorita. A woman hasn't the capacity for mixing wine and cards that man does. But I understand you also play at dice, a riskier game. Will you chance that?"

Catherine drifted toward the table, pulses racing. Instinct told her he was more the gambler than the gentlemen who had faced her earlier. He was shrewd. She could see a measure of truth in what he had said about men's heads being turned. Yet the statement had come out a taunt, a challenge. She found it hard to resist.

"You are a soldier, Señor Valdivia. The stakes have been high tonight—"

In answer he tossed to the table a purse as fat as any she'd seen. Amusement touched his mouth as she fingered the ruff at her neck, uneasy.

"Will that do, señorita?"

She found his very confidence irritating. He showed not the least discomfort at being a soldier amid this roomful of landed gentlemen.

"Very well." She picked up the wine goblet untouched by her in earlier games, and with a defiant look of her blue-green eyes she drained it. The wine went through her like pleasant fire. She smiled provokingly. "Will you have the first toss, Señor Valdivia?"

The first toss was over before the room's other occupants sensed a new game in the making. Catherine had won it, and she won twice more as men gathered around the table laying bets. This victory excited her as none of the others had. Rodrigo de Valdivia had been quite confident of his prowess, and now with every loss he was growing more annoyed. She met his scowl with a smile.

"More wine," he snapped to Rose who stood nearby with a pitcher. "Perhaps the lady wishes more too?"

She knew he did not expect her to. She raised her cup prettily, ignoring the fruit punch Alonzo Sanchez had brought her.

"I would not wish you to think I take advantage of you," she said. The men around the table laughed as Valdivia's tanned skin darkened. Though she sipped at her cup he drained his quickly and called for another. When she had won six throws of eight he swept aside the dice.

"What now, Rodrigo?" joked the marquis. "Will you quit while you are losing? I have never known you to do so."

"I quit only to challenge the lady to another game of cards—a different game."

His dark eyes smoldered with his anger. He himself was feeling the effects of drink now, Catherine guessed. A wave of black hair fell across his forehead.

"What game, señor?" she asked, leaning forward. Never had she enjoyed a contest so much, for she sensed herself pitted against not just a rival but a masculinity frustrated by the inability to win, frustrated by luck more than her own powers, but by her nevertheless.

"*Tute,*" said Valdivia.

She nodded. The game was tailored perfectly for two. She

had often played with her father. Holding his eyes with her own she raised her cup for wine, though she knew she would not drink it. She was forced to accept the humiliation brought to her by her brother and Don Luis. She would not endure the jeers of this wanderer who lived by the skill of his sword and the horse beneath him.

Valdivia gulped down his wine.

"Deal," he ordered.

He proved far more skilled than the men she had played against earlier. A fine dew covered Catherine's brow as she nudged forward her bet, one finger lingering on it uncertainly. Noting her hesitancy Rodrigo de Valdivia stretched and grinned. His eyes caught hers, communicating satisfaction with his own power, deriding her indecision.

But when the cards were on the table Catherine proved the winner.

"I hope, Señor Valdivia, that you are more prudent in battle than you are in gaming," she said. "Have you had enough!"

The spectators laughed. Catherine realized they were dwindling now.

"Your luck cannot last," said Valdivia shortly.

Indeed it did not. The next game fell to him. But Catherine took the next hand, and the next. As she did so he flung down a sorry assortment of cups and batons.

"Won't you sit another hand?" goaded one of the men who watched them.

The soldier's eyes were flashing. He swung his leg across the bench and stood.

"No," he growled. "I'll leave her to whatever devil made her."

Turning, he strode out of the room with a man Catherine had not noticed before, another soldier—judging by his rough attire—a barrel-chested man with bushy hair the color of rust.

The Marquis de Zurbarán took Valdivia's place and a larger game began, but after several hands Catherine excused herself. She was exhausted. Surely Juan had met his goal tonight. With Doña Teresa she crossed the gallery to her room.

Ana lay curled on a bench. She rose sleepily and helped her mistress undress, then left with the dueña for whom she would perform those same duties. Cool in a nightdress of thin lawn, her hair loosed in deep waves, Catherine blew out the candle beside her bed and slid under the sheet.

She was asleep almost immediately, falling deep, deep, toward an unconsciousness which was avoided only as her ear caught in the stillness the squeaking of a door. Her door.

3.

Catherine raised on her elbow. Fear seized her. Who would come at this hour, with this stealth?

The gleam of a candle appeared in the doorway. It moved, and behind it she saw the looming figure of a man.

"Juan?" Her voice sounded hoarse.

The door snapped closed and the candlelight moved up, revealing a face to her.

"No, Doña Catherine, it is not your brother," said Luis de Alvarado.

Catherine set upright.

"Get out of my room! There are servants around. I shall summon them!"

Don Luis gave an ugly laugh. He took a step toward her.

"Try if you like. The only one near is your dueña, and she does not much like you. For the proper amount of silver, she will be quite deaf tonight."

"What—what do you mean?"

Catherine slipped from her bed. She was conscious of the sheer lawn nightdress she wore but instinct told her there was more danger in being trapped than in being immodest. She was frightened. She could not forget the insulting way Don Luis's hands had lingered on her waist. She tried to find a way around him, but he continued slowly toward her.

"Only that I have come to collect my debt," he said smoothly. He set the candle holder on a table.

Catherine shrank back.

"The debt is canceled," she said nervously. "Juan collected enough from the tables tonight to pay what he owes. He has money drafts from Spain as well. Now leave me!"

She saw his loathsome smile, the stirring of his mismatched eyebrows.

"Little fool! Do you believe Juan would part with money for your sake? It is he who told me in which room I would find you waiting. A man like Juan does not cavil at the sale of his sister. Even if he should be overtaken by some sense of honor and offer gold in lieu of you, I would not take it. Your body is even more pleasant than I had first judged, now that I see it more clearly."

28

Shame suffused her. Catherine tried to force sound from her throat and couldn't. It was impossible that this was happening to her under Juan's roof. Yet she knew now the deceitful creature her brother was. He had sent her to the gaming tables with lies, then left her to this fate.

"It will take me many months to tire of you," said Don Luis, moving still closer.

She could not avoid him. To her side was the wall and in front of her was the ever-advancing councilman. She darted on impulse in the opposite direction, around him, but he glided easily into her path. His laugh filled the room and seemed to suffocate her.

"There is no escape. In a moment you will lie beneath me. I will expose every inch of your white skin. You will lie naked to my eyes like the meanest of tavern whores. Then we will see what happens to your haughty manner."

Again Catherine tried to duck past him. His arm caught at her waist. His long fingers groped for the flesh beneath her nightdress and his laughter, like a living creature of the darkness, curled toward her.

With a cry of rage Catherine jerked free of him. She heard the rip of lawn, felt the air strike her shoulder and the breast which now swayed free of its covering.

"Doña Teresa! Doña Teresa!"

She heard Don Luis curse angrily. The room around her had become a nightmare setting, with patches of wavering light. His face was a dark shape above the white line of his ruff.

"Doña Teresa! Come at once!"

The call ended in a sob. A dull despair told her Don Luis had spoken the truth. He had bribed her dueña. Doña Teresa had abandoned her.

Her attacker closed in again.

"Your Doña Teresa will not come!" he snapped. "You are helpless!"

Catherine held a torn piece of fabric to her, trying futilely to cover herself.

"You beast," she gasped. "How dare you call yourself a gentleman? I—I would sooner be touched by the boy who tends the stable than by you!"

She saw his face contort with rage. Suddenly she was in his grasp, struggling wildly. His open hand slapped smartly against one cheek and then the other. Her senses faltered beneath the blows, and she felt herself thrust backward onto the bed.

"You have a fine opinion of yourself!" snarled Don Luis. "Little bitch, you shall pay for resisting Luis de Alvarado. I might have dealt with you easily, but now it will be a pleasure to break you. This is for your insolent tongue—"

He hiked up her nightdress, exposing her body.

"And this is for your arrogance—"

His hand caught her breast and squeezed, then ran one finger tip around the nipple.

"And this is for your fine opinion of yourself—for daring to spurn me!"

The flat of his hand moved coarsely down, down, to her curling hair. His fingers dug in and he shook her.

"I will teach you how little consequence a woman is in this world!" he hissed.

Each act brought new shock to Catherine as she felt the violation of all her private parts.

Don Luis now lowered himself upon her. She felt a swelling between his legs.

"I will draw your blood," he promised. "I will use you again and again until it flows."

His breath was hot on her face. Her hands were imprisoned. Still she could not submit to what was happening to her. In desperation she gathered her strength and tried to roll. The sideways movement jarred loose his hold for a moment. Jerking and twisting she slipped from the bed and she was free.

He lunged in pursuit of her. She stumbled and stumbled again, intent upon the door. Neither of them had fully recovered their balance. She felt his hand close over her wrist and she writhed from his grasp.

But she could not elude him fully. He had missed her wrist but caught her opposite shoulder. She was unable to twist from his grip, but he could not quite detain her. He swung her around and around, bringing his body closer to hers.

"You will—regret this!" he panted.

He ground her against him, trying once again to raise her skirt. There was no appetite in him but for violence. She felt its echo in her own blood. She concentrated on nothing now but hurting him, anything to save herself from a fate which seemed too certain.

The candle, in a heavy silver holder, rested on the table by her bed. She snatched at it, smashing the heavy holder toward his temple.

It missed its mark. But the flaming stick of wax, as it fell free, touched the wide white ruff flaring out from Don Luis's neck. The fluted fabric ignited. Catherine, flung to the floor, looked on in horror as a fan of flames leaped up at the face of the man who had attacked her.

With a piercing cry he threw himself to the floor. He rolled on the carpet like some maddened animal, beating his face. After a moment he only crouched there, gasping. His hands worked with mute agony in his hair.

Slowly he staggered to his feet. It was totally dark in the room now, and she could not see his cheek, only the faint line of the hand he held pressed against it.

"You will—pay for this!" he choked with effort. "If you were a man I would kill you outright, but you will pay for this. You will rue the day you ever lifted a finger against me—you and your brother as well!"

Still staggering with pain, he stumbled from the room.

4

Catherine huddled in the darkness, dazed and sick. The feel of Don Luis's hands still lingered on her body like festering flesh she longed to rip away. The knowledge of what had almost happened to her made her dizzy. It was the realization of what she had done which frightened her, however. He deserved to have had his whole body in flames, she told herself savagely. But now she recognized the impending doom which she most certainly had brought down on her head.

Luis de Alvarado would have no interest in her body now. He would want revenge. The fact she was a woman would be no deterrent. She had marked him for life, and there was no telling what he would do to get even. He would probably invent some lie about what had happened—claim she had invited him to her room, perhaps, say she had tried to kill him. His was a voice which would not be disputed in Lima. At any moment now soldiers might pound on the door of the courtyard below.

With quick decision she rose to her feet. The penalty for rebuffing Don Luis's ardor might well be death or prison. She would ride for the port of Callao. Even if she were caught before she could board a ship about to sail she had nothing to lose.

Throwing open the shutters she dressed by starlight in a velvet riding costume. How she would saddle a horse she was not quite sure. There had been a stable boy. Perhaps she could bribe him. She wound her hair up quickly, securing it with a minimum of pins. There was no time to lose.

In a scarf she folded all she could carry, a comb, some pieces of jewelry she could convert to cash, and the lone bank draft she had withheld from Juan. A wave of rage swept over her. How stupid she had been to believe her brother's seeming change of heart.

She paused for a moment, thinking about young Ana. The girl was so inept. Would someone take care of her? Catherine shook her head. She must not think of that. The bank draft in her scarf would pay for her own passage back to Spain, no more. With a catch in her throat she wondered if anyone there would take her in. She was too young to be a dueña, the usual role assigned to females thrown on the charity of their relatives. Putting that thought too from her mind she opened the door.

The night air was cool against her fevered skin. She stole along the gallery, her slippered feet making not a sound. She did not even know behind which door her brother slept with his English wife, she thought with a stab of irony. How unimaginable her first, and possibly last, days in the New World had been.

As she left the stairs and started across the courtyard Catherine realized several hours must have passed since she left the gaming room. The deep black of earliest morning lay around her. The air smelled sweet. Her sight adjusting to the dark she made her way toward the back of the house and the stables beyond.

All at once she stopped, heart fluttering in her throat. On a bench near the back of the courtyard she saw the form of a man. Stretched on his back, his chest heaved with sleep. Even as her straining eyes made out the rust red of his beard a voice spoke from beneath the gallery.

"Have no alarm, señorita. A falconete firing at his ear would not wake Rojo when he's sleeping."

Rodrigo de Valdivia stepped into the starlight, blocking her path.

"So," he said, teeth flashing. "First Don Luis rides off in a fury and next you appear, set on stealing away somewhere, it would appear. You have learned of the bargain made by him and your brother, then, and do not approve it?"

"Get out of my way," she said coldly.

He shook his unruly black hair.

"So you may run, señorita? Don Luis would see your throat slit for that, and you are much too lovely."

Desperate even beyond fear, she started around him. A hard arm caught her waist.

"I am serious, señorita. He will kill you. There was a girl in Córdoba who refused him, and she was sent before the Inquisition."

"What business is it of yours? And what are you doing here this time of night?"

Catherine was panting. She had never been held like this, calmly, unrelentingly. Don Luis had seized her with violence, never quite securing her because he had sacrificed the ele-

33

ment of surprise. This man had not. She had to get this soldier out of the way.

Valdivia's dark eyes stared down at her. His lips parted over even teeth.

"What am I doing here? Trying to forget the defeats you handed me, señorita. Juan often lets us a room by the stables, but Rojo prefers the outdoors and I found sleep eluded me."

His arm tightened just a fraction. She felt his thigh against hers. Belatedly she remembered the wine he had drunk, thinking he must be half tipsy.

"Please," she whispered. "Please let me go."

His voice was a growl which turned her blood to water.

"It strikes me you should pay me something for the gold you took off me tonight. And for saving you now from a foolish move."

"No—"

She saw what he meant to do and tried to turn her head. It was hopeless. Calmly, with no great haste, he drew her toward him.

"A kiss is a small price to pay," he said against her lips. "Far less than what Don Luis will require of you."

She thought of crying out, but then her flight would be discovered and now it was too late, for already Valdivia's mouth was covering hers, soft yet demanding her response. Catherine struggled beneath it, trying to wrench her head away. Her nails clawed at his arms. This sudden forcing came too close on the heels of Don Luis's, and for a moment she lost all reason. Her pounding fists touched Valdivia's dagger. In an instant she pulled it free, plunging it with all her strength toward his ribs. Its point embedded, stuck, and he caught her wrist, laughing softly.

"Little tiger! So you would kill me, would you? Then you must start the blow lower, aim it up so it will not be deflected by the corset."

She fought him with a fury, hating him for his laughter. She had forgotten men too laced in the boiled leather corsets to give them the form of fashion. Her hair had come loose in her struggle and fell across his arm as he drew her toward him again, the dagger clasped safely in his fingers.

This time his kiss was harder, savoring her resistance, and it seemed to draw out all of Catherine's strength. She trod on his foot but he seemed not to notice. Freeing one arm she brought a fist smashing against the side of his hand, struggling not only against her captor, but against new physical sensations which she knew intuitively were treacherous.

Valdivia drew his head back with an angry exclamation.

"By my beard, you struggle as though you were a virgin."

She tried to free herself, too frightened to speak. A strange expression passed over his face. The glaze which came to his eyes was not a product of wine.

"You are—too lovely a prize for a debaucher like Don Luis. If you strike out at him he will deal with you harshly. God forgive me, what I am about to do is for both our sakes."

As the last words ripped in a soft whisper from his throat, he swept her into his arms. Catherine felt the tireless strength in them, knew her struggle was futile. Rigid with fear she looked up into his face, acknowledging the handsomeness in his bold jaw even as her mind screamed out against what was about to happen. Already she could feel the fire in his body, hear his breathing quicken. He held her as if she were a toy, one hand clamped across her mouth to still her voice. And he was smiling.

"There are worse fates," he whispered. "What does it matter to you whether I am the first or Don Luis? I will give you greater pleasure, I promise. When he finds you have been used—and by me—he may no longer want you."

Each word was a caress, filled with desire. She shook her head. The man was crazy. She felt instead of saw herself carried over a threshold, heard the door kicked shut behind her. They were in a room which smelled of hay and staleness. He let her slip to her feet, slowly so that her body swung in a tantalizing arc across his own.

"Scream all you like," he said, freeing her mouth and, stroking his hand down the curve of her neck. "We're in the servants' quarters now. If anyone hears you they will only think one of the stable men is making his latest conquest."

With his other hand he was unfastening his shirt.

"Please, Señor Valdivia—"

"You have a body to drive men mad. Even tonight when you sat tormenting me across the table in the gaming room I longed for the feel of your flesh against mine more than any favor of the dice."

"I didn't—"

He stripped off the leather undergarment which had turned aside the dagger. A shaft of moonlight through a crudely shuttered window struck him and she stood, entranced by the gleaming whiteness of his skin, the muscled shoulders, the black hair curling thickly at his chest whereon there gleamed a small silver cross. Here was a vision of maleness which made the heroes of romances pale in memory. This man was no part of the civilized world which was hers. Even in this uncertain light she could see a thick, jagged scar at his waist.

Then she realized she had lingered too long appreciating the very ruggedness which would enslave her. She turned and ran.

Valdivia's arm flew out and caught her to him, a sob escaping her as she felt him seize the velvet of her riding costume. His two hands rent the heavy cloth as if it were paper. Gentle and moist his lips began to move in every-widening circles down her neck, toward her breasts. With a flash his dagger slit through her corset laces. The clumsy garment fell to her feet. Rodrigo de Valdivia's fingers moved beneath the ribbons of her petticoats, drawing out her breasts, stroking, arousing, and then with a lunge he threw her backward onto the rough cover of a straw-filled bed and fell on top of her.

She fought against the sensations awakening inside her. His only response was laughter soft in his throat as he drew her arms above her head, where he held them effortlessly with one hand.

"You are beautiful," he whispered. His free hand traced her contours, savoring the tightness of her nipples, her waist. "You were meant for this, doña, but not with some weak-chinned aristocrat. You've too much spirit."

Helpless now she awaited his brutality, but he did not hurt her. His tongue curled toward the swelling tips of her breasts. She gasped as a liquid pleasure shot through her and he looked up smiling.

"There, my lovely *Sevillana,* let us end this suffering."

Purposefully, without effort, his fingers twisted in the petticoats at her waist. Filmy fabric yielded to a single jerk. The powerful thighs which could master a great bay stallion forced her own resisting flesh apart with ease. Catherine was aware of nothing but the shock of rigid flesh against her own and in confusion she found her body arcing toward the very one she sought to escape.

"Yes, *preciosa,* exactly!"

Cupping his hand beneath her buttocks he brought her quickly against him, around him, and she cried out at the hot, hard pain. For a moment his arm went taut as though he struggled for control, and then he commenced a rhythmic movement which drew her senses out toward some abyss over which she knew now she must fall. She bit her lip, resisting. Then consciousness seemed to elude her and her body curved upward. Blindly she caught at the man above her in an effort to stave off the fall, but he fell too, and they lay together shuddering on the bed.

The night, the darkness flowed through her mind, a stream of time which now seemed meaningless. She became aware of moisture beneath her fingers, realized she clutched Valdivia's shoulders, tried to draw away. Rolling onto one elbow he caught her hand.

"Easy, doña," he soothed. "Rest a minute."

She was crying, soundlessly, the tears hot paths of shame along her cheeks. She had drawn his blood and she was glad. She hated him. Not only for what he had done to her, she thought, a sick feeling rising in her throat, for Don Luis had meant to do the same. Her hate of this man was sharpened by the easy competence with which he'd handled her, and which Don Luis had lacked.

The hand imprisoning hers brushed up against her cheek, wiping her tears. He kissed her palm.

"Hate me then," he said against her hair. "Tonight is for the good. You will have less reason to struggle now when Don Luis demands you. You will come to no harm."

"You think you've not harmed me?" she asked, hoarse with loathing. Did he suppose his act was any more forgivable because it might spare her a blow or two from Don Luis? Did he think she would yield herself up freely now that he had forced himself upon her?

"Very little." His voice held suddenly a cutting edge.

"You are disgusting! No decent man would do what you have done."

His anger burned clearly now. The hand which held her fingers almost crushed them.

"No man of family and manners, do you mean? How innocent you are! Do you think because you are a doña you value your honor more than the serving girls who are every day set upon by the rich men who employ them? More than my cousin, a girl of fourteen and devout as any nun, who died in jail because she dared refuse Luis de Alvarado's ardor?"

He had drawn her harshly to him. His dark eyes glittered.

"Of course there is no proof he was the one who accused her to the Inquisition, but who else would have bothered with a lowly cook's assistant? If I had not been in Peru and he in

37

Spain he would have tasted my sword then. Be very careful, *preciosa*, to tell him who it was who stole his trophy."

Catherine shrank from the deadly purpose in his manner—and from the tale he was telling. By the hard set of his mouth she knew it must be true.

"This was—your revenge, then?"

"And my pleasure," he said smiling with a sudden change of temper.

Releasing her hand he drew her hair like a rich and silken curtain across her breasts. It was a curious gesture, strangely tender. Catherine waited for him to speak. Instead he lifted a silken strand and watched it drift back into place. She trembled.

Rodrigo de Valdivia frowned. "Are you frightened? But why? Surely you see I will not hurt you."

"May I—go now?"

Droll amusement curled his lips.

"You are hardly dressed for it, doña. Is sharing a bed with me so distasteful?"

His blithe manner was the hardest thing of all to endure.

"Yes!" She wrenched away from him. His hand stayed her back, loosely imprisoning her.

"Strange, no other woman has ever thought so. A month with me and you would come to me as willingly as any Indian wench. You would offer me your favors and your heart as well."

"I would not in a lifetime!"

His teeth flashed.

"We have something still left of the night. Enough to give a hint which one of us is right in this wager."

Her cry of rage as she fathomed his meaning was muffled quickly against his lips. This time they did not bruise but brushed back and forth, now slowly, now with increasing tempo and his passion grew, until resistance left her and her own were parted in response. He savored her, and as he shaped her to him, Catherine let her mind grow limp. Like one who did not know a dance she let him guide her, a foil for his desire, unable to deny the curious pleasure which slowly lifted her toward the inevitable fall.

It was the coolness of night air against her cheeks which finally woke her. Slowly she stirred from that drowsy world in which she had found a refuge. Why she left it with such reluctance she couldn't remember until she felt the strong arms holding her and the scent of male flesh in her nostrils.

She was being moved with great care. As her eyes flew open she found she was in the courtyard. She was in Valdivia's arms, her nakedness completely covered by the folds of the cape which he had tucked around her. The stars above were dimming in a prelude to dawn.

She lay completely still. Valdivia was a frequent bather, she thought sleepily. Perhaps he did have Moorish blood. Doña Teresa had warned darkly that Catherine herself might be accused of such a crime for her insistence on a monthly bath, and it was, in truth, from an old Moorish nursemaid that she had acquired the habit. In a man such behavior was even more unusual. She wondered idly about the man who was her captor.

While seeming still to sleep she studied the dark head above her. She knew about his cousin, knew he was eager for a clash with Don Luis, knew he had slept with Indian women. Never had she known so much about a man, save for her father. Bitter and hysterical laughter rose to her lips.

It did not take sound. Nevertheless Valdivia seemed to sense that she had wakened. He glanced down at her. For a long moment she lay looking up into eyes which mirrored the night skies above. Then he gave his raffish grin.

"Where are you taking me?" she asked.

"To your room. You've wakened very handily. It will save me the trouble of opening doors until I find the right one."

Catherine sighed. The man would joke on the gallows. She turned her head half toward him, too worn to think about the future.

He mounted the stairs with the stealth of a cat. In a low voice she pointed out her door. What would happen if he was discovered here, she wondered. Anything? She felt a final hardening of the heart toward Juan.

Valdivia paused for a moment inside her room. He noted the trunks, the mirrored dressing table, the canopied bed in its alcove, and with a sudden soberness of expression he bent his head to search her face. She wondered as a frown appeared between his brows just what it was he sought there.

Guided by the last pale light of night he picked his way from shadow to shadow until he reached the bed where he eased her gently down. Wordlessly he drew the cape from her. As it unwound, her corset and the scarf which held the money draft tumbled free.

The ghost of another lifetime, her nightdress with its row on row of lace lay discarded at the foot of the bed. Valdivia

39

picked it up, letting the fine cloth slip between his fingers, strangely quiet. Sitting beside her he searched her face again with that same puzzled, vaguely troubled look.

"You are a beautiful woman. A lady," he said, handing over the nightdress. "You seem intelligent as well. Why did you come to your drunken fool of a brother? What had you done?"

Catherine pushed up sharply on her elbows.

"Nothing!"

Again there was a sense of intimacy between them which went beyond the physical. She found herself answering though she did not know why.

"I—I would have had to marry a man I found abhorrent if I'd stayed in Spain. Juan wrote that he was married, that his wife needed help in running a large household. I—found the prospect of coming here exciting. . . ."

She bit her lip, which trembled at her own folly.

Valdivia's chuckle was muffled by the darkness.

"Exciting? A dangerous luxury for a woman."

Burning with unshed tears, her throat wouldn't allow speech. At last she faced the question of what would happen to her. There was little left of the night, too little for running. Despite her show of defiance she clung to her sanity by only the slimmest thread. The smell of hay, the feel of Valdivia over her, came back in a wave of nausea. The rushing horror left her dizzy, on the brink of madness.

No man would ever welcome her lovingly into his arms. Don Luis, after what she had done to him, might see her in jail. And if not, what then? Would decent people shun her? She wound unfeeling fingers into the nightdress, wishing they instead held Valdivia's dagger that she might plunge it into her chest.

After a moment Valdivia said in irritation:

"Come, come. You are hardly the first woman ever taken by force. You'll survive."

Her voice now had the brittleness of old leather.

"Indeed? Are you trying to soothe your conscience?"

"I have none," he said, lounging across her agreeably, hips on one side, arm propped on the other. "For twelve years I've fought with Indians and lived with men who would kill at the drop of a glove. A man's life can be pinched out as quickly as a candle and I do not mean to dim what's left of mine with the nuisance of a conscience."

He swung himself off the bed and went toward a table

where a pitcher of wine sat, left from when Catherine had dressed to go to the gaming room. She watched him move, the rhythmic grace of a man accustomed to the saddle, thinking that if he had been twelve years in Peru he must have come here very young, for he could be no more than twenty-five or six.

"Here," he said, thrusting a cup of wine into her hands. "Drink deeply and sleep. You show a becoming concern for your good name, but there are those of us who have managed without one. If Alvarado still claims you, you will be well provided for. If not, some *hidalgo* will be asking you to be his wife. Alonzo Sanchez is smitten by you already by the way things looked tonight, and his family's coffers overflow."

Not for hours had Catherine had cause to think of the gentle Alonzo Sanchez with his lame leg and his love of poetry. Flushed from the wine cup she looked up angrily.

"He would hardly be interested now, when he learns about me."

"I'm not so lacking in honor that I damage a woman's name, *preciosa*."

"Nor am I so lacking in it that I would hide the truth from a man who wanted to marry me!"

Valdivia was silent. Then, in the hall, there was a noise. Someone moving. Immediately his hand was on his sword. His fingers were loose, relaxed. The footsteps passed and, arm dropping to his side, he turned back to the bed.

"Remember. Tell Alvarado it was Rodrigo de Valdivia who robbed him of his prize," he said. Without another glance at her he let himself out the door.

The cup in her hands was empty. Her body felt leaden, beyond despair. Dragging her nightdress over her head she sought oblivion in sleep. Let daylight come. There was no hope left.

5

The crashing of her door upon its hinges catapulted Catherine into the reality of daylight. Half waking she rose on her pillow just in time to glimpse her brother striding toward her. Then his hand closed on her throat and she was jerked violently from her bed.

"What have you done?" he cried hoarsely. "You fool, you bitch, you have ruined us! What have you done?"

Red patterns wheeled in her head as her air was cut off. Juan shook her. He flung her backward against the wall. Gold spots exploded in the back of her skull and she crouched there on the floor at his feet, looking up into a dissolute face contorted with rage. Rage at what she had done to Don Luis, she quickly perceived, for now she was all too fully awake to the harsh scene around her.

Don Luis himself stood in the doorway, his left cheek bandaged, and at the edges of the bandage his skin showed ugly pink. His eyes were cold and deadly. In front of him stood two men she knew at once for hired ruffians despite their fine attire. One now caught Juan's arms and pinioned them. The other dragged her unresisting to her feet.

"What's this? No fight? No haughty manner?" asked Don Luis moving toward her.

His voice held the fatal softness of a slashing sword. She knew by his look that he would like to kill her, and that no such easy fate awaited her. He walked around her, cruel satisfaction showing on his lips. With effort she forced herself to meet his eyes, which now held nothing but anticipation for her punishment.

"Last night the pleasure of my company would have been overpayment for the debts Juan owes you. Today you will find it exactly what you deserve. I am no longer a virgin."

She was surprised to hear the spirit with which she spoke. For a flashing second as she looked levelly at Don Luis she experienced a strange and bitter triumph. It was, in a way Rodrigo de Valdivia could never have anticipated, a victory of sorts for her and she did not care now what happened.

Juan had made a strangling sound at her announcement. "She lies!" he hissed.

He tried to lunge toward her, but Don Luis's man restrained him. The councilman showed white-lipped fury. In all the room no one seemed able to speak, or even move. Then Rose, who had been hovering sullenly in the background, hurled herself toward the bed from which her sister-in-law had been dragged.

"She cannot have lain last night with a man! She was even now abed!"

The Englishwoman looked frightened, and if she had hoped to help her husband, her words produced the opposite effect. Slowly Don Luis moved toward the bed. He twitched aside the sheet, his hard eyes searching for the telltale signs. Catherine saw the knuckles whiten in his hands. Hot with shame she raised her head still higher.

"Who?" demanded Don Luis.

"I do not know his name."

Don Luis's fingers closed around his sword. He drew it from its sheath.

"Indeed? Are you so free with your favors?"

Catherine smiled, glad to oppose him until he ran her through.

"It suited me better to dispose of them at will than to have them taken from me by someone like you."

The henchman holding her arms jerked one so violently she gasped.

"Who?" repeated Don Luis.

Half blind from pain she shook her head. She had no intention of serving Rodrigo de Valdivia's purpose in the quarrel between him and Don Luis. She drew more satisfaction from withholding the information from Don Luis, from letting him suppose she had destroyed her own honor rather than yield it to him.

The drawn sword touched the hollow of her throat.

"A name, señorita."

"It was some soldier passing in the street. Perhaps you can inquire of every soldier that you meet and see if one remembers."

She felt the shudder of his sword as anger shook him. Then Don Luis stepped back. He made a little bow. Without warning his arm darted out, sinking the steel blade of his weapon through Juan's chest until the point came out on the other side dripping red.

Even the unfortunate Juan was too stunned to cry out. He stood for a moment skewered like a piece of meat. Then Don

43

Luis with a careless twist of the wrist withdrew his sword and Juan fell to the floor with fingers spread in a futile attempt to dam the outward flood of his life.

Catherine found herself on the floor beside him, holding him. Rose had begun to shriek.

"English bitch! Get away!" he gasped as Rose bent over him. "Catherine! Catherine!"

She caught the blood-slick hands which were hunting her and held them tightly.

"Hermanita, help me! Bring a doctor."

"Yes, Juan. Quickly."

She knew a doctor would not help. Juan clung to her like a frightened child. Great convulsions wracked him as he struggled still to speak.

"Bautista—he has murdered a Bautista. You must avenge it, Catherine. You must make him pay for his infamy. You must—avenge—our name!"

His head dropped onto her arm. Juan was dead. Dazed, aware of the clamor of servants, Catherine got to her feet. Don Luis watched with scorn from beneath his thin, disparate eyebrows.

"The next time I ask a question you will answer," he predicted.

Catherine looked from him to her blood-drenched hands. His words trailed off in her ears. She collapsed.

A heavy light pushed through the shuttered windows when she woke. It was oppressively hot. She was in her own bed and Ana sat beside her bathing her hands. The maid's small face was swollen with crying. Catherine closed her eyes.

Had she caused Juan's death? She tried to care but couldn't. The part of her that felt and cared had stopped functioning, and the knowledge frightened her. She seemed hollow inside. A shell.

"Señorita?"

The terror in Ana's voice was too much to ignore. She opened her eyes again, waiting.

"Señorita, they have locked us in! It is well past noon and no food has come. They—they mean to starve us!"

"I think not," Catherine said listlessly. "You are in no danger, Ana. It is only I who have acted unwisely. Don't be afraid."

Ana twisted the cloth in her hands.

"You—you are ill, señorita?"

"No."

Her whole body ached. Hardest to ignore was the tenderness of the flesh between her legs.

Catherine's gaze wandered over the room. Juan's body had been removed. A dark stain covered the carpet where he had lain. The house was quiet.

Strange, her whole life seemed to have been spent in this house. Already her father's large home, which she had managed from the age of thirteen, belonged to some impossible tale told to children. Here in these dark walls she had been raped and her brother had died. Here she herself now faced an uncertain and unpleasant end. Would anything have been different if she had told the truth about Rodrigo de Valdivia?

Again the memory of hay and naked flesh came back to her and she gagged, cold and shaking beneath the sheets. Hearing Ana's sob, she fought against the welcome wave of darkness which threatened to drown her.

It would not pass immediately, but when it did she thought about the soldier with his mocking eyes and sense of wounded honor. Perhaps all honor was an illusion. Her poor, pathetic brother had courted it at the last, begging her to avenge him. Rolling her head from side to side in feeble despair she closed her eyes, pretending sleep.

Hours later she did sleep. The sound of Ana's moving across the room roused her at last. Day had fled and the sky beyond the window Ana had opened was as dark and lifeless as her own spirit. Someone was at the door, and as it opened Catherine recognized one of Don Luis's strongmen.

"Get your mistress up and dressed," he growled to Ana. "Don Luis is in no mood for excuses from anyone. If she's not ready when I return he'll have your ears for it."

The door was snatched shut under Ana's hands. She stifled a whimper.

"Pay no attention, Ana," Catherine said, swinging herself to a sitting position. "I will dress and go to him. The man who brought the orders is a bully. No one is angry with you."

Across the room Ana fidgeted.

"Shall I unpack the new corset that you brought, señorita? I tried to repair the old one, but—"

Catherine sighed, interrupting. Ana was slow with needlework. She wondered what the maid must be thinking about the neatly slit corset laces. Slipping off the bed she went to stand by her trunks, studying with little interest the dresses spread across them. The silks and velvets seemed to belong to some other woman, one who laughed and trusted. Not one with this terrible hardness at the core.

"Where is Doña Teresa?" she asked absently.

Ana gave a painful shrug of embarrassment.

"In her own room, señorita. She—she says she will take employment in another household."

Catherine's words were calm. "Of course. I've heard that Spanish servants are worth their weight in gold here. You'll find a fine job too, Ana." She made a faintly irritated gesture with her hand. "Bring me some water. Let me wash my face."

She chose a dress of stiff black satin parted in the front to frame a pearl-gray underskirt which shimmered softly. The night was warm and she slipped her arms through long slashes in the black satin sleeves so that they fell about her shoulders like a cape, affording the slightest coolness to arms encased in white lawn undersleeves. She had put on the colors of mourning. The face looking back at her from the mirror as Ana arranged her hair was pale, the eyes rimmed with shadows. Yet her chin retained its willful set. Frowning, she asked herself how that could be. Then, with a shrug, she retired to a corner where she said a rosary for Juan's soul.

At last there were footsteps in the corridor. Catherine felt her fingers tense. She willed them into loose repose.

"I have little to leave you, Ana," she said, speaking quickly. "These clothes and the jewels are yours if you can get them. If not then you must take this." She flourished the bank draft, then slid it back into its hiding place in the trunk lid. "Present it to a banking house, Ana. They will give you gold for it. Do you understand? And let no one else know of its whereabouts. It is yours."

The maid's face was white as she stared at her mistress.

"But, señorita, you—you—"

The door burst open. Don Luis's man stood outside, thumbs hooked through the belt which held his dagger.

"Goodby, Ana," Catherine said softly. She touched the maid's shoulder and walked with head high toward the door.

The man who was waiting seized her roughly by the arm. Her impulse was to draw away, but she thought better of it. Let them treat her like the prisoner she was. She would go with dignity.

In another minute she was at the door to the gaming room. She felt herself pushed inside. The bright glare of candles and the lack of nourishment combined to leave her feeling suddenly weak in the legs.

Don Luis de Alvarado sat easily in the room's only chair, his sumptuous costume of black edged with silver defiant, it seemed, of the unnattractive bandage plastered to his cheek. At the table around him sat some half-dozen men from the night before. The other tables were empty.

There was an air of expectancy in the room, yet Catherine found her attention drawn to the fireplace where Rodrigo de Valdivia stood, one boot upon a stool, exactly as he had the night before. He gave no sign of recognition, though the bull-chested man who was with him gave the faintest shake of his rust-hued head. He was the man who had lain sleeping in the courtyard, the one called Rojo, Red.

"A great calamity has befallen Doña Catherine," said Don Luis, his thin fingers peeling an apple with his dagger. "Her brother Juan died suddenly this morning. The lady has no place to go. I have taken it on myself to provide her with a protector. Alas, I cannot say a husband, for the lady is flawed."

A murmur made its way around the table. The gazes which were turned on her were bold, assessing, different in every way from the previous evening.

All but one of them. Alonzo Sanchez sat among the men, and his expression was stunned. Catherine felt a hotness on her cheeks. She looked away, unable to meet his eyes.

"Doña Catherine's brother owed me something over twenty thousand crowns," resumed the honeyed tones of Don Luis. "You, my lord marquis, you like a lady. This one reads and plays the cittern, so I am told. Will you make good her brother's debt?"

Humiliation blurred her vision. The councilman was selling her like some African slave. Yet note how subtle were his words; he did not soil himself by asking payment for her, but rather couched his demand in flowery phrases alluding to her welfare. Once, Catherine thought, she would have challenged his hypocrisy. Now she had no spirit left.

The Marquis de Zurbarán, stroked his thinning beard. His watery eyes were thoughtful. They moved over Catherine with the eagerness he had shown for gambling with her the night before and his smile attempted to charm her.

"Ah, Don Luis, you know my weakness. I would like to find this wicked little angel ever ready when I craved a game of cards. But twenty thousand crowns? Impossible. I'll give you ten."

"Come, come, my friend," said Don Luis. "You would pay that much for a merchant's daughter."

"Exactly!" agreed a round, sweaty man who had been watching Catherine hungrily. He sprang from the bench. "See here, my lord. Firm fleshed!" He raised Catherine's arms in the thin undersleeves, to a chorus of muttered admiration. His thick hands circled her waist and squeezed. "Nor is the lady laced past breathing. You are a poor judge, my lord marquis. She is worth at least fifteen thousand."

The men around the table laughed agreeably, some of them jostling the marquis, who sat undecided. Then a voice spoke from the fireplace.

"It would seem, Don Luis, that your profits might be higher if you put the lady up for auction."

Catherine glanced with a last flare of anger at Rodrigo de Valdivia. His dark eyes mocked them all. Her color deepened as she realized that he had judged the morals of these so-called gentlemen and found them little better than his own. Don Luis, who seemed to guess something similar, looked at the soldier with dislike. His voice, though cold, was even.

"Your choice of words betrays your lack of breeding, Valdivia, yet what you are suggesting is perhaps the fairest. Well, Don Pedro? Would you give fifteen thousand?"

The fat man, with his hands still on her waist, gave a nod.

"Very well, I will give sixteen," burst out the marquis.

"And I seventeen," said a third man at the table.

Catherine looked with mute shame toward Alonzo Sanchez. Would he not bid on her? He would not court her now, but would he make no effort to spare her this horror? His eyes were filled with pity and with anger, but he did not speak.

"Eighteen thousand crowns," Don Pedro said uncertainly, scratching his head.

The marquis tugged at his limp little beard.

"Twenty, then. But not a penny more."

Catherine knew then there would be no deliverance. What did it matter which of them she went to? She watched their faces bitterly. The third man who had bid now shook his head. He could not spend as freely as the old marquis. She heard Don Pedro give a sigh which marked defeat.

"Twenty-five thousand," came the offer from across the room.

Catherine gasped. The color drained from Don Luis's narrow face. Valdivia, who had spoken, looked faintly bored. His boot still rested on the stool. He did not even look at her.

The question she had asked herself a moment earlier resounded in her frightened mind, re-forming itself. Would it not be a thousand times better to be the property of the cultured old marquis than of a soldier? She could coax the marquis with a look—

"I think, Valdivia, you can scarcely afford such a costly mistress on soldier's pay," said Don Luis with silken insult.

As Valdivia set his foot down Catherine knew all was lost. His eyes were smoldering. Picking up a saddlebag which sat beside him on the floor, he flung it onto the table. Incredulous, one of the men who sat there opened it and watched the gold spill out.

Don Luis's long fingers formed steeples between his hands. "My lord marquis?"

The marquis shook his head. Catherine watched Don Luis's cruel mouth harden at the way all this had been maneuvered.

"Do not believe that after she has lived as a soldier's wench you can expect to sell her for more than the price of a loaf of bread," he warned sharply.

Valdivia, sauntering toward the table, looked at him with contempt.

"I will hardly be selling. I intend to marry the lady as soon as a priest can be found."

For the first time he allowed his eyes to encounter Catherine's, very briefly, and she saw the shadow of amusement. He took her arm.

"I will send for her trunks in the morning," he said as the men at the gaming table looked on, too stunned to speak.

Her degradation was complete. By a hand which was all too familiar Catherine felt herself led toward the door. The huge soldier Rojo stretched his arms before the fireplace, clearly ready to silence any protest at this outcome of events.

Like some blind beggar Catherine was drawn toward the stairs, down into the courtyard. Valdivia did not speak. A stable boy, appeared from the back with the large bay horse, who haughtily resisted this control by someone other than his master.

"Boabdíl!" commanded Valdivia. The great beast grew quiet at once.

What rashness of nerve, thought Catherine, naming a

horse for a Moorish king. Was this Valdivia defiant in everything he did?

They passed out into the street. Valdivia took the horse in hand.

"Can you ride in that attire?" he asked.

"No."

She felt wretched and shy before this man who knew her body so completely and who now claimed her. She could not raise her head to face him. Desperate in the silence which hung between them she reached out a hand to Boabdíl, thinking, too late, that she could not bear it if the horse pulled away. He snorted nervously but did not move. She stroked his silken nose.

"You did not name my name to Don Luis," said Valdivia with grim authority. "Why?"

Her fingers found their only strength in the horse's warmth.

"It was the one thing that he wanted. I didn't know that he would kill my brother when I refused."

Valdivia, studying her, gave a puzzled shake of the head. "The rumors are true then? He ran Juan through?"

"Yes."

"And the injury to his face—whose work is that?"

"I—I struck him with a candle holder and he was burned."

"The devil! You're lucky he did not kill you too!"

Biting her lip Catherine held back the urge to say her fate had been much worse.

"Señor Valdivia, I—I appeal to your honor. I have jewels I can sell—friends in Spain. I will repay what you have spent for me tonight, if you will only allow me the refuge of a convent. . . ."

Her voice trailed off at the amusement in his eyes.

"You do not understand, do you, *preciosa?* I want you. I wanted you even before fate cast you into my arms last night. I want you now—"

Interrupting himself he swept her to him and kissed her. She hung limp as a doll as his lips drew out all her thoughts.

"I have spent a fortune for you," he said, releasing her at last. "Far more than a man in my position can afford. I have no intention of letting you go, and even if I did, *preciosa,* there is not a convent nor even a nun in all Peru. Accept your fate. I am after all offering marriage."

Catherine winced at the magnanimity of his tone. He was sparing her the disgrace of living in sin, it was true, and by the sound of it he thought she should be grateful. None of the other men in the gaming room would have given her their name. But how could she be grateful to him when he was the one who had ruined her? That she could never forgive him.

They had reached the central plaza, walking through streets where at this hour only a few candles flickered. In the stillness she could hear the soft rush of the River Rimac. The cathedral faced them, its roofline hung with stars. On every side there were fine palaces.

"Where are you taking me?" she asked, and blushed remembering how she had uttered that question the night before.

"I will place you in the protection of the Marquesa de Zurbarán." As a cry of protest escaped her Valdivia said calmly, "There are in the city no more than a handful of women with backgrounds similar to your own, and I know none of them. As the lady of greatest status in Lima the marquesa also will be most compelled to render help. Moreover she is a religious woman. She will not turn from her duty."

"But her husband—"

"Sought you as mistress? He will hardly speak of that to the marquesa. The marquis is somewhat ridiculous, bringing his flowery manners here where there is no time for them, waiting only to make his fortune and return to Spain, but there is no harm in him."

As he spoke he stopped at a vaulted door heavy with carving and raised the knocker. The sound of it thundered through the night. They waited some minutes before Valdivia knocked again. This time muffled footsteps sounded on the other side of the wood. The door inched open and a wizened servant peered out.

"This is a decent house," he said. "Who dares disturb it at this hour and to what purpose? Speak quickly! We number at the ready a dozen armed men."

Valdivia flashed his smile.

"Señor, I crave your pardon for the intrusion. I come to beg the mercy of the good marquesa in sheltering a lady newly arrived from Spain."

The servant scowled at Catherine.

"The marquesa has retired to her chambers."

"In the name of charity see if she will receive us. This lady has lost her family and has no place to go."

The servant wavered.

"Only tell her that Doña Catherine Bautista de Caño of

51

Seville awaits her generosity. If your lady chooses not to see us we will leave."

With doubt still evident in his face the servant turned and started for the stairs. A sleepy stable boy came forward and took the halter of Boabdíl.

It mattered not to Catherine that minutes turned into eternity. She watched them pass with detachment. An hour ago she had anticipated her own death. Now, without feeling, she awaited whatever befell her.

There was a rapid shuffling of feet as the servant returned twice as quickly as he'd gone. He held a candle before them.

"The marquesa will receive you," he announced.

Valdivia gave Catherine his arm. As they were ushered along the main gallery to a smaller one overlooking a second courtyard, his eyes took in the rich tiles covering the walls, the wood carved with extravagant elegance. The servant opened a door before them and they entered a sitting room complete with carpets and tapestries. Wall sconces blazed.

Before them, attended by two women, stood an austere, small woman with bright hawk eyes and a mole on her chin. Her white hair had been pinned hastily up, leaving a few escaping wisps which on a woman of lesser rank might have destroyed the impression of absolute command. A sumptuous cloak with deep silver borders had been thrown on over her night clothes, and she looked for all the world as if she had been up and dressed for hours.

At sight of her Valdivia sank to one knee, his dark head bowed.

"My lady marquesa, I ask your pardon for disturbing your household. I am Rodrigo de Valdivia, and I come here not on my own account, but for this lady soon to be my wife. Her brother was killed today, leaving her without family. An inn is no place for a decent woman. As I know you to be a good christian I beg you by the blessed Virgin to grant her shelter."

The politic speech surprised Catherine, who unconsciously turned her head to look at the lips which had uttered it. This was an altogether different man from the mocking soldier. His face was grave, his tone respectful.

The marquesa looked over his head toward Catherine.

"Where is your dueña, señorita?"

Catherine had no desire to lie. Words to explain her situation simply came slowly.

"Her dueña felt it beneath her to chaperone someone

betrothed to a soldier," said Valdivia before she could answer.

Tapping a bony finger saddled with a ring of pearls too large for it, the marquesa sighed.

"This was one of those matches kept from you until your arrival, then," she said. "A disgusting practice, if you will overlook my saying so, Señor Valdivia, but one which is with us nevertheless. And where, pray tell, are the lady's trunks?"

She made an impatient gesture for him to rise. The mole on her chin gleamed like a cherry pip in the candlelight. Valdivia stood, dusting his breeches.

"At her brother's house, marquesa. Her brother's wife is there, an Englishwoman of loose repute."

The marquesa snorted.

"Marguerita, show this lady to a room then, and attend her. If she came on the ship arrived yesterday she is no doubt still quite tired, so hold your chatter."

She turned in dismissal as Catherine started after the maid who had been addressed. At the door from the room the marquesa looked back.

"We shall expect the lady's luggage tomorrow, Señor Valdivia. You may call late in the afternoon if you desire."

Catherine would have followed her at once, but Valdivia stepped forward to detain her.

"Your dueña—shall I engage her as housekeeper? You will need one and there rarely is a Spanishwoman to be had."

The first reawakening of emotion stirred in Catherine. Her head went up. Her voice shook with her anger.

"No," she said. "I will not have her near me. She proved disloyal and I never want to see the woman again."

6.

Marguerita, the maid, brought fruit and milk sops at midmorning. Catherine could see the worry in her face when she did not touch them. With poignant remembrance she thought of a maid much less skilled, and frightened, Ana. She wondered whether Ana would make her way in the world alone.

A strange lethargy had settled over Catherine. She could not move her head from the pillow. Soon she would wed Rodrigo de Valdivia. She would be provided for. She ought to be grateful, but she wasn't. Listlessly she fixed her gaze upon the window, wondering how many women ended up like this, going through all the motions of living when their spirit had gone out.

In memory Catherine heard her father's voice: *I have prepared you to wed nobly, daughter. You read, know something of history, ciphers and music, and your expertise in running this household equips you easily to manage one three times its size.* How she had failed his hopes!

Knuckles rapped sharply at the door. Marguerita fluttered forward to admit the marquesa.

"You have little appetite," observed the marquesa, noting the tray beside the bed. Today she was an imposing figure, small but carrying her dress of heavy silk with its jeweled pendant as if neither weighed more than a feather. Not a strand of snowy hair escaped its elaborate coif this morning.

"I—I grieve for my brother," said Catherine.

"Yes, and for betrothal to a soldier, too," the marquesa said shrewdly. "But come, others have shared your fate. Many of these soldiers hold great grants of land. Lieutenant Valdivia's is one of the smallest, it is true, worth scarcely a thousand ducats a year I would judge, but you will not starve. You are young. Quite pretty. Perhaps he will be killed—the life of a soldier is short. There are plenty of men of wealth who would court such a charming widow."

Catherine blinked in amazement. The pragmatic marquesa fanned herself with energy, barely missing the mole on her chin.

"Moreover," the marquesa added, "Rodrigo de Valdivia is a religious man. I recognize his face from Mass, which is more than I can say for most. Get up from your bed. I am sending Doña Mercedes, a cousin of mine, to be your dueña."

At a look from the marquesa Marguerita opened the door. Doña Mercedes, a plump, placid woman who had been waiting outside, was admitted.

"The marquis and I will expect you to join us for lunch," said the marquesa, known before her marriage as Doña Beatriz from Salamanca.

Catherine gasped at the prospect of facing the marquis.

"I—could not tax your hospitality, marquesa."

"You will tax it if you choose to stay in your room and make work for the servants. Good morning, doña."

She was almost out the door before Catherine drew courage to speak.

"My lady marquesa, might I have a tub sent up for a bath? It is the custom, I believe, before marriage."

At birth, before marriage, and after the birth of a child. Those were the only occasions when most women bathed save for the final cleansing prior to meeting God. The marquesa's dark eyebrows had gone straight up.

"A custom, yes, but on the day before." Amusement touched the matriarchal lips. "However, as it's the first sign of interest I've seen in your forthcoming match, I see no harm. Who knows when the wedding will be, anyway? Things are done with absolutely no regard to form here."

An hour later, before a roaring fire and protected by a great screen to ward off fatal drafts, Catherine stepped into her bath. It was enough to turn one into a stew, she thought. The day was warm enough without the fire. Yet tears of gratitude sprang to her eyes as she covered herself with the warm, clear water.

She sought to wash away not only the residue of months of travel, but all trace of Valdivia, knowing full well that in the latter she failed. She could recall his touch, his strength defeating her, and she thrust the memory violently away. She would rather be in hell than to be his wife, subjected to his whims and listening to his taunts.

Doña Mercedes came to watch as Marguerita dressed Catherine's hair and readied her. Her borrowed dueña was a good-humored woman who no doubt occupied an inferior position in the household and seemed grateful for this minor diversion. She tactfully asked few questions of Catherine and seemed undisturbed by her silence. Catherine welcomed her stolid presence when it came time to present themselves for lunch.

The marquis's dining room was in truth a banquet hall, capable of seating sixty or more. The ceiling was brilliant with tiles in a Moorish design, each painted with touches of silver. On a dais at one end a table was spread with a snowy cloth on which there rested silver plates and goblets. A servant was filling the marquis's goblet from a ewer of wine. Another servant held a napkin at the ready for any who summoned it.

"Well, señorita, you look considerably refreshed," said the marquesa in greeting. "Allow me to present my husband, the Marquis de Zurbarán. Doña Catherine Bautista de Caño, my dear."

The marquis rose gravely, betraying not a wink or a flicker of recognition.

"It is a pleasure to welcome you into our house, Doña Catherine. You are from Seville, did my wife say? We have many friends there."

The four of them sat down together, and over duck and salad Catherine's nervousness gradually fled. Once she sent a look of gratitude to the marquis. He answered with a courtly smile. He would not publicize her shame.

Afternoon was waning when a maid knocked at Catherine's door with great excitement.

"Señorita, a—most peculiar individual asks to see you. The marquesa sent him to the drawing room."

"Most peculiar," Catherine thought. Was that how Valdivia would be regarded? But when she and Doña Mercedes arrived in the drawing room she found waiting not Valdivia but his red-haired friend.

"Señorita Bautista," he said, bowing deeply. "I am known as Captain Rojo, a comrade of Rodrigo de Valdivia. He sends me to present you with this gift in his behalf."

Extending his hand he moved a few steps toward her, uneasily, as though the polished floors beneath his boots felt unpleasantly foreign. The marquesa, fanning herself in one corner of the room, watched curiously as Catherine stepped forward to meet him.

He was huge. Her head did not come to his shoulder and the width of those shoulders looked as though they might fill a doorway. His nose was hooked, his beard square and rough, and as he came near a powerful odor invaded her nostrils. It was not the normal male smell of sweat and horses, but one strong with garlic and something else hot which brought the tears to her eyes.

"I—thank you, señor," she gasped, as he dropped something into her hand. Retreating a few steps backward she looked at her palm. It held a gold ring set with an emerald, deep green and as large in size as the nail on the finger which would wear it. Never had she held a more costly jewel.

"I don't understand," said Catherine, as Doña Mercedes and even the marquesa came forward to see.

"It was part of his booty from a campaign in the north," said Rojo simply. "He has had it set in a ring for you."

Catherine continued to stare at it.

"Come," said the marquesa. "Put it on."

Slipping it onto her next smallest finger, Catherine watched it flash. It was a jewel befitting the very rich. Valdivia's extravagance in bestowing it upon her took her breath away.

"A fine fit," said the marquesa. "Now, where are Señorita Bautista's trunks?"

Rojo's bushy mustache rose over a smile.

"They will be here shortly, marquesa. Upon my word."

When he had gone the marquesa's attendants and Doña Mercedes crowded closer, examining the ring.

"It is the most beautiful betrothal ring I've ever seen," said Doña Mercedes.

Catherine could not deny it was beautiful. Had Valdivia brought it to her himself she wouldn't have known what to think; that he sought to win her favor, perhaps. The fact that he sent it by Rojo showed it meant nothing to him.

Why he had chosen so costly a gift she could not imagine, unless it was intended as some sort of compensation for the wrong already done her. Despite his boasts of having no conscience she began to suspect he had purchased her as his wife out of some distorted sense of duty. He had been filled with wine the night he forced himself upon her. That was the source of his lust. So in atonement he had condemned them both to a future neither would choose.

On invitation of the marquesa she stayed in the drawing room, plucking idly at a cittern while her hostess busied herself with needlework, speaking from time to time in abrupt staccato snatches.

"Disgusting, the crowds in the streets today. Always the same when new silks arrive. . . . The cathedral needs altar cloths. . . . More fruit would end half of the gout complaints."

They were occupied in this lopsided conversation when a maid appeared, announcing breathlessly. "My lady, the luggage is arriving."

The marquesa inclined her head in invitation toward the mirador, the narrow balcony whose finely carved sides afforded them clear vision of the street while hiding them from all who passed. Through the breaks in the wood Catherine watched half a dozen pairs of Indian men approaching, each pair of them carrying one of her trunks between them. In front of them came Valdivia on the bay horse Boabdíl. Rojo brought up the rear on a grayish mount.

"Receive Señor Valdivia in the rear courtyard," ordered the marquesa with a softening of the lips. "I will not put my legs to the unnecessary exercise of going down to greet him. Wish him good day."

Obediently Catherine left with Doña Mercedes for the rear courtyard. Valdivia was being ushered in as they arrived. He watched them descend the broad stone stairs and move past lilies, carnations and tubbed fig trees to the central fountain where he waited. His legs were planted slightly apart, emphasizing the angular muscularity of his body. The sun broke on the dark crests of his hair, scattering its blackness with the fire of amber and rubies.

"Doña Catherine," he said, nodding.

"Señor Valdivia. I—trust that all goes well with you today?"

She felt as stiff as wood. What went on behind Valdivia's smoldering eyes she could not determine, save when they mocked her. Doña Mercedes had stopped at the edge of the courtyard and settled herself on a bench, apparently choosing the role of an indulgent dueña eager to allow young couples their own sweet and private words.

"The ring fit well enough, I suppose?" said Valdivia, his voice evincing little interest although he glanced at her hand.

"Yes, very well." Catherine carefully equaled his indifference. She drew a breath for the speech she had been preparing. "Señor Valdivia, I beg you to take back your gift. Let me return to Spain. Already the servants in this house gossip about us. Soon all Lima will do likewise. For you—for a man—things are forgiven. In a woman they are not. You are condemning me to a life of perpetual disgrace if I remain here. I beg you to have mercy. I appeal to your honor—"

"What honor could I claim if I let you bear a nameless child?" he interrupted softly.

58

Her heart took a frightened tumble. Color leaped to her face. Valdivia, watching her, shook his head.

"Is it possible that thought had not occurred to you?"

Catherine moistened her lips.

"I—will seek shelter in a convent. It will not matter."

"A convent three months away? And what if you were found to be with child on the voyage? You would be the prey of every man on ship. No, *preciosa,* I am your only hope of safety. It's true I have given you some cause to dislike me, but I have dealt with you generously in amends. Both of us will survive a little gossip."

His casual attitude angered her. Had she lost all pride that she begged mercy from this man, who spoke as though he were some benevolent parent and she the petulant child?

"No doubt the prospect of scandal appeals to you, Señor Valdivia," she suggested with heat. "Your contempt of society is all too evident!"

"And your fear of it surprising. Tell me, is it gossip about your sins you fear, or about a marriage beneath you?"

The taunt was all too accurate.

"I have not sinned!" she cried.

"No? The society you so esteem would say you had, in playing cards with the good marquis."

"You are contemptible!"

She whirled away but his quick grip stayed her.

"And losing my temper," he warned. "Tread carefully."

Catherine tried to twist free of him. His hold on her wrist was hidden from Doña Mercedes by the wide spray of the fountain.

"I have offered you the decency of marriage," he said sternly. "If that does not suit you I can easily make you my mistress. Shall we start now? It would end the need for a dueña."

He had drawn her against him. Catherine shrank back, frightened by the hardness of his face.

"You—pretend noble motives for offering marriage when it is clearly to your own advantage!" she panted. "By marrying me you gain for your children the titles of don and doña."

"I am less than interested in titles."

"But I would guess you are interested in the law which requires a man to marry if he retains an *encomienda!*"

"That law is flouted."

"Then—"

"Silence!" His free hand captured her chin and forced it up

toward him. "I want the use of your body, nothing more. And I will have it. Married or not you are going to warm my bed."

She felt the sudden tensing of his body, recognized it. The nearness of his desire set her heart racing. Suddenly footsteps, light and running, sounded in the courtyard.

"Señorita!" cried a voice.

As Valdivia released her, Catherine, in astonishment, saw Ana hurl toward her. Flinging herself to a stop, the maid caught Catherine's hand and, weeping, pressed it to her lips. Catherine hugged her, tears in her own eyes as she stroked the frail young shoulders.

"Oh, Ana!" she choked. "Ana." She looked across Ana's head. "I do thank you, Señor Valdivia. I am most grateful."

"I see. No word of thanks for a ring most women would envy, yet tears for a serving girl who looks to be less help than bother."

"She is a human being!" Catherine hissed.

She caught the sudden flash of his grin.

"Oh, señorita!" sniffed Ana, straightening. "You should have seen Señor Valdivia! Don Luis left two of his men to keep your trunks from leaving and they drew swords on him, they and two servants with them. Señor Valdivia fought them all and ran one through."

Rodrigo de Valdivia squinted at a fig tree, whistling softly.

"The Englishwoman, your brother's wife, took the bank draft."

Ana sat on a trunk lid, tears welling from time to time as she told her story. Marguerita and other maids of the marquesa's had been in Catherine's room for a long time after the trunks arrived, helping with the unpacking. It was only near dinnertime, when even Doña Mercedes had withdrawn, that Catherine and her maid at last were alone.

"She came to the room the very night you left," continued Ana, twisting the handkerchief Catherine had given her. "She went through all the trunks and everything. She found the paper. There was no way I could stop her, señorita." Ana began to cry.

"There, there, Ana. It doesn't matter. We don't need the money."

It was a lie, but it lifted Ana's spirits. She blew her nose.

"Señor Valdivia has money. I hadn't thought of that. He says he will provide a proper house for you. It's why he brought me to you."

This was the first that Catherine had heard, or even thought, about a house. With a shudder she realized Valdivia might well have planned to install her in rented rooms, or even an inn. But could he truly afford a house, she wondered.

"The redbeard, Captain Rojo, he said Señor Valdivia was a fool to plan so grandly. He said that feeding me would be a waste of good money, and he called me a silly little goose."

Ana blew her nose again, this time indignantly. The sound was the first thing in days to bring a smile to Catherine's lips.

"You are not a goose. And how did you manage to save so many of my mother's jewels?"

"I sat on them, señorita. You had said I was to have them. I—I heard Señor Valdivia had taken you away. I was gathering things to leave myself when I heard someone coming. I dared not hide all the jewels, so I took the best ones and left the others. When the Englishwoman came in I sat in the corner. She hardly noticed me. She thought that I was too afraid to move. But she found the bank draft."

The corners of Ana's mouth turned down again.

"By rights the jewels should be yours now," said Catherine. As she saw Ana start to protest she smiled. "As I see you are about to refuse, you must have at least this for your loyalty."

From her own hand she took a delicate pearl ring and held it out to Ana. The brilliant emerald eclipsed the pearl. Besides, thought Catherine sadly, the ring which she was offering Ana was a girl's ring, and she herself was no longer a girl.

Ana's face shone with pleasure. Color washed her cheeks.

"Oh, señorita!" she exclaimed.

By the time she had retired that night Catherine had decided if Valdivia would not release her she would escape him. She seethed with the memory of his arrogance and the blunt way he had told her he sought her for one thing only. She would sell a piece of the jewelry Ana had saved and escape to the port.

Two days passed before she had the opportunity. After Mass the marquesa planned a social call. Catherine, returning to the house with Doña Mercedes, pleaded a headache and retired to her room.

"Send for the horses," she ordered.

Ana, when Catherine had sent her out to sell a necklace, had found a man with horses to rent. A signal had been arranged, a piece of paper bearing the marquis's coat of arms, which would be sent by one of the Indian boys forever visible in the streets. Upon receipt of it two horses would be left in an alley near the marquis's residence.

Now Catherine drew on her riding dress—the only one left her after her other futile attempt at escape—wishing as she did so that it were anything less noticeable than this expensive deep, dark blue. There had been no time to secure a proper costume for Ana. She would have to make do with a loose-skirted dress. And she would have to manage despite the fact that she had never sat a saddle before, Catherine thought grimly.

As they let themselves out the back door of the household which had sheltered them, she drew a breath. This time she was flying brazenly in the face of convention, slipping away from the kindly dueña who had been generously given her, betraying the marquis and the good marquesa. There would be no returning to decent society.

Ana wept the first hour in the saddle, as terrified of the horse beneath her as she was of falling. Ignoring her, Catherine tried to keep her bearings by the rough map drawn up by the man who rented the horses. Finding their way to Callao would have been no trick; they could follow the river. But Catherine had specified back roads out of Lima and they threaded their way past small houses, irrigation ditches and finally the Indian gardens which fed the city.

Once on the open road Ana could not keep any sort of pace at all. She slipped this way and that in the saddle. Catherine tugged crossly at the white lawn at her throat, further aggravated by the nervous perspiration trickling down from her temples. Finally, after coaxing and threatening Ana to make greater speed, and seeing patient instruction in the art of riding was in vain, she smacked Ana's horse across the rump and watched with satisfaction as the animal took off, its rider, for all her shrieks, maintaining a seat.

They were to leave their horses at an inn well frequented by sea travelers. There, Ana had been assured, they could easily learn of any ship about to sail. Catherine hoped so. After these few hours she already saw the staggering effort required to care not only for herself but for Ana. Nor was she unaware of the looks cast in their direction by the men who passed them on the road, especially as they at last reached Callao and their pace was slowed.

In the event Valdivia should trace them, they would not stay at the inn where they left the horses, she decided. As soon as they booked passage they would look for lodgings elsewhere.

It was scorching hot in Callao. The midday sun was reflected in blinding sheets from the long shoreline with its hodgepodge of buildings. As they drew up to look for the inn a sailor detached himself from a group drinking wine in a spot of shade and stepped into the street, seizing Catherine's bridle.

"Say, pretty one, if you're lost I'll take you in."

"Let go of my horse," said Catherine coldly.

"Not very friendly, are you?" He inched toward her. "Paid for by some rich captain, by the looks of those clothes. Turn your nose up at an ordinary sailor, do you? Seems to me you ought to be a little more polite."

Catherine's heart beat raggedly at the glitter in his eyes. As his hand neared her stirrup she jerked sharply on her horse's reins. The animal reared, throwing the sailor to the ground. As the hooves struck the ground Catherine sent him galloping forward and Ana's mount followed, so abruptly that the maid herself was almost left behind.

Racing up one street and down another, they lost their bearings. But when they reined their winded horses, in a street where there were no loiterers, they sighted the inn in the distance.

A woman carrying slops from the kitchen directed them to the man who would collect their horses. He sat beneath a lean-to propped against the stable, a hat tipped over his eyes as he whittled a piece of wood. At sight of them a curious expression stole across his face. He came toward them rubbing his fingers on his shirt.

"Luis Gomez?" inquired Catherine.

He nodded, grinning boldly at her. She tossed him the reins.

"You are to receive these horses, which we rented in Lima this morning. Also I am told you can inform us of any ships making ready to sail."

He continued to grin, a sensual, heavy-lipped gesture.

"Aye, I can tell you, as soon as you pay for the horses."

Catherine, just dismounted, stared at him.

"We paid when we received them."

"A down payment only. And look, you have ridden them hard—it is extra for that."

"Nonsense! Take them and good riddance. Even if we had money to part with we wouldn't."

He caught her as she started past.

"Any woman who travels alone can offer payment better than money."

He leered at her with yellow teeth.

There was a gleam, quick and silver, in the sunlight. The man holding Catherine staggered back from her cursing and clutching his arm, which ran red from wrist to shoulder. Her throat frozen with fear, Catherine turned to look into the steely face of Valdivia.

"Draw your sword," he commanded.

The man with the horses snarled like some maddened animal.

"With pleasure, meddler!"

He jerked his sword free.

Catherine watched with a sense of unreality. Valdivia could not be here, unless he was some familiar of Satan who could divine the future. Yet it chagrined her that in the instant she had recognized his presence she had been glad of it. There had been no feeling in his face. He had not even glanced at her. And now, almost with disgust, he thrust at his adversary, who parried clumsily.

It was over almost at once. The man of the rented horses struck in a rage at Valdivia, who with the slightest shift of body ran him through. Stooping, he wiped his sword on sun-scorched grass. The still air was filled with the death moans of his opponent. Catherine shrank before the brutal gaze of the man who had saved her.

"Another life against my soul," he said, "and all for the sake of your rashness. Does it please you, Doña Catherine, to see the ground run red?"

She could not answer him. Her hands were pressed to her mouth, her face was wet with tears. In the background she heard Ana gasping.

"You, girl, bend over and let your head drop before you are senseless," Valdivia ordered the maid. He took Catherine's arm.

Numb, she let him guide her toward a table placed in the shade outside the inn. There were other men nearby drinking wine and ale, and while they looked at her with curiosity she realized there was in their looks nothing of the danger which brief experience had shown her awaited a woman alone. She sat across from Valdivia with downcast eyes.

Undisturbed he ordered wine and cheese, motioning impatiently for Ana to join them. He had complained of another life against his soul, thought Catherine, dizzily, yet how many other men he must have killed to move so quickly and without emotion. She shuddered with revulsion.

"The marquesa and Doña Mercedes were greatly upset by your disappearance," he said, ending an interminable silence. "They feared for your safety."

"How did—how did you find us so quickly?"

The stern look had not left his face. He speared a piece of cheese with his dagger.

"Your dueña went to your room to inquire after you. Even as you were slipping away from the back of the house, I have no doubt. She sent for the marquesa and the marquesa sent for me. I am well acquainted with the few places one may hire horses, and also where one leaves them. I no doubt was out of the city ahead of you."

A sob of angry defeat hung on Catherine's lips. She could not escape him. And now . . . what would be the penalty for trying?

He proferred a piece of cheese on the sharp silver blade.

"Eat and drink. I will not have you fainting on the ride back. It would be too distressing to the household which has shown you kindnes."

She stared at him, certain that she had not heard correctly. "Am I to return to the marquesa's, then?"

"On the assumption you will cause no further trouble."

"I—I have learned the impossibility of traveling without a man's protection."

"And that I do not let my property slip through my fingers—you have learned that too, I trust?"

Pressing her lips together she nodded. Valdivia reached across the table and touched the emerald ring.

"What did you sell for money if not this?"

"A necklace."

A cold shudder gripped her again as she wondered how many men he had killed for the glittering emerald. Why had she not sold it?

She could not read his expression. "Come," he said. "There is a silk shop near here. We will take a length of material back to your dueña for the worry you have caused her."

Exhausted and confused she went with him through the dusty streets. She was his property. He would not let her go. The man who had been killed on her account had been an animal, but his death weighed heavy on her conscience. She would be the cause of no more bloodshed.

The interior of the silk shop was dark, lighted by only a single window. Catherine stopped just inside, unable to see. A dim shadow turned toward her.

"Why, Doña Catherine," came the mincing voice of Elvira Berruguete. "I hardly thought to see you again. Your dueña Doña Teresa came to us seeking employment. She left us with the impression you would be going to—what is the place?—ah, Cuzco."

The malicious satisfaction in Elvira's eyes was visible even in the poorly lighted silk shop. Her dimpled smile bespoke superiority. Was Cuzco not the gathering place of soldiers? Doña Teresa had no doubt told her something of Catherine's being carried off by a soldier.

Almost by instinct Catherine's head went up. She forced a smile.

"To Cuzco? Why no, we will remain in Lima. Surely Doña Teresa told you I am betrothed? Come, meet the man I am to marry."

Gracefully she reached out the hand which wore the fiery emerald and drew Elvira forward, at the same time turning slightly to slip a hand through Valdivia's arm. She glanced up apprehensively to see his mocking smile.

"Doña Elvira Berruguete, allow me to present Señor Rodrigo de Valdivia, lieutenant of cavalry."

Her slight mouth slack with disbelief, Elvira pulled her eyes from the ring and stared at Valdivia.

"Señorita Berruguete. Ladies."

He bowed in turn, first to Elvira and then to her straight-backed dueña and attractive maid.

"Señor Valdivia," said Elvira, recovering enough to stress the undistinguished title. Her eyes slipped sideways to Catherine's. "You are betrothed? How interesting. But—ah—surely you have rather prematurely dispensed with a dueña?"

Catherine's laugh, if it was brittle, did not sound so to Elvira, judging by her sour expression.

"I have a new dueña, a darling. She is a relative of the Marquesa de Zurbarán in whose house I am staying."

"We have slipped away from her for a few minutes only to buy a length of silk with which to surprise her," Valdivia put in. "Now if you will excuse us. . . ."

Elvira's perfect little face was rigid with annoyance.

"Of course," she sniffed. "I personally find the merchandise here lacks quality." With a flounce which set her skirts to wobbling she marched out, accompanied by her ladies.

"So," said Valdivia, grinning down, "you have consented to the terms of marriage, then?"

Catherine met his eyes briefly.

"Did I not say I had learned the folly of being a woman alone?"

"A pretty act you put on for that plump little parsnip. She must think you are mad for me."

As Catherine blushed a laugh welled in his throat.

"I told you you could still the gossips, *preciosa*. Remember, the only one who can rob you of your pride is you yourself." Stacks of silk on a table hid them from the shop owner. Valdivia's eyes were flames. "You have not thanked me for the ring," he said. "Nor for the length of silk I am about to buy you to replace another riding dress which you once wore."

Catherine hesitated.

"Be quick," he said, "or I could well ask more than a kiss."

Miserable, she recognized she had no choice except to yield her body. Trembling, she raised her mouth.

He kissed her slowly, savoring her surrender. There warred inside her anger at herself for her defeat and outraged fear as she began to feel her senses melt and flow together. When he released her she would have lost her balance had she not clung to the arms around her.

"Nothing compels me to marry you," she whispered breathlessly. "I carry no child."

"For which you are no doubt grateful. Nevertheless you will marry me—or be my mistress. Say it!"

As he spoke he shook her shoulders. Wondering what had drawn that rush of words from her, Catherine looked into eyes half crazed with desire. She realized now there would be no escaping.

Wearily and with pounding heart she nodded.

"Yes. I will—marry you."

7

In the early morning sunshine Catherine listened to the clamor. From the marquesa's kitchen came sounds of servants preparing curded beef soup and jellied fowl, parsley bread and tansy cake, dates fat with wine and eggs and cheese, the foods to celebrate her wedding feast.

Far from disowning her after her futile, unchaperoned ride for freedom now more than a week in the past, the marquesa was claiming her as a welcome charge before all Lima with this lavish show. At times Catherine wondered whether this had been selected as punishment for her misconduct. She and Valdivia could have exchanged their vows with virtual privacy. At other times tears crept to her eyes at the thought of the marquesa's goodness. Of her own mother Catherine had but a fleeting memory, for the woman who had borne her had succumbed to plague not many years later. In the marquesa she seemed to have found a ruthlessly unsentimental and always pragmatic second. Of course one could not express such presumptuous thoughts to the marquesa.

"Señorita! You will catch a cold!"

Ana's cry from the gallery above the courtyard where Catherine sat brought her inescapably to the present. The maid was dancing on the air this morning with excitement over the wedding. And also, Catherine suspected, with the prospect of being not only maid but housekeeper, a position of authority which must seem ludicrous to all but Ana herself. Sighing, Catherine rose from the last sweet minutes of privacy which she might ever know.

Assisted by Ana and Marguerita and half a dozen other maids who could not bear to be excluded from this festive occasion, Catherine dressed for her wedding. Her petticoats were newly sewn, so lavish with lace that, as Marguerita laughed, it was a shame to hide them. Doña Mercedes, joining them just then, predicted that vanity would one day overcome propriety and lace would make its appearance on outer garments just as it had done on the edge of handkerchiefs in recent years.

Merrily, and with many romantic sighs, the women arranged her dress, a creation of soft black velvet so smooth and glowing it could only have been made in Spain. Its hem was edged in the finest silver embroidery, the tiny stitches depicting small roses. The sides of the overskirt were gathered up, yielding deep points front and back which caught the sheen of the velvet. A row of silver buttons decorated the bodice, and at her throat Catherine wore a brooch her father had given her, set with pearls and centered with a small but lovely emerald which matched the one on her finger.

"The cart is ready," announced the marquesa coming into the room.

With a heart which beat more from fear than from anticipation, Catherine stepped into the cart which would carry her and the marquesa to the cathedral. The marquis, on a horse sporting silks of scarlet, rode beside. How would Valdivia appear on this occasion, Catherine wondered. Would he wear the red breeches? His armor? She felt the stirrings of anxiety over how he might feel about these genteel plans of the marquesa and whether he might rebel.

But when he met them on the steps of the cathedral she viewed him with surprise. He had exchanged his soldier's attire for the silk suit of a gentleman, beautifully cut. It, too, was of that most fashionable color, black, with trim of deep, dark wine which was repeated in silk stockings. At his neck he wore a modest ruff and from his belt, gleaming handsomely, hung the etched silver sword case which had belonged to Catherine's father and which had been her wedding gift to her bridegroom.

At least she could never complain of lacking a handsome husband, Catherine thought as her throat closed over. The memory that he sought her only for physical pleasure caused a small ache inside her. He bowed to her stiffly and with cool possession took her arm.

All Lima, it seemed, waited in the cathedral as they entered. In this raw, young country, the farthest removed of any spot in the Indies, a wedding was a welcome excuse for merrymaking. But first the couple about to be joined went separately before a confessor.

"I do not wish this marriage," whispered Catherine as she knelt before him.

She expected no comfort and she received none.

"Would you neglect your duty to the church? To Spain?" asked the priest. "By adding christian souls to this heathen land you do God's will."

While candles flickered and saints and supplicants looked

on, Catherine Bautista de Caño was bound irretrievably to her husband. In absolute silence, aware of the marquesa's smile and many curious eyes, she left the church on his arm, stepping out into a brilliant, cloudless day.

Across the street from the cathedral a horseman waited. At sight of him Rodrigo stopped. A frown spread quickly across his face.

"What is it?" asked Catherine, feeling the sudden tenseness of his body.

He did not answer. The horseman sped away.

"Nothing," he said. "It's nothing."

At the marquis's palace places had been laid for fifty guests, a modest banquet. Catherine was relieved that Viceroy Blasco Nuñez was expected to arrive tomorrow and that the grand reception the marquis planned in his honor precluded a larger celebration on the present occasion. Also, she felt certain, the marquesa knew the wisdom of restraint. Even her position as the highest-ranking woman in Lima could not completely still the gossip about her charge.

"I have heard that he carried her off—and that she did not protest!" whispered a woman behind her fan as they moved through the banquet room receiving congratulations.

"I have heard she offered herself in payment of her brother's gambling debts!"

Catherine held her head erect, lips pressed together. She glanced at her husband. He was oblivious to the whispers, more silent and withdrawn than she had ever known him. From the time they left the cathedral he had not looked at her, and his eyes, in which she had thought to see approval of her careful toilette, burned instead with savage triumph.

"My dear, you have not met our governor," said the marquis, making his way to her side with a tall, mild-looking man. "Doña Catherine Bautista de Valdivia, his excellency Vaca de Castro."

Answering to her unfamiliar new name Catherine curtsied low to the man who for three years had governed Peru, putting down civil war, establishing order. That he had not been named viceroy when the position was established seemed a slight. She wondered what his feelings were in the matter.

"I wish you happiness, Doña Catherine," said the governor. "And to you, Señor Valdivia, prosperity."

Rodrigo nodded.

The marquis had turned away to other guests. Vaca de Castro hesitated.

"Tell me, Señor Valdivia, how will your friend Pizarro receive the crown's new representative? With friendship?"

Rodrigo's voice was sharp, almost defiant. "I do not know the general's sentiment toward the viceroy."

"I have heard that certain *encomenderos* of Cuzco have summoned him to that city, that fearing the viceroy they urge revolt, which Pizarro wisely resists."

"It's long since I have been in Cuzco," Rodrigo answered with caution.

The governor inclined his head in a thoughtful pose. His shrewd eyes studied Rodrigo. Then smiling he took his leave.

The only soldiers present in the banquet hall were a few of the high-ranking captains. With their gaudy doublets and restive stances they stood apart from the other guests, a tight little enclave not quite at ease. Rodrigo joined their company.

"Eh, well, Rodrigo, your wedding feast serves also as a fitting meal for condemned men," joked one, dropping a hand onto Valdivia's shoulder.

"Hush, fool, the governor will have you arrested for such disloyal comments," warned another.

"Who's disloyal? Those of us who have shed our blood to win an empire, or the king's representative who would take what little we've won for our work?"

It was a blessing the viceroy's arrival was so much in everyone's mind today, thought Catherine. It drew attention from her. She couldn't endure another of the assessing looks which many women in the room turned on her. She welcomed Doña Mercedes's friendly presence, but her dueña's conversation passed through her head and left no impression.

"You are pale," said Rodrigo, at her side again.

As she started, he caught the goblet of mulled wine which threatened to slip from her hands. He held it to her lips. She drank like a small child, aware of his fingers near her cheek.

"Are you not enjoying the celebration?" he asked.

She could not see beyond the darkness of his eyes. Was he mocking her? She knew he looked with contempt on this society which had produced her. However much he might desire her he no doubt held contempt for her as well.

"It is most pleasant," she lied.

He would have spoken again, but a figure in the crowd caught his attention. It was the tall archbishop of Lima in brocade robes. To Catherine's amazement the man she thought so lacking in reverence dropped quickly to his knees and bowed as the archbishop dispensed his blessing. Then guests, jovial with the freely flowing wine, drifted between them and Catherine and her husband were separated again.

After a time she found herself at the side of the room while one of the marquis's servants held a ewer to her goblet.

"You make a lovely bride, Doña Catherine," said a man near at hand. Alonzo Sanchez had come up behind her.

With bruising impact their gazes met. There was agony in Alonzo's face. He shifted on his lame leg while Catherine, with a terrible thickening of the throat, found herself unable to speak.

"I wish you hearty congratulations," Alonzo added awkwardly.

The eyes which once had held her own so urgently, which had spoken more loudly than his words his intent of paying court, rested on her even now with admiration. Catherine felt the grief she had tried to conquer welling through her. Lest she betray it, she sought protection in coldness.

"Please spare me the insult of all these pretensions," she said, voice low. "You know the circumstances of my marriage; you know how little congratulations are in order—knowledge shared by every person in this room, I have no doubt."

Alonzo took a step toward her. "Doña Catherine, I beg your forgiveness. I meant no harm. If there were anything I could do to save you from this—this marriage—"

"You could have bid on me," said Catherine shortly.

There was a silence. She turned to leave. Alonzo spoke quickly, the grave set of his mouth intensified.

"I wanted to marry you, do you not understand? But a marriage where the bride is purchased—what chance has it of happiness? The barriers it creates are insurmountable for those who would—love."

Catherine looked away. Did he speak the truth? Or when Don Luis had spoken of her as flawed, had that made her distasteful in Alonzo's eyes?

"I believe it is time to sit to table," she said, and pressing her hands against her skirts to stop their shaking, she made her way toward the raised platform and seats of honor.

The table before her held goblets which were extravagant bubbles of glass, more precious than gold. A servant with napkin stood behind each guest. The platters of fish, fowl and roast as they began to arrive were fragrant with precious spices, but Catherine had no appetite. She pushed roast capon in cream sauce about with a cardamom cake, pretending to feast, while Rodrigo, beside her, ate placidly in utter silence.

The banquet lasted through the afternoon. Jugglers were brought in, and musicians. The marquis applauded his delight at each performance, as joyous as a child. Rodrigo began to show signs of restlessness. At length he looked pointedly at Catherine, who rose and with mingled relief and sadness took her leave of the marquesa.

Use of the marquis's cart had been pressed on her for the trip to her new home. Rodrigo went ahead to see to its readiness while Catherine lingered over goodbys to Doña Mercedes. Then, greedy for the fresh air and solitude which waited outside the banquet hall, she stepped onto the gallery.

Two women stood before her fanning themselves at the railing. They appeared to have been watching something and their backs were to her.

"How can he afford a household? He's not a captain," one said with comfortable superiority. "Mark my words, they'll be begging bread if they attempt to live in any sort of style."

Catherine flushed, aware it was her husband's passing through which had prompted the remarks. She smoothed her skirts noisily, and as the women turned in guilt, she gave them a level look. She was still her father's daughter.

Catherine looked up at the dressed stone front of a small but handsome home. There was an open grill shaped like a fan above the door, and although that door would easily have admitted the cart, she was guided by Rodrigo's waiting silence and alighted to enter the courtyard on his arm.

There was no stable boy. A lantern had been lighted, and by its glow Catherine could see the desolate bareness of the courtyard. Then there was the sound of hurried footsteps.

From the kitchen quarter a woman appeared, eyes lowered deferentially. She was slender and shapely in a gown of cheap black cloth. Her round cheeks glowed in the lantern light. There were small plugs of gold in her ear lobes and her hair was a gleaming coil around her head.

"This is Magdalena," Rodrigo said. "Her husband, Carlos Rodriguez, fell at Salinas. She has been baptized and will serve you well."

Magdalena curtsied deeply.

"Welcome, señora."

As she spoke Ana came flying down the stairs from the gallery and, with a terrified eye on the Indian woman, called out, "Señorita! A gentleman waits to offer congratulations to you and Señor Valdivia."

Catherine saw her own surprise reflected in her husband's face. In a lighted doorway above them a man appeared, dressed in boots and a rough linen shirt.

"I beg you, Rodrigo, forgive my untimely arrival. I did not know that you would be a-marrying today." He bowed. "I wish you happiness, señora."

"Will you take some wine?" she offered uncertainly. "You look as though you have ridden far."

"So I have, doña. From Cuzco."

A look that was gone in a blink passed from him to Rodrigo. They all stepped into the *sala,* the drawing room. Catherine scarcely noticed her surroundings, for in the light she now recognized the horseman who had waited outside the cathedral that morning. An apprehension she could not name quickened her heart.

"Why have you come here, Díaz?" Rodrigo asked bluntly.

"Can you not guess, my friend?"

"If I guess correctly I want no part of it."

"Rebellion is inevitable, my friend," said Díaz. He squinted into his wine cup. "The country wants Pizarro, not some viceroy who knows nothing of the country, who comes with a set of laws which will be the ruin of all of us."

"The viceroy is the legal representative of the crown."

"The crown knows nothing of conditions here. How are we to work our land without the services of Indians?"

"I am loyal to my king, Díaz."

"As are we all!" Díaz replied indignantly. "Loyal to King Carlos, to his excellency the governor, to Pizarro—not to some viceroy who already makes trouble at every stop."

Catherine sat down fighting for breath, the scent of danger sharp upon the air. This man who stood before them preached insurrection!

"The men of Cuzco do not intend to relinquish the fruit of their toil without a fight," he said. Although he had checked his passion the words sounded ominous in the quiet room. "I wonder that you would, Rodrigo, so newly wed, so agreeably housed." He glanced toward the door, then lowered his voice. "Pizarro has been named captain-general by the officials of Cuzco. His army numbers four hundred seasoned soldiers. You know Pizarro would not seek power himself. This is pressed on him by circumstance, by loyalty to the men who fought for him and his family. By loyalty to Peru!"

"Enough, Díaz!"

Rodrigo waved his hand in angry dismissal. The other man's lips grew narrow with satisfaction.

"Enough to make you see the sense of what I am saying, to judge by your temper."

"I will not join your cause."

"You will, and bring others with you once you see that reports about the viceroy are true. I will call again next week—I or someone else."

Rodrigo, to Catherine's consternation, did not refuse the visit.

"Make certain no one sees you leave," he ordered grimly.

Díaz swept a bow to Catherine.

"Doña, for keeping you from your husband's company I crave your pardon."

He left the room.

Catherine sat in frozen silence. Surely Rodrigo de Valdivia was not so rash that he would join in out-and-out rebellion. Yet why had he not forbidden Pizarro's man to call at their house again? She saw the indecision in his face, swallowed back her disbelief. All her life had been lived in the fullest sunshine of unquestioning loyalty to church and king. Now she felt a shadow.

"What—what will you do if he comes again?" she asked, dry lipped. "They are arresting men for any display of sedition—"

"Quiet!"

The angry storm passed over his features. Stepping across the bench where she sat he settled facing her.

"Does the thought of me swinging from the gallows as a traitor distress you, *preciosa?* I am truly touched. But no. I will not join Díaz. I have joined with other caballeros here in Lima in petitioning for suspension of the New Laws. If the viceroy is a fair man he will grant that request."

"But if Díaz comes here—"

"It is hardly treason. My house is open to all who call me friend."

Catherine bit her lip, quite sure such simple honesty would not stand up in times of trouble.

He caught her chin between his thumb and fingers, drinking in her loveliness.

"You are a woman. Don't worry yourself with such matters."

Precisely because she was a woman Catherine could not obey. The wife of a man accused of treason could herself be

75

jailed, or turned out into the streets. Vaca de Castro's question at the wedding banquet suggested Rodrigo was known already as a partisan of Pizarro.

There was a timid knock at the door as Ana entered.

"Señor, señorita. The supper tonight is cold. . . ."

The maid moved quickly aside as Magdalena entered with a tray.

"Señorita, here is the book which you required," Ana whispered, pressing a leather-bound volume into Catherine's hands.

Her mistress nodded. She was not unmoved by Valdivia's generosity in dealing with her. Since very few marriages were contracted with an eye to happiness Catherine had resolved that her own, unwelcome as it was, would be at least an alliance of mutual respect. She had thought at length and hit on an offering to end the hostilities between them. Today was a day for starting anew.

When they were alone she held out the book. Owning a book was the advertisement of a prosperous household. The pages were printed, run off on the great press in Zaragosa.

"I beg you, señor, to accept this gift in return for the many you have given me," she said. "I am told all men enjoy the adventures of Amadis, though you may not find them half so fantastic as those you have had yourself."

Rigid of face Valdivia took the book. He turned it over slowly.

"I thank you, doña, but I have not learned the art of reading."

He pitched the volume back into her startled hands. "Call your maid," he said abruptly. "Get ready for bed."

8

Catherine felt the heat on her face as Ana unlaced her. A few hours later and both of them could have pretended that these were simply preparations for sleep. By donning a nightdress now she advised the entire household that a visit from her husband was imminent.

Mingled with her uneasiness over the night ahead and the servants' gossip was a sharp distress over her blunder with the book. Why had she assumed Valdivia could read when even many noblemen could not? It had been an innocent mistake on her part. Yet by the hard set of his face when it happened she knew he believed she had deliberately embarrassed him.

Her husband's knock was loud and impatient. He opened the door before her lips had even parted to bid him enter. A rebuke for the lack of courtesy died on her breath. He was master in this house. He could do and demand exactly as he wished.

"Go," he said sharply to Ana.

"But—señor—I have not combed Doña Catherine's hair—"

"It will have more need of combing in the morning, I assure you."

He jerked his head. The maid scuttled under his arm and out the door, her pale face crimson. Eyes shining, Rodrigo closed the door.

"You have embarrassed her," said Catherine, vexed by his amusement.

"I will not put on airs for servants, *preciosa*. Both you and they will have to learn it."

He had removed his coat and sword. The white shirt at his chest was open. Looking away, Catherine was aware of a trembling inside her. How would she feel if she did not have some knowledge of what lay ahead of her, if she were an ordinary bride?

She could feel the heat of his gaze upon her. The thin white nightdress which she wore seemed suddenly ridiculous, so low was its neck, so transparent its folds. As if he had read her thoughts her husband's teeth flashed. Struggling for composure she moved gracefully from the spot where she stood and sat on the edge of the bed.

It was a handsome piece of furniture set in an alcove and canopied in dark green velvet edged with gold. And in a moment he would join her there. . . . For a moment Catherine's eyes fell closed.

"Take off your gown."

The command jerked her back from the thoughts which had left her pulses racing. Rodrigo came toward her, bare chested. His shirt was in his hand. Rebellion rose in her, but as quickly as it came she knew that it was useless. Slipping from the bed she caught the skirt of her nightdress and with a difficult breath to summon courage, raised it over her shoulders to stand before him naked.

He took the gown from her and dropped it on a bench with his shirt, holding her lightly by the wrist.

"It will spare you torn gowns, doña, if you wait for me like this. I may not always be so patient as I am tonight."

His fingers were like a bracelet of fire encircling her. She offered no resistance as he brought her slowly toward him. There was the slow shock of flesh against flesh, the moist friction of her breast against his chest. Memory stirred within her, memory not only of hay and fear, but of sensations. She fought to put it down.

"You are lovely, my little *Sevillana*," Rodrigo whispered against her hair. His fingertips moved fluidly down her shoulders on to the narrow curve of her back and the softness below. "A taste of you has given me an appetite it will take many a night to satisfy."

He lifted her gently, kissing her throat as her head fell back. He knelt with her on the bed. Her eyes had closed again, and as she opened them Catherine saw him slipping easily out of his breeches. She tried to speak as he rolled toward her but no words came out.

"For this I would fight a thousand battles," he said, lifting a glistening mass of her hair and watching it tumble through his fingers. He rested on an elbow, the candlelight dancing in yellow pools across the hard planes of his body until the sight of him there above her sent Catherine's senses whirling.

"You are a treasure, my lovely one," he said. "A luxury greater than this bed beneath me and one which my tastes can better appreciate. I count owning you good payment for the years I've spent in armor."

The satisfied words made Catherine aware of the swelling

softness of her own body, subject to his superior strength. They were different. His acknowledgment of it stirred a response as sharp as the upward movement of his thumb against her nipples. She caught a hoarse breath and he smiled, the flame of the candle flickering in his eyes.

Briefly Catherine fought against the quickening tempo of her own blood. The look in his eyes filled her with excitement. Almost involuntarily she parted her lips.

Valdivia smothered her against him, his mouth extracting its plunder with barely checked force. Her arm dropped nervelessly across his back. Her fingers felt the movement of muscles. With wonder she traced the smoothness of his skin until a rough and knotted patch brought her up abruptly.

"Don't be alarmed, *preciosa*," he said, freeing her lips as her hand recoiled. "It's not the mark of some dread disease I carry, only one left by an Indian spear which passed through me."

Catherine stared up at the vital, laughing face. This man who was her tormentor was also mortal, his life as tenuous as a straw in this wilderness. It was shocking to think of.

"You could have been killed," she whispered, distressed in a way she could not explain by the realization.

"But I wasn't."

With lazy confidence he eased her thighs apart. He rolled his weight on top of her. A thousand candles danced in her brain as their bodies melted together and Catherine felt the scorching heat of abandon, of dark and reckless sweetness which she would have tasted at the cost of her own soul. In the end it was some other woman, obeying body instead of brain, who finally lay near oblivion on the sheets.

In the darkness Catherine awoke, terrified by the feeling of being imprisoned. She had been dreaming of the soldier Díaz, of fighting, of clashing swords. Now she could not move. The candle near the bed leaped with the drunken frenzy which presaged its burning out.

Slowly, as the night air through the window freshened her face, awareness returned to her. She was not alone. Valdivia, her husband, lay beside her, face down, one arm flung tightly across her. In the shadows she studied him, the dark crest of his hair, the mouth which in repose was guarded and grave. Was its quick smile only an armor like the cuirass he had worn the first time she saw him? Would she ever know him, she wondered. It didn't matter. A woman wasn't expected to understand her husband, only to keep his household, to satisfy his lust. But she was curious about this man who on the one hand seemed so simple and direct and yet was given to such puzzling whims.

Why had he married her? If out of some sense of responsibility for what he had done to her, then it was a gesture worthy of the proudest hidalgo. It had cost him dearly, too, she thought, remembering the bag of gold he had handed over and the whispered talk of his limited resources. Or was it pride which had caused him to claim her? He had called her a luxury, spoken with satisfaction of owning her. Catherine frowned. Perhaps she should accept the explanation which he had given, mere physical desire. Raising the hand which wore the emerald she searched its glitter, as though she might find there an answer.

"So it pleases you after all, does it?" Valdivia drawled beside her. At his low chuckle she dropped her hand with angry guilt. He had been watching her. "There are small stones which will make you earrings if you're nice to me." He rolled onto his back. Folding his arms behind his head he looked comfortably up at the canopy.

"I do not sell myself for trinkets," Catherine informed him coldly. Catching the sheet she pulled it up over her nakedness.

Unperturbed, Valdivia reached out a hand and flicked back the sheet.

"Your favors are not yours to dispose of, doña. They are mine to take, whenever it pleases me."

Catherine felt her hands curl. As if he could see them Valdivia smiled.

"Come now, *preciosa,* you don't find the situation entirely unpleasant, judging by your behavior a short while ago."

"You are—"

"—no gentleman? I've never claimed to be."

He reached over and pinched out the candle. Her fists pushed into the sheets and she did not answer. She could not keep her balance, so quickly did his mood shift from desire to humor. For the one there was no recourse but submission. For the other. . . .

"The emeralds were payment to you for service, were they not?" she asked, struggling for a calm she did not feel. "Why didn't you sell them?"

He turned toward her. She could make out nothing of his

80

features now except the reflection of starlight on his cheeks and the shining pools which were his eyes.

"Some things are too attractive to sell," he said.

Catherine was quiet. She wondered whether the day might come when he regretted that attitude. A soldier's pay was nonexistent in times of peace.

Rodrigo too was thoughtful. "You are better than fair as a rider," he acknowledged. "You made the ride to Callao in respectable time despite being hampered by that idiot of a girl."

Catherine's lips curved at the memory of Ana. Her husband could not see her.

"The white mare is yours to use whenever you like," he continued.

"The mare which made the crossing with us?" Catherine asked in surprise. "She belongs to you?"

"She does. I have an *encomienda*—land with which to make a livelihood. I intend to raise horses on it. Fine horses. I will breed the mare as soon as a stallion can be had, though how long that may be I do not know, as His Majesty Carlos himself insists on authorizing every export of a horse."

Catherine nodded, quickly understanding. There was in Spain some fear of the horse's becoming extinct, of the pure breeds at least disappearing. Eager for profit, too many men were putting their mares to stud with donkeys, raising not foals, but the sturdy mules in demand for pulling commerce and the heavy artillery of armies. She had not known the king was guarding every export from the country.

"But why not Boabdíl?" she asked. "He is a magnificent animal."

"Magnificent, but of uncertain breeding." The irony in his words was unmistakable. "Somewhat like our own situation, is it not, my lovely doña?" With an angry movement he began to make love to her.

Unaccustomed to an open window while she slept, Catherine toward morning curled in unconscious retreat from the cool, damp air. The sunlight found her stiff and shivering.

"Here, *preciosa*, come near and be warm," said Valdivia with drowsy languor. He turned over, shaping himself around her, his arms still heavy with sleep. Catherine instantly was awake.

"What are you still doing here?" she demanded breathlessly. "Ana will see you." He should long ago have returned to his own room.

"So Ana will see me," he agreed with little interest.

"You are naked!"

"Then Ana is lucky indeed. It will give her an excellent standard for judging men."

Catherine brought her elbow back against his abdomen. He caught her, laughing.

"Please. You must go," she said, rolling onto her stomach.

He flung an arm behind him, lifting his head to look at her through narrowed eyes.

"Do you know you're most provocative when you plead? Coax me, *preciosa*. Perhaps you can persuade me."

Strangling him with the sheets would be sheer delight, Catherine thought. A little experience of him had taught her the futility of opposition, however. Nor could she quite ignore the faintly pursed mouth above his beard. Hesitantly she leaned toward him, wondering if this concession would win his compliance.

This morning his kiss was sweet, devoid of passion. She tasted it with curiosity. But the passion followed quickly. His hands brushed down her arms and up again, each time more roughly than before.

The timid knock was more startling than a gun. Catherine jerked from his grasp.

"Ana!" she exclaimed.

Knowing that if she did not answer, the maid would likely slip into the room to leave the tray she carried, Catherine whirled off the bed, drawing the sheet up to cover the laughing Rodrigo. Frantically she tugged her discarded nightdress over her head. The door cracked open before the hem of it had settled around his ankles.

Ana's eyes went from her to the bed.

"Oh!" she said as they widened.

"You see, I told you your mistress would have need of a comb this morning," Valdivia said.

Ana took in Catherine's disheveled curls with something approaching awe. The tray she was holding tipped.

"That's all, Ana," said her mistress, catching it in time. "In the future you may leave the tray outside the door."

Wordlessly Ana nodded, backing from the room.

Catherine slammed down the tray, which held cheese, coarse bread and fat pink grapes.

"You have embarrassed her," she railed, picking up the cheese and bringing it toward him. "She is little more than a child and easily scared. I beg you, señor, spare her your whims of humor even if you will not spare me!"

Valdivia had turned comfortably onto his elbow. She saw his face darken.

"You will use my name," he ordered sharply.

A cold certainty of having erred filled Catherine's stomach. His eyes were closed to her, their laughter gone.

"I—beg your pardon—"

"I have no concern for the embarrassment of a serving girl, even less for those who are so slavishly afraid of impropriety," he informed her, drawing on his breeches. "I had thought you different from those other simpering women of good family who dare not call their breath their own. It seems I was mistaken. As you value your morning privacy so highly, Doña Catherine, you may have it."

Thrusting his arms through his shirt he strode out of the room. Catherine stared at the door, fighting back an impulse to call out to him. What would she say? That she welcomed him here? It was not true. Yet she stood there with a bitter sense of having let an opportunity slip through her fingers.

9

The house was small, about the size of a prosperous merchant's, beautifully built but unlived in, desolate. Dared she make any changes, introduce any color, Catherine asked herself? Perhaps her husband, accustomed to inns and the hard life of out of doors, found shelter alone sufficient. If so he likely would misconstrue any effort she made at improvements, taking them for criticism, thinking that she sought to emphasize the difference in their backgrounds. It would further the hostility between them. Tears of frustration welled at her eyes. She was more this house's prisoner than its mistress.

She moved toward the *sala familiar,* the one room she had not yet seen on this first morning of inspection. Furniture in even the finest homes was scarce, and this room held but a single item. The beauty of it took Catherine's breath away, however. Disbelieving, she traced a finger along the gleaming *vargueno.* With its huge iron lock removed the front of the cabinet would hinge down for a writing surface, revealing drawers inside.

"It was made for Don Luis, but a bribe and immediate payment rerouted it here," said Rodrigo behind her. "Causing him to wait for another seems small revenge for all he has done, don't you agree?"

Catherine had jumped at the sound of his voice. She watched him come into the room. His manner was reserved, neither angry nor personal. Reaching past her he dropped the front of the *vargueno,* then opened a drawer to reveal pen and ink.

"It is . . . a handsome piece," she said.

Clearly it was meant for her use and she was awed by the extravagance of it.

Valdivia shrugged. His expression told her nothing.

"Are you ready?" he asked.

Catherine searched her mind for some forgotten obligation.

"The viceroy arrives this morning," he supplied impatiently. "We shall want to see."

The prospect of joining the crowd at such an event both surprised and delighted her. She did not think her father would have permitted her to attend such a public spectacle.

"I will get my riding clothes," she said with a quick turn toward the door.

"Riding clothes are unnecessary. I'll fasten on a pillion. Come."

Though she sorely resented his neglect in not hinting of these plans ahead of time, she smothered the feeling. Following down into the courtyard and back into the stable area, she watched him saddle Boabdíl with easy skill.

"A stable boy would be of help to you," she ventured as he brushed dust from his breeches with a curse.

"And an unnecessary expense." With a glance of irony he added, "I earned my bread as a stable boy when I was younger, doña. I have no need of help."

Catherine stood aside for the great bay horse, avoiding her husband's eyes. Rodrigo mounted and reached to lift her onto the pillion cushion fastened behind the saddle. At his summons Magdalena came running to open the door to the street.

A pillion had always seemed a far less reliable seat than a saddle to Catherine. She was forced to keep an arm around her husband's waist. But she held her balance well and within minutes they had joined a crowd pressing out toward the city gates.

Catherine looked with interest at the Indians. There were hundreds of them, some dressed like Spanish peasants and others in white cotton shifts which came to their knees. Their faces were serene, not frightening in the least. They were jostled aside by the Spanish who came, on foot and on horseback, to receive the viceroy.

Governor Vaca de Castro and the city's officials had gathered at the gate. They were robed in cloaks of scarlet. Reflecting back the sun's own fire a great gold cross from the cathedral glinted at the head of a body of clerics. Catherine was aware of a pageantry such as she had never seen before.

"Why, these might be the preparations for a prince!" she murmured.

"They say the viceroy conducts himself as if he were one," Rodrigo answered, turning in the saddle.

His words were cut short by the movement of a horse toward them. The massive Rojo drew up beside them, expression grim.

"They have jailed Martín Suarez," he announced without a word of greeting.

Catherine caught her husband's exlamation.

"Jailed him? What for?"

"Sedition. He was visited by Juan Díaz yesterday."

Catherine felt the hand around her husband's waist grow chill.

"Since when is that a crime?" Rodrigo asked, his voice kept low. "Suarez is as loyal a cavalier as ever the crown could ask."

Rojo nodded his rusty thatch of hair. "The air smells dangerous, my friend."

Abruptly he smiled, revealing yellowed teeth. "Forgive my manners, doña. You were the loveliest of brides. At your convenience I will call on you and Rodrigo with a small gift to convey good wishes."

Preoccupied with her question of whether Díaz's visit to their house had been noted, Catherine barely nodded.

"You are most welcome any time, captain—" She stopped, distracted by the realization she did not know his surname.

"In truth I have answered to Rojo so long my real names escape me," he said, then roared with laughter. The three of them rode forward toward the front of the crowd.

An arc of triumph bearing the coat of arms of Spain and of the city had been constructed of braided green velvet. At one end of it, in her cart, stood the marquesa. Doña Mercedes was beside her, and nearby, the marquis. Catherine nodded greetings, but her thoughts had turned from the pomp around her to the knowledge of Díaz's visit, which hung like a guilty secret over her conscience.

The sun was hot. She had ample time to grow aware of curious eyes turned toward her. At last a trumpet sounded heralding the man whose voice would be supreme in all the land.

Vaca de Castro and the dignitaries of Lima went forward on foot to greet the viceroy as he advanced on a horse caparisoned in yellow and scarlet. Eight of the city officials carried staffs embellished with silver, on top of which fluttered a scarlet canopy. His excellency the viceroy Blasco Nuñez took his place beneath the canopy, looking neither left nor right. Ahead of him came a mounted cavalier who carried the mace of authority. The viceroy stopped before the assemblage waiting inside the gates and with his hand on a missal held by the archbishop swore to uphold the laws of Spain.

"A hard day for Don Luis when he must work," muttered Rojo as a procession started toward the cathedral. They were closer to the canopy now, and Catherine recognized the councilman, his left cheek red and ugly, shouldering one of the heavy silver poles.

The procession which wound through the dusty streets stopped at its destination. After the cross had gone inside the cathedral the citizens followed. The dark walls echoed to the chant of the Te Deum and Blasco Nuñez Vela was confirmed as viceroy of Peru.

"A fetching bride, Rodrigo," boomed a voice as they strolled afterward toward the imposing palace of the late Francisco Pizarro. Now frequented on occasion by his brother Gonzalo, the palace faced the cathedral, and the courtyard before it was currently filled with horses left in the charge of Indian grooms.

Valdivia acknowledged the compliment with a nod. The man who had spoken appeared to be an *encomendero,* a land holder, as were most of the men in the group now moving toward the courtyard. A few were ordinary soldiers, captains of rank, but most had been landed gentry in Spain, men of good family with skill at arms. Some, like the man who had spoken, greeted her husband with an affable familiarity which Catherine suspected must spring from acquaintance at the gaming tables.

"I did not expect to see you out today, Rodrigo," joked one of the captains, striking a note of merriment for those around them as he winked.

"A man of commendable duty," said a hook-nosed old Asturian with a twinkle. "Don't you agree with us, Don Luis?"

Ahead of them Luis de Alvarado paused in the act of swinging onto his horse. His thin mouth curved.

"Perhaps Señor Valdivia finds fresh territory in the duty he performs today," he said with heavy suggestion.

Catherine saw the color leave Rodrigo's face. His hand shot out for the councilman's bridle. Rojo, walking beside him, tried to check the gesture, but too late.

"I beg you explain," said Rodrigo. His voice was quiet and deadly. There was a stir of apprehension in the crowd.

A slight sneer covered Don Luis's features.

"Would you have me speak more clearly when your wife herself is present, Valdivia? Let go my bridle."

Rodrigo did not move.

"Apologize for your insinuations or draw your sword," he said in ringing tones.

Catherine saw the satisfaction come to Don Luis's eyes.

"I will not apologize for the truth, Valdivia. If you're eager to taste my sword let's not delay."

Rodrigo swung aside, still gripping the bridle, while the councilman dismounted.

Catherine turned to Rojo.

"Stop him," she whispered through lips which barely moved.

"I cannot, doña. The man has questioned your honor."

Her nails dug into Rojo's sleeve. She shook it angrily.

"All Lima questions my honor! You know the circumstances of our marriage. This is absurd!"

She saw compassion in the rough face of the man beside her but the situation was beyond them both. Already a space had cleared at the back of the courtyard and in the center of it her husband and Don Luis were stripping off their jackets. Their leather vests or corsets were also discarded. They faced each other in thin shirts ruffled by a slight, hot breeze.

"Let me take you into the church," Rojo offered, taking her elbow.

Catherine shook free of his hand.

"No. I am the cause of it. I'll stay."

She was the only woman present. The men in the courtyard were forming a ring around the two combatants. Rodrigo had not looked in her direction since the altercation started and the knowledge was a weight upon her heart.

"Is he—is he a good swordsman?" she asked.

The time in Callao he had been pitted against an ill-bred stableman little skilled in soldierly arts. What were his chances of surviving this current act of rashness? She wondered that she should care about it, for the two of them meant nothing to each other. Still her mouth was dry.

"There are few to equal him," Rojo answered. "But he is a fool to take on Don Luis. Don Luis has powerful friends. They will have revenge."

The clang of steel on steel now cut across his words. Catherine watched her husband feint backward with a grace which belied his strength. Don Luis's blade flew back and forth like silver in the sun. His movements were faster than Rodrigo's and utterly cool, controlled. Every thrust of Rodrigo's sword, in contrast, showed a brilliance possible only when a man held his personal safety in utter contempt.

He did not care about the outcome of this duel, Catherine thought. It was exactly this sort of confrontation which he had sought to provoke when he raped her. It was not so much her honor which he was fighting for as that of his long-dead cousin, and her own presence, here or in his life, meant nothing.

At that exact instant she saw Don Luis's sword glint wickedly as Rodrigo stumbled. A gasp escaped the hand pressed to her lips.

In relief she saw the steel had missed him. Rodrigo spun around to face the councilman, and for a moment his eyes met hers. Suddenly the style of his swordplay seemed to change. She could see the deathly intensity with which he circled. Then he seemed unaccountably to let his guard slip. Don Luis's weapon plunged forward.

With savage force the sword which had seemed unwary struck. Don Luis fell backward, a red spot showing on his arm. Rodrigo put a sword point to his throat.

In a moment now it would all be over, Catherine thought sickly. She had never seen a duel before, but she knew that the winning came in death, not injury. She waited.

Her husband's voice rang in her ears.

"Apologize to my wife, Luis de Alvarado."

She started at the words.

Don Luis lay in the dust, rage stamped across his features. His look was haughty. He did not speak. The sword point pressed against his flesh.

"An apology!" Rodrigo demanded more sharply.

She did not expect one, could not believe it when at length she saw Don Luis's mouth open.

"I apologize, Señora Valdivia, for any slanders I may have offered to your good name."

She thought she heard sarcasm in his tone.

"I accept," she said, setting her nerves for the final blow.

Rodrigo let his sword travel downward, onto the untouched white of his opponent's shirt. Slowly and deliberately its point moved down and up, not claiming a life, but etching on Don Luis's chest a bloody V.

"Remember to whose name you owe your life," he said. Then turning, he wiped his sword on his boot and sheathed it.

A murmur went up from the circle of onlookers. Rojo shook his head in disbelief. The crowd parted with a rustle of commendation as Rodrigo came toward them.

He held his jacket in one hand. A wave of black hair fell across his forehead. Satisfaction burned still in his eyes.

"You should not be here," he said shortly to Catherine. "Rojo, why did you not take her away?"

"I insisted on staying," said Catherine, aware of a sudden weakness spreading over her. "I had to see—"

"It was not proper. This was no concern of yours."

"It concerned me most directly!" She bit her lip. "I thank you for sparing his life. I do not wish to be the cause of further bloodshed."

"I will try to honor those wishes."

"You will not duel again on my behalf then? Our marriage was contracted under—unusual conditions. Gossip is inevitable."

She frowned as he did not answer.

"My pride is as great as any man's, *preciosa*. Take care to remember that."

Dismissing her abruptly from his attention he called for Boabdíl. Rojo gave another of those wags of the head which made him resemble more than ever a great, slow-moving bear.

"You may not relish the thought of bloodshed, doña, but Don Luis is one man safer dead than shamed."

10.

"Oh! There is dirt on my cheek," wailed Ana.

Catherine sighed. A cutting from her father's favorite fig tree, carried across the sea with them, stood newly planted, and as a result of the work Ana now looked anything but her role of housekeeper. The knock at the front gate sounded again.

"Shall I answer it, señora?" offered Magdalena. She came back with a quickness to her steps. "Señora, two ladies wish to call on you. They are Doña Isabella, a wife to the lord Pizarro, and Doña Marina, another Indian lady."

"A wife." That must mean a mistress or concubine, thought Catherine. The mere name of Pizarro filled her with awe. She was curious to see what manner of woman had caught the eye of so powerful a man, more curious still to see what kind of woman would be openly known as a mistress. By merely coming to her door the women had given cause enough for rumors of the Valdivias' sedition.

"Show them to the sala," she said, dusting her skirt.

The room held benches and two folding chairs. There were several trunks in the corners, her own and one of Rodrigo's. Blue and yellow tiles ran waist high on the walls and fireplace front. Catherine looked about nervously, listening to the approaching footsteps.

Magdalena opened the door. A woman with the high, round cheeks of the Peruvian race came into the room, followed by another, slightly plumper, each of them accompanied by an Indian maid. The dresses of the ladies were black, their waists sharply cinched, the ruffs at their necks finely made. But on both there was a degree of ornamentation not found in women of Spain.

"I am Doña Isabella, lady to Gonzalo Pizarro," announced the first. Great pendants of gold, each set with three emeralds, hung from her ears, and her bodice was heavy with chains of gold. The woman with her wore a heavy necklace of gold with a pendant of pearls.

"I am honored to greet you," said Catherine, though her heart was racing now that she stood face to face with these exotic creatures. "Please, will you sit down?"

A look passed from Doña Isabella to her companion which Catherine could not read. Was it uncertainty?

"Bring orangewater for our guests," she said to Ana.

Shoulders set in resignation Ana slipped past the Indian servants.

"Forgive me, I do not remember your name, though Magdalena told me," Catherine said to the other women as they seated themselves.

The plumper of the ladies folded her hands. "They call me Doña Marina. My husband is a captain in the service of lord Pizarro."

"Your husband, Rodrigo de Valdivia, is much loved by Pizarro," said Doña Isabella. "When my lord heard of your marriage he asked that this gift be sent."

She clapped her hands. The door to the sala opened and three Indians entered, young boys in cotton shifts who knelt at Catherine's feet. In their arms was a full table service, plates, cups and bowls, all of it hammered from silver. Catherine stared, her breathing suspended.

"The lord Pizarro is too generous," she said.

There were dishes enough for twenty people, and a pair of handsome candlesticks as well. A bribe, she thought quickly. But Gonzalo Pizarro could have no way of knowing Rodrigo resisted his cause. This must be simply a gesture of largess, and one which she greatly appreciated. Her only other wedding presents had been a tapestry from the marquesa and some personal items made by Doña Mercedes.

"I am glad it pleases you," Doña Isabella said. "Shall I send them to the kitchen?"

Catherine managed a nod and the Indian carriers left, passing through the door just before Ana entered with a tray.

The orangewater tasted sweet and surprisingly cool. Catherine made a mental note to find out how that was accomplished. Along with it Ana (or Magdalena) had had the presence of mind to bring a plate of grapes which Catherine now passed.

"A fruit from your land which we greatly admire," said Doña Marina, popping one into her mouth.

They well deserved the title of doña which they had usurped, thought Catherine. Both women sat erect beneath their glittering jewelry, conversing easily, taking the attentions of servants in stride. In some ways their manner was even more aristocratic than the marquesa's.

"What city do you come from?" asked Doña Isabella.

"Seville," said Catherine. "And you?"

"From Cuzco. Doña Marina is from Tumbez."

As another question formed on her tongue there was the sound of hoofbeats in the courtyard. Catherine felt apprehension flash over her. Her guests turned their attention too as booted feet climbed the stairs. A moment later Rodrigo entered the room. Catherine leaned back weakly.

Rodrigo looked somewhat nonplussed at the scene before him, the three ladies sipping orangewater, each of them attended by a maid. He gave a deep bow.

"Doña Isabella, Doña Marina."

His obvious pleasure did not quite erase the grave look he had worn when he entered.

"The lord Pizarro has sent us a handsome wedding gift," Catherine told him.

"And his wishes for many heirs," added Doña Isabella.

Rodrigo inclined his head.

"Send him our thanks, and our hope of expressing it soon in person."

Pizarro's mistress had a voice which was beautiful, like the night rush of a river. She spoke again, watching him intently.

"You are troubled, Señor Valdivia. What is the news?"

Rodrigo gave a turn across the room.

"The viceroy has refused our petition to suspend the New Laws."

"He will seize all lands then?" asked Doña Marina.

"He says he will fulfill the letter of the law. What that means, madam, I do not know. The governor urged suspension, intimating rebellion might follow any refusal, but the viceroy insists he is not empowered to suspend the ordinances, though he generously offers to join us in addressing a petition to the king."

The last words were filled with disgust. A great silence followed them.

"The governor is a wise man," Doña Isabella said. "He has sent much of this city's artillery to Guamanga, away from the reach of angry hands. The viceroy would be well advised to listen to his counsel."

By some prearranged signal she and Doña Marina rose, as regally as queens. Catherine and Rodrigo saw them out into the courtyard. There Catherine watched in fascination as the two women settled themselves on litters and were carried aloft out the gate and into the street.

"Will there be rebellion?" asked Catherine, still watching the place where they had disappeared.

"I do not know."

He was looking with disapproval at the courtyard. His eyes had stopped on the pile of earth abandoned at the announcement of visitors.

"We were planting a fig tree from my father's orchard," said Catherine, annoyed that without a word from him she felt compelled to offer explanation. "I trust you will not object?"

He shrugged.

"What you do with the house is your concern. I have no interest in it. So long as there's food and wine when I call for it I'll not complain."

His tone set her direction firmly in her mind. He could scorn beauty and comfort all he chose, slight her role in housekeeping if he wished, but she would make him aware of her as something more than a vessel to be used when need overcame him. She would make the barren garden bloom. She would make this house warm and alive until he could not help but see her hand in every room he entered, until it wrung from him an admission of improvement.

"I will buy some sweet orange trees," she said. "Perhaps a citron. And I will hire a boy to pluck the grass. The women cannot do it."

He considered something.

"Come with me," he ordered and went past the sala to the room with the *vargueno*. Taking a key from his belt he unlocked a small trunk which had been moved in. He reached inside and withdrew a number of *reales* which he placed into her hands. "This will be your housekeeping money for the quarter year. I regret it can't be more. Although I've long invested half of all my earnings, the income involved is small. Most of it was required to purchase this house."

And me, thought Catherine, wondering why she felt guilty.

"This is more than enough," she said, though the sum in truth was frightfully little. She bit her lip. "Señor—Rodrigo," she said as he turned toward the door.

He looked back at her.

"This house and all that's in it is very handsome, and I thank you for your generosity. I promise I shall make this household one which is looked on with envy."

His expression told her nothing. For a moment he stood

94

looking at her. Then he went from the room and she listened to the soft click of his spurs against the stairs.

For the rest of the day Catherine worked with unrelenting energy. With Ana's help she hung the tapestry from the marquesa in the sala. After some debate she set the half-dozen books which comprised her library on a shelf in that same room, rationalizing that whatever damage they could do between her and her husband had already been done. She longed to transfer the carpet which was in her bedchamber to the bare floor of the sala, but instinct told her not to. If Valdivia had seen to it that her own room was attractively and completely furnished perhaps she should not question it. He would be paying many visits there, she thought with a sigh.

By night she was bone weary. The wood in the sala and the dining room were fragrant with polish and the silver dishes from Pizarro gleamed on shelves. The courtyard was picked as clean as a goose. Yet despite her earlier confidence Catherine wondered now if anything she did could win her husband's approval. He thought her a spoiled and pampered woman, suitable only for pleasure.

It was late, the dinner hour, before she heard his footsteps on the stairs. As soon as Ana had finished combing her hair, which was much disarrayed by the day's activity, she went out to meet him.

He was in the sala, a goblet of wine in his hand. If he noticed any change in the room he did not show it. A brooding look was on his face as he stood in the *mirador* staring down at the street.

"You have found the wine, and the food will be ready shortly," she advised him with weak humor.

He gave her the slightest of smiles.

It was awkward, Catherine thought, being alone in a room with a man, knowing you would be together for the rest of your lives. What could she say to break the deadly silence? She knew nothing of his daily routine or interests and he would hardly care to hear her chatter about domestic details. It was a relief when Ana's knock and summons called them to dinner.

They sat on stools at either end of a long trestle table. The silver plates were before them and the silver candlesticks held brightly gleaming tapers. Ana had even arranged a bouquet of sorts in a squat wooden bowl. All in all things were very attractive, Catherine concluded wearily. Her husband made no comment.

Magdalena served the meal, which consisted of salad and a stew unlike any Catherine had ever seen. It was very thick, the result of some coarse yellow meal which had been added along with the carrots, turnips and mutton. Catherine's appetite deserted her at her first sampling of it. The taste was not bad, she told herself miserably, but the feel of it—the heaviness on her tongue!

She became aware of her husband watching her. With effort she forced a few bites into her mouth and swallowed quickly.

"The yellow meal, is it the maize which Oviedo writes about?" she asked.

"I know nothing about Oviedo, but it is maize, yes."

He was eating the dish with relish, accompanying it with bites of thin yellow cakes made also from maize.

"And the—the stew?" asked Catherine, spots of color burning in her cheeks.

"Puchero. A native dish, as you may have guessed."

His mood was darkening. Catherine ate another spoonful of the *puchero* and knew she could face no more. She picked at her salad, exhausted, feeling on the defensive, aware she was failing some crucial test whose meaning she did not know.

"Magdalena," said her husband. "Bring rum."

Magdalena's eyes crept fearfully to Catherine's, then lowered quickly. She left the room, returning with a pottery bottle shaped like a stirrup. Rodrigo poured from it into his goblet and there was the smell of strong, potent liquor.

He drank the rum in silence as Catherine forced down her salad. When they adjourned into the sala he took the bottle with him. Nervously Catherine looked around the room for something to do. With her father she had read after dinner or they had played chess. She looked wistfully at the gleaming chess men she had also set out in the room.

"Would you care for a game of cards?" she asked. "There is much of the evening left."

"I am not in a mood for cards."

He looked at her directly, peering into her as if to drag some secret from her. Catherine locked her hands together and lowered her eyes.

"You look tired," he said.

She shrugged awkwardly. "A little, perhaps."

"From oiling furniture? The room reeks of it."

She sensed displeasure in his words.

"I'm sorry if the scent annoys you."

He was opening his mouth to answer when Ana appeared.

"A lady waits below to call on you," she said. "She says she is a friend of Señor Valdivia's."

Rodrigo stopped in surprise with his cup halfway to his lips.

"Of mine?" he said.

There was laughter rich as molten gold.

"The trouble with a cage as fine as this one is that you'll find yourself often trapped in it, Rodrigo," teased a voice just beyond Ana's shoulder. A woman stepped around the startled maid and into the room, smiling roguishly.

"Francisca!" Rodrigo exclaimed as if the breath had been driven from him. "What the devil are you doing here?"

"Offering my congratulations on your marriage. Bringing gossip from Cuzco." Uninvited she flung back her cape, not looking yet at Catherine.

The woman called Francisca was an intriguing mixture of villager and aristocrat. Her gown was beautifully cut with silver trim and a dainty ruff, but it was open slightly at the throat and her hair hung free in glistening curls across her back. Her ripe red cheeks gave her an unmistakable beauty, underscored all the more by the quick, unsheltered humor in her eyes. Catherine smiled at her agreeably, but all the time alarm bells sounded in her mind.

"Catherine, this is Francisca Griega, wife of Captain Griega. My wife, Doña Catherine Bautista."

Rodrigo made the introductions with near disinterest, almost pointedly rude in his failure to rise. Francisca, her high spirits undiminished, now studied Catherine with bold appraisal.

"Won't you sit down?" asked Catherine, blushing under the other woman's gaze. "Will you take some wine?"

"If Rodrigo will put the scowl from his face and make me feel welcome," Francisca said, settling herself on a stool. His only answer was a dark look and a deep drink from the rum cup. Francisca raised her eyebrows in question to Catherine, who shifted uncomfortably.

"Ana—bring wine," said Rodrigo.

Ana jumped at this unaccustomed order from the master of the house. Her eyes darted quickly to Catherine's before she hurried out to obey.

Francisca burst into a peal of laughter.

"You've taken on a great task civilizing this one, Catherine," she said, giving a pretty shake to her unbound curls. "Don't expect me to tax my poor woman's brain wondering what I have done to displease you, Rodrigo. I'll tell my tale of how the bishop caught virtuous Captain Díaz bathing with an Indian woman to Catherine's ears alone."

Catherine struggled to keep her composure at this bawdy story and this newcomer's immediate use of her christian name. Yet already she could see the remote and brooding mood which had held him all evening loose its hold on Rodrigo, though he still looked far from pleased. As the story of the errant Captain Díaz progressed his mouth relaxed, reluctantly, she thought, into a smile.

"Francisca, you have no business speaking of things like that," he laughed when she had finished.

Francisca gave an impudent shake of her curls.

"Ah, but the things which are supposed to be a woman's business—running a household and living up to all the little conventions of society—are so dreadfully boring. Forgive me, Catherine, but how can you stand it?"

"I am glad to see to my husband's comfort after his years in the field," answered Catherine, recognizing immediately the stiffness of her words.

"Of course," agreed Francisca lazily. "If comfort has come to be important to him. I hadn't realized, Rodrigo, that you were yet in your dotage."

Rodrigo laughed. "That I am hardly, Francisca. As to the field, I would just as soon be in it. This town is becoming tedious."

Catherine listened aghast. He had not once hinted of any dissatisfaction with Lima.

"Then come to Cuzco," said Francisca, eyes narrowed and glowing. "There is excitement there."

"Pizarro is massing troops. We have heard."

"And will you join his party? You and Rojo and other men of the capital?"

Rodrigo looked at Catherine and away. Setting down her wine cup Francisca glanced at the door.

"Do your servants listen?" she asked.

"Of course not!" said Catherine, outraged more than she cared to show at the mere suggestion.

"I came to Lima several days ago in the event Juan Díaz was taken prisoner, as now has happened. A woman's comings and goings are not looked on with as much suspicion as those of a man, and I have spread the word about that we will open a house in Lima. My trips between here and Cuzco will not be questioned. I have come to you to carry your decision to Pizarro."

Rodrigo was silent. Catherine felt her heart pounding wildly.

"I will wait and see what the viceroy does," he said at last.

Francisca regarded him. Her full lips parted to offer argument. Then with the quick decision of one who knew her adversary well she simply rose.

"Then perhaps I will delay my return for a few days more," she said smiling. "If you would be so good as to fetch my horse, Rodrigo?"

When he had gone she tilted her head and studied Catherine.

"You are as pretty as I'd heard," she said. "But cold. If you choose to be so for long, it will be your undoing. Rodrigo is a man of passion. He will demand the same of you—or begin to look elsewhere."

"You seem to know my husband very well," said Catherine, her light tone masking the shock she felt at the other woman's boldness.

"Yes, very well," Francisca agreed. "Though I see less of him since I have married. I pity you, truly, for his humor changes quickly. My husband I find much more agreeable in that respect, though not half so pleasing—"

She checked herself with a sly smile, laughing a little breathlessly. Catherine's hands pressed rigidly together. The words might as well have been spoken. Francisca had slept with Rodrigo.

The door opened on them then and Rodrigo came in.

"Your horse is ready."

Francisca smiled up at him.

"They're singing at the inn tonight, a merry group. Bring Catherine and come to listen."

Helpless, Catherine watched a long look pass between her husband and the woman who could so easily coax him to laughter. She saw the reluctance in his face as he shook his head.

"Then I will bid you goodnight," said Francisca gliding past him. "Please don't trouble to see me out."

In a moment the sound of her horse's hooves sounded

outside the *mirador*. Catherine stood without speaking while emotions boiled inside her.

Once again they had been visited by a spy from Pizarro, but this time her reaction was less fear than anger. Already she recognized that the woman Francisca was not bound by any convention, not by fear of a rebel's fate or by marriage vows. Was her coming here a challenge? Why had Rodrigo not married her? The questions seemed to glue her in place.

"You waste no sweetness on a woman you consider less than equal, do you?" Rodrigo demanded.

"I find it hard to pretend special friendliness for anyone rude—whatever their station!"

"Rude? In what way was Francisca rude? In that her story offended your delicate ears? In view of the things you know, sweet doña, that is laughable."

Catherine felt the blood rage in her temples. He had been deaf to Francisca's provoking innuendos. He had not heard her near admission that they had been lovers. And if that was over, why was he now in such a fury?

"Do forgive me," she said coldly. "Perhaps I should sleep with assorted men so that I, too, have amusing stories to tell you."

He took a step toward her, his jaw clenching dangerously. Then whirling he strode out of the room. A few moments later she heard him call sharply to Magdalena and Boabdíl clattered across the courtyard.

She lay awake many hours, gripped by a despair she could not explain. With the dawn she finally slept. Her husband's footsteps still were absent from the stairs.

11

An omelette and fresh bread came to Catherine next morning still warm and fragrant. She ate them without tasting.

"Where is Señor Valdivia?" she asked Ana.

"Out with the large Captain Rojo, señorita. He left very early."

Catherine swallowed her breakfast in silence. There was no reason for this perverse melancholy over her husband's absences. They were not meant to live together. Closeness bred only quarrels. Furthermore they felt no affection for one another. Why did she concern herself over Francisca? Why could she not resolve to make a life of her own?

Her muscles ached from yesterday's flurry of housekeeping. She could not look forward with enthusiasm to resuming it.

"We will go to Mass today," she added. "Tell Magdalena she's coming with us."

She thought with guilt of the marquesa's comment that Rodrigo rarely failed in attending Mass. Her own obligation had slipped her mind since her marriage. Even now she realized her decision to go was born not of piety but of the need for those rituals which would mold them as a household. In Seville she had gone to Mass daily, accompanied by Doña Teresa, her father, and various servants, and if she did not think always of God, she found a respite from turmoil which strengthened her.

Catherine felt a certain satisfaction as she and her two women walked toward the plaza. Until this morning the fact of being mistress of a household of her own had not sunk into her. There was a certain freedom about it. She had no need for a dueña but could choose whatever female servant pleased her mood. And she need be restricted by no one's judgment save her own.

Along the way there was an occasional greeting from someone she had met at the marquesa's, and on the cathedral steps from one of the captains who knew Rodrigo. The soldier bowed low. Catherine was aware of heads turning toward her. She held herself straighter, smiling all the while.

Afterward, in front of the church, Catherine waited to greet the marquesa and Doña Mercedes.

"My dear, I am pleased to see you," said the marquesa. "I have just been acquainting myself with some of your friends from the crossing." She nodded to Elvira Berruguete who now appeared with her father and brother.

"Why Doña Catherine!" exclaimed Elvira with a delight which seemed contrived to Catherine. "What a pleasure to see you. I have not yet offered congratulations on your marriage."

"Nor have I," said a soft voice as Doña Leonor García, who had made the crossing with them to wed a soldier, appeared behind them on the steps. "I wish you great happiness, Señora Valdivia."

Catherine looked at Leonor, hoping the shock she felt did not show in her face, for Leonor seemed to have aged by years since they last met. Dark shadows ringed her pretty eyes. Her face, always grave, looked strained and ill.

"Doña Leonor," smiled Catherine. "I saw you in church the day of my wedding. It was pleasant seeing a friend."

In fact the two of them had spoken not half a dozen times in the months on ship, but Leonor García accepted the compliment with a weak smile of her own.

"Another friend from the crossing?" inquired the marquesa, looking very pleased.

Leonor made a graceful curtsy.

"Yes, my lady marquessa. I am Leonor García de Silva."

De Silva. So that was Doña Leonor's married name, thought Catherine. Her unhappiness was unmistakable. Catherine wondered if those same traces someday would be found in her own face.

"You must join me, all of you, for refreshment," said the marquesa. "We are eager to hear how Doña Catherine finds her role of housekeeper, are we not, Doña Mercedes?"

Elvira Berruguete's doll-like face showed consternation. Catherine knew the girl would relish snubbing her and Leonor but her desire to win the marquesa's favor was just as strong.

"As I already count your husband the marquis as a dear acquaintance, I would not dream of refusing," said Don Francisco Berruguete, settling the decision for his family. Behind his features there was a keen satisfaction. Catherine knew he was savoring the thought she had received the punishment she deserved for her willful ways.

"I—I regret, marquesa, that I have no one to send to inform my husband of my whereabouts," said Leonor. She made a small gesture toward the single withered maid who accompanied her. A lady always required the company of a female servant. This one could not be sent with a message.

"Magdalena will be returning to my household," Catherine said. "Could she not stop at yours and leave word?"

Leonor seemed to hesitate.

"That would be most generous," she said. "The house is there."

She indicated a modest door facing across the plaza from the place where the viceroy himself now resided.

"On the plaza itself?" said Catherine. "What a stylish location!"

"Yes," said Leonor, looking at her hands. "My husband is very pleased to live in style."

All the way to the marquesa's Catherine wondered about the comment. What did it convey? Leonor seemed almost frightened.

On the way into the marquesa's lavishly furnished sala Diego Berruguete pressed close to her, the indolent charm enlivening his face.

"You are absolutely blooming, Doña Catherine. Marriage must agree with you, whatever the circumstances."

So he had heard of the auction which had been her final shame. Catherine looked at him coolly. His low laugh answered her.

"Come, come, you are too pretty for such fierce looks. And why turn them on me? Why, I have persuaded my father that certain unkind rumors concerning you are only exaggerations. Otherwise be certain he would not allow my sister to speak to you."

"The gallantry of you both is touching," Catherine answered, her voice like a sword's edge. She swept past him to a seat in a folding chair.

"What of the Audencia, Don Francisco?" asked the marquesa while they awaited orangewater. "We have heard that one of its members is taken ill."

"That's why the Audencia stayed in Tumbez while his excellency the viceroy came ahead. We have been relieved to learn the member who is ill is not my cousin. The delay is unfortunate; the Audencia's presence would lend weight to the viceroy's decisions, though why this unruly populace should take it upon themselves to question those decisions escapes me."

"Let us hope the judges arrive before there is trouble," said the marquesa.

"Trouble?" Leonor's concern was magnified by the dark circles under her eyes.

"Yes." With a shrewd look at Catherine, Don Francisco added, "Your husband, Doña Catherine, no doubt knows of the unrest in Cuzco. Does he approve it?"

A now familiar chill ran over her. That they were under suspicion of communicating with dissatisfied soldiers was evident.

"If there is unrest in Cuzco he has not spoken of it to me," she said, struggling for an air of mild indifference. "Though he undoubtedly has heard something of it in the natural course of his business. You men are fond of discussing such things on your daily rounds, are you not, Don Francisco?"

"Yes," said Don Francisco drily.

Catherine knew the weakness of relief. He had the bored tone of a hunter who has discovered the absence of game.

But Elvira, unconcerned with her father's chase, now inquired with malicious brightness, "What is your husband's business, Doña Catherine? I thought he was a soldier."

"So he is. However he also has interests in various business ventures."

"Mining?" asked Diego lazily. "I've heard that every *encomendero* who wishes to be well thought of engages in the search for gold or silver."

"We cannot afford such sport," said Catherine bluntly. "My husband has chosen to use his land for the raising of horses."

She knew full well that the admission might separate herself and Rodrigo still further from the social circle which the people facing her represented. In Peru men were attempting to raise cattle on terrain which was ridiculously mountainous and mining for precious metals in the most unlikely places simply because those were the genteel occupations.

"Diverting," said Elvira. "But hardly what one thinks of as more than a hobby. What of his other ventures? Shipping? Spices?"

"I must confess I do not know. We have, after all, been married less than a week, and it's not the sort of subject a wife introduces." She gave a bright smile.

Elvira, undeterred, said sweetly, "But surely you had occasion to talk of such things in the weeks before your wedding?"

As her spine stiffened Catherine with effort tilted her chin and laughed.

"You have not yet been betrothed, Doña Elvira," she said in her most tolerant tones, casting a look of pretended secrecy to Leonor García.

Not only Leonor laughed, but also Doña Mercedes and the marquesa. The betrothal, it suggested, was a time for tender glances and words of endearment, not for discussing the nature of business investments. Elvira colored furiously, her small eyes crackling.

"Now if you will excuse me, there is still much to be accomplished in the settling of our household," Catherine said rising. Impulsively she paused. "Marquesa, Doña Mercedes, it would give me great pleasure if you would call on me next week that I might return a small measure of the hospitality you have shown me. Doña Leonor, Doña Elvira, will you join us? Shall we say Monday?"

"Monday it shall be," agreed the marquesa with a faint lift of her jeweled fingers.

"I look forward to it," said Leonor. "And now, my lady marquesa, I too must go."

Elvira Berruguete made no reply. Don Francisco, his mouth set severely, stared through Catherine as though she did not exist. Accompanied by their maids, Leonor and Catherine descended the stairs.

"I fear Doña Elvira does not much like you," said Leonor. "It will be interesting to see if she accepts your invitation."

"Yes, I myself am curious to see what my status will be as a woman of notoriety," Catherine said calmly.

A pathetic ghost of amusement touched Leonor's lips.

"There have been rumors about you," she admitted. "But what does it matter? Your husband is splendid to look at, not bothered by gout or missing teeth. As long as he treats you well, let people talk."

Catherine knew she had made a rash decision. From the doorway she watched Rodrigo, standing with an arm on the *vargueno,* intent on thoughts.

"I—came to inquire how your day was," she said.

His head raised slightly.

What did one say to a husband? Catherine felt a sharp and

unexpected irritation with her father for failing to instruct her in such matters.

"Well enough," Rodrigo said. He watched her come into the room.

Her index fingers formed a point as she locked her hands together. "Did you know Magdalena has a son?" she asked.

"No, I did not." He was clearly baffled by her question.

"His name is Mateo," she said, drifting toward the *mirador*. "He looks to be eight perhaps. I—I have told Magdalena he may stay here with her as she has no one—no relative—to care for him. He could be of some small use, I think, in the garden and about the stables. I hope you will not forbid it."

Relieved of the words she chanced at last a look at him. One corner of his mouth curved with amusement.

"If your tender heart leads you to feel he should be with his mother then I have no objection. How is it, *preciosa,* that you're so easily moved by everyone but me?"

Catherine blushed, all words eluding her. His directness could leave her confused, and he was aware of it.

"Put him to chores in the garden if it pleases you," he continued before she had recovered. "But I have no wish to see him in the stables. There's nothing a boy of eight can do."

Argument swelled Catherine's breast but she held it back.

After the easy resolution of an encounter which she had dreaded, Magdalena's beautiful dinner was almost more than she could bear. The Indian woman had supervised the grilling of shrimps in oil and garlic, and there was rice and goose and a succulent yellow fruit which Rodrigo gave the name pineapple. Things were going to work out, Catherine told herself, relaxing. This household could run smoothly. There could even be peace between her and the man who faced her across the polished table.

"If you keep eating like that you'll need that ridiculous corset which you wear," he said as she sank her teeth into the sweetness of another wedge of pineapple.

Catherine smiled. "The Moors say one will never get fat eating fruit." At ease, she changed the subject. "I visited the marquesa this morning after Mass."

Briefly, so as not to bore him, she described the gathering.

"Do you know a soldier named de Silva?" she asked.

"Captain de Silva? Yes. He's newly married. His home is on the plaza. Why?"

"His wife was there. She came on the ship from Spain with me."

"And?"

Her husband was more perceptive than Catherine liked. She avoided his eyes.

"Only that she looks—homesick, perhaps."

Rodrigo said nothing. They continued the meal in silence until a quick knock interrupted them. Ana came into the room without being bidden.

"A message for you, Señor Valdivia," she said breathlessly and stepped aside, revealing a mestizo youth in Spanish attire.

The youth spoke rapidly in the clattering Indian tongue. Rodrigo rose.

"Forgive me, a matter of business has come up," he said. At the door he paused, his back toward her. "Expect me quite late."

His words were too casual. Catherine frowned. As soon as he had gone down the stairs Magdalena appeared, concerned, no doubt, about the status of the meal.

"Ask who sent the message to Señor Valdivia," said Catherine, nodding toward the mestizo youth who was just leaving.

Magdalena spoke to him. She listened, unblinking.

"He says it was a woman at the León, señora."

Catherine looked away, determined not to let her expression show. The León. An inn. What else could it be but a summons from Francisca, the woman they had quarreled over the night before? Going into the sala she stepped into the *mirador* and through its carved wood watched her husband ride away. She was glad of the privacy of that closed, narrow balcony. It hid her humiliation, the hurt she was suffering. Her fingers traced the curves of the open spaces through which she peered.

It seemed impossible rejection should cut so deeply. Catherine lay sleepless watching the moon gild a path across the far wall of her room. From her old Moorish nursemaid she had learned not only the art of bathing, but some small skill in medicine, and she had mixed herself a powerful sleeping draught, yet still her eyes were wide.

It was not just her body which Valdivia rejected, Catherine thought. That, in fact, was the single fragile thread which bound them. Apart from it, her husband seemed to find her displeasing—a disappointment, at best. What was it that she lacked? Courage? Resilience? One arm tucked behind her head, her nightdress rising and falling with her shallow breaths, she pondered the question. Even if she could avoid further quarrels like the one which had sent him to Francisca the night before, instinct told her it would not be enough. What was it her husband sought in her and counted missing?

12.

The sound was ominous in its very smallness, as controlled and menacing as the cocking of a crossbow. Rodrigo stood in the door connecting their rooms, his powerful nakedness gleaming like the candle in his hand. Drowsily Catherine struggled to rouse herself from the deep though tardy grip of the sleeping draught. The room around her loomed and wavered dizzily. Then, as her husband moved toward her, a cold fear swept across her at the terrible anger in his face.

With a low cry she flung herself aside, away from the demonic form which towered above her. His eyes blazed like coals, unfeeling. His hand caught her across the throat and she was slammed back hard against the sheets. Was he drunk or merely insane, she wondered, as the steel grip stopped her air. All around her there were spinning shadows. This was a dream, a nightmare brought on by the sleeping nostrum. Then his fingers forced apart her jaws as if she were some horse resisting the bit and he began to kiss her and Catherine knew it was no dream at all. His free hand found the neck of her nightdress and ripped it, exposing her breasts. He tugged again and with insane possession fitted his body to hers.

As breath was restored to her Catherine stopped her frantic struggle. She lay beneath him dimly charting movements whose pattern she already was beginning to know, moving with him toward the end despite all resistance, until they at last lay still, the feel of his sweat against her skin, the taste of blood on her lip.

When his own breathing had returned to normal he kissed her brutally, winding his fingers in her hair.

"Look at me," he commanded.

Pale and shaking she obeyed.

"Did you suppose for a minute you could escape my attentions by retiring? This will prove to you otherwise, I trust."

"You—said you would return late," Catherine protested, chagrined to find there was no force behind her voice.

"I also told you to expect me. What did you suppose I meant?"

Catherine stared at him, confused. "I—certainly not this!"

"Why?"

The question was so sharp she shrank from it.

"You did not come last night—or the night before," she whispered. She could not bring herself to raise the name Francisca.

Rodrigo's face was grave.

"On both occasions I had drunk too deeply of rum, the *aqua vitae* of the New World, *preciosa*. I would not force my company upon you in those circumstances. Nor would I cheat myself by being less than aware of every breath you draw, whether in hate or desire."

Releasing her hair he rolled over on his shoulder, brushing the back of his hand against her frightened cheek.

"Bewitching Catherine," he said softly. "Did you suppose I'd tired of you already? Were it from anyone but Rojo I would have ignored that summons tonight."

"Rojo?" she repeated, hollow with his lie. The boy with the message had said it came from a woman. While her unhappy eyes saw nothing but the dark hair of his chest his words continued warm above her.

"Yes, the wench who serves drinks at the León sent word for me to come to him in secret." Her eyes leaped up in time to catch the slight curve of his mouth. "You see the extremes of caution my friends press on me now that I am married?"

Her heart began to beat with a new kind of fear.

"And was the caution necessary?"

He was silent for a minute. Then he did not answer the question directly.

"The viceroy, in the name of the crown, has taken back extensive lands belonging to Juan Portero, not only a brilliant soldier but a man from the finest of families. It does not argue well for the future."

Catherine listened, surprised less by the words than by her own reaction. Could she so easily forget the ruthless way he had used her not five minutes past? It was true he had explained his absences, but why was she so willing now to lie beside him calmly, so quick to think about his safety? She hated him for causing that reaction, for making her safety one with his.

"You're frowning," he said. "There is no need. The Audencia will come, the viceroy will be forced to temper his acts. The times are unpleasant but they will pass."

"And Rojo would speed their passing?" she suggested, careful to keep emotion from her voice.

"Not Rojo. There were others there tonight who would, but they're mad. We are but a handful of men when the viceroy's troops are counted. The others will no doubt stir up impossible plans till dawn. I chose to come here. Does that make you feel less abandoned, *preciosa?*"

She turned her head away.

"A husband comes and goes as he chooses, does he not?"

She heard the laughter in his voice.

"You are stubborn, my lovely doña—or hopelessly innocent. Do you not realize my desire for you cuts through me like a sword's edge? There will be no release from that pain—for either of us—while I draw breath. Do you understand?"

She nodded slowly. With his forefinger he touched her chin and turned it back toward him. His eyes, night fires in which she could see nothing but her own reflection, probed her own.

"You do not," he said. His lips moved gently across her mouth as he drew her closer. "You do not understand at all."

Tears trembling in her eyes, she flung her head aside.

"How can you—kiss me like that—subject me first to your anger and then to—to—"

"To tenderness, Catherine? Because I am resolved to tear down the wall you have built between us. I will do it by force if I must, though I find this way much more pleasant."

His lips touched the vulnerable flesh at the side of her neck. Catherine quivered. At the back of her mind a question screamed, but she dared not voice it. She dared not even give it her own ear, she was so fearful of the answer.

In the morning, sitting before the small table which served for her toilette, Catherine thought about the wall which Rodrigo had mentioned. There was one, it was true. But should she seek its safety or help destroy it? If only she could forget the taunts he had made about arousing her own passion. If only his touch did not seem always a weapon in some war between them.

The comb between her fingers had fallen still. Rodrigo, lounging behind her on the bench where she sat, retrieved it from her. He drew it somewhat clumsily through the curls cascading past her shoulders, watching the black waves ripple into place.

"You're pensive," he said. He studied her reflection in the oval mirror framed in gilt which hung before her on the wall.

On a corner of the table sat the tray which had held their breakfast. Ana had shown commendable sense in guessing her master's whereabouts this morning, Catherine thought. The tray, announced by a knock and left outside the door, had held not only her omelette, but thick slabs of bread and cheese and a larger than usual pitcher of wine. Rodrigo had shared the omelette at her invitation and did not yet show any inclination toward leaving, though Catherine had wrapped a dressing gown around her waist and for many minutes had sat working tangles from her hair.

"What are you thinking?" he asked, easing her back against the warmth of his bare chest.

She closed her eyes against the pleasant sensations flooding through her.

"I was trying to guess what prompted the thirst for rum you spoke of last night," she said.

"I'll spare you the guessing then. On the first occasion it was the duel with Don Luis, which I would have welcomed save for the suffering exacted from you. On the second occasion I was bitterly angry with myself for bringing you to such circumstances as I have, a house without sufficient servants where you yourself must oversee the arrangement of rooms and the cleaning of furniture."

Catherine twisted to face him.

"I have made no complaint and I have none! I realize you think me spoiled and fond of leisure, but you are wrong. I like nothing better than work, Rodrigo, whether with my hands or with my brain. The prospect of running this house— exactly as it is—delights me. I'm not one of those creatures who can sit for hours with needlework."

She half expected laughter to reward her ridiculous shortage of restraint. Instead, as she turned back toward the mirror he lifted the hair from the nape of her neck and kissed her scented skin.

"Thank you," he murmured.

"For what?" she asked, surprised.

"For what you have just said. And now, my pretty doña, get dressed, or there will be no one to run this house for the rest of the day."

He rose before she could speak and went to his own room, closing the door between.

When Ana came to dress her, Catherine again decided to dispense with the formality of an overblouse or jacket. She expected no callers today, the weather was warm, and besides the white lawn underblouse looked well on her, she thought, admitting her vanity. Perhaps Rodrigo would not ride out today at all. She sent to the kitchen and ordered a vegetable gruel for lunch.

While Magdalena was with her receiving the instructions, Catherine took a silver coin from the housekeeping money and handed it to her.

"Do you know the place where trees are sold?" she asked. From conversations at the marquesa's, Catherine knew the amount she was giving over would buy no more than a single tree, yet she was reluctant to part with more. "Buy a citron," she said. "No, a sweet orange would be more practical. Buy that. And if you've anything left over buy a clump of bulbs."

Magdalena pocketed the money without reply and left.

Mateo, who had followed her from the kitchen, lingered for a moment staring curiously at Catherine. Frail legs topped with small knees showed beneath his white cotton shift, and yet there was an air of pluckiness about the boy for all his size. He was *mestizo*, a mixture. He had his mother's face and coloring, but his lovely dark Spanish eyes and the wave to his hair must have come from his dead father. Stubbornly Catherine resolved to show her husband just how useful this boy of eight could be.

After lunch, in her room, Catherine found she could not rest. The memory of the business which had called Rodrigo out the night before came back to her. Through the viceroy, the lands and Indian workers which the crown had given its citizens in payment of service were being reclaimed. Small wonder that the New Laws were unpopular. Men who had risked their lives to win a country could hardly be expected to give up their sources of livelihood cheerfully. Yet surely the crown understood the situation better than she did. Surely it was fairer than it seemed.

More immediate than the question of fairness was that of her own position. Would Rodrigo lose his small *encomienda*? Would he turn rebel? The house which she was laboring to set to rights could be snatched from them in an instant, gone forever. The orange tree which she hoped to plant today could tomorrow be uprooted. She got up resolved to plant.

Halfway down the stairs she stopped to stare in disbelief at the sight which met her eyes. In a shaded corner of the patio stood a citron and a sweet orange tree, both nearly as high as her shoulder. Beside them lay clusters of brilliant pink bougainvillea which Magdalena and the kitchen maid were fitting carefully into glazed pots filled with earth.

"Magdalena!" she gasped.

Magdalena's dark eyes dilated with fear.

"If you do not like the color, señora—"

"No, they're beautiful! But how—how did you manage to buy so much? You didn't subtract from the food money—"

"No, señora. The trees I bought from a grower who sells much more cheaply than the stalls where your countrymen buy. It is in a market for my people. At this time of day there were no Spanish out to see me, so it will bring no discredit to this household."

Catherine stared at her. Magdalena had taken pains to avoid being seen shopping at a place less than fashionable. Surely this was loyalty such as one rarely found in a servant. What had she done to deserve it?

The first tree was in place and the earth firmed around it when Rodrigo rode in.

"What is this? A veritable forest!" he exclaimed.

Catherine could not decide if the words were mocking. He was eyeing the freshly turned earth as he swung down.

"There is another tree, I see. Let me stable Boabdíl and I will dig the hole for it."

"There is no need, señor—" Magdalena began.

"No need, perhaps, but I will do it. My back is stronger than the kitchen maid's. I can do the job in half the time. Captain Rojo promises to pay us a visit later this afternoon. I would not like to have him see us with dirt piled everywhere."

Catherine could not imagine that Rojo would even notice the dirt. She smiled in appreciation at her husband and walked with him to the stable. He lifted Boabdíl's heavy saddle with ease. She watched in silence as he rubbed the horse.

"The water is fresh. Mateo brought it," she said as he reached for the bucket.

"I suspect it will be the limit of the chores which he can handle. Now come and show me where to put this tree. I hate the sight of servants scuttling to and fro."

Rodrigo removed his doublet and the leather shell beneath it. After a moment or two of digging he also unfastened his shirt. Catherine watched the movement of his muscles under the rough white linen. Beneath her own clothes her breasts were sore from his touch. Resting a foot on the shovel he looked at her, eyes narrowing with a sudden gleam as if he could guess the course of her thoughts. There was a knock at the gate.

114

"Rojo," he murmured, unperturbed.

But when the gate swung open a lightly built horse appeared, and on it was Francisca. Her deep plum riding suit was molded to her body revealing curves far more generous than Catherine's.

"How domestic you are these days, Rodrigo!" she laughed in greeting. She dismounted and hands on hips surveyed the courtyard. "Sweet orange. How charming," she said with a curve of the lips which deprecated the words. "How clever you must be, Catherine, to turn a soldier into a gardener."

Catherine felt her nerves tense. Then just as quickly she told herself she must not be lured into this trap. She must not again allow this woman to provoke her into words Rodrigo might criticize.

"I'm afraid he could not bear the length of time it was taking the servants to put things to rights," she answered with her broadest smile. "He has finished the job in half the time, which is all the better, as the afternoon is growing late. Won't you come inside and take some refreshment?"

With an intuition of triumph she saw Francisca's eyes close into sparkling slits.

"I'm afraid I have no time to spare. I leave at dawn for Cuzco. I came only to get Rodrigo's answer to the matter we discussed the other night." Giving her attention now to Rodrigo she flicked a finger against the open front of his shirt. "Frankly, *hombre,* you look as if a bit of fighting would agree with you. Your disposition is sour and you are plump."

That she could call Rodrigo's hard muscularity plump amused Catherine. It also angered her that Francisca should take such shameless notice of his body.

"Nothing would agree with me less," Rodrigo informed her blandly. "You may tell the general as much."

Francisca's sensuous face exploded with rage.

" 'Rigo, you are a fool! They have taken Juan Portero's land; they will take yours! Why are you, of all men, now playing the role of the cosseted townsman?"

Rodrigo's jaw hardened.

"I have no desire to see another civil war, Francisca."

Already she had gathered up her skirts.

"There will be one, whether you like it or not," she snapped, finding a foothold in the stirrup unassisted. She jerked her horse up with a heavy hand and would have ridden away had Rodrigo not caught her horse's bridle.

"If there is war, then you will find the townsmen whom you

115

scorn are ready, Francisca *mía*. A group of them are meeting here tomorrow night. We do not spoil for a fight as the men of Cuzco seem to, but if it comes we will not turn from it."

Catherine struggled to suppress the gasp which hovered in her throat. Rodrigo had led her to believe he would not take part in the treason whose odor grew ever stronger on the air around them. Now she learned that their own house would shelter it.

Lazily Francisca smiled her satisfaction. She swung her gaze toward Catherine.

"Be careful you're not betrayed," she warned Rodrigo, her meaning unmistakable.

"I won't be," he assured her.

But as he looked at Catherine she could see the question in his eyes. She met them blindly. She felt numb, shocked, trapped.

"Expect a visit from me or someone else in a fortnight," Francisca said. With a smack of the whip she sent her horse leaping forward into the street, followed by the sharp-chinned serving woman who always accompanied her. She did not even pause at the sound of a voice which hailed her from beyond.

A moment later Rojo rode in, his expression worried and quizzical as he looked at Rodrigo.

"That was Francisca?"

"Yes."

Catherine felt a tension in the briefness of his answer. Rojo gave one of those wags of the head she had determined indicated his disapproval.

The sweet orange stood abandoned by the hole dug to receive it. There was dirt heaped on the cinnamon-colored tiles. In the engulfing silence those signs of work suspended assumed significance out of all proportion to themselves. They were symbols, in Catherine's mind, of life abruptly interrupted, its direction changed forever.

13

"I believe we shall complete our altarclothes by June," announced the marquesa.

She took her needlework from a tapestry bag and peered at it critically, the mole on her chin jutting forward as she pursed her lips. At her feet the oriental rug which had been Rojo's gift to Rodrigo and Catherine glowed deep blue in the sun-filled sala.

A month had passed since Catherine first entertained the group of women she now considered her friends—the marquesa, Leonor García, Doña Mercedes, and, to her amusement, Elvira Berruguete. Now, on a bright May morning, she watched the light flood Rojo's wedding present and bounce from glistening blue and yellow tiles which ran around the room waist high. Her mind was not on this peaceful sewing project the marquesa had set for them. She could not rid herself of the feeling that any moment any of these women might look into her face and see there the guilt of a traitor.

For such had Catherine come to regard herself. She could not deny the course her husband had chosen. She could not pretend ignorance of the midnight meetings held in this house of late.

"This room is charming," Elvira said. "There is that intimate feeling—as though we're in a sitting room."

Catherine knew what was insinuated—the room was small. Still, in her less troubled moments she could look on it with satisfaction. Had she termed Elvira a friend? She knew the girl came only to curry the favor of the marquesa. And Catherine admitted she feared Elvira's probing eyes more than any others.

"You are quiet today, Doña Catherine," observed the marquesa.

Catching the speculative glance at her waist Catherine shook her head, smiling wanly.

"You must pardon me, marquesa. My thoughts were occupied. My husband has ridden to meet the ship which docked this morning. We're hopeful it carries the stallion we're awaiting."

Elvira cleared her throat, a sign she found this suggestion of sex and breeding indelicate.

Catherine had not slept well in weeks. With growing frequency men opposed to the viceroy's high-handed rule came together in this very room. Cloaked and under cover of darkness they came and drank wine and talked in heated voices, captains of rank, *encomenderos* with great grants of land at their disposal, and ordinary soldiers like her husband. Determined to enforce the New Laws, the viceroy had seized more lands. He had freed many Indians needed by the Spaniards to work their mines and run their farms. Catherine felt sure now there would be trouble, and her own house was sheltering its seed.

"Let us hope, Doña Catherine, that your husband's occupation with his animals keeps him from the treachery so common to cavalrymen just now," said Elvira bluntly.

Leonor sent Catherine a quick and uncomfortable look. The recent defection of two detachments of cavalry to Pizarro's forces was the scandal of the city. Puelles, the military commander at Guanuco, had been the first to turn openly against the viceroy. Receiving some warning of Puelles' intent, the viceroy had sent another detachment of horse to intercept him, and that body too had gone over to the rebels. The loyalty of every household, or every one which housed a soldier, now was coming into question.

"One scarcely glimpses gallantry in politics today," lamented the marquesa. "Imagine, turning against one's commander."

Elvira sniffed. "It's a blessing the Audencia is finally under way. Perhaps this disgusting populace will show a little more respect for the viceroy's authority when they arrive."

Catherine smiled over her needlework. Rumor had it that the judges of the Audencia were at no pains to obey the New Laws which the viceroy was enforcing. They were said to show no qualms about appropriating Indian labor whenever it was required, less concerned about freeing the natives entrusted by God to Spain than they were about finding ready backs to carry their luggage.

"Do you find the viceroy amusing, Doña Catherine?" Elvira asked coldly. Her bright little eyes waited, eager to judge.

"I was thinking," Catherine answered, "that I could not imagine a populace less inclined to show respect."

The men drank in the streets. They were loud and outspoken in a way men in Seville had never been. Conquering this land had forged a new breed, afraid of little. How could they know fear when eight of every ten of them had died in the winning of this country? Apart from their politics Catherine awarded them grudging admiration. Elvira's belief that things would ever be here exactly as they were in Spain was fantasy.

"They'll begin to act like Spanish citizens or pay the penalty," the Berruguete girl predicted. "My father's cousin says so."

Leonor García, with a yawn of pointed boredom, changed the subject.

"It amazes me, Doña Elvira, that you have time to occupy your mind with politics. I hear you are being courted by half a dozen suitors."

Each week it surprised Catherine to see how Leonor's face, as they sat sewing and chatting, lost its haunted look, until gradually flashes of humor appeared beneath the tired lines. She was glad to see the change now. It made Elvira's answering show of coquetry more endurable.

"The men who call come mainly to see my father, I am sure," she said with a flutter of lashes.

Leonor's smile held a hint of mischief.

"Ah, and your father summons Alonzo Sanchez to dinner out of a passionate interest in the history he is writing, I have no doubt."

The marquesa and Doña Mercedes laughed heartily. Elvira's face was red.

"Gossip is a discredit to those who spread it and those who hear it," she said, furious.

"But inescapable," Leonor assured her blandly.

Catherine listened with frozen expression. She had tried not to think about Alonzo Sanchez. Her distress over hearing he was courting Elvira angered her. What did it matter?

"My father wishes me to marry well," Elvira said, laying down her needlework to fan herself with petulance. "Don Alonzo seems to qualify. His father is highly placed in the government of Hispaniola. Don Alonzo, of course, will inherit extensive holdings there, and has lands in his own right here.

"If he suits my father I suppose I shall marry him. It matters very little to me, one way or another."

At her superior tone Catherine saw anger flash in Leonor García's eyes. Neither she nor Leonor had had the luxury of statements such as that. By the time her guests departed Catherine's forced composure had left her with a headache.

She had retired to her room to rest when Ana came to her breathless with the news that two men sent by the viceroy waited on her in the courtyard. Catherine sat up, pulses pounding. Men from the viceroy—it could only mean the meetings held beneath their roof had been found out. Aware her manner would set the tone for the household, she got up calmly. She smoothed her skirt and held her head erect.

The scent of sweet orange met her nostrils when she stepped onto the gallery. It seemed impossible that just a month ago the patio had been so bare. Now the orange and citron looked as if they were long-time residents, the bougainvillea erupted from their shiny pots in an explosion of blossoms, even the fig tree appeared to be taking hold. For a moment tears misted Catherine's eyes as she looked down on the peaceful scene, shattered by the waiting forms of horsemen inside the gate. She descended the stairs with a determined appearance of unconcern, Ana at her heels.

"Señora de Valdivia?" asked one of the horsemen, moving his mount a few steps forward before she had a chance to speak.

Catherine could only nod, for she recognized the other horseman, the one who remained behind, as one of Don Luis's hired thugs, the one who had restrained her brother on the morning of his death.

"We are pleased to receive you," she said, amazed at the steadiness of her own voice. "Will you come into the sala? The sun is warm."

Across the way she saw Magdalena watching silently from the kitchen. Magdalena must know well enough the nature of the secret meetings in this house. The air itself seemed to wait for something to happen.

The man who had spoken was a jaundiced-looking individual with the bearing of a *bachiller,* the lowest-ranking form of lawyer. Ignoring her he flipped a thin book open.

"This is not a social call, señora."

Catherine's mouth curled with contempt at his failure to dismount. A man of breeding would have done as much from simple habit.

The *bachiller* took a pen from Don Luis's man and held it poised.

"Your husband holds a grant of land from the king, señora. I have orders to learn its exact location, as well as the number and breed of any livestock on it."

"Orders from the viceroy?" she inquired.

"From Don Luis de Alvarado, a member of the Cabildo now aiding the viceroy—"

"I am acquainted with Don Luis," interrupted Catherine with a look at his man, who now sat grinning. So Don Luis was beginning to exact revenge on her and Rodrigo. What was the purpose of the list he was compiling? To seize a great many pieces of land under pretext their owners were treasonous? Or was this largely some innocuous accounting job which he had taken charge of to settle scores with a few?

"I regret I cannot help you," she said coolly. "I have never seen the land in question."

Beneath his sallow skin the *bachiller* grew red.

"I would hardly expect a woman to have seen it, señora. I asked only its location."

"Why would I know its location if I had never been there?"

"You know something, surely, of the animals. There is said to be at least one very fine horse, and possibly more."

"For which we have been justly taxed," smiled Catherine. "Yes, there is a horse, señor, but I do not think you'll find it on the land in question. I expect my husband pastures it somewhere closer to the city. Where, I could not say."

Her heart was beating against the sides of her throat. A shadow of surprise hung over her to find that she was lying for her husband. Just the week before she had gone with Rodrigo to see the white mare. She knew where it was. But what did these men intend to do? Their very omission of threats left her increasingly nervous.

"You know little about your husband's affairs," the *bachiller* snapped as he closed the book.

Catherine inclined her head just enough to show that the charge did not ruffle her.

"Don Luis, I am sure, knows more. Perhaps you should ask him for answers. Of course you could return when my husband is home."

"So we will," said the man as he swung his horse around.

Catherine let her shoulders sag as they rode out the gate. She had entertained no thought of politics in the moments just past. Now she realized she had defied the viceroy in her hate for Don Luis.

The sweet orange cast long patterns on the courtyard floors before she heard Rodrigo return. She could not readily find Magdalena to tell her dinner would be wanted soon, and by the time she located her Indian servant and continued to the stables, her husband was not there.

But what she saw held Catherine motionless for some moments. The two stalls next to Boabdíl's were occupied, both by Andalusians, both by mares. Quickly her mind arranged the story of what must have happened. The ship which had docked had brought not the hoped-for stallion, but another mare, and Rodrigo, somehow getting wind of Don Luis's interest in their animals, had brought both of them here. Strangely the thought of him angry and disappointed made her more anxious to find him.

He was in none of the usual rooms. With some hesitation she knocked at the door of the single room she had never entered, the one adjoining hers.

Her husband wore such a frightening expression when he opened the door that she looked quickly away. Shock filled her as she saw the bare walls of his room. Whereas her own room was finely furnished and even carpeted, this one held nothing but a wardrobe of inferior workmanship and a floor-high frame filled with straw which served as a bed.

"You have not been sleeping there!" she cried, her immediate thoughts forgotten. "But why? It is unthinkable, with furniture in every other room!"

For a moment she expected anger at this thoughtless outcry. Instead she saw an easing of the tension in his face.

"I would have no better in an inn. Here at least nothing nests in it, but perhaps you will be less eager now to banish me from your comfortable mattress. What is it, *preciosa?* It is seldom you come hunting me."

She blushed, annoyed that she had failed to keep her mind on business.

"I saw the horses. You must have heard the viceroy has shown interest in them. It is well you did not come earlier, for two of his men called here."

"Here?" His head jerked up.

"They wanted to know the location of your *encomienda* and the number of animals pastured there. I told them I did not know. One of them was Don Luis's man. Don Luis is no doubt responsible for the inquiry."

"No doubt." Rodrigo removed his sword and scabbard, tossing them onto the bed. "Frankly, *preciosa,* I am surprised you lied for me. It was an act against the crown, you know."

Although the words were casually spoken, Catherine was stung by them.

"I am your wife," she said. "I owe you loyalty, and you shall have it."

His look was scathing.

"How fortunate I am you pay your debts. Now order dinner."

As he seemed bent on being unpleasant, Catherine took her place at the table with no intention of making conversation. They dined in heavy silence. At last, reluctantly, she said:

"I am sorry there was no stallion. At least the mare came safely, and that is something."

"Another mouth to feed, that's all, until she serves a purpose."

Catherine winced, wondering whether similar thoughts were directed at her. Without legitimate heirs Rodrigo's *encomienda,* should it escape the threat of the New Laws, would revert to the crown on his death.

"I heard rumors that inquiries were afoot about our mares," he said. "They would be too easily spotted where the first was pastured. They will be safer on the *encomienda.* I'll take them there tomorrow."

Catherine frowned.

"But if the viceroy intends to take the land—"

"He is going methodically through the list of those who took part in the civil war, starting of course with those whose gains were greatest and whose names have gained some prominence. By virtue of holdings as well as birth I am low on that list. There will be ample warning."

Catherine put down her spoon. The almond-cabbage soup before her had lost its appeal. Even now, when it seemed to their advantage, she could hear the bitterness in her husband's voice as he assessed his status in society. Suddenly it struck her how far he had come, from stable boy to master of his own house. She could not fault his bitterness. Indeed she shared it, having learned from her own experience how one was judged by convention, appearances, anything, it seemed, but worth.

When the dishes had been cleared in front of them she said in a low voice, "I want to go with you tomorrow."

Rodrigo regarded her over his wine cup.

"Impossible. The ride is too much for you. More than twice the distance to Callao."

"I am capable of it. I want to go."

Even to herself she could not say why.

"I'm sorry, *preciosa,* it is too far."

"Francisca makes the ride from Cuzco—much farther."

"Francisca is a different breed of woman."

Catherine's anger flamed and she stood up. A weakling, suitable for little except amusement in bed—was that how he saw her? She despised the role.

"I have a right to see the land," she said. "My children will own it one day!"

His eyes fixed on her rigid form with no expression at all that she could see.

"Is there to be a child?" he asked.

"They generally occur in marriage. One is not on the way at present, which is all the more reason why I should make the trip at this time. Another is that a second rider would be of use, with two extra horses to lead."

"In that case you will be relieved to know that Rojo is coming with me."

There were no arguments left her. Resentment growing at his inexorable position, Catherine started from the room. He rose behind her.

"Catherine."

He put his hands on the delicate shoulders so forcefully squared.

"Listen to me, Catherine. I have no desire to see you exhausted, tired when there is no reason. I would rather find you waiting for me, rested and smelling of violets, when I return."

She did not weaken to his touch.

"And what I want—that doesn't matter?"

"Do you know what you want, *preciosa?*" He turned her toward him, peering into her eyes. "No, I think not," he said. "You are still too angry, your resentment of me too keen."

Depression settled over her. He did not understand that what she resented most now was his attitude, his refusal to see her as anything but a costly toy. Perhaps she should be glad he required so little of her. Still she wanted to prove herself more than the useless creature he imagined her. But she was weary of argument. More than anything she wanted peace.

He gave her his arm. They walked in silence down into the courtyard where the young trees beat a leaf tune on the night breeze fanning them. Stars glittered like a fortune in silver *reales* flung against the heavens.

"Who will care for the horses?" asked Catherine.

"I hired a man—this afternoon when I decided to move them. I know little about him except that he was looking for work. He rode out today. He should be there when we arrive tomorrow. Already I am thinking better about the expense of it. The mares could both be dead before a stallion comes. Unfortunately I see no other choice."

Catherine touched a finger to the fig tree. The gesture made her feel somehow closer to her father. He had wanted her to prosper. Perhaps it was time for her to think of that, though a time of less promise she could not imagine.

"I've been thinking," she said slowly. "My father has a cousin of some position in India House. He also raises fine horses himself—or did when I was a child. Perhaps if I wrote him he could end whatever delay it is that's holding up the export license for the stallion."

She held her breath. This was straining her husband's pride and she was aware of it. She was offering the chance of help through business connections and family name, avenues not open to him.

His body had tensed at her suggestion. The night was still around them.

"All that I've ever gotten, I've gotten by my own efforts," his deep voice answered. "Still, we must make our peace with one another's backgrounds, mustn't we, *preciosa?* As this would benefit you as well as me, do whatever you like."

Catherine pressed his arm in a rush of relief which she herself had not expected. She did not want them to be enemies. As they were bound in marriage, could they not work together?

"My father's cousin is a wonderful man," she said, scarcely aware of the words she uttered. "I think you would like each other."

Rodrigo laughed. "Let us hope we won't have to wait the six months or more it would take this relative of yours to set things right." He clenched his teeth. "Hell's fires! Why, when I've ordered but three animals, do I get two of a single sex?"

Made bold by her success Catherine smiled at his ire.

"It could take six months; we must face that. Let us turn some profit on the mares in the meantime."

"What are you suggesting?" he asked warily.

She shook her head. "Not Boabdíl again, if that's what you're thinking. It occurs to me there might be, among the *encomenderos*, a fine horse or two. A stallion. Not Andalusian, perhaps, but of good blood. Some arrangement could be made for breeding."

"Just now I feel too distracted by politics to make such arrangements."

"Then let me make them for you. It is not uncommon for women to engage in business, I believe, so long as they remain behind the scenes."

"Some are silent partners in investments, it is true. But a lady can hardly discuss the breeding of livestock—"

"I will make our requirements known to an agent, then. He can advertise our needs and send any prospects to us. What do you say?"

"Catherine—"

"Please, Rodrigo."

She felt his violent sigh of resignation.

"Very well. If it pleases you. Now come inside."

14

The stable area smelled hot and dusty as Catherine entered it. She moved toward the stall with the rented horse kept for her. Let her husband reassess her hardiness when he caught up with her, already well ahead of him on the road to the *encomienda!*

The dark of night was lifting just enough for her to make out shapes of horse and saddle. She turned up her palm and the mare bent to it. Catherine stroked the animal's muzzle, then deftly coaxed a bit into her mouth. So far, so good. If she could but saddle her mount unaided, she would prove to her husband she was made of sturdier stuff than he believed. And that she had no intention of being the docile creature he expected.

She strained but could not lift the saddle perched on a partition between stalls. She jerked and it fell in a heap. Panting, she looked at the mountain of leather. A wisp of hair fell across her face. She swung the saddle up and up with awkward motion, felt it hit the mare and hesitate, and grunting angry words she pushed.

Now it was done. No more would she endure Rodrigo's smugness at her frailty. Shaking with exertion she wondered whether the saucy Francisca had ever saddled a horse.

There remained but to tighten the girth. Catherine tugged until it lay snug against the horse's belly. She pushed a stirrup to test the fit, and cried in alarm as the saddle slipped dangerously to the side. Puffing with effort she pushed the saddle back into place and tried once more.

Behind her a chuckle sounded in the silent stable. She spun, and in the grayness which surrounded them saw her husband. He was leaning against the partition, arms crossed lazily.

With patronizing calm he came into the stall. Taking the saddle girth in one hand, he brought his knee up sharply against the mare's belly. Catherine heard the animal expel a breath and saw the strap jerked tight.

"There, a simple matter," Rodrigo grinned. "But tell me where did you think to ride at this hour, *preciosa?*

Catherine felt heat flood her entire body. He was laughing

127

at her. Her competence in bridling the horse and lifting the saddle were all negated by this intervention, and angry humiliation filled her at the defeat.

"I am going to the *encomienda!* I had thought to be well ahead so that you had no choice when you caught up with me, but as you have discovered me, I give you warning: If you refuse to take me with you I will make the trip on my own, and it will be on your conscience if I lose the way."

Her chin was turned up and she met his eyes with a challenge. In the mockery of his expression she saw now a shade of surprise. The knowledge rekindled a certain sense of triumph, which wavered as she watched the slow spread of his smile.

"Very well," he answered lightly. "If you insist on such punishment, I will not stop you. Neither will I make concessions for you. Which means, my lovely, that if I am inclined to have you tonight, I will not let the presence of Rojo interfere."

Tossing the reins of her horse to her, he moved whistling toward Boabdíl's stall.

Catherine stood speechless. He would not dare make good his threat! Her mouth settled into a firm pink line. He would not use this ruse to force her submission.

It did not take long for her to see her husband meant to make her repent her stubbornness. Once clear of the city he and Rojo put their horses to a steady gallop, the slender-limbed Andalusians running behind. She kept pace with them, exhilarated by the morning air and the sight of the rising sun in the east, beyond the Andes. In no time at all they turned toward those mountains, following the broad road built for messengers in the Indian empire. She had heard that roads like it traversed the highest mountains.

The sun, as it rose, grew blistering. They were in a desert, barren and formless. The only strip of green was the narrow track of the Rimac River stretching up the valley which now they followed.

"You are a passing fair rider, Doña Catherine," grinned Rojo when they stopped to rest their horses.

She nodded her thanks. Already her throat was dry from the air and dust. She longed to slip down from the saddle and walk a bit to stretch, but she did not do so. Rodrigo, lounging against the front of his saddle, looked at her and tried to hide his amusement.

He and Rojo rode in the manner of soldiers, with shortened

stirrups. At rest their legs bent almost double, but when they put their horses to the gallop they stood in the stirrups, towering well above the horses' heads. For most of the afternoon she watched them, for they were often ahead of her now. She kept them in sight, and at intervals they slowed that she might once again catch up with them. Her body was aching now, but she made no complaint.

"We might make camp here," suggested Rojo as she caught up with them on a small draw. "There is a tree, and Doña Catherine must be tired from riding."

Rodrigo's lashes slanted lazily over his eyes.

"What do you say, *preciosa?* Are you weary?"

Catherine gritted her teeth.

"I am quite agreeable to further riding if you prefer."

"Ah, good. We have kept such a slow pace that a little distance more would be most welcome."

She gave a bitter slap to her horse's rump and set off ahead of them. A slow pace indeed!

When at last they stopped, every bone in her body was weary. It seemed to her that Rodrigo held her a moment longer than was necessary after he had helped her from her horse, but the strength of his arms was such welcome support that she did not take issue. He went to tend the horses while Rojo built a fire. She sat on a blanket and watched, too tired for emotion. Before he even set food over it, her eyes fell closed and she slept.

When she awoke the sky was black above her. She felt her cloak tucked snugly around her and the welcome warmth of a blanket. Her husband lay beside her. She slipped back into welcome slumber.

In the morning a round, cold object prodded her ribs. She sensed what it was before her eyes came open. With sharp annoyance she struck Rodrigo's boot away.

"Will you sleep the day out?" he grinned.

"I will answer to a civil summons," she answered, shivering and sitting up. "I remind you I am not some animal, in need of blows," she added, recalling the mare.

He continued to watch her with needling expression.

"Animals are more reasonable. They do not forget their supper."

She stood and brushed out her skirts and turning her back to him began to arrange her hair.

That day the way ahead of them grew hilly. Catherine sat grimly in the saddle, too sore and fatigued to notice her surroundings. It was not just to prove her endurance to Rodrigo that she had come, she thought. She wanted to see the things he had seen, to look with his eyes, to understand a little his world. And she wanted him to see that despite their differences she sought to share his vision.

The sun was high in the sky when Rojo dropped back to join her.

"How much farther, my friend?" he called to Rodrigo, who was still ahead of them.

Rodrigo stopped his horse and the white mare behind him stopped too. His face held a pleasure he could not hide.

"We have been on the land since mid-morning."

He extended his arm. "There, just over that ridge, we should find the *estanciero* if he has not lost his way."

They rode quickly up a gentle swell. Ahead of them a meadow spread, the land beyond it rising in the foothills of the Andes. The barren desert was long behind them. A few trees punctuated the rich grass, and a man on horseback sat beneath the trees. With relief Catherine followed the men and the white mares toward the peaceful spot.

It was cool in the shade of the trees. Rodrigo, having already greeted the *estanciero*, lifted her from her saddle.

"Well, *preciosa*," he said with dry amusement. "Here is your land. Tell me, is looking at it worth the punishment of the ride?"

She had slipped from his grasp and stood staring about her with hands on hips, until she realized it was his own pose she had adopted, and one which ladies shunned.

"Yes!" she breathed drinking in the lonely splendor which surrounded her. "Oh, yes!"

He turned away. Behind her Catherine heard Rojo chuckling. She could not tell if he was laughing at her, or at Rodrigo.

Rodrigo and the hired man set out at once to search for timber, and a spot for the corral. Rojo, when he had hobbled the horses, came back and sat beneath a tree.

"I am going to rest now," he said pulling his hat low over his eyes. "If you are wise, Doña Catherine, you will do likewise."

She stood for a moment studying him. The great bear of a man was offering her a chance to succumb to weariness without losing face. Just then it seemed to her the height of gentility.

By the end of the day a crude corral was taking form, two sides of it made by the rocky fingers of a high ridge rising to the east. The men had felled all the trees in sight save one, and now they labored, stripping the branches and bringing in rocks for posts. Catherine set a twig from one of the trees in the earth and carried a bowl full of water from a nearby stream to pour around it. Perhaps it would grow. Perhaps there would be more trees.

All through the next day she watched the men work. Their bare backs glistened in the sun. Their laughter filled the meadow. She felt useless, unable even to cook the strange foods which they ate here in the open.

As the heat of the afternoon abated, she grew restless. She walked toward the high ridge, past where the men were working, and picked her way around boulders, climbing. The course she followed did not seem steep, but when she reached the summit she caught her breath at the grand sight down below her. She could see the corral and the meadow, the narrow stream which splashed down from the mountains. She could see far, far back in the direction they had come. Never had there been a sky so blue or grass so green. For a long time she stood lost in awe of such beauty.

Her ear caught the sound of a falling pebble, and she turned to see Rodrigo coming toward her. His open shirt was tucked loosely in his breeches. She looked quickly back over the valley. She was afraid he would not see the beauty she saw, and she wanted to be a part of this spot, to make it hers forever.

He stood beside her, his shoulder brushing hers. His gaze moved out, as hers had done.

"There is room for a house here," he said. "I have measured."

She realized it was a question, and she turned toward him with a gladness she could not explain.

"There is room for vineyards," he said. "And fig trees."

She laughed and caught his hand as he smoothed back her hair.

"Oh, Rodrigo!" The hand which touched her cheek was vibrant with intensity. Her fingers pressed it tightly as they looked at one another. Fig trees would not grow here, where nights were cool, but it did not matter. For a golden moment she felt all barriers between them slipping, and they were close, united.

"We will need more than Magdalena and Mateo to help us if we have vineyards here," she said, smiling at the completeness of his plans. The land around them was so vast, their funds so limited.

131

"We will have a dozen servants," he said, the words reverberating in the stillness which was binding them together. "And the house, *preciosa*—men will see the house from miles away!"

She turned her lips toward his hand, but suddenly it was gone. He had straightened and was looking past her, to the south. She followed his gaze. Two specks were visible on the horizon.

"Men on horses," said Rodrigo. He started toward the path which led to the meadow. Catherine for a moment could not believe the spell which had surrounded them was ended. Then she hurried after him.

By the time they reached the corral the *estanciero* had already ridden out to see who came there uninvited. The travelers proved to be two priests on mules. For more than a year they had worked among the Indians, and now they were bound for Lima.

When Rodrigo rose that night to scatter their campfire, he spoke to Catherine.

"There is nothing for you to do here, and it is no place for you. You have seen the land which you longed to see. I am sending you back with the priests."

The words came so unexpectedly that she gasped.

"And you?" she ventured.

"Rojo and I will stay until the corral is built. Perhaps we will help the *estanciero* build a shelter."

"I see," she said.

Already she thought she must have imagined that moment on the hilltop.

It was mid-morning. Catherine sat with thoughts far from the needlework in her lap. Four days had passed since her return from the *encomienda,* and still there was no sign of Rodrigo. Surely he had expected to be here by now. Could Don Luis's men have followed him?

She dismissed the idea as too disturbing. It only cleared the way for other worries. Had she been foolish to pay an agent to locate a suitable stallion for the Andalusians? Horses still were scarce in the New World. Even if there were blooded stallions in Lima their owners might have no interest in a business proposition. The thirty *reales* she had given the agent yesterday could have been better spent. Rodrigo would regret letting her take any part in business.

At least the letter to her relative connected with India

House might bring results. She had spent much time in penning it, all too aware it was the first notice she had given anyone in Spain that she was married. Her mouth firmed as she imagined the shock with which her relatives there would view her new condition, wed to a soldier. Well, let them scorn her. She would not run from what she was.

"Señorita?" Ana slipped into the room, her expression uncertain. "There is a gentleman to see you. He says his name is Sanchez and that you must not disturb yourself if you are resting."

"Alonzo Sanchez?"

Ana nodded.

Catherine felt a curious fluttering in her breast. Why should Alonzo Sanchez come to see her? In a great flood every word they'd ever spoken to each other came back to her. She saw again his slightly uneven gait, his gentle eyes so different from her husband's.

"Señorita?" Ana prompted, looking at the pale face of her mistress, who sat as if in a trance.

Catherine jerked her attention firmly back to reality.

"Yes, Ana, show him in."

Alonzo Sanchez might have saved her and had not. With great deliberation she resumed her needlework. When the door opened again she looked up, took two more stitches and laid the cloth aside before she rose in greeting.

"Señor Sanchez," she began, conventional words of welcome on her lips. Then he reached out and took her hand and she was aware of nothing but his presence.

He did not overpower her with his masculinity as Rodrigo did, yet facing him Catherine felt an intimacy such as she had never known with her husband. It was was if Alonzo had known her always and could peer into her very soul.

"How—kind of you to call," she said around the terrible thickness in her throat.

Alonzo's fingers tightened over hers.

"I would have called much sooner, Doña Catherine, had I the least excuse."

Whatever had brought him here now, Catherine knew it was a mistake. This moment should never have been. It had, she could sense without knowing why, unlocked a door to suffering. To pain.

His eyes still on her face, Alonzo released her fingers.

"Señor Ortiz, the agent, contacted me about the business

133

interests of a client. I see by your expression that you understand."

Catherine sank back onto the bench she had occupied prior to his arrival and gestured toward another.

"You have a stallion, Don Alonzo?"

He smiled, making no effort to take a seat.

"I do, in Hispaniola. It is the closest Andalusian you will find, I think. Señor Ortiz has told me there were none to be found in Lima. He came to me only because he thought I might have an animal of suitable lineage, though of some other breed."

Catherine pressed a hand to her throat. Fate seemed to be laughing at her, that of all possible men it should be Alonzo Sanchez whom she faced in this business venture of her own making. By taking on a project in their mutual interests, she had thought to dispel the differences between herself and her husband; to make their marriage something more than a series of encounters in the bedchamber. And no one made her more aware of those differences than Alonzo Sanchez.

"Hispaniola is very far away," she said, and hoped he would express a similar sentiment.

"An easy voyage," he said. "I would have no objection to it. The animal could be here in a month's time. What terms did you have in mind?"

His fair beard shone like gold in the sunlight beyond. Catherine shook her head. She should cut the matter off here. There was more to be lost by this venture than gained. The pounding of her heart assured her of it.

"I—am not sure of the terms, Don Alonzo. You would have to talk to my husband. In truth I think we could not put you to the trouble of shipping an animal—"

"Would you think my terms too severe if I asked for first right of purchase to any foal brought to light?"

She made a helpless gesture. The quiet of his voice, the warmth of his unfading smile as he looked at her—those made it impossible to fight against him as she was wont to do with other men. A laugh escaped her. She had begun to acquire some skill in dealing with Rodrigo's own particular brand of fire, and now Alonzo Sanchez, with mere gentleness, had backed her into a corner.

"Those terms are much too lenient," she said.

Alonzo, taking her laughter for proof of high spirits, laughed too.

"I will present them to your husband, then. When do you expect his return?"

Catherine turned toward the window, quickly hiding her frown.

"I do not know. Today, perhaps."

He considered her for a moment, uneasiness in his gaze. He spoke abruptly, his words held low.

"Send your maid away. I must speak to you alone."

Startled, Catherine stared back at him.

"You are in danger," he said tersely when she did not respond.

The impossibility of what he was suggesting flew through her mind. She could not comply.

"Ana—leave us, please," she said.

She saw the expression of disbelief on the little maid's face. Ana edged out of the room. A silence filled it. What had she done, Catherine asked herself? What if Rodrigo should find them thus? She had never been alone with any man but him, and every convention said she should not. Had she taken leave of her senses?

She got up and went to stand at the *mirador,* her pulses pounding with nervousness.

"You spoke of danger, Señor Sanchez."

He pivoted on his lame leg. The suede of his shoes brushed the floor as he came toward her.

"I beg you not to put the formality of a surname between us, Doña Catherine. I am your loyal—and very devoted— friend."

He stood so near she could feel the warmth of his body. Wisdom told her she must not turn and face him. Words were impossible in the strain of breathing.

"You and your husband are under heavy suspicion of conspiring with the rebel Pizarro," he said. "It is rumored you receive his couriers. I myself know secret meetings have been held here. You must beg your husband to end such activities at once."

Catherine's breast pitched rapidly.

"You are kind for your warning, señor. But a woman has no right—"

"A woman has every right! To safety. To freedom from anxiety. To consideration!"

His mild voice held such wrath that she looked at him in amazement. His eyes swept back and forth across her face, drinking in each detail.

135

"You must tell him, Catherine. He would not want you exposed to danger. He rescued you from the infamy Don Luis would have subjected you to, and though I disagree with his method, I do not for a second question his gallantry."

Unconsciously Catherine pressed her fingers to her throat. The emerald on her hand sent flashes of green light across the floor, unspoken reminder of the barrier between them. The tension was unbearable. She stepped past him quickly, moving toward the door.

"I thank you for your warning, Don Alonzo. And for your willingness to enter some agreement regarding the stallion. My husband will discuss the terms with you when he returns."

15

"Valdivia!"

Catherine heard the name called as she walked along the street on her husband's arm. She looked up and there, smiling broadly, was Alonzo Sanchez riding toward them. Beneath him was a pure white stallion, head tossing and dancing as though the presence of a rider were something to rebel against. Recalling his lame leg, Catherine wondered with some alarm about Alonzo's ability to control such an animal. Yet, mounted, he showed no hint of infirmity. On he came with apparent ease.

"What do you think, Valdivia? I met the ship which brought him at Tumbez. He should be gentler for the ride overland. When will you take him?"

Rodrigo's eyes were shaded with surprise. Catherine guessed the thought of Alonzo's making the long ride from Tumbez had occasioned it. Even without the handicap of a bad leg Alonzo seemed more of the temperament of a scholar than of a rider.

"I have a few matters which must be settled first," said Rodrigo. "I could come for him tomorrow, or the following day."

As he spoke Catherine tried to shut out the memory of Alonzo's warning. Tonight another meeting was scheduled for their house. The governor Vaca de Castro had been arrested by the viceroy's order and charged with treason, a charge which everyone in the city knew was false. It would draw many cavaliers to their home tonight. If the meeting was not discovered—if there was not the midnight visit by viceregal soldiers which she always feared—then Rodrigo could ride with the stallion to the *encomienda* as he was arranging.

"Will you ride with me?" he asked Alonzo.

Catherine sensed hesitation in the other man's manner. His eyes moved briefly toward her.

"I would only slow you down, and this weather causes stiffness in my knee. Perhaps I will ride with you when you collect him. I would like to see the mares."

"I assure you they are more than suitable dams," Rodrigo

said, an edge to his voice. He did not like Alonzo; Catherine knew that. He had entered rather grimly into the breeding arrangement, but his manner was one of reserve whenever Alonzo was around.

"I have no doubt of that," Alonzo answered with a smile. He bowed to Catherine. "Doña Catherine, have you formed an opinion yet of the first works of the poet del Río? I've just finished reading him and I find myself impatient for more."

Catherine shook her head. The world of poetry seemed as remote to her as her own homeland. No, farther still. Her thoughts were often in Seville, but her eyes had not scanned a line of poetry since the night she met Valdivia. She had scarcely read at all since they were married. The pleasure she once had taken in it had almost been forgotten.

"I have not seen the volume of which you speak," she said.

"Then allow me to send mine to you for your enjoyment."

He touched his hat to both of them and rode away. Rodrigo set off so impatiently that Catherine was forced to ask him to slow his pace.

"Why are you angry?" she asked.

"I do not like the free way Sanchez uses your christian name."

"Rojo does likewise," she reminded, though with a guilt she could not explain.

"Of Rojo I have no objection. But I am not such a stupid man, *preciosa*, that I cannot see the much you and Sanchez have in common. Your backgrounds are similar; so are your tastes. He is a gentleman, while I am not."

Catherine's voice caught in her throat. "You can forbid the sending of the book to me, if you think such communication between us improper."

He looked down at her, a harsh smile on his lips.

"It isn't necessary. I'm sure you do not want another life—his in particular—upon your conscience."

A shudder gripped Catherine there in the hot, still street. Her husband's casual utterance of the words was frightening. Cruel. She felt sick inside as his free hand came up to imprison hers possessively against his arm.

The evening meal had a brooding stillness to it. Magdalena glided in and out like a candle flame, serving wordlessly. When the hourglass in the sala said ten o'clock she would bring up wine. Mateo would open the gate behind the stables and wait to receive the horses of the cloaked men who called.

138

Rodrigo rose and came around to stand behind Catherine's bench.

"You're frightened," he said, pushing aside her scarcely touched plate.

"Yes," she admitted. Her gaze was on the candle. Its golden glow highlighted the definite lines of her mouth, now set and quiet, its velvet softness lost in thoughtfulness.

"You have never been frightened before."

"There has never been such unrest before. The whole city—" Unable to form her thoughts she gave a despairing gesture. "Forgive me."

Rodrigo's hand slipped under her elbow. He drew her to her feet, turning her into the protective circle of his arms.

"You disagree with what I'm doing, don't you, *preciosa?* You would prefer that I suspend these meetings."

She kept her eyes from his.

"You have given much thought to your position, I'm sure."

Yet in her heart Catherine told herself it was an easy one for him. He was a soldier. The prospect of war, of danger, was nothing to him. Had he not told Francisca he found the life of a gentleman boring? He would welcome the chance to take up arms, though in fairness she was not certain he himself recognized it.

"Here, have another glass of wine to give you courage," he said pouring it for her. "Believe me, what we do is necessary. And we've not yet turned rebel."

"But we will," said Catherine. "It is only a matter of time before you declare for Pizarro. Waiting will not make us seem more innocent."

Rodrigo, who had turned back to the table with the empty wine pitcher, swung toward her savagely.

"The appearance of innocence does not concern me. Nor am I so eager to join the rebels as you would like to believe. I know my duty, and my duty is to the crown of Spain. The viceroy is its representative. I owe him my allegiance. I dislike him, I dislike the New Laws, but how can I call myself a Spaniard and defy them both?"

He stopped and ran his fingers through his hair and looked away with brooding weariness.

"On the other hand, all that I am and all that I have, I owe to Pizarro. He has given freely of his own land to men who had none, and never in my life have I known so fair and brave a man."

There was nothing Catherine could say. She closed her eyes and drank the wine.

Why Rodrigo always bid her stay and listen at the meetings in their sala, she didn't clearly understand. Did he think that she might come to accept the need for organized opposition to the viceroy? She had not, even though the arrest of Vaca de Castro, a legally constituted officer of the crown, had shocked her. Men simply did not take the ruling of a country into their own hands. They went to the courts, to the king; they waited. In France and in heretic England lord still warred against lord, but in Spain there was order, and recourse for every need.

One by one soldiers and a scattering of townsmen arrived. As Catherine had expected, their number tonight was nearly double that of any previous meeting. While they milled about, talking in low but passionate voices, Rodrigo came to her frowning.

"No one has yet arrived from Cuzco. I am loath to leave the rear gate unbarred much longer, but with so great a gathering Mateo can serve us better at the front entrance."

Catherine nodded understanding. When the last man was admitted to these meetings Mateo was sent to the end of the street as a lookout against unexpected visitors. What would happen should he ever sound an alarm, Catherine could not guess. She immediately saw the need both to leave the rear gate open and to watch the front.

"I will watch the rear gate," she said.

Her husband's frown did not diminish. Now, in fact, it seemed to deepen. He traced his thumb along the firm line of her cheek.

"You would be alone. You're frightened."

"I will manage."

He seized her hand and kissed it fervently. The ache which gripped her was now a familiar enemy, a breach in the wall which kept her from his total domination. She turned from the fire in his touch and hurried out of the room.

The night was heavy, fog soaked. Catherine picked her way down the gallery more by feel than by sight and crossed to the kitchen where Ana and Magdalena sat sewing by candlelight.

"I am going to relieve Mateo," she said. "Ana, you know your instructions."

She could see the trembling of Ana's hands as she nodded. As housekeeper it would be her duty to answer any summons

140

at the front gate. The girl had never questioned the nature of these late night meetings, but Catherine thought she must know they were dangerous. The hour and the need for Mateo's vigil in the street were proof of that. Catherine had told her that if ever a summons came in the midst of one of these meetings that she, Ana, must answer calmly, say her master and mistress were entertaining, and delay unbarring the gate until Magdalena had had a chance to race up the stairs with a warning.

Ordinarily her own near presence would be enough to strengthen Ana's courage for such an ordeal. But tonight she would be at the stable door, at the back of the house. Looking at the frightened young face turned toward her, Catherine felt a growing weight of apprehension.

Magdalena spoke in soft tones.

"Go with God, señora. We will be calm and guard the door."

Catherine shot her a brief look of thanks and moved through the mist to find Mateo. The lantern in her hand cast a feeble light. The candles on the gallery were mere pinpricks.

Mateo looked up without the least trace of uneasiness at her approach. On her instruction he scampered off, never questioning orders, which he habitually obeyed with diligence.

Catherine shivered. She longed for her cloak though the night was stifling. She could feel the moisture in the air turn the hair around her face into soft curls. Never before had one of the couriers from Pizarro been delayed. Had he been discovered? Had they? Long minutes passed, and then she heard the faintest sound of footsteps in the alley.

By their sound she took them to be yet some ways distant, and jumped at the unexpected knock on the gate in front of her. Her heart began to batter against her chest.

"Who calls at this hour?" she inquired, determined to keep her voice from shaking.

"By my beard! A woman!" exclaimed a man on the other side with a hint of laughter. "Tell me, señorita, have you fine mares for sale?"

With relief she heard the phrase which marked identity. She opened the gate for the rebel courier.

He slipped in and, before she could appraise his features, swept a bow. As he straightened Catherine was struck by the openness of expression in a rather handsome face.

"You will be Señora de Valdivia herself," he said. "I swear

Rodrigo came to light under lucky stars to have acquired such a lovely lady for his wife."

Catherine barred the gate.

"You've caused us great anxiety," she admonished. "Pizarro's couriers usually are on time."

"Pizarro's couriers seldom take the trouble to hide a horse and move with stealth, as I have done," he answered. "Will you show me the way?"

His frankness and the easy friendliness with which he spoke caused Catherine to relax despite the tensions of the evening. It was true the other men who had come in the rebel cause had brought their horses. This one showed admirable courage in parting with his single means of escape. They climbed the damp steps to the gallery and Catherine, with a glance to the man who followed her, pushed open the door to the sala.

Rodrigo, standing by the entrance, saw them first. His foot came sharply down from the stool on which it had been resting and his face was flooded with disbelief. Catherine in sudden alarm saw it reflected in the expression of every man in the room.

Then there were muffled exclamations, exultant, amazed.

"Pizarro!"

"Pizarro!"

"Pizarro!"

Catherine turned with a questioning look. The man who had followed her into the room was smiling broadly.

"Had someone reported my death," he asked, "to merit such surprise at seeing me?"

Rodrigo, recovering, said fervently, "General, you are most welcome! But do you not risk too much by coming here?"

"Tell me, Rodrigo, have you ever known me to take a risk which was unwise?" Pizarro inquired, dropping an affectionate arm across Rodrigo's shoulder. He turned to Catherine. "Forgive me, madam. I did not earlier introduce myself. I am Gonzalo Pizarro, native of Trujillo, at your service."

As he spoke he bowed over her hand and kissed it. Disconnected thoughts about the man before her raced through Catherine's mind. Here was the one who, with his famous brothers, had won this land of gold for Spain. He had lived, half starved, for six months in some distant land called Chile. He had slept with the aristocratic Indian woman named Doña Isabella. And of all the men in Peru, their house could shelter none more dangerous.

"My lord Pizarro," she said simply. "You will honor us if you take some wine."

She poured it with a hand which shook. Yet having met him she could easily see why men were rallying under his banner. He was gallant, warm, courageous, and he spoke not as a leader but a comrade.

"Your home is most attractive, Doña Catherine," he observed. "I see you have men for the game of chess, which I have long desired to learn."

His eyes moved quietly across each detail of the room. Then, with another bow to Catherine, he went to stand before the fireplace and the focus of the gathering at once was business.

The arrest of the governor proved, as she had suspected, the breeze which had fanned sparks of rebellion into flames in many breasts.

"The viceroy has shown his own contempt for authority!" declared one cavalier who only the week before had argued for prudence. "Arresting the governor, acting without the Audencia—he is assuming the powers of a very dictator. I say it is he who is a traitor to the crown!"

Murmurs of approval sounded in the room.

"Do we make a revolt then?" another man asked. "I say yes!"

Pizarro had detailed the condition and the sentiment of his own forces. They were richly equipped, their expenses met by appropriation of the public treasury in Cuzco, and they were eager to throw off the viceroy's yoke. Now he listened without comment. Either he truly did not wish to sway these men, thought Catherine, or he was the shrewdest of leaders.

"I agree the viceroy has shown himself unfit to serve," said Rodrigo. "But who are we to judge him? None of us holds any writ of authority from the crown. The Audencia must condemn him, or the Cabildo. If we take up arms without their support, we proclaim ourselves rebels aginst King Carlos, no matter how just our cause."

Pizarro studied him thoughtfully.

"You draw a fine line, my friend, for one who is always first in battle."

Rodrigo flushed.

"There is merit in his words, however," sighed a thin Dominican friar who was the only clergyman attending.

At that moment footsteps sounded on the gallery, running. Ana burst into the room.

"Señorita!" she gasped. "There are soldiers at the gate! The viceroy's soldiers. Don Luis is with them!"

Their fate inevitable, Catherine felt surprising calm.

"Control yourself. Where is Magdalena?"

Agitated past speech Ana wrung her hands. Catherine knew intuitively what had happened; the girl had panicked.

"Listen to me!" she said sharply. "Go down. Admit them. Keep your wits."

Ana fled like an animal flushed from hiding.

"It's hopeless," said Rodrigo. "That fool of a girl will give us away."

Steel whispered in the room as men moved their sword cases to the ready.

Catherine flung back her hand.

"Give Ana a chance. Give me a chance. I will delay them."

"Catherine—"

Rodrigo caught her arm.

She broke away and stepped out onto the gallery. The gate at the front of the house swung open. She saw Ana scurry aside as a body of horsemen poured in.

"Ana, what is this commotion?" she demanded with innocent indignation.

The mist had lifted. She could count at least a dozen men. The leader wheeled to look up at her.

"Catherine de Valdivia? Instruct the members of your household to do as they are told. Anyone who attempts to leave through the rear of the house will be shot."

The house was surrounded. She fought an urge to look behind her on the gallery where the shadows might now be sheltering the movement of Pizarro toward the stables.

"Who is giving orders? What is the meaning of this interruption?" she asked in her most ringing tones.

The men were dismounting, swords drawn. She hurried down the steps to block their way.

The men in the lead wavered slightly.

"Let them pass," snapped their commander.

Now she saw him clearly, the white-haired viceroy himself. Behind him stood a figure which gave her an excuse yet for delay.

"My lord bishop," she said with genuine surprise. She genuflected. "I did not realize you were a member of this company—nor his excellency. Of course you may pass. But I do not understand the meaning of this visit at this hour."

Soldiers brushed past her, accompanied by the viceroy.

Spite gleaming in his eyes Don Luis swaggered forward next to the bishop of Lima.

"There are grave accusations against you, madam," the bishop said gently. "I pray they may not prove true. Shall we go up?"

Catherine turned on the stairs and returned to the sala, soldiers in front of her, the bishop and the man whom she now recognized for a mortal enemy at her rear.

Nerves tensed she stepped into the room. She stared about it in disbelief. There was no trace of Gonzalo Pizarro. Two stools had been drawn up to a table, the chessboard was out with pieces in play, and stacks of money gave evidence of betting on the outcome of a game. A jovial *encomendero* named Carbajal sat on one stool. The one across from him was empty.

"My lord bishop," said Rodrigo, repeating his wife's earlier gesture of reverence. "What is the meaning of this invasion? What is going on?"

"Señor Valdivia, I am informed that you hold treasonous meetings in this house," announced the viceroy. "And that tonight the rebel Pizarro himself is among you."

Rodrigo's courtesy was forced. "Your excellency, I hardly think the general is so great a fool that he would come into a city where his life is forfeit. Someone has misinformed you—and slandered me."

His gaze turned pointedly to Don Luis.

"Search the rooms," Don Luis ordered brazenly. "You have an uncommon number of guests for this time of night, do you not, Valdivia?"

Catherine saw the anger smoldering in her husband's eyes and wondered if he was thinking he might have better killed Don Luis. At the chess table the man named Carbajal laughed.

"Forgive me, your excellency. We do not come here to plot, but for a chess game. You no doubt are familiar with the time which one entails, and as I appear to be losing, I am in no great hurry to see this one end."

The viceroy's haughty manner remained unchanged.

"And who is your opponent?" he inquired looking shrewdly at the chess board.

"It grieves me to confess I'm losing to this lady, whose strategy has proved formidable."

Catherine felt herself stiffen. The ploy was a desperate one and might soon prove so. Someone—Pizarro, perhaps—had assumed she had some skill at this game, when in fact she barely knew its moves.

"You, señora? You were playing for money?" asked the bishop.

She nodded, spots of color rising in her cheeks as she guessed the judgment her lie would cost her. Rodrigo moved to stand behind her. Her shoulder sought support against his chest.

"Such behavior in a woman is extremely wanton," the bishop cautioned. "I shall expect you to call on Father Talavera tomorrow to purge your soul."

Catherine nodded, her eyes downcast, her misery overflowing. Tomorrow . . . if there was a tomorrow. Where was Gonzalo Pizarro?

Carbajal, the chess player, now looked uncomfortable. She saw apology written in his face for this embarrassment to her.

"Still, your grace has been in this country long enough to know how readily men are wont to fight because of a bet," said Don Luis, his eyes aglitter. "I suggest you let the game proceed to its conclusion so no blood is shed. It will while away our time."

Catherine's lips curled with her hate of him.

"Exactly, Don Luis. In Spain I might have furnished music at my keyboard. Here chess and conversation are the only entertainments I can offer to our friends."

Blasco Nuñez, the viceroy, subjected her to an arrogant scrutiny.

"You play the keyboard? A soldier's wife?"

Rodrigo's fingers tightened on her arm.

"My wife's father was a mayor of Seville."

They were interrupted by a clear voice in the doorway.

"Señorita?"

Catherine looked in amazement at Ana. The girl's spine was as straight as the marquesa's, and she looked levelly ahead. Only the white of her knuckles in tightly clasped hands betrayed her terror, and that, Catherine thought, to her eyes alone.

"Señorita, shall I bring refreshment for these gentlemen?" she asked.

More innocent an act could not have been asked on anyone's part. The toll on Ana's nerves of coming into this room when she could have avoided it was incalculable. Catherine nodded, silently saluting the little maid.

"Very well, resume your game," said the bishop sighing.

As one who went to her execution Catherine took her place on the stool across from Carbajal.

To her dismay Don Luis strolled forward to stand beside the table. The passage of months had seen the fading of the large scar on his cheek, yet its very presence had caused a metamorphosis in his looks. Before, his had been a handsome if cruel face. Now it was one from which any woman would turn. He watched the table closely. Any attempt to inform Carbajal of her lack of knowledge, or of her opponent to coach her, would be immediately spotted.

"You had, in your last play, captured my bishop," Carbajal said smoothly. "My answer will be this."

Adroitly he nudged a knight forward in one of their erratic moves.

Catherine frowned at the board before her. All ability to concentrate seemed to have fled her. Stricken, she looked up at the man across from her.

Carbajal's eyes widened slightly as if he understood her dilemma. All eternity seemed to pass. Then, beneath the table, his booted feet came down on both of hers.

It was not the amorous advance of a rogue. The pressure of Carbajal's boots brought tears to her eyes. Gradually the pressure eased and he tapped her left foot lightly. Catherine realized he had devised a system of helping her, however inadequate it might prove.

She stared now at the left side of the board. Again she felt a single tap. What piece should she move a single square? After a moment's study she saw a tower in peril from Carbajal's knight. She moved it forward a square and Carbajal smiled.

The shaky system guided her along. Her toes, in their thin slippers, soon smarted from the pressure of Carbajal's boots. Sometimes she misinterpreted the signals and moved the wrong piece, but as yet she had not made a serious blunder. Ana brought the wine. Some of the men in the room moved closer to watch the game. Her nerves were stretched to breaking. She let her thoughts bounce from the chessboard to the farthermost parts of the house. Where was Pizarro? The viceroy's soldiers must be turning each floorboard, examining each piece of lint.

Carbajal pressed her foot three times. She moved another tower. Almost imperceptibly he winced. Then his queen came sweeping across the board and he said with satisfaction which sounded forced, "Check mate."

"A stupid move. I did not see the opening," Catherine

147

murmured. She was so relieved at the ordeal's end that she could not move. Various of the onlookers came forward to claim their winnings.

"Do not forget your visit to Father Talavera," the bishop admonished. "Perhaps the vanity which led you to wage this game led you also to lose it."

A moment later one of the viceroy's men came in, saluting smartly.

"The man we sought is not in the house, sir. The stable shows no sign of an extra horse, save those accounted for by the men here present. And none of the horses has been hard ridden."

The viceroy looked provoked.

"I thought you swore your information in this matter was accurate, Don Luis."

"So it was," the councilman said blandly. "Our lack of quarry proves only that we came too late."

Catherine saw the anger in Rodrigo's face and feared that, as on another occasion, he might demand apology. Prudently he held his temper.

Blasco Nuñez rose and flipped the wrinkles from his cape.

"Be advised, Señor Valdivia, that you are under surveillance."

Rodrigo answered with the sketchiest of bows.

There was silence in the room as the unexpected visitors filed out. The door to the gallery stood wide behind them. Rodrigo nodded to Rojo and the two went out, returning only when the final clatter of hooves had sounded in the courtyard.

"They are gone," announced Rodrigo.

With a grunt and a thump the figure of a man landed on the floor of the fireplace. Gonzalo Pizarro ducked out of his hiding place in the chimney.

"Holy Mother, I thought my back would give way before they did," he said cheerfully. "Doña Catherine, I thank you for your gracious and loyal support of me and my cause. Whatever you ask of me, now or ever, will be my great pleasure to give. I am your servant."

Shaking with the aftermath of tension, Catherine got up from the chess table. Rage washed over her in waves, beyond control. This handsome, smiling man who spoke so casually of danger epitomized the lust for power at the core of every man. Don Luis, the viceroy, Pizarro or her husband—each of them hungered for it in some degree—and the innocent, like herself, were trampled in the getting of it.

"Nothing you could do would make amends, my lord Pizarro," she said, her voice at once imperious and quivering. "I long ago was ruined in the eyes of decent society. Tonight I have been ruined in the estimation of the church as well. You have left me nothing. And let me add that what I have done was done not for your sake, but for the safety of my husband—and myself."

Every eye in the room was upon her, and every man looked uncomfortable. An apology was forming on the lips of Carbajal. She turned her back on it and left without a backward glance.

Torn by shame and anger she began to run along the gallery, moving by instinct, blindly. Her toe caught in a rag and she threw her arms out to preserve her balance. From the floor there came a wretched, animal sound. Scanning the darkness her eyes picked out a shape, a human form. It was Ana's black dress over which she had almost fallen, and now Ana's face rose, white and miserable, from the bucket over which she had been retching.

"Ana, what is it? You are ill!" cried Catherine dropping to her knees. The maid was shaking. Catherine put her arms around her.

"I—I was afraid," sobbed Ana. "When the soldiers came I ran instead of sending Magdalena. They might have killed us! And I—am still—afraid!"

She gagged, twisting her face from Catherine's view. Catherine held her nearer. She was moved past speaking by the loyalty of this timid girl whose nerves had suffered so much before giving way in this nausea.

"I am frightened too," she soothed. "Every man in that room was frightened. What you're feeling is natural, Ana. These are terrible times!"

As she spoke she passed her linen handkerchief across Ana's mouth. She hiccupped, but her trembling ceased.

"Let us wash and try to put this day out of our minds," said Catherine, lifting her gently to her feet. "I am exhausted. I know you must be as well."

Ana blinked at her. Catherine smiled, wondering if Ana had supposed her above fatigue.

In her chamber it was Catherine who lighted the tapers and held a towel for Ana while she bathed her face. The girl went through the motions as meekly as a child. Her emotions

149

seemed spent now. Was she truly calm, or was she only obeying what she discerned as her mistress's will?

The sound of the last departing guest had ceased. Catherine wondered how Gonzalo Pizarro would make his escape as the viceroy's men undoubtedly still watched the house. But though she wondered she did not care.

When Rodrigo's knock came at her door she lifted a hand to Ana in signal not to open. The door opened anyway. He came in uninvited. By candlelight she could not see him in the mirror, yet she sensed his presence.

"I am sorry," he said simply.

She made no reply. He walked across the room to stand beside her. For the first time Catherine was aware that tears were sliding down her cheeks.

"Preciosa—"

He reached out to touch her. She drew away.

"Please," she whispered. "If you are truly sorry, leave me. Let me be."

He studied her, his features taking on the set lines of a mask made out of bronze. When he next spoke it was to Ana.

"You performed with courage tonight," he said. "This shall be your reward."

He held out seven gold *escudos.*

Ana's eyes, in her child's face, rounded in surprise. Then some storm of emotion swept through her, as perceptibly as if she had been buffeted by a sudden wind.

"I did only my duty to my household, señor," she said, drawing herself erect. "I want no reward."

He stood, his broad form dwarfing both of them, and Catherine knew he felt the sting of the rebuff. With anger breaking in his eyes he strode out of the room.

"Go to bed," she said to Ana.

When she was alone she traced the sign of the cross before her, then traced it again. Her tears fell softly. She could not give her thoughts the shape of prayers.

16.

An ominous quiet filled the city. It was the hour after mass, but no bells pealed. As Catherine and Ana watched, the workmen lowered the last of the church bells from the spire of the cathedral and rolled them across the plaza toward a bonfire. There, by the viceroy's order, all the bells of Lima were being melted into guns.

Catherine watched the glistening bodies of shirtless soldiers as they toiled in the August sun, aware not so much of preparations for war as she was of human skills. Until quite recently the men who settled the New World had not known the luxury of gunsmiths, shipbuilders, surgeons. They had performed all tasks themselves, turning their hands to whatever was required for survival these thousands of leagues from home.

She was startled from her thoughts by a small sob from Ana. The maid struck a defiant pose which she had assumed with increasing frequency since Pizarro's near-disastrous visit. Her mouth, however, was quivering.

"What is it?" Catherine asked quietly.

"I do not want to go on a ship again," said Ana. "I do not want them to burn our house."

Impatient with fears she could not herself dispel, Catherine started with brisk steps for home.

"That would happen only in the most extreme of circumstances," she lied. For weeks the viceroy had been assembling a squadron of boats, his eye to loading women and household items onto them and burning the city rather than let it fall to Pizarro. "Besides," she added, "I have heard the Audencia very much disagrees with his plan."

That much was true. Only a few days earlier the Audencia had arrived, and already rumors were rife that its royal judges were at odds with the viceroy. She had heard that some of them argued for suspension of the New Laws, and that all of them were outraged at the arrest of Vaca de Castro and the seizure of lands. They had even walked into jails and freed some of the viceroy's prisoners.

"Señor Valdivia will leave us if there is war," sniffed Ana. "We will be alone."

"That much is often required of women," Catherine said.

Ana looked at her with such misery that Catherine felt guilty. At times she had envied Ana for knowing so little of the troublesome events around them. Now she wondered if living in ignorance made the ordeal more wretched. A servant could go to her death not knowing her mistress's politics—not knowing why she died. Catherine resolved that must not be so with Ana and Magdalena. She must talk to them. They had shown her great loyalty; she must offer what protection she could to those in her household.

"Which side will the señor fight on if there is war?" Ana asked, the corners of her mouth turning down.

Already betraying her new resolve, Catherine said with pretended lightness, "The winning side, of course."

Ana picked up her skirts and hurried, with head bent, down the street to their house.

"Ana!" called her startled mistress.

If she had any reputation left for deportment this should finish it, Catherine thought, running through the streets in pursuit of a serving girl. Even as she thought it, she knew she did not care.

She caught up with Ana just as Mateo was opening the gate. The maid dropped onto a bench with dry little sobs in which Catherine, to her amazement, heard the sounds of frustration.

"Ana, I am sorry," she said, catching breath. "I spoke glibly because I can't honestly say which side Señor Valdivia will choose. He has not enrolled in the viceroy's forces, though a handsome bounty is being paid. If there is war, I fear he will turn rebel.

"The dangers in that I acknowledge fully. This house will be unsafe. I will give you my blessing if you choose to go to the marquesa's household. I am sure she would give you employment, and I can manage with Magdalena."

Ana sought the dignity of her handkerchief.

"Whatever the señor's loyalties, I am proud to make them mine," she said with uncommon force. "He is brave—and good—and above all your husband! I do not want to run away like a rabbit. It's only that . . . I am afraid. Not just of the viceroy's soldiers, of everyone who calls at this gate! I am afraid of men, I am afraid of strangers. In your father's house I was afraid of the cook and Doña Teresa and even Señora Vasquez!"

Catherine smiled briefly, recalling rumors that Ana had

fainted once when Señora Vasquez, the housekeeper, called her staff together for some minor reprimand.

"I am a disgrace to you!" Ana concluded, wiping her nose as if to rid her face of it.

Catherine sat down beside her, slowly gaining insight into this complex, frail creature. She saw things Ana possibly did not see herself. A moment before, in the street, she had thought of Ana as a serving girl, and that was exactly what she was. A serving girl, yet one with promise; young, yet struggling to nurture in her small frame a giant's spirit.

"There are more important skills than receiving guests," Catherine said. "You have never disgraced me, and the day you do I'll dismiss you. Now go dry your eyes."

As she had expected, the threat of dismissal, far from frightening Ana, served better than praise to reassure her of her present worth. She moved as briskly as Catherine had spoken, and if she looked dogged, she was no longer on the brink of tears.

Catherine ran distracted fingers through her hair. Slipping her arms free of the heavy green silk oversleeves of her dress she began to walk, from the sweet orange to the fig tree, up and down, the length of the courtyard.

In the large house in Seville Ana's faintheartedness might have been amusing. Here it was dangerous. Though Ana had rallied valiantly on the night of Pizarro's visit, her initial panic that evening had posed too great a threat to chance again. The meetings of discontented cavaliers had lately been held at inns, places which offered far less privacy, greater risk. Rodrigo had warned her that their house might be required again soon.

Catherine knew the logical solution to the situation. It had crossed her mind before and she had dismissed it, determined to retain some scrap of genteel status. Now, resentful of the suspicion that her entire way of thinking had been altered by Rodrigo de Valdivia, she considered survival instead.

Has it come to this, Catherine Bautista de Valdivia? A simple matter of survival?

She knew it had. For herself and for the handful of unfortunates who served her. She summoned Magdalena and announced her intention to give over to her the duties of housekeeper.

The Indian woman expressed quiet gratitude. Save for the shabbiness of her clothes she already looked the part of a housekeeper, dignified and discreet, thought Catherine.

"And now there is something I must show you," Magdalena said. "You have said the times are perilous, señora. I fear you do not know how much so."

She led the way to the servants' quarters and indicated a small window looking out on the alley behind the house. At first Catherine was puzzled. Why should Magdalena want to show her the alley?

Then, as her eyes moved along toward the distant street, she froze. There, nearly hidden in a clump of trees, patches of sorrel showed. A horse. A man. Someone watching.

Catherine whirled. Magdalena did not let the question leave her lips.

"It is one of Don Luis's men. Sometimes Don Luis himself is there. Sometimes one is in the front as well. By day and night we are watched."

"Why—why have you not mentioned this before?" gasped Catherine.

Magdalena met her gaze directly.

"Had it become a matter of safety, I would have told you. I have kept silence for fear that you would tell your husband. His temper is quick, señora, and he would challenge the man. I have no wish to see you made a widow. I know too well how difficult such a life is for a woman."

For an instant the quiet Indian eyes blazed with anger, bitterness. The lines of her face were drawn in sharp relief. As quickly as it had come the expression was gone, but not before it had stamped its impression of suffering on Catherine's mind.

"You must not tell Señor de Valdivia," repeated Magdalena. "You also must see to it there are no more meetings in this house."

Catherine's mind was reeling. She was impressed by the depth of Magdalena's wisdom. If Rodrigo knew of this surveillance he would, indeed, take issue, and by the sword or the legal influence of Don Luis he would perish. Before she could voice her thanks Magdalena spoke again.

"I will send Ana to you."

A first step toward equality, thought Catherine with shaky humor. It was the first time Magdalena had used Ana's name without a title.

She wasn't prepared to see Ana. Her mind was preoccupied with the knowledge that their house was watched. Consequently she hadn't composed her words when Ana arrived.

"I have been thinking, Ana," she began, "that there is a

154

solution to your nervousness over receiving guests which may please you and which certainly would give me great delight."

Ana watched her meekly. It was strange, Catherine reflected, but she was starting to suspect that opposition might be encountered in Ana just when it was least expected.

Catherine drew a breath.

"I have often found myself wishing of late that you were more convenient to me when I called. Your duties downstairs often leave me quite alone. I've been wondering whether you would mind relinquishing them to Magdalena."

Ana gaped, face falling.

"You recall how dear Luisa was to me," said Catherine, hurrying on. "She was my closest friend. My confidante. So I have come to regard you, Ana. In short I realize that I treasure you far more as a personal maid and companion than I do in the role of housekeeper, which anyone could fill. Why not let Magdalena perform those duties? I cannot make conversation with her as I can with you, and I grow impatient every day that we haven't the time to talk as we did at the marquesa's."

In truth she and Ana had talked very little in those days. She doubted they would do so now. But the argument seemed to sway Ana, if not convince her. The maid seemed caught between delight and bewilderment at the compliments heaped upon her, yet disappointment was apparent too.

"I would have to give up my keys," she said, fingering the heavy ring of them pinned at her waist. Apart from the pearl ring her mistress had given her, the keys were her only ornamentation. "And I look like a house maid, not a lady's maid. Elvira Berruguete's girl looks at me as if I belong in the kitchen every time we go there."

"Then Elvira Berruguete's girl is as great a snob as her mistress," said Catherine quietly. "Tell me, Ana, what would it take to make you look the part I am offering you?"

Ana answered with surprising certainty.

"A dress of finer fabric. With buttons. Some earrings suitable for a lady's companion. New slippers."

Catherine could scarcely contain her laughter. The little minx! Ana's brown eyes shone with avarice.

"We will shop for silk tomorrow," she said. "And we'll ask a cobbler to come in. For the present, I believe there's a gown of mine which might with a few tucks fit you."

Going to one of the trunks she unearthed from the bottom a

simple black silk. She gave it a shake and held it up in front of Ana.

"It was a present on my fourteenth birthday. I have always thought to alter it to fit me now, but the task would be an endless one. What do you think? Would it suit you as a second dress?"

Ana clutched it rapturously.

"Oh, señorita! It is much more handsome than Doña Elvira's girl's! Why, even Doña Teresa never wore such silk!"

Catherine smiled. The change in her household had been accomplished. She opened her jewel cask and after a moment's deliberation took out a pair of small gold drops made in the three-pronged fan shape characteristic of Spain. Along with a simple gold pin for neck or waist, she handed them over to Ana.

"Take these," she said.

By the time she gave earrings to Magdalena—probably the great gold hoops—she would have few left. The prospect didn't alarm her. She watched Ana at the mirror, trying the earrings and murmuring endless words of thanks. The pale little shadow had been transformed into a bright little shadow, Catherine thought fondly. Then she jumped at a sudden roar from the courtyard.

"Oh, that is Captain Rojo's voice," Ana said, looking back for a final glance in the mirror. She sighed in contentment, then stepped out onto the gallery, serenely unconcerned by the rumbling voice below.

Catherine, having followed her, looked down. Rojo had not dismounted. The sun blazed on his fiery head, and by the prancing of the horse beneath him she sensed Rojo himself was on edge about something.

"Rojo, will you not step down?" she called in greeting.

He looked up with quick salute.

"Is 'Rigo about?"

Alarmed by his manner she shook her head. She hurried down the stairs.

"He said he would return for lunch," she reported, nearing his horse. "Will you not wait and join us?"

Rojo hesitated.

"I will not intrude upon your meal, Doña Catherine, but with your permission I will wait. I must talk with him."

Fear tightened its hold on her.

"Rojo, what is it?" she demanded. "Has fighting broken

out? Shall I order my ladies to the windows with their weapons?"

Weakening to this impertinent humor he gave a ponderous wag of the head. His huge form slumped in the saddle.

"No, doña, nothing so grave as that. Still, it is troublesome. You recall young Suarez de Carbajal with whom you played chess when the viceroy called? He has disappeared. There are rumors he was called before his excellency, suspected of treason."

There was more, she felt certain. Rojo avoided her eyes.

"Get down," she said again. "Your horse will enjoy a rest if you do. These are poor times for you to slight me by continuing to refuse my hospitality."

The robust soldier, his chest made broader still by the heavy steel cuirass which protected it, fell prey to an expression of awkward helplessness. Recognizing he was her husband's closest friend, Catherine had on several occasions invited him to take meals with them, but always he had declined. Now she watched his face take on the very hue of his beard.

"By the blessed Virgin, Doña Catherine, I meant no slight," he protested, climbing from his saddle. "In truth I have lived so long at inns that I thought it wiser to spare you my clumsiness at the table."

"I do not judge people by their manners," Catherine said.

"No, doña, I'm sure you do not. You are as noble a woman as ever it's been my honor to meet, and one of the bravest. I do not mind telling you I thought Rodrigo a fool when he—when he married you," he said, stumbling as he skirted the mention of how she had been bought. "But you have proved a model wife, turning this rundown house into one of the most comfortable I've ever known, performing with courage when the lives of all of us depended on it. If any woman can tame 'Rigo, you will be the one, and I would sooner cut off my own arm than offend you in any way."

Catherine smiled. She could not imagine ever feeling at ease with this great, rough man, but his sincerity was unmistakable. She reached out a hand to him.

"Then let us be friends, Rojo."

He squeezed her fingers warmly, and then kissed them, the sharp and fiery odor which engulfed him bringing tears to Catherine's eyes.

Rodrigo found them in the sala, where Rojo crouched with

furious concentration over the game of cards which Catherine had suggested as a means of passing time.

"Well! How often do you turn my house into a gaming place?" Rodrigo asked with evident surprise.

Rojo's mustache lifted in a grin.

"If you showed proper concern for the appetites of your luncheon guests, such sport would not be necessary. My belly's growling."

Rodrigo, to his wife's amusement, could only blink. But the humor of the moment was short lived. Rojo's face grew quickly grave.

"Forgive me, 'Rigo, but I had to speak to you. Doña Catherine insisted I stay."

Reluctantly Catherine rose to order the serving of lunch. Rodrigo stopped her with a gesture.

"Wait, *preciosa.* I have a feeling I know what this concerns. You might as well hear."

Rojo cleared his throat uncomfortably.

"You've heard of Suarez de Carbajal's disappearance, then, Rodrigo?"

Narrow eyed, Rodrigo nodded.

"I have heard that he has not been seen for several days. There is a rumor afoot that he was summoned to the viceroy's palace under cover of darkness, and that he's not been heard from since. Carbajal is well liked. The prospect of his being jailed with such infamous secrecy is causing unrest."

"There may be more than unrest if what I've heard is true," said Rojo. He hesitated, glancing at Catherine. "His excellency Blasco Nuñez is no more loved by his servants than by the rest of us. Several of them are telling tales of that night. They say the viceroy accused Carbajal of treason, and that when Carbajal with equal haughtiness denied it, insults were traded."

Catherine felt her breathing dwindle to nothing.

"And?" Rodrigo prompted.

The red-haired soldier spoke impassively.

"They say the viceroy in his anger struck Carbajal with the tip of his poniard. The viceroy's attendants took the gesture for a signal and fell on Carbajal with their swords. His body was carried from the house by a private staircase and lies buried beneath the floor of the cathedral."

Rodrigo took a turn across the room, his face devoid of color. Catherine wound her fingers tightly together.

Murder. That was how the disaffected men of Lima would

see the event, and she could not disagree with them. She had been angry over the chess game, but she had liked Carbajal. He had been so gallant as to send her two bottles of wine and a note of apology, begging her forgiveness over the bishop's reprimand. She felt shock and horror at the thought his body might lie lifeless in some hastily dug grave.

"Surely the Audencia will act now to unseat the tyrant!" she gasped.

Rodrigo shot her a cynical look.

"I would not count on the Audencia, *preciosa*. See to lunch."

Her nerves quivered at the veiled threat of his words. Perhaps the malcontents of Lima would not wait. What if they took matters into their hands?

Yet the silence on that subject by the men during lunch made it all too likely such would be the outcome. Rojo praised her lavishly on every course. Rodrigo watched with amusement his friend's attempts at genteel deportment. No mention of Carbajal or the viceroy was made until the arrival of a great platter of grapes which was dessert.

"We will want proof," said Rojo. Biting into one of the purple globes he squinted at the half remaining as if to auger the future.

Rodrigo nodded slowly.

"When will you go?" asked Catherine quietly.

Both of them, completely startled, looked at her.

"Go?" repeated her husband, but with evasion.

"To the cathedral. There can be no proof of murder unless you see Carbajal's body, can there?"

Silence stretched over the table for a moment, agonizing.

"No," said Rodrigo, "there cannot. We will go tonight."

How ironic, Catherine thought, that on this, of all evenings, she longed to go to the cathedral. The need for that peace which devotions brought her weighed heavily upon her heart. Rodrigo had left long ago to rendezvous with Rojo and two other comrades. Ana, by her instruction, had retired. Only Magdalena, down in the kitchen, kept vigil with her. She tried to calm the nervousness which filled her.

Rodrigo said he would not expect to find her waiting tonight. Yet she couldn't bring herself to go to bed. Settling onto a bench near the wall she asked herself why she resisted. Was she so anxious to hear bad news? Opening a book she stared at the page before her.

The book had slipped from her hands and her neck was stiff

when she heard the quiet clink of spurs against the stairs. Rodrigo turned into his room and closed the door. She was out of her seat before she was fully awake. Her knuckles struck the wood of the door between their rooms, and then she opened it, as lacking in forbearance as he had sometimes been.

He turned, his features drawn with weariness. The sleeve of his shirt was smudged with dirt and a harsh light burned in his eyes.

"Did you find him?" she whispered moving toward him.

He moved his head in assent.

"I am sorry," she said. "He seemed a very pleasant man."

She raised her face to him, hoping he would read the words of sympathy she could not form. Rodrigo extracted his own sort of solace. Catching her chin between his fingers he kissed her with painful roughness until she cried out. Then he thrust her away.

"Did you—did you kill him?" she asked, shaking with the knowledge of the violence burning in him.

"Who?" he asked sharply, his eyes fixed on her as she pressed the back of her hand against her bleeding lip.

"The viceroy." She dropped her hand.

"We are not assassins, we're soldiers. We'll meet the viceroy and his troops as such. Rojo has ridden tonight to inform Pizarro."

The dry taste of futility filled Catherine's mouth.

"Could you not go to the Audencia before you act?"

"Why?"

The question was as cutting as a sword. Rodrigo, shirt unlaced to the waist and boot cocked on a stool, had never looked more the unruly soldier. There was an arrogance in the tilt of his dark head, contempt in the curl of his lips. In that quiet room his defiance was directed not just toward the viceroy, but toward her.

"To avoid bloodshed, to stay within the law," she said, controlling the words though his expression mocked her.

Rodrigo's voice was harsh with ridicule.

"Sweet doña, the law will not protect your lands from seizure by the crown. Pizarro will."

"I do not care about the lands!" she flared. She despised his suggestion that she would be swayed by gain.

"You care enough for the respectability those lands can buy!" He seemed bent on cruelty. He flayed her with his words. "You live in a world of dreams. You believe that respectability is a gift from God, the just reward for conduct. I know it can be bought!"

Bitterness hung on the air between them. Catherine did not answer. She saw again how far removed she was from this man, how improbable agreement or even liking was. Yet sharply she felt the sense of being yoked to him, in this as in other matters. She waited.

When he spoke again it was almost indifferently.

"There will have to be another meeting here. An inn is too public for setting the time and place of attack."

Her reply was cool, as unemotional as his own.

"We cannot have a meeting. Our house is watched."

His eyes snapped toward her.

"By whom?"

"One of the viceroy's men," she said, skirting the truth.

"Then at Juan Portero's, perhaps. We are all of us watched, no doubt. If you wish to go to the marquesa until this danger is past, I'll make no objection."

Whatever her husband's politics, a woman of honor was expected to stand beside him. Rodrigo's bland assumption of her weakness was the deepest cut of all, and it made her reckless. He would see just how much a coward she was!

"If all are watched then an open gathering will arouse the least suspicion," she said calmly. "Is it possible from among your friends to obtain a cittern?"

"Yes, of course." Rodrigo was clearly vexed by this unrelated interest in a musical instrument.

"Then bring me one," said Catherine. "We will have the meeting here. We'll hold a great party to cover it, and half the town will come—not because they are our friends, but because they are so curious to see the style in which we live."

17

Music from hired musicians filled the sala. The table in the dining room groaned with food and drink, much of it thoughtfully provided by the men who would meet here tonight. A party had, indeed, been welcome to the weary citizens of Lima, and Catherine listened with relief to the gaiety of her guests.

"It was a brilliant idea, *preciosa*," Rodrigo murmured at her arm.

Together they stood at the gallery railing greeting the last, late arrivals. For the first time since their wedding her husband wore the clothes of a gentleman. The rich silk and velvet gave him an aura of sensuality which Catherine couldn't ignore. She shook her head to rid it of such thoughts. The hard and ruthless man beneath the silk would never change. Sometimes her own contradictory feelings about Rodrigo puzzled her.

"Now we will let them drink their fill," he said. "We must encourage merriment to run full tilt. De Silva will clamor for you to play the cittern when the time has come. Go in; enjoy yourself till then."

How little feeling he must have to think she could enjoy a single breath tonight, thought Catherine. For a moment tears pricked at her eyelids, though she could not name their source. As she turned he put a hand to the thin silk of her sleeve, detaining her.

"What is it, *preciosa*? I understood women delighted in parties."

Catherine strove for normality.

"My status tonight precludes it," she said, thinking that the role of hostess was in itself unnerving enough without adding that of conspirator.

Her husband's hand fell away.

"Of course," he said sourly. "It had not occurred to me how much you would miss the freedom to flirt which you knew as an unmarried woman."

Snatching up her skirt so sharply that it wrinkled in her hand Catherine went into the sala.

She refused to give a moment's reflection to the scene with

Rodrigo. In a corner by the fireplace she watched Elvira Berruguete holding court with half a dozen admirers, though the girl's conversation was clearly directed at Alonzo Sanchez, who was among them. Catherine looked quickly away.

"My lord marquis, you are out of wine," she said to her old friend, slipping her arm through his with unaccustomed familiarity.

The marquis beamed.

"Upon my honor, Doña Catherine, I have never seen a more tastefully furnished house. You have a perfect little jewel. Perhaps you and your soldier have done well by each other."

Her breath caught only slightly as she laughed.

"Here, Magdalena, fill the marquis's cup." She beckoned to the housekeeper.

"A charming house," said a staid old doña whose name she could not remember, as Catherine passed. The woman's eyes moved jealously along the row of borrowed chairs. "Your furnishings are uncommonly fine in a place so small."

"We've been uncommonly fortunate in many things, including friends," said Catherine with a wry enjoyment. For a moment she delighted in considering the shock of these proper men and woman if they knew they sat on chairs provided by Pizarro's mistress.

The silver goblets which had been her wedding gift from Pizarro flashed as they were raised and emptied. Other vessels had been borrowed, and many of Rodrigo's friends had brought their own. With the gifts of wine and meat from men who had secret business here tonight, the Valdivia household seemed a very prosperous one. Catherine could see the surprise in some of her guests' expressions. A few, like Don Francisco Berruguete, looked plainly displeased.

"An excellent party," he said. "I trust you have not overextended your husband's resources trying to match the scale of entertainments in your father's house."

Catherine bit her tongue to keep from pointing out that the present party could scarcely compare to the lavish affairs of her youth. Instead, certain he knew as much, she smiled brightly.

"I am glad you enjoy it," she said. "As to my husband, have no fear. He has an admirable head for business."

"Most admirable," agreed Diego Berruguete with shameless insinuation. He grinned at her furious glance. "Tell me,

163

Doña Catherine, would you be so kind as to guide a guest to the refreshments? I seem to have forgotten the way."

He offered his arm, but Catherine ignored it.

"Certainly," she said.

The room was crowded and Diego pressed close to her as they covered the length of it.

"Such a pale shade of green becomes you," he whispered. "You look more than ever a goddess."

Catherine could not decide whether to be vexed or amused by his outrageous flirtation. It was impossible to determine what motives lay behind his facade of lazy charm.

"I think you unkind to so callously allude to my—sale," she said, her head held high.

They had stepped onto the gallery. Diego flung an arm in front of her, laughing as she stopped short, preventing him from circling her waist.

"I swear, Doña Catherine, I meant no disrespect. Your marriage to Valdivia amuses me. I can't help wondering if he didn't get more fire than he bargained for."

Before, Diego Berruguete's actions had seemed harmless. This intimate stance, though it might show no more than thoughtless high spirits on his part, Catherine knew instinctively was dangerous. She turned quickly back into the sala.

Plunging into the crowd she caught sight of one of Rodrigo's friends standing with empty cup.

"You need wine, señor," she said, looking about for Ana or Magdalena.

Catching her eye the soldier shook his head.

"I will wait for wine on another night, Doña Catherine."

She understood his intent of remaining clear witted and she smiled.

"There is no need to wait for meat and cheese, however. You will find some very fine pickled eggs at our table."

With a nod of respect she found welcome after her brush with Diego Berruguete, he took his leave. Scarcely a moment later the *encomendero* named de Silva held a cittern aloft, capturing every eye as he called to her.

"Doña Catherine, your hospitality this evening is superb. Will you not provide the one thing lacking and furnish us with your music?"

Approval broke out from those few she could count her friends—the marquis and marquesa, Doña Mercedes, Alonzo Sanchez—and from the men who would shortly meet with

Rodrigo. Feigning modest surprise she reached out for the small stringed instrument.

"I will gladly play, señor, if Jaime Lopez favors us with song."

Jaime Lopez had early thrown his support to Pizarro. His presence with her, it was hoped, would keep it from becoming evident that those with suspect loyalties were absent. Smiling broadly he swaggered forward.

"I will sing, but first a solo, Doña Catherine."

Complying, she set her fingers to a lilting serranilla. As she played the first bars, to the obvious enjoyment of her guests, she caught sight of Rodrigo standing near the door. Then she was forced to concentrate on her music, and when she looked again he was gone.

Now, slowly, Catherine began one of the love songs written by the poet Bernart four centuries earlier. Jaime Lopez sang along, not in the flowery Provençal in which the poems had been written, but in an honest Spanish, haunting in every note. With elation she knew they had captured the attention of everyone in the room. From the corner of her eye she watched two men drift inconspicuously toward the dining area. Another followed, and another.

The song ended and Jaime Lopez looked at her, his eyes piercing and intense. A faint, damp line glistened between his lip and mustache. Striking several gay chords Catherine eased into another Bernart tune, confident they were succeeding. Even so her heart was starting to beat more violently. She felt the strain of keeping her audience diverted, and longed suddenly for the anonymity of darkness. Every man who had ever come to this house in secret had vanished from the room. Automatically her fingers moved now in a *cantiga,* a song of religious devotion.

Applause surrounded her as the cittern fell silent. She heard the marquis's voice.

"Uncommonly lovely!"

"Indeed," Elvira Berruguete agreed politely to one of the young men beside her. "Though I have always found the Bernart goes more smoothly if more quickly fingered."

The comment was just loud enough to carry. Catherine seized on it with unexpected relief.

"You play also, Doña Elvira? You must favor us with a sample. I fear my own skills are quite limited."

There was a murmur of complimentary protest. At the same time Elvira demurred.

"Only if my brother sings with me," she consented at last.

With a curtsy Catherine relinquished both chair and cittern.

"Forgive me, I must take some air," she said to Jaime Lopez.

"This works to our purpose," he whispered. "When they have finished I will loudly demand a rebuttal. Unexpected luck."

She nodded and slipped unnoticed out onto the gallery. In her bedroom the revolt against Blasco Nuñez was being planned. In the sala Diego Berruguete sang in Provençal. Leaning weakly against the railing she breathed deeply of solitude.

The man who came up behind her spoke softly.

"Catherine."

She whirled, immediately on guard. Her heart seemed prepared to jump free of its cage tonight. Her tension did not diminish at the sight of Alonzo Sanchez.

"You—you startled me," she faltered.

His face, half revealed by starlight, only intensified the alarm she was already feeling. A determined look blazed there which was at odds with his mild bearing.

"I must speak with you," he said. "Now. In there." He nodded toward the dining room, which stood deserted.

As Catherine shrank back, stunned, he caught her shoulders, his eyes with all earnestness seeking hers.

"Catherine, I know what is afoot here tonight. I watched the men melt away as you played, and I could guess. No, don't look frightened. No others will have guessed, for few, I feel confident, share my preoccupation with your safety. Will you come?"

A terrifying weakness seemed to grip her. She could feel the pulsing of his fingers through the thin material of her dress. Dazedly she broke away and turned into the dining room.

Alonzo stepped through after her and closed the door. He leaned against it. The openness of his gaze unnerved her more than her knowledge that the rebel meeting had been discovered.

"What do you want?" she whispered with trembling lips.

"There is going to be civil war, Catherine. What I've seen here tonight confirms it, does it not? I want you to come away with me—now—tonight—before the horror of it starts."

She shook her head, disbelieving.

166

"Don Alonzo, I can only suppose you have drunk too deeply of our wine."

He took a step toward her.

"You know I have not. I love you, Catherine. Say you will come."

She put out a hand to check him, but he ignored it. His arms encircled her, lightly, tenderly.

"Say it, Catherine!"

In the distance she was aware of Diego Berruguete's voice raised again in song. She was aware of her own noiseless tears.

"You said—and rightly so—that there could be no future with a purchased wife. What sort of life could there be for either of us if I became your—mistress?"

Agony filled his face.

"Catherine, I beg you not to call yourself—"

"It is what I would be," she said flatly. Fear had left her now. How little hold it had when all pretenses were down. "It fades the blush of romance, does it not, Alonzo? You would have a woman who could not even show her face in decent society."

He drew a wavering breath. "I am quite prepared to turn my back on that society, should it prove necessary. I do not think it will. I believe your marriage to Valdivia can be set aside as invalid once the dishonorable circumstances of its contraction are made known in Rome. But if not I will count myself content to merely have you by my side and love you freely."

This declaration of love, so honest and fervent, sharpened the pain of her tears. It shattered the iron self-sufficiency which she had so carefully built these last, long months. She averted her face, but not before Alonzo had seen there her loneliness and despair, and she felt herself gathered closer against the swift beat of his heart.

Confusion swept her. She knew that this was wrong, yet her heart cried out that Rodrigo would never hold her with such tenderness nor speak such words of love. Alonzo loved her. The life he was offering could carry no more suffering than she now endured. With a sob she broke away from him.

"Please," she whispered. "I beg you, Alonzo, never speak of this again. What you suggest is impossible."

"Are you happy with your marriage, then?"

She shook her head miserably.

"You know I am not."

"Then in the name of all that is holy, come with me. Escape the madness that is about to sweep this land. Let me bring you happiness, Catherine. Let me make amends for not claiming you as my wife as I should have done."

"Rodrigo would kill you."

"We will go to Hispaniola. There will be no need for killing."

She recognized that he spoke not in cowardice, but from humane regard both for her feelings and for Rodrigo's innocence.

Long seconds passed. His eyes held hers. Even their very breathing seemed to issue from a single breast.

Summoning all her strength Catherine turned away and went to stand beside the door.

"I could not betray my husband now, when war is coming. What you have offered, I will always cherish. I—I must return to my guests."

"Your answer is no, then?"

Throat bursting with the intensity of emotion, she nodded.

Alonzo straightened. His eyes had darkened but were resolute. Stepping past her he opened the door.

"Then I must ask you in what room your husband and his friends are meeting."

She froze, a new anxiety gripping her.

"Why? What do you intend?"

He smiled ironically.

"Since boyhood I have lived in the New World. I would not see it destroyed by unjust laws. As I have no reason, now, to take me from Peru, I mean to join the rebels."

18

"Read back what you have written," Rodrigo said.

He stood by the *vargueno,* the hand which rested on it curling tightly in a fist. There was a brooding look about him. The polished cuirass fastened around his torso reflected images of the candle at Catherine's hand.

It was early evening. Catherine put down her pen and lowered her eyes to the words her husband had dictated.

" 'I, Rodrigo de Valdivia, native of Granada, do by this document swear my loyalty to His Majesty King Carlos, ruler of Spain and the Low Countries and of all the Indies. In his service have I fought the legions of the Inca Atahuallpa and the levies with which his successor, Manco Inca, laid siege to Cuzco. And it is as a loyal subject to His Majesty and the laws of Spain that I now take up arms against the viceroy Blasco Nuñez, who by the act of murder discredits his office and by violating the rights of Spanish citizens threatens to plunge this country into civil war. I do so with no thought of gain, but as that which is required to serve my king.' "

A silence filled the room as she concluded. Rodrigo nodded slowly.

"Let that suffice. Where is the notary?"

"Perhaps he was out. Magdalena will find him. There is plenty of time."

She wore the lightest dress she owned, the green silk she had worn the night of the party, yet she was perspiring. Tonight a score of men throughout the city were fastening on their swords. Many would be requiring notaries for statements like Rodrigo's. In the hours past midnight they would storm the viceroy's palace.

Rodrigo was calm. He had eaten well at dinner, his hand betraying no tremor. His temper seemed better than it had for weeks. Still, thought Catherine with amazement, his manner suggested that he was having second thoughts about this undertaking.

"Your declaration is well worded," she ventured.

His head jerked as though he had forgotten her.

"Are you—concerned with the rightness of your act?" she asked, and held her breath.

"No," he answered, so quickly that it startled her. "It is necessary. It is just." He hesitated. "There is no doubt that we are turning our backs on the law, that we are setting ourselves above the king, perhaps; but there are times when God in his wisdom requires such of us as we cannot understand."

Catherine looked up at him. How often he seemed a stranger to her, a mystery. Even now she could not determine his feelings. He appeared all too ready to fight. The reluctance in his words surprised her.

Ana knocked timidly at the doorway.

"Your bag is ready, señorita."

Rodrigo looked at Ana sharply.

"Your bag? Where are you going?" he asked Catherine.

Earlier he had suggested that she spend this night with the marquesa. She had refused. If tonight's action failed she did not want the respectable couple who had shown her so much kindness disgraced by harboring a rebel.

"Leonor García de Silva has invited me to keep her company," she said. "Her house is on the plaza. We will know as soon as the attack begins."

She had not known Leonor's husband was among the conspirators. Having seen him only once, she did not recognize the man. But he had attended the meeting during their party three days earlier, and the following day, the attack being set, Leonor had come to her with the invitation.

Rodrigo studied her.

"As safe a place as any, I suppose, since you ignored my preference in the matter. I have borrowed a horse for you. Mateo can take him to de Silva's. If our attempt should fail ride for the port, and pray that you can find a vessel about to sail."

A fine fear quivered in Catherine's throat. She did not answer. There was a rush of voices in the courtyard, footsteps on the stairs, and Magdalena came into the room followed by the notary, young Señor Bocanegra.

Catherine doubted he remembered her from the morning he had come to Señor Ortiz's office to witness their contract. Nevertheless he nodded politely. To her surprise he bowed.

"Señora de Valdivia, I thank you for recalling my name when you had need of a notary's services."

"Do you take care to keep your services confidential?" Rodrigo cut in.

Señor Bocanegra answered firmly and without pause.

"I do, señor."

Rodrigo considered him and seemed satisfied. A slender and rather attractive young man, he smiled slightly, not in the least disturbed by the obvious tension of this household.

"There, señor, is the document you are to witness," Rodrigo said, gesturing to the *vargueno* and the stool which Catherine had vacated. "My wife has written my statement. I will ask you only to add a clause stating that she is free of any sympathies with my political views."

The notary's eyes became alert, and without comment he seated himself. It had grown darker now, and Catherine gestured to Ana to hold the candle nearer in order that he might see. His face betrayed no emotion as he read the graceful script before him. Taking up the pen he added the requested clause which, though Catherine knew it had little value, caused her to feel an unexpected affinity toward her husband on this perilous night.

The scene in the *sala familiar* seemed to press itself into her mind. There, straight and striking in his soldier's garb, stood the man who had occasioned in her both hate and gratitude. There was Magdalena, woman of this land and yet with her neatly dressed hair and gold ear hoops very much the dignified housekeeper of a Spanish household. Though Ana's hands were trembling, there was in her too some faint new element of growth.

Suddenly they all seemed part of a tightly woven circle in which she could not imagine a breach. Her eyes misted over.

"Bring the candle closer, will you, señorita?" said Señor Bocanegra to Ana as he bent forward to affix the date and his notary's seal.

Ana moved quickly, and in the room's charged atmosphere her gesture was jerky. As Catherine gasped, a stream of melted candle wax cascaded onto the notary's outstretched hand. He dropped the pen, which made a dark blotch on the page.

"Oh, señor! I am sorry! Forgive me!" cried Ana. Her face, which a moment earlier Catherine had thought surprisingly pretty, went as white as the fine new ruff at her neck.

Señor Bocanegra had clasped his hand to his chest as the first pain hit him. Now with jarred professionalism he reached quickly out to reclaim the pen.

"Give no thought to it, señorita," he said, his calm belying the pallor around his lips. As the look of dismay continued on Ana's face he forced a smile. "We are all a little nervous tonight. If Señor Valdivia does not object to a small spot on the page, no damage is done."

Ana stared at him incredulously. Then she blushed as red as an apple.

Unaccountably the rest of them began to laugh, even Señor Bocanegra as he set his burned hand to the moistness of his mouth. He got briskly to his feet.

"Señor Valdivia, if this document signals what I think it does, I wish you well tonight. I am of the sentiment that Blasco Nuñez is a tyrant. Forgive me if I do not shake your hand."

Rodrigo paid him, and with a slight bow to the women the notary left.

"Bring your mistress's bag," Rodrigo said to Ana, who was nursing wounded pride. "I'll see you to the de Silva house."

The streets were quiet as they walked along. A faint breeze blew from the distant sea and in the back of Catherine's throat there was a fierce ache for the beauty of the evening and the tangle of emotions she could not sort. She and her husband did not speak until they reached the gate of Leonor's house.

"Where will you go?" she asked as he raised a hand to the door.

"Now, to the cathedral. After that, to the León until the appointed hour."

"Will it not arouse suspicion, so many of you in armor?"

Before he could answer the fat Spanish woman who served the de Silva household opened the door.

"Let me go with you to the church," said Catherine impulsively. "I will find my way back alone when it is time."

Rodrigo looked uncertain. Then he shrugged. Catherine spoke quickly to Ana.

"Tell Doña Leonor I will arrive when a little more time has passed."

She slipped her hand through Rodrigo's arm. She longed to wish him safety, to let him know that for all hostility between them the fear for his life lay sore within her tonight. But the words formed in her mouth were insufficient. She could not speak.

Inside the dark cathedral only a few candles burned. Rodrigo de Valdivia knelt with his wife beside him. She raised the silver rosary at her waist, and he, from a pocket, drew one of wood and iron.

Beneath her lashes Catherine studied him, marveling how

the hard lines of his face relaxed when he knelt there. His eyes were tightly closed. With unaccustomed freedom she looked on his rough, proud beauty. The strong jaw undisguised by his beard, the waving darkness of his hair. In these moments, cut off from the outer world, he was as fierce in his humility as he was in his arrogance. There was a part of her which forgave him all injury—and a part which did not.

Her rosary beads forgotten, she let her mind race to the night ahead. There would be the screams of horses, the clash of swords, danger and confusion, and in the thick of it would be Rodrigo.

Another image came to her unbidden. There, sitting a horse with a grace which belied his infirmity, would also be Alonzo Sanchez. Formless and flashing her prayer went up for both of them.

At last Rodrigo opened his eyes.

"What do you think about when you are here?" Catherine asked as a feeling of closeness to him washed over her.

He frowned as if the question made no sense to him.

"I think about my sins," he said simply. "And the infinite wonder of God, who delivered this land into the hands of men such as me."

He rose and helped her to her feet. Wordlessly he walked with her back across the plaza.

"Go with God and Santiago," said Catherine as he knocked again at Leonor García's door.

He smiled at her.

"Good night, *preciosa*."

"The assault will not come till near dawn," said Leonor, when they had sat for some time visiting in her neatly furnished sitting room. "Let us put on dressing gowns that we may wait in comfort. Or, if you prefer to rest, there is a bed made up for you."

Catherine shook her head.

"I could not rest tonight."

"Even opposing what is to come?" asked Leonor lightly.

Catherine lowered her eyes.

"How did you know?"

"I only suspected. Your mouth took such a stubborn set whenever the subject of politics was raised in our little sewing group."

"And you, Leonor? Do you support the revolt?"

"I do," said Leonor, rising. "I am starting to believe I have always been a rebel, in many senses. Now it will be quite respectable, with the Audencia joining in."

"What do you mean?" asked Catherine, shocked.

"Have you not heard? Word came to us at supper. The Audencia this afternoon passed a decree for the viceroy's arrest."

Catherine felt her heartbeat quicken. What did this mean for Rodrigo and the others? Would the two groups join forces?

"Let us call our girls," said Leonor, "and be rid of these corsets."

With Ana and Leonor's maid they went into Leonor's bedroom. Ana had spread a cool lawn dressing gown out, anticipating this desire for comfort. The excitement of the evening had fired her cheeks, and she chattered eagerly as she unfastened Catherine's dress. She was helping her mistress out of her petticoats when her gasp made Catherine turn.

Ana's eyes were fixed in horror on something across the room, where Leonor was undergoing similar change of clothes. Glancing across her shoulder, Catherine came too nearly let a sound of dismay escape her, for Leonor's back was to them, and on it were the long, red gashes of a whip. Other welts had already healed into scars.

Catherine's lips were numb as she spoke.

"Leonor!" she cried. "He whips you?"

Leonor turned, a fixed smile on her lips.

"He also beats me, Catherine dear. Marriage is a charming condition, is it not?"

"But why?"

"Sometimes from anger, sometimes to—arouse himself for—"

Her voice broke and she looked away in shame. Catherine sank down on a nearby stool.

"You are a lucky woman, Catherine," Leonor resumed in normal tones.

"Yes," agreed Catherine, guilty she could not fully appreciate her fortune.

A knock at the door cut short conversation.

"Señora," said the fat housekeeper, curtsying apology. "Jaime the stable man is downstairs. He says he must speak with you, that it is most urgent."

Leonor frowned, an uneasy look passing from her to Catherine.

"If it is urgent then send him up. We will be in the sitting room."

Catherine sat nervously on the edge of a bench. Leonor stood in the manner proper for receiving a servant. The stable man made his entrance with hat in hand and multiple bows.

"Señora de Silva, forgive me. I would not trouble you this time of night except I fear there's danger to the master. I passed the back of the viceroy's palace, and upon my word there are preparations for battle underway there. I saw armed men riding in, and there was much activity. I stayed a moment in the shadows and heard plans being made for arquebuses to be fired from the windows of the upper floors. If you know where the master can be found I'll go and warn him that the revolt has been betrayed."

Leonor, the circles under her eyes seeming darker than ever, looked at Catherine.

"I do not know where they are gathering, do you, Catherine?"

"No. Perhaps they could be found at the León. Rodrigo was going there."

"The León has put out its lights," said the stable man. "It is very late, señora. Near dawn."

Near dawn. The time of attack. And the viceroy was alerted, waiting, with several hundred troops at his disposal. If only Pizarro's own forces were nearer the city, thought Catherine with aching head. But those troops were several days away. The Lima rebels were riding into a massacre.

"Let us go to the window and wait," said Leonor. "I did not realize that time had passed so quickly. Perhaps you should petition God for your husband's safety. It is the only recourse left."

Laying trembling fingers across her mouth, Catherine thought wildly.

"We cannot let them attack, Leonor. They will be butchered!" She addressed herself to the stable boy. "Saddle my horse. I will circle the plaza. Surely there will be some evidence of their advance—"

A sound on the night air interrupted her. It was the sound of horses.

"I fear it is too late," said Leonor, running to the *mirador*.

The windows of the wooden balcony looked out onto the plaza, giving a splendid view of the viceroy's palace. From the front the huge building was dark and unsuspecting.

The rumble of hooves filled the quiet streets and horsemen

burst into view, the moonlight reflecting silver from their helmets and breast armor.

"Liberty! Liberty!" a voice yelled hoarsely. "Long live King Carlos and the Audencia!"

Catherine's eyes were fixed on the tiny company of men. At the front of one flank, with sword drawn, she could recognize Rodrigo, by the size of the horse beneath him more than any other feature. All around the plaza heads appeared at windows. Other women, and men as well, ran onto balconies. A general din blotted out coherent speech as servants and homeowners snatched up weapons and poured into the streets.

"Look—there is the marquesa!" cried Leonor, pointing to a window across the way.

"And there is someone waving a scarf," said Catherine. Taking up her handkerchief she did likewise, a prayer on her lips for the outnumbered rebels.

The attackers and their swelling ranks had reached the palace. They halted, no doubt preparing to storm the gates. The ominous thunder of arquebuses drowned out all other sounds as a volley of shots rained down from the palace windows. Gunpowder lent its sickening sharpness to the air.

Catherine suppressed a sob. The revolution had begun.

19

As the smoke from the arquebuses lifted, Catherine strained to see by the first light of dawn. It seemed, impossibly, that no one had been injured. Rodrigo, on Boabdíl, was still in the fore.

Suddenly the heavy gates to the palace swung open and soldiers streamed forth, dozen upon dozen in viceregal livery, led by officers in extravagant costume. Too frightened to look, and yet too frightened not to, Catherine gripped the spindled wood of the *mirador,* watching grimly as the rebels drew their swords against appalling odds.

"Look! Look!" choked Leonor, seizing her arm. "See how it goes!"

And then as the wave of palace soldiers parted, and the rebel forces surged ahead into the viceroy's residence without the least beginnings of opposition, Catherine slowly realized what must be happening.

"Surely the viceroy's own men cannot have turned traitors!" she exclaimed.

"They must have!" laughed Leonor. "Listen to the cheers!"

Leonor embraced her friend, who alternately laughed and wept. Below, the great plaza of the city filled with people as candles appeared in the palace windows against the still-dim sky. Someone was sounding merry notes on a flute and people were dancing. A few men reappeared through the palace gates brandishing what Catherine knew must be wine kegs. Without the loss of a single life the mood throughout the city had gone from one of fear to one of joy.

"Let us dress," laughed Catherine. "It will not take our husbands long to pillage the palace. Why, do you realize, Leonor, we have not even been to bed!"

"An exciting evening this has been!" sighed Leonor.

Vitality had returned to her face, rendering her a pretty young woman. Seeing her, Catherine was filled with rage at memory of the welts on Leonor's back. There should be recourse for a woman when she was so mistreated. How could the law uphold a husband's right to treat his wife in a manner not even befitting a horse?

Wishing that she had more solace to offer, Catherine caught Leonor's hands between her own.

"Do you realize, Leonor, what a good friend you have been to me? I am lonely here, as you must be, and though some women bring themselves to speak to me, I am aware of a sly contempt in every manner but yours."

"And the marquesa and Doña Mercedes," Leonor said, smiling faintly.

"Yes, certainly, but they are women apart. Your acceptance of me has given me a strength without which I could not survive."

Leonor shook her head.

"Examine yourself before you speak as one with so little courage, Catherine. You are a woman of enormous strength. You could defy any obstacle, and for that I salute you. Now let Ana help you with your dress."

True to Catherine's calculations those of the de Silva household who had managed to sleep through the commotion in the plaza were shortly wakened by the arrival of horsemen in high spirits. Chiding Ana for her slowness, she hurried out onto the gallery. Great torches burned in the courtyard showing Rodrigo and Leonor's husband as they dismounted. She ran down the stairs.

"A most impressive victory!" she said, stopping, short of breath. "I congratulate you both."

"And I," said Leonor from the stairs.

High spirits glowed in Rodrigo's face. The fluted edge of his helmet reflected the dancing torchlight. His arm caught Catherine around the waist.

"Didn't I tell you there was nothing to fear, *preciosa?* The viceroy even now is being sent under guard to an island off the coast for safekeeping. We have all sworn loyalty to the Audencia as the provisional government, with the Berruguetes' relative as its president. They promise to suspend the New Laws until consultation can be held with the king."

He reached into his pocket and drew out a small gold chain. "Here. Rojo sends you this as a trophy of the evening. One of the viceroy's ladies seems to have left it behind in her haste to flee."

"No lady would wear it," protested Catherine as he put it around her neck. But his spirits were infectious. She fingered it in delight.

Meanwhile Captain de Silva had drunk thirstily from the wine cup brought by a servant.

"Every house in the city is putting out food for celebration," he said, finally rousing himself to speech. "Leonor, do likewise."

"The plaza is like a grand ballroom," Rodrigo said. "Come, let's join the party."

Eager to sample such uncommon scenes, Catherine turned to Leonor.

"Will you come too?"

Leonor looked longingly toward the sounds of merrymaking which could be heard through the open gate.

"It is late," said Captain de Silva.

The light went out of Leonor's eyes.

Leading Boabdíl, Rodrigo ushered Catherine out into the street. For an instant she drew back, repelled by noise and crowds such as she had never seen so near. Rodrigo seemed unaware of the movement.

"Rojo has carried off a whole keg of wine, which he promises to finish by sunrise," he said, putting his lips to her ear to make himself heard.

She felt the magnetism of his body and laughed.

"Come," he said. "Let us visit the marquesa."

Though the distance was short the going was slow. Catherine stopped in fascination to watch a soldier and a serving girl engaging in a dance. As the flute notes which accompanied it grew quicker and men applauded, Catherine's eyes widened. The movements of the dancers, subtly disguised, she recognized only too well from her nights with Rodrigo. She looked quickly up at him to find him laughing.

"The *zarabanda*, a dance brought from the northern Indies. Shall I teach it to you, my proper little doña?"

Before she could make indignant answer one of the men who had often come to her house rode up. He bowed from the saddle.

"Señora de Valdivia, as your bravery has often aided our cause, I beg you to partake of the viceroy's wine cellars," he said, holding a cup down to her.

"I will drink to your victory," Catherine answered.

It had escaped her notice that Rodrigo also had a cup until he held it up for his comrade to replenish. That accomplished, the horseman rode off.

"To your courage, Valdivia," shouted a passing soldier. "And to that of your wife."

In the excitement of such surroundings Catherine drank

her wine down quickly. Her heart was singing and her head felt light.

"Here, *preciosa,* this is not a night to go thirsty," said Rodrigo, stopping to shoulder his way to another keg with her at his side. Then they set off again for the marquesa's.

That lady was, as usual, taking all with equanimity.

"Ah, Doña Catherine. We have been waiting for you," she said in greeting, as though the entire evening had been planned and invitations issued. Two long trestle tables had been brought from the house and were covered with food. "Take nourishment," she said, gesturing. "We have much to celebrate. I fear the man deposed had been corrupted by power."

Catherine felt amused vexation. Had the marquesa's sentiments long been on the side of the rebels, or did she graciously adapt to any change ordained by God?

"A brave assault you made, Valdivia," commended the marquis, himself pouring liberally into their cups. "I regretted I could not get saddled in time to join you, once I saw what was afoot. By my beard, I regretted it!"

They were swept along by a group of soldiers singing an old war chanty sung in wars against the Moors.

"Let us escape this madness for a little!" Catherine laughed, glad for her husband's arm around her shoulders.

"There *is* no escape," he answered, shouting above the noise.

Nevertheless he steered her into a side street where the crowd seemed thinner and another couple was dancing not the suggestive *zarabanda,* but the dances of Spain.

"There are some who will have aching heads tomorrow," Rodrigo prophesied, watching cloudy liquid splash from a jar into waiting cups.

"What is it?" asked Catherine.

"Chicha, a native corn liquor made for the heathen gods. Look, is this not the house of your friend Doña Elvira?"

Catherine looked up. Indeed they were in front of the Berruguete house.

"I cannot imagine Doña Elvira venturing out tonight—or rather this morning," she smiled, her mood grown reckless.

"A pity. They have good sausages," said Rodrigo, sampling.

Catherine recognized now her own hunger. She ate one of the greasy sausages, wiping her fingers on a handkerchief trimmed in lace. Her wine cup had been refilled again; she did not know where.

A passing soldier cuffed Rodrigo on the shoulder.

"Why do you drink that invalid's drink, Valdivia? There is good rum just two houses up."

Rodrigo grinned. "Fine news. I'll make my way there if you'll stay a moment with my wife to bear her company. I've worn her slippers through tonight showing her this celebration."

Catherine put a hand against his arm.

"There is no need to provide me with company. I'll wait for you there, and rest a moment from the crowd. Then who knows?" she added gaily. "I may be willing to go quite barefoot to see more sights such as these."

She had indicated a narrow wooden gate which opened into an alley between two houses. Rodrigo, with a quick squeeze of her waist as she voiced pleasure at this wandering, pushed open the gate and found the alley deserted.

"There is even something for you to sit on," he said, noting hay piled hip high. "I'll close the gate and be back shortly."

Catherine sank onto the hay and closed her eyes. Her head seemed to sway a little, but it was most delightful. It had been a most delightful evening, this sampling of unbridled revelry such as she had never known existed.

The creak of the gate brought her back to alertness. Had she dozed, that Rodrigo returned so quickly?

But by the faintly lightening sky above her she saw it was not Rodrigo, and she stiffened. Then as she recognized her companion her nerves relaxed, though her wariness in no way diminished.

"Don Diego, you gave me a start," she said.

"Then I am a poor host. Do you like the party, Doña Catherine?"

As he spoke he came toward her. Catherine rose and dusted her skirts.

"I confess I do. I have never seen anything like it."

"Your tastes delight me. Most women of your class would not be able to grasp the excitement of it." As he spoke he reached out and caught her, laughing under his breath. "I have waited a long time to kiss you, Doña Catherine."

Catherine now recognized Diego as a man who thought only of amusing himself, whatever the cost.

"My husband would kill you for it," she said disdainfully.

"Which is exactly why you will not choose to tell him! How fortunate that I saw him go. He is bound for the rum at the end of the street, I have no doubt. It will take him some time to return."

Laughing still he sought her lips. His mouth was hard and brutal. He shifted his arm, slipping it under hers to bring her closer against him. His thumb, as his grip on her tightened, moved greedily over the soft skin waiting just beneath her sleeve.

Her reactions were slow, Catherine thought as she fought him. She had drunk too much wine. Diego Berruguete pressed her backward against the hay, almost bending her double.

Contemptuous of her weakness, he had freed her arm when he took her waist. Her flailing hand struck the wine cup she had abandoned on the hay where she had been sitting. She snatched at it and flung its plentiful contents against the cheek of the man who held her. He stood back with a curse, his ardor momentarily reduced to anger over his sodden finery.

"Damn you, madam," he snarled.

"And you, likewise, Diego Berruguete. You shame the label of gentleman!"

Still clutching the empty cup she turned on her heel and stormed angrily out of the alley, furious that Diego had judged accurately. She wouldn't dare tell Rodrigo of the incident. Diego's drenching had been her only satisfaction.

Halfway up the street she met her husband and the placid Boabdíl.

"I was sure you had lost the direction," she said to head off inquiry.

Rodrigo's eyes were bright. Obviously flattered by the greeting he circled her waist with his arm, more forcefully than propriety would have dictated. When Catherine leaned against him, he swept her around and kissed her, a gesture noted by some of the crowd, who cheered.

His teeth flashed wickedly.

"Here, Doña Catherine Bautista, taste this rebel's brew if you would sample all the wonders of tonight."

He raised his cup to her lips. The fire of rum was far more potent than the rare drinks of her father's *aqua vitae* which Catherine had been permitted. It purged her mouth of all traces of Diego Berruguete. It made her reckless. She stayed Rodrigo's hand and drank again. Warmth and abandon flooded through her.

"Should we drink the health of the Audencia in the liquor

of the New World or the Old? What do you think?" she queried, leaning back to scowl with mock intensity.

Rodrigo's fingers traced the curve of her back with a sudden pressure which made her shiver, every inch of her responding to its message.

"I think, my prize, that you are better kept at home, away from such carousing," he said in reply. He swallowed down what remained of the rum in a few quick gulps and lifted her onto Boabdíl.

"I am not dressed to ride," she protested, laughing.

"A pity you are dressed at all," he murmured as he found a seat behind her.

She was drawn back sharply against him. With every movement of the horse she felt his thighs encircling her. As they left the area of the plaza and turned into empty streets his arms moved tighter around her, resting against her breasts. Dawn was breaking in strips of orange, pink and crimson. Catherine longed to wrap herself in the brilliant colors and dance the *zarabanda*.

Their little house stood peaceful, already astir with the activities of the day. As Mateo opened the gate Magdalena, Ana and the kitchen girl came running out with excited congratulations for their master.

"What a party your mistress has seen!" he called to Ana as he dismounted. "Though in truth we nowhere saw a notary being burned."

Everyone laughed and Catherine slid down into the arms upstretched to her. This morning she could marshal no resistance to the quick sensations he produced in her: the warm downward rush of her blood, the tensing of nipples encumbered by layers of clothing. She was glad it was daylight and they would go their separate ways.

With a jerk of his shoulders Rodrigo loosened Boabdíl's saddle and slung it onto the tiles.

"See to Boabdíl as best you can," he said to Mateo. And to Ana: "Your mistress had not yet been to bed."

As if confident no more need be said, he swung Catherine into his arms and started with her toward the stairs. The swift act took her by surprise.

"I have good use of my feet," she protested, reddening at this outrageous behavior in front of the servants.

"Do you, Doña Catherine? It had occurred to me you might be a little tipsy. You drank an unseemly amount of rum."

183

"Is it possible you feel your own capacity threatened by a woman, señor? Have no fear."

He grinned at her mockery and with a kick of his boot which almost cost him his balance he sent the door to her room crashing open.

"For doubting the gallantry of my concern you had better make amends," he said.

Demurely she raised her lips and kissed him on the cheek.

"Not precisely what I had in mind," he said beneath his breath as he set her on her feet.

"But all you ought to have in mind. It is daylight."

"You are beautiful by daylight. You are also drunk."

"Would you take advantage of me, then?"

"With utmost pleasure, unless you oppose it."

His hands moved up her arms. He kissed her, not so roughly as he had sometimes done, but slowly, probing, his lips teasing hers. Catherine tried to rally herself against this man who sought nothing but to dominate her completely, but she lost the effort. She was drunk with his nearness as she had not been with the rum. If only he would go!

"Shall I leave, *preciosa*? A word from you is all it will take."

Involuntarily her nails had buried in his sleeves. She wet her lips, trying to answer. She saw his dark eyes narrow with victory.

"Deny, if you can, that you want me," he said, easing her forward until his thighs were pressed against her own.

Catherine groaned, eyes closed at the sharpness of the ache inside her.

"I—cannot deny your body pleases me," she whispered thickly.

She had not capitulated completely; she had not showered him with words of love, nor even begged for this encounter as he so long ago had taunted that she would. Nevertheless she was aware of having placed a powerful weapon in his hands.

There was no more to be lost at present. She raised her parted lips. This time they were crushed, and the passion in them matched his. She was only faintly aware of it as his fingers loosened the laces at the back of her dress, and as she, for the first time, attempted the unbuckling of his armor. He shrugged it off, and her fingers moved to the laces of his shirt, pausing when it was half open to slip beneath and trace the warmth of his chest.

"High-born bitch," he laughed softly against her ear. "Have you no manners? Do you not know the man should lead?"

"You are leading too slowly," she said brazenly.

Releasing her, he removed his boots and breeches. The shutter of the room was open and she saw every line of his body in sharp detail. Then slowly she loosened a string and dropped the last of her petticoats to the floor.

Even before it settled he caught her to him, the grace of the movement somewhat marred by the night of celebrating. He kissed her throat and felt her shudder in response.

"Confess you cannot live without me," he whispered fiercely.

She pressed herself against him, trying to ease the torment inside. With her last strength she put a note of lightness in her voice.

"How can I say? I have not lived with other men."

Her answer was to be tossed none too gently onto the bed. Rodrigo's lips traced their familiar path across her shoulder. He nudged the sensitive petals waiting to enfold him and then eased back, repeating the gesture until her head thrashed from side to side at the breaking tumult. Then control left him too, and he entered, and their separate convulsions left them for a moment united.

20.

Catherine felt shamed by her response to her husband. More grievous than the rape which brought them first together was this now undeniable admission that he brought her pleasure. She was angry with herself for betraying her weakness. She was angry with him for causing it. Physical desire bound and bruised them, and by morning it made their encounters seem cheap, too humiliating for confession. She had yielded everything to him except her heart, and she would never yield that. The small comfort brought by her resolve was smothered by the dismal voice which whispered her husband did not want it anyway.

Attempting to forget the night of the viceroy's overthrow, Catherine sought refuge in weariness. Not only did she oversee the most minute details of her household, but she regularly accompanied Magdalena to the market, memorizing foods and prices and all the streets in the city. Twice weekly she went with the marquesa to minister to the sick. When day was done she studied, rereading every book she owned and all which she could borrow. She strove to exhaust both mind and body.

Rodrigo did not seem to notice her resolute activity. He was busy too, and happy with it, checking on his investments in spices and Toledo steel in the new air of peace which pervaded the city. When the time of month arrived which banished him from Catherine's room, he did not give his usual grimace. Instead he rode off eagerly to the *encomienda* to check on the well-being of the precious mares.

For four days Catherine enjoyed the almost forgotten luxury of breakfast in her bed, receiving the news of the morning from Ana, who had gotten it from Magdalena. On the fifth day the maid barely managed to set the tray beside her mistress before bursting into speech.

"Señorita, you will never guess the terrible occurrence! Three men, all fine cavaliers, have been found hanging in a tree at the edge of the city. Magdalena says they are men who fled the general Pizarro and aided the viceroy, and that this is Pizarro's warning that the Audencia must quickly meet his demands."

Catherine frowned. For several days she had heard rumors that Gonzalo Pizarro, far from disbanding his forces once the viceroy was deposed, had answered the Audencia's request that he do so with an ultimatum: Unless he were made governor and captain-general of Peru, he would attack the city of Lima. She hadn't believed those rumors. How could a man of such limited learning expect to govern a country? Having met Gonzalo Pizarro, she could not believe he was so great a fool—or so hungry for power.

She shuddered at the thought of hangings. Even though she had opposed Pizarro's politics, she had admired his courage. She found it hard to imagine his stooping to such an act.

"Rodrigo, of course, will support him," she said more to herself than Ana. Unhappily she pleated the sheets between her fingers. It had been possible to recognize the Audencia's new-won power as somewhat legitimate. The judges, after all, had been appointed by the crown. But Gonzalo Pizarro— how could anyone support his demands and not be disloyal to Spain?

Church that morning was tedious. The comfortably stout old doña who occupied the other end of the pew which Catherine entered drew herself more erect and edged further away. Accustomed to such slights, Catherine fixed her attention fiercely on the priest.

On their return home an excited Mateo met them.

"Señor Valdivia is back!" he said, eyes shining. Señor Valdivia had in no time at all become his hero, and the boy worshipped him.

Catherine lifted her skirts and hurried up the stairs. She went first to the sala and then to the *sala familiar,* but her husband was not there. Perhaps he was in the stables, she thought, and started down again.

"No, *preciosa,* over here," called a lazy voice from across the way.

Looking, she saw that the door to her bedroom stood open. A faint flush warmed her. He had been watching! Had she seemed overly anxious to welcome him home?

Deliberately she slowed her steps. When she reached her room her breath caught at the sight which met her. He lay on her bed bare chested, one arm folded behind his head and his crossed boots resting on the green velvet spread.

"I swear the life of a townsman is making me soft," he drawled. "I could scarcely wait to feel a bed beneath me after four nights on the ground."

"We must get a proper bed for you," she murmured, putting down the fan and handbag she had carried that morning.

His gaze followed her movements.

"I believe I'd still find this one more to my liking. Come here and sit down so I don't have to tax my neck."

He was in fine humor, his black eyes glowing. Catherine could not tell whether it was the state of things at the *encomienda* or merely a return to the rugged life he knew which had pleased him. She obeyed, and when he made no move to touch her she found herself more nervous than if he had.

"What of the mares?" she asked. "Are they well?"

"Well and with rounding bellies," he said, unable to keep the pleasure from his voice. "Don Alonzo's stallion is in the stables. I'll return him shortly."

"I am glad." She smiled at him. "Soon you will have a real herd."

"We will have a real herd, *preciosa,"* he emphasized, reaching out at last to take her hand.

The vibrant touch of him caused such a quick response in her that she bit her lip.

"Much has happened while you were gone," she said. She told of the hangings.

"That sounds like the work of Carbajal, not of Pizarro," he said. Anticipating her confusion he added, "This Carbajal is related neither in blood nor manner to the one the viceroy murdered. Some in fact would say he is born of the devil. He has already seen eighty years, an unnatural age for a soldier. I had heard he was with the general. I'd hoped it was not so."

Catherine sat twisted to face him. Her husband had rolled onto his side.

"Will you support Pizarro in his demands to be made governor?" she asked, holding her breath.

"I will disappoint you if I say yes, will I not?" he asked, watching. He drew her back to lean against him, his expression earnest as he traced the sober line of her chin. "I am beginning to fear it will take a strong hand to keep the country together, *preciosa.* The Audencia does not have it. Judge Alvarez has been sent with the viceroy to Spain to justify the judges' action; Judge Zarate is too ill to leave his house and will certainly die soon; Judge Tepeda is indecisive and Judge Cepeda, I suspect, ambitious. We have half an Audencia at very best, and the judges know nothing of the country outside Lima. The general is familiar with every mile of it."

She struggled to disagree with what he was saying, but his words were so positive that she sighed. He laughed and pulled her down across him, kissing her until her heart was racing.

"Now," he said, his fingers hunting the fastenings at the back of her dress. "You had better get up and close the door."

Three men stood together in the courtyard, the foremost of them clutching a battered felt hat between his hands. They wore linen smocks and long brown stockings, and only the leader boasted a *capa* or short cape.

"Lieutenant, lady," he said, jerking his head in a shy bow. "I am Valdéz. You will probably not remember me."

"I remember you quite well," said Rodrigo. "You sold me Boabdíl when my other horse had gone lame."

A wide smile spread across Valdéz's anxious face. He bobbed his head vigorously, long hair dancing.

"Aye, lieutenant. Then you know me to be an honest man, just as I know you for a good judge of horses."

Rodrigo frowned, clearly puzzled.

"Yes?"

The felt hat moved half a revolution through Valdéz's fingers. He glanced back at the men with him as if to gain support.

"These are Ramirez and Sandoval. They work for me. They are good workers, lieutenant, gentle with animals, and Sandoval doctors well."

Now Rodrigo was growing exasperated.

"What is it you want?" he asked.

It was Ramirez, the youngest of the three, who spoke.

"Our families are starving, Señor Valdivia. We need your help."

Catherine could see her husband's amazement was as great as her own. Valdéz, taking advantage of it, spoke quickly.

"For five years we have run a small stable with horses for hire. We have had a few colts born, of which your stallion, lieutenant, was by far the finest. We were far from rich, but it was a living. Then his excellency the viceroy took our horses when he was preparing for war. We have nothing to hire, only three mares and a stallion, and two colts too young for riding. Señor, we have no money to pay the rent. Our children are starving!"

"The viceroy took your horses?" Catherine interrupted. "Do you mean he didn't pay for them?"

Valdéz repeated his awkward bow.

"Not a copper coin, señora. He took them for King Carlos. We are loyal Spaniards and would make no objection if we were richer, but it was our living he took—the bread from our mouths!"

She listened with a new and ugly comprehension. The tyrant viceroy had been overthrown. Most people were rejoicing. But the action had come too late to spare men like Valdéz and their families.

"Surely you do not want me to reclaim your horses for you," Rodrigo said uncertainly.

Again it was Ramirez who spoke up.

"We want you, señor, to buy Señor Valdéz's stable. If you do not they will put him into prison as a debtor, and we, having no work then, are sure to follow. You have money, Señor Valdivia. And it is not charity we are asking, for you will see the business turns a handsome profit.

"I cannot afford it," Rodrigo said. "By my beard I can't, Valdéz!"

The hollow male anguish which touched the faces in front of her was so unfamiliar to Catherine that she slipped a hand through her husband's arm.

"Surely you can borrow money," she suggested.

In Valdéz's eyes there seemed no spirit now.

"I have already borrowed, señora. Don Luis has called the money due tomorrow."

Beneath her fingers she felt Rodrigo's arm stiffen.

"Don Luis?"

Valdéz gave a final turn to the hat in his hand.

"Aye, Don Luis de Alvarado."

"You may know him for a gentleman," young Ramirez burst out bitterly. "But I tell you he makes more in a year from the loans he makes to desperate men than he does from his own income, and more from selling *encomiendas* than he does from both of those."

Valdéz opened his mouth to silence the stable man, but Rodrigo cut him off.

"No, Valdéz, let him speak."

Ramirez shrugged. "What is there to speak of? We are too weak to stand against a man like him."

"As was my brother," Catherine murmured. She raised her eyes to meet Rodrigo's.

"How much is the loan?" he asked Valdéz.

"Three hundred *escudos.*"

"Impossible. I could not raise a hundred."

There was a curtness to his words which Catherine guessed came from frustration with his own limitations. She watched his rigid expression as the three men took their leave with many apologies. When they were gone he walked the length of the courtyard.

"Three hundred *escudos* and I do not have it. Damn it. How can I in conscience enjoy what I have when I cannot help three honest men like those? I would to God I had killed Don Luis when I had the chance!"

She heard bitterness in his voice and could not bear it. She was not used to seeing him helpless, without resources.

"How much could you raise?" she asked.

"It is exactly as I told Valdéz—not a hundred, even if I spent every penny needed for running this house. Not even to stop a man who preys on the weak and makes a mockery of all of us by selling *encomiendas.*"

Catherine stood quietly. It was illegal as well as scandalous to sell or buy *encomiendas.* Don Luis engaged in a thoroughly despicable traffic.

"You must borrow the money," she said.

Rodrigo's head jerked up.

"It is too dangerous. We could lose everything. If anything happened to me, you would be once again at the mercy of Don Luis."

The succinctness of his argument betrayed him. He had already thought of a loan. For her, and for the household which she ran, he had spent all that he had. She could not let it stand between him and a duty he wanted passionately to fulfill.

"Borrow the money," she repeated firmly. "Do you forget I too hate Don Luis? In a few months we'll have foals which we can sell for a handsome sum. If all else fails there is this."

She flashed the emerald ring which lay against the whiteness of her tapered fingers. Rodrigo caught those fingers in his own and held them tightly.

"You will see me dead, *preciosa,* before that ring is sold. But as you will, then. Returning Don Alonzo's horse can wait a few hours more. I'll go into town and try to arrange a loan."

They left a short time later, Rodrigo for a spice merchant's office which dealt in banking matters, and Catherine, accompanied by Ana, on the pretext of visiting Leonor García. To herself she admitted that she was anxious about the loan and could not bear having time on her hands while she waited for an answer about it. It was also true, however, that she was concerned about Leonor. Her friend had missed their weekly sewing session the day before, and even simple politeness would have suggested that Catherine should call and ask of her health.

Rodrigo saw them as far as the plaza. At Leonor's gate Ana knocked twice before there was an answer. Then the fat Spanish housekeeper who appeared looked out at them but did not ask them in.

"Good morning. Is Señora de Silva at home?" asked Catherine, puzzled by this lack of hospitality.

"Señora de Silva has been taken ill," the housekeeper said, and she started to close the door.

Catherine spoke quickly.

"Ill? I am sorry to hear it. Would you send word to her that we are here? Perhaps I could look in on her just for a minute—"

"She is sleeping."

"Ah."

Something in the woman's behavior made Catherine uneasy. She seemed too eager to be rid of them. As Catherine started to offer some delicacy from her own kitchen, there came from the depths of the house a high and splintering groan, one uttered by someone in great agony.

The housekeeper glanced back nervously.

"I will tell Señora de Silva you have called," she said, and almost slammed the door.

"What do you make of that?" asked Catherine, pursing her lips.

Ana's eyes were as round as eggs.

"That—that was Doña Leonor's voice that cried. She was not asleep!"

Catherine nodded, certain they both were recalling the ugly welts on Leonor's back.

"I'm afraid you're right. I'm afraid she must be suffering."

A silk shop nearby was rumored to have new goods. Catherine turned into its darkness seeking to purchase nothing but a chance to think.

How seriously injured was Leonor? She had never missed their weekly gathering before, though by the looks of it she must often have worn fresh whip marks beneath her dress. The prospect of still more brutal treatment was bad enough, but was it possible her friend was also being held a prisoner? Leonor's life might slip away if she were cut off from what little social life she had.

As soon as the first pair of eyes picked her out, Catherine heard a whispering begin. It was scarcely discernible from the soft sound of silk being lifted up for inspection by delicate fingers.

"That is Catherine de Valdivia. A doña. She is married to a common soldier, not even a captain. Duels have been fought over her, and I have heard she gambles."

The clucking sound which met such delicious gossip brought a smile of irony to Catherine's lips. The tale was meant to be damning, but it had a ring of romance. Beside her, Ana's mouth was opening on an indignant comment.

Shooing her maid outside, Catherine interrupted her. "Let us stop briefly to see Doña Elvira. I saw lavender silk and she has been complaining for weeks that she wants some."

"It will make her look like a dead woman," Ana said.

"I agree. I also doubt that she would do a similar favor for me. But perhaps her father will be there, and if he is I will speak to him about the way Doña Leonor is mistreated. A word from a man like Don Francisco can go far in tempering a husband's brutality, so I am told."

The doorkeeper at the Berruguetes' admitted them promptly and they were shown into the sala. Catherine sat down in a chair. From somewhere near at hand she heard the buzz of voices. Looking about she saw a door ajar which led to an adjoining room. Ana, standing near it, noticed too, and suddenly she gave a little gasp and motioned frantically.

Aware of the impropriety of what she was doing, Catherine went to her.

"What is it?" she whispered.

But before her maid could answer, Catherine herself recognized the voice which was speaking and froze.

The voice was that of Don Luis, and though she could not see him, she could just make out the features of the man to whom he spoke. The long chin and weak mouth barely able to support the mustache above it belonged to Judge Cepeda, president of the Audencia and cousin to Francisco Berruguete, who on his arrival had taken up residence in this household.

"Are you proposing we give in to Pizarro?" he asked now,

clearly shocked. "Forgive me, Don Luis, but I find the present arrangement more to my liking."

"Do you, Cepeda? Sharing your position with three other men?" The velvet voice of Don Luis was full of mockery. "Listen to me. Pizarro can take this city. Win his favor now and there is money to be had. Money and influence—more of both than are in your reach as a paltry Audencia judge."

Cepeda's side was to her and she could not see his expression, but she could hear the tremor in his voice as he reacted to both dismissal and avarice.

"What are you suggesting, Don Luis?"

"That you go to Pizarro in person. In secret. Offer to use your influence with the other judges so that he can be confirmed quite legally. I am confident it will appeal to his vanity more than the prospect of snatching the honor. And of course once confirmed he will welcome an adviser of your superior education and experience with the laws."

"It is a risk," said Cepeda. "And you ask me to take it? You ask me to relinquish certain control and rely upon the whims of some soldier?"

"Better than relying upon the whims of this city! Perhaps he will be murdered in his house like his brother before him. Perhaps he will prove unpopular in time and have to be replaced. Meanwhile there is much to gain and nothing to risk."

A silence fell.

"My fine cousin Don Francisco would never approve," said Cepeda.

The two men started to laugh.

Catherine tore herself away, aghast. She did not stop to consider whether it was a sense of betrayal or the danger of being discovered there which made her move. She crossed the room without thinking, Ana at her heels, and stepped out onto the gallery.

The housekeeper was returning.

"I am sorry. Señorita Berruguete had been resting and was not yet attired for receiving guests," she said, with evident surprise to see them leaving. "She will be along directly."

"Please ask her not to trouble," said Catherine with her most charming smile. "We were on our way to another engagement and unhappily cannot stay. We stopped only to inform her there is lavender silk in the shop which faces the Rimac. She has been hunting some for several weeks. Would you please tell her?"

"Of course," said the woman, still slightly bewildered. With great propriety she ushered them out.

As they reached the street Catherine drew a shaking breath.

"I pray, Ana, that it's never suspected we heard that conversation."

From ill-clothed stable workers to the president of the Royal Audencia, the control of Don Luis was making itself felt in this city today. And she and Rodrigo thought to oppose him?

Ana skirted a puddle and looked behind her.

"Do you think . . . will Judge Cepeda. . . ." She floundered, her young face wracked by the enormity of it all.

"It seems that Judge Cepeda is a man of great ambitions, just as my husband suspected," said Catherine, putting thoughts into words for her. "I believe we shall see Pizarro in power—and in Don Luis's pocket."

"But that cannot be!" cried Ana. "The general thinks highly of Señor Valdivia. Surely he would not listen to someone who is his enemy!"

"I hope you are right," said Catherine.

She did not, however, share Ana's confidence. Once she might have believed in the unswerving loyalty of a man like Pizarro. But once, too, she had believed in the incorruptibility of royal judges. Now she wondered how she ever could have been so blind. She quickened her steps toward home.

Rodrigo was in the courtyard. His flashing smile told her all she needed to know.

"I never realized that borrowing money was so easy," he laughed. "I took three hundred and fifty *escudos*. You must buy yourself some silk." He paused, his eyes on her face, and his forehead wrinkled. "What is wrong?"

"Leonor García's husband whips her cruelly," she said, flinging down her handbag on a bench. "And your friend the general is about to become a puppet ruler."

She saw the challenge darken in his eyes.

"I find it hard to imagine the general being any sort of puppet."

"What, then, do you make of this?" In flat, quick words she repeated the conversation which she and Ana had just overheard.

Rodrigo looked more troubled, she thought, by her reaction than by what she told.

"The general will not be governed by anyone, *preciosa,* nor

195

does he forget his friends. Don Luis and Cepeda will learn so to their displeasure."

His trust was so simple it touched her, and she prayed as they walked together up the stairs it would not prove misplaced.

On the twenty-eighth of October, fifteen hundred and forty-four, Gonzalo Pizarro entered the city of Lima, by invitation of the Audencia and accompanied by the cheers of the people, to be installed as governor and captain-general of Peru. Ahead of him came thousands of Indian slaves dragging heavy artillery. They were followed by twelve hundred Spaniards, a formidable army for the New World. Lines of arquebusiers followed lines of spearmen, and last of all came the cavalry, at the head of which rode Pizarro himself.

The man who had sprung from a family of swineherds to rule the richest of Spain's possessions was covered chin to boot in gleaming armor. A richly embroidered surcoat floated about his broad shoulders, and a crimson cap sat on his head. His horse was powerful, his bearing was at once generous and filled with authority, and Catherine, watching the procession, could not deny that he was a handsome and impressive leader.

Before the new governor came the royal standard of Castile, the house of King Carlos. To the right of it fluttered a banner showing the arms of Cuzco, and on the left another displaying the coat of arms granted by the crown to the Pizarros. The cannon which once might have been turned against Pizarro now boomed in greeting, and there sounded on the air the jubilant chimes of a few small church bells spared by the viceroy.

From her vantage point in the saddle Catherine thought of another pageant which she had watched enter the city, more ostentatious but less impressive, less joyously received. How much had happened since that first spectacle when she was a bride of one day!

As if he shared her thoughts, Rodrigo reached over and covered her hand.

"Now we will get to the building of the land," he said.

There were the oaths of office and services in the cathedral, and then Pizarro rode into the palace where his brother had lived and died and where Doña Isabella waited, and the capital gave itself up to celebration.

This time the festivities were more lavishly planned than

on the night of the viceroy's overthrow. Rough barricades had been thrown up to provide arenas for bullfights. There were parties at several houses. Soldiers contended with one another in prowess just as they had in tournaments of old, and everywhere there was music and dancing and drinking in the streets.

But somehow, in the full glare of day, this celebration seemed tawdry compared with the other, Catherine thought. She held tightly to Rodrigo's arm when they left the horses to walk through the crowd. She was so preoccupied she did not even notice Elvira Berruguete and Alonzo Sanchez until Alonzo spoke.

"Rodrigo, Doña Catherine, can a person get through in the direction you have come without getting crushed?"

"Only if he goes sideways," Rodrigo answered, even his antagonism toward Alonzo forgotten on this day.

Alonzo laughed. Elvira was holding sedately to his arm, accompanied by her dueña and a maid.

"Then perhaps we had better turn back. Doña Elvira does not much like the crowd."

Catherine was surprised at the irritation which filled her in seeing him so plainly paying court to Elvira. It would be easier living and moving in the society they both must share if Alonzo would marry, but his interest in Elvira dismayed her. The girl was quarrelsome, cold-natured and petty—everything which he was not. Now, settling her arm more closely through his, she gave a jealous look in Catherine's direction.

"They are racing at the end of the street," said Alonzo. "We've just now come from watching. I tell you, Rodrigo, there's not a horse running that will be able to match those foals we'll have next spring!"

"I hadn't thought to race them, but I hope you're right," Rodrigo answered. He made the effort now of nodding to Elvira. "Señorita Berruguete, I trust your father and brother are doing well?"

"Quite well, thank you. Come, Don Alonzo, let us brave the crowds again."

Spoiled little adder, thought Catherine. She spoke to Rodrigo as if he were a footman!

"A moment more," said Alonzo patiently. He turned again to Catherine and her husband. "Are you coming to the marquesa's entertainment the evening after tomorrow?"

Rodrigo shrugged. "Whatever Catherine wishes. I have little interest in parties."

Elvira fanned herself with excessive energy.

"Come, and persuade your wife to bring her cittern and sing for us," Alonzo said. "It should be fun to see if her voice is as fine when there is nothing at stake."

The two men laughed as Catherine blushed. Elvira withdrew her hand from Alonzo's arm.

"The sun is too warm for standing, Don Alonzo. I believe I will rejoin my father."

"No, no," said Alonzo hastily. "Let us be on our way."

Catherine watched them walk a few steps and then stop to talk with a well-connected grandee and his wife, Elvira's voice rising in delighted chatter, all objection to the sun forgotten.

"I marvel he would put up with such an ill-tempered creature," said Rodrigo. "He would not in a horse, I'll warrant."

Catherine smiled despite herself.

"Perhaps he loves her."

"Any man who loves a woman is a fool."

She kept her eyes upon the ground.

"Why do you say that?"

"Because he loses control of himself as well as her. If I were to fall in love with you, *preciosa,* it would prove quite fatal. You would use my weakness against me. It is preferable to have none."

What he was saying frightened her with its accuracy. Care too much and there was pain. She must never let herself in for that trap. Yet she hated him for the calm with which he could say it; for the ease with which he clung to safety. At the same time she felt strangely sorry for a man who had never been touched by tenderness.

They found their horses again and started for home. Still passing various remnants of the celebration, Rodrigo reined unexpectedly. Catherine, beside him, looked in the direction of the dancers who had caught his interest, and her heart suddenly plummeted.

There, laughing and whirling, her hair flying free, danced Francisca. Though the cloth in them was costly, she was dressed like a woman of the lower classes in skirt and bodice. Her uplifted arms accentuated her full breasts. As she turned in the dance she caught sight of them, and her head jerked sharply up in recognition to Rodrigo.

It seemed to Catherine that Francisca's movements took on increased sensuality. Her partner was a young man, slim and virile. Certainly not her husband, Catherine thought. Francisca's skirts brushed his thighs as they passed each other.

Against her will Catherine's eyes sought her husband's face. He wore a brooding look in which there seemed to be some trace of longing.

The music stopped and Francisca, rumpling the hair of her young partner, turned gaily to Rodrigo with hand uplifted.

"What a merry city you have," she called. "I shall not mind living here. Come, 'Rigo, let us see if life as a gentleman has spoiled you as a dancer."

Rodrigo's face twitched. With the jibe, his wife suspected. He was oddly silent. Was it so hard to refuse, Catherine wondered, heartsick. She saw knowing grins exchanged among the men as they looked from her to Rodrigo, grins which said of course Valdivia would dance except for his aristocratic wife.

She turned to him.

"Please do, if you like."

He looked at her in sharp surprise.

"You would not object?"

The flesh around her eyes strained with the effort of facing him, of lying, of seeing the quickness of his response.

"Object? Not in the least," she said coldly.

A cruelty she had never seen before touched his features.

"I was hoping for such an invitation, Francisca," he called back.

Catherine heard the stir which passed through the crowd. She kept her eyes straight ahead, struggling for an outward appearance of calm. Rodrigo joined Francisca in the clearing, and with a sardonic look toward his wife kissed the other woman's hand. A flute and cittern began to play, no other dance than the *zarabanda*.

A moment and Catherine could bear no more. She turned her horse away from the spectacle.

Another rider blocked her path. It was Alonzo. His eyes met hers with sympathy and pain.

"It will never be any different, Catherine," he said softly. "The two of you are from separate worlds."

Her lips pressed together.

"Perhaps you would be so kind as to tell my husband I've gone home?"

"I'll see you there," he said.

She shook her head. As memory of their surroundings touched her she added, "Where is Doña Elvira? You should not have left her."

"Doña Elvira is with her father. She makes but a poor replacement for what I cannot have."

The words deadened the ache of Catherine's hurt pride. She smiled sadly, the fragile strength of her face transcending even its beauty.

"I thank you, Don Alonzo. Please let me pass."

He moved his horse aside, but as she started past he spoke again.

"Catherine. Are you sure I may not see you home?"

"Quite sure."

"Then will you grant me one favor—as a friend? I am growing impatient to send the first part of my history to Spain to see if it will find a sponsor at the court. Will you read it for me and give me a true opinion? I know that you are acquainted with similar works, and that you have an interest in this country."

Catherine hesitated.

"Doña Elvira, I think, would give you an honest opinion."

Rueful amusement touched Alonzo's mouth.

"Doña Elvira reads poorly at best. I should have to tell her every third word. Moreover I fear her feelings about this country disqualify her as an objective critic. Will you take on the task?"

Just then a measure of music from the *zarabanda* rose loudly to catch her ear, mocking her. It made Catherine reckless. How long since she had been told she did something well, her thoughts and opinions solicited? A voice of conscience warned her what her answer should be, but she could not—did not even want to—resist the chance to feel useful, in however small a way. In trusting her with the history he had written, Alonzo was trusting her with a part of himself. Her bruised heart longed for such sharing with another human being.

"If you think my reading would be a help at all, I would count it more a pleasure than a task," she said.

21

Handing her dressing gown to Ana, Catherine slipped into her bath. Her hair was freshly washed and pinned loosely up. Afternoon sunshine filled the room. She yawned and leaned back in the water half dozing, wondering what it would be like to swim in the cold waters of the Rimac as Rodrigo did.

These were placid days. Pizarro was firmly in power and had replaced many city officials with men of his own choosing. There were great dinners in his palace to which the gentry, though scorning him in private, were eager for an invitation. Catherine and Rodrigo would be his guests again tonight.

Even between herself and Rodrigo all was tranquil, the incident with Francisca being avoided by both of them until it was almost forgotten. Their nights together were perfect, not only in passion, but in humor and in the brief bursts of conversation which sometimes followed. If by day such a coming together seemed to elude them, they at least achieved a strange sort of peace.

Rodrigo's appetite for activity had found its match in the work needed on the Valdéz stable. It proved run down and sadly in need of repairs. There was no question at present of stocking it with rental horses, but with effort it could be made suitable for boarding animals. Stripped to his breeches, Rodrigo worked side by side with Ramirez and Sandoval repairing corrals and shoring up the buildings. If he heard the whispers suggesting such labor did not befit a man who aspired to life in the upper classes, he betrayed no hint of it. He was determined to make the venture pay.

As her thoughts floated pleasantly there was a firm knock which she recognized immediately as her husband's. Ana, who was nearer the door, yelped with the rage of a misused puppy. Through a crack between the panels of the screen surrounding her, Catherine could see her maid attempting to block Rodrigo's intrusion.

"Your pardon, señor," gasped Ana. "Señora Valdivia is in her bath. You cannot see her."

"I cannot imagine a better time for seeing her," Rodrigo

answered. He strolled past the horrified maid as she fell back.

Catherine's hands gripped the sides of the tub. She was stunned. No man of tact would walk into his wife's room while her maid was dressing her, let alone while she sat completely naked. What would the servants think?

His grin flashed as he caught her look of outraged propriety.

"Such extravagant preparations for a party," he said coming nearer.

Catherine felt her cheeks and forehead blazing at his gaze, though it held far more amusement than desire at the moment.

"It is customary to allow a lady the privacy of her chamber," she said shortly.

"A ridiculous custom. One no doubt responsible for the number of dons who frequent certain rooms above the León. My appearances now and then insure a certain honesty on both our parts, I think."

He was doing this only to provoke her, she suspected. She lowered her voice. "Get out!"

He stopped beside the tub looking calmly down at her.

"Do you suppose Ana thinks I've never seen you naked?" he inquired, imitating her whisper. Aloud he said, "It pleases me to have some conversation with someone when I come home. You were not waiting; I sought you out. Would you quarrel with such devotion in a husband?"

Using his foot he hitched a stool up near the tub and took a seat. Catherine, in the futile hope that he might end this visit if she showed indifference, bunched her washcloth and began to soap her neck. Dismayed strangling noises were issuing from Ana's throat.

"I too have made great efforts for this party," Rodrigo said, clasping his hands behind his neck. "Do you approve?"

Some instinct warned her that if she looked at him directly her own embarrassment would grow acute. It was struggle enough maintaining her composure with Ana witnessing all this. Why she did not send the maid away escaped her.

Furtively and with an almost forgotten shyness Catherine glanced at her husband. He was newly barbered, his beard no longer in its usual squarish cut but stylishly pointed. It gave him the aura of another class, of genteel manners. Yet the bold masculinity which touched every inch of him made it a

fleeting impression at best, and she found herself unexpectedly glad.

"You would set hearts fluttering no matter how you trimmed
your beard," she said mildly. "As no doubt hundreds of
women have told you."

"Most somewhat more adoringly," he said. "Tell me, *preciosa,*
do I not flutter yours?"

"No." She scrubbed vigorously, splashing him. He did not
move. She gritted her teeth and tried another tactic. "Are
repairs at the stable finished? I cannot recall that you have
spent less than an entire day there since you purchased it."

"The roof is no longer in danger of falling down," he said. "I
grew bored."

"Oh."

Ana stood stolidly by with towel in hand, looking, Catherine thought, as ridiculous as she herself felt. Again she
attempted to find the safe refuge of conversation.

"What news of the viceroy?" she asked. "Are the rumors
true? Has he landed?"

Blasco Nuñez, the overthrown viceroy, had been sent back
to Spain in the care of Judge Alvarez. However word had
come that Alvarez, no doubt having second thoughts at the
prospect of justifying the Audencia's actions, had freed Blasco
Nuñez and placed the ship which carried them at his
command. For several days it had been rumored that the
viceroy was now ashore in the north and raising an army.

"The rumors are true," said her husband. "Blasco Nuñez
landed in Tumbez. He has proclaimed the general and all
who support him rebels. The general will march against him
when the New Year comes, in April."

His eyes grew narrow, and dark with amusement. "Tell
me, *preciosa,* why so many questions? And why do you refuse
to look at me? Do I make you uncomfortable?"

"I—want only to finish my bath," she protested. But she
knew she did not have the courage to stand before him while
Ana rinsed her.

He leaned forward—dangerously close—his voice lowered.

"You are irresistible with those droplets gliding down your
skin, you know. Shall I send Ana away?"

Eyes shaded she nodded, raging inwardly at this control he
had over her.

"Here, Ana, give me the towel," he said cheerfully. "I
believe I can manage the use of it when your mistress
desires."

Ana hovered for a moment, undecided. Then she all but threw the towel into his hands and marched out of the room, skirts crackling.

"Why, *why,* did you do this?" Catherine asked, her lashes still pressed together in weary defeat. "You'll have created a minor scandal among the servants."

"It is well for the servants—and you too, perhaps—to sometimes be reminded who runs this house." His tone was matter-of-fact. "This bucket—is it the rinse water?"

"Yes."

Catherine opened her eyes and saw him stripping out of his shirt. She stood, shaken by an overpowering sense of intimacy just when she thought that she was growing accustomed to him. He lifted the heavy wooden bucket with ease and water, cooler than it should have been for rinsing, cascaded over her shoulders. He turned her gradually until it ran down her front, his hand sliding over the contour of her wet waist. The bucket fell to the floor. With a single movement he freed her hair from the pins which held it, then he lifted her, dripping, into his arms.

"My towel—" she objected, struggling.

"Be still or I'll drop you. You're slippery as a fish."

He laughed at her breath of frustration and fell with her onto the bed.

Afterward, as she lay in his arm with the sheet tucked securely around her, Rodrigo said, with unexpected seriousness:

"Could you teach me the game of chess?"

"Chess?" repeated Catherine languorously. "I can show you the rudiments, though if you remember my game with Carbajal you'll recall I have little skill. But why?"

His voice was casual; his gaze was on the ceiling.

"It's more acceptable than other forms of gaming, is it not? The men often play it at the parties given by your friends. And it appears to be a game enjoyable without the need of wager."

She lay quietly, digesting this small crumb of insight into the man beside her. By her friends he did not mean true friends, but acquaintances of background similar to her own. This was the first intimation she had had that his attitude toward them would ever be other than thinly veiled defiance. His allusion to wagers made her realize, too, that he must miss his old habit of dice and card playing, a habit not compatible with the cost of a household such as theirs and limited funds. Touched by the same pride in him which so often exasperated her, she pressed his arm.

"I am loath to teach you something at which you will so quickly best me," she teased.

But he was in a pensive mood, she recognized now.

"I went to see the general today," he said.

Remembering his statement that an army would be raised against the viceroy, her heart missed a beat.

"What business had you with Pizarro?"

His face was untroubled, but there was the slightest darkening of his eyes. He drew forward a strand of her hair, caressing it with his thumb.

"With all the changes he has made among municipal officials, he has not yet replaced Don Luis. I was troubled by the conversation you overheard. I thought perhaps if I talked to the general he might grant us the small favor of replacing him."

"And?" Her interest quickened. She was somewhat awed that her husband made such a bold request to the man who ran the country.

Rodrigo sighed and folded an arm beneath his head.

"The general, of course, was curious why we should object to Don Luis. He is a man who appreciates frankness, *preciosa,* and I told him the whole of what Don Luis had done to you." His jaw tightened briefly. "The general has little use for his character after hearing that. But he maintains that Don Luis is an honest and duly elected member of the Cabildo. He cannot replace him. He did, however, give me his word that Don Luis will have no say in anything regarding us or our property so long as he rules the country."

Catherine weighed the promise. Was Pizarro a man of his word? The men who had flocked to his cause seemed to think so. And certainly he had moved with great discretion since becoming governor. While it was true he had named new officials in place of old, they were thought to be honest, and such an act was not uncommon when powers changed. Moreover, while he had ordered the arrest of some who had been most ardent in their opposition to him during the viceroy's rule, he had executed not a one of them. His leniency had surprised the city.

"Perhaps all will be well," she murmured.

"Perhaps," he agreed. There was a pause and then he added, "The same rider who brought word of the viceroy's landing also promised a ship on the horizon by afternoon. It should land tomorrow."

There was no need to mention the stallion. She knew that both their minds were on it. At least perhaps this time there would be a letter from her father's cousin in India House saying the export had been approved.

Rodrigo's call as he rode in from Callao the following afternoon brought Catherine running. She knew at once he had good news; he used her name.

"Catherine, damn it, will you come?" he called again.

She hurried along the gallery. Through its arches she could see the horse he led, fine boned, dancing with spirit, its coat as white as milk.

"At last!" she laughed. "At last!" Then her eyes, examining the precious horse, stopped with a shock. She looked at Rodrigo in horror. Had he not noticed?

"Another mare!" she gasped.

"She is a beauty, is she not?"

He had dismounted and was fondling the mare's fine nose. Catherine stared at him, unprepared for this calm in the face of what could only be a disastrous mistake.

"But—are you not angry?" she stammered.

"Why should I be?" He grinned, enjoying her confusion. "This one, it seems, is your affair."

With that he reached beneath his doublet and produced a letter which he held out to her.

"This, I am assured, bears your name. It was sent in the charge of the same man who delivered the horse."

Ana and Mateo had crowded close, aware of drama. Magdalena, too, had left her chores to see what good news caused this commotion in the household. Even the kitchen maid hovered in the doorway to the courtyard.

Catherine broke the seal on the letter with trembling hands. Eagerly, and still bewildered, she unfolded it.

"Why, it's from my father's cousin!" she said glancing up. She read the sentences penned in the land of her birth, then read them again when she could not believe what they conveyed.

"This horse is a gift," she said. "A wedding gift to us from Don Raimon and other cousins. I cannot believe it!"

Catherine shed happy tears. Far from the censure she had expected, these relatives had sent congratulations, and to her spirits it was a gift more precious than the horse.

"This too comes for you," said Rodrigo. For the first time she noticed the small trunk of carved and polished walnut which he had balanced before him on the saddle. "And these as well." He handed her more letters. Smiling warmly he placed the trunk on a bench.

"Open it, señorita!" Ana cried, clapping her hands. Even reserved Magdalena came closer to see what riches it held as Rodrigo turned over a key.

"Look, a tapestry!" Catherine exclaimed. "And scissors . . . laces . . ."

Ana knelt beside the trunk making cooing sounds at the treasures revealed. Catherine hugged the letters in her fingers joyously against her. News—of people who were dear to her.

"Oh, but I am sorry!" she said, suddenly sober as she thought how bitter Rodrigo's disappointment must be in contrast to her own elation. "I can think of no words to console you," she said. "My relative Don Raimon says it is hard to get an export license for a stallion. In the meantime perhaps we can have use of Don Alonzo's once again."

"The mare is yours," he said. "You may do whatever you wish."

The negativity in his words was so strong, that it surprised her. He raised his voice.

"Rojo!"

From beyond the gate there came the rush of hooves. Rojo rode in grinning, and Catherine, with dawning understanding, saw behind him another white horse.

If confirmation were needed, she saw it now in her husband's face. It was relieved and full of hope. The next thing that she knew his arms were around her waist and both of them were laughing and spinning like children.

"By my beard," rumbled Rojo. "What presents come to this house, and Twelfthnight still a month away! I swear the bankers will be borrowing from you next."

There was merriment in the house for the rest of the day as the letters were read and Ana wept at news of those now so distant. The source of each gift in the walnut trunk was made known to them, and while Catherine and her maid again examined each item, Rodrigo and Rojo looked on indulgently, apparently enjoying this female commotion as much as the wine they were sipping. As the afternoon waned the stallion was installed with great preparations in the stable behind the house. The mare, lest she prove a source of trouble, was removed to the boarding stable and the attentions of a devoted Valdéz until the time arrived to take her to the *encomienda*.

By dinner the quiet joy of optimism had settled over the household. Catherine let her thoughts range back across the letters from Spain—her maid Luisa's pending marriage, her cousin's new baby—relaxed in the knowledge that Rodrigo's mind was occupied with plans for the future and there was no need for conversation. She had not stopped smiling, and as often as he looked at her, she could sense his pleasure in it. It was puzzling, then, when after only a brief time together in the sala he went out and did not return.

At length Catherine grew restless. She put down the needlework which busied her fingers but not her mind and went outside. It was a lovely evening, and not since her marriage had she felt such wellbeing. Thinking Rodrigo might have gone to the stable, she turned her footsteps down the stairs.

Halfway across the courtyard she stopped. Her husband sat straddling a bench beneath the fig tree. His arms were folded and he was deep in thought.

"You do not have the manner of a man who's seen four valuable horses cross the sea without a single loss," she said softly.

He smiled and moved back on the bench to make room for her. Uncertain now whether she should have interrupted him, she joined him.

"It would be all too easy today to feel like King Carlos himself," he confessed. Yet a faint line of worry, or perhaps it was only of fierce concentration, stretched across his forehead.

"You came here to be alone and I have intruded," she said, starting to rise.

He took her hand.

"No, only to think. Stay, *preciosa*. It is seldom enough you seek me out."

She grew quiet, certain now that something was troubling him. In their months together she had learned it was impossible to gain admission to his thoughts by pressing.

"You have much to consider now, with foals on the way, the stallion and the Valdéz stable," she ventured after a silence.

She heard him sigh.

"Exactly, *preciosa*. I sometimes think there is too much to consider. With the investments in spices and wares from

Toledo, my head grows weary reckoning our costs and profits."

The question of why he did not keep records sprang to her tongue and was just as quickly caught. Of course he did not keep records. He could not write. She looked at him with a new amazement, wondering how accurate his reckoning could be.

"The steel and spices—are those investments worth the effort?" she inquired.

He gave a wry smile.

"They are the most reliable of all our incomes, *preciosa*. The spice trade turned a profit of some twenty-five thousand *escudos* last year, of which we receive the hundredth part, two hundred fifty. From steel our profit is twice that. Together they nearly equal what little the *encomienda* brings. Valdéz's stable will bring in fifty *escudos* this year if we are lucky. That makes us four hundred short of two thousand annual income, less the loan on the stable and our expenses, which are not small."

The precision with which he listed all won her admiration. Their income was not great, but their investments were diverse. Guided by nothing but instinct her husband had come a great distance from his beginnings as a stable boy.

"Perhaps the expenses of the house, at least, can be reduced," she said. "I will look into it."

"No."

He spoke so sharply that she recoiled.

"It was not the running of this house which I was thinking of," he said. "It was the cost of buying further mares. Of putting something aside for the house we will build one day. And of hiring a *mayordomo* to manage these business affairs."

He stood up as he said the last and walked a few steps with his thumbs hooked through his belt, his back toward her. Catherine watched him in stunned silence.

"A *mayordomo!* But why? You have just now shown how easily you handle them yourself."

"It will reflect better on you if I cease to do so and hire a man, as anyone with gentleman's pretensions is expected to. Soon there will be a practical reason for it as well. The general intends to ride north to defeat the viceroy when the year turns. I will go with him."

Dismay followed the shock coursing through her. She barely

stilled the impulse to cry out. All the day's joy was gone in an instant. Rodrigo turned to look at her.

"Come, come, sweet doña," he said, his smile quick. "I am flattered you look so forlorn. But that is my life, after all, to be a soldier. I have played the townsman too long; I am losing the taste for it. A few months of fighting will be most welcome."

His tone was so light it seemed to mock her. There was no hint of regret in it, and only eagerness in his words.

A lonely bitterness flooded her as she watched his careless stance. She had come very close to persuading herself that he felt some affinity for this house, for her. Now, from his own lips, she heard how little it all meant. In April he would leave.

Lest he fault her for not showing the mettle expected in a soldier's wife, she drew herself up. Her chin was held firm, her words calm.

"You are kind to think of my status when you mention a *mayordomo,* but I scarcely think that consideration worth what you would pay to hire a man. If you are gone you cannot manage your affairs, that is true. Can you not trust me? I would willingly keep a written record of the various accounts, and it would cost you nothing."

He struck his knuckles thoughtfully against his chest.

"An interesting suggestion, *preciosa.*"

"And practical as well."

Suddenly, winning her way in this assumed the greatest importance. Her household duties, her charitable works with the marquesa, would not be enough in the months ahead. She wanted to leave herself neither time nor energy for thoughts of this man whose face and voice were stamped upon her life like an illness for which there was no cure. She wanted to show him her strength.

"It is not a wife's place," he said. "It is not even woman's work."

"No one need know. If I do not object, why should you? God knows there is little enough that I do."

He was silent.

"It is difficult to think of you as capable of what you are suggesting," he murmured. "Yet thinking on it I can see you must be. If you are certain that you want to—"

"I am certain."

"Very well. But half of what we save you must spend freely on new gowns for you and Ana."

She got up, nodding stiffly. He caught her hands and searched her face. For what she did not know.

"You are not frightened of my going with the general?"

"No."

It was to be expected. It was for the best. She had been in danger of growing too fond of a man who would never tolerate a similar weakness in himself.

"There is no need to be," he said. "The foals will be here, or very near. Their sale will pay off the loan on the stable. All will go smoothly, I am sure, and we have still three months together."

22

"Señora, you must come to the stables. Señora de Silva is there."

Catherine looked up in surprise as Magdalena came in. "Leonor? In the stable?" She saw anger in her housekeeper's eyes. "But why did she not come to the sala?"

"I believe she did not wish to be observed, señora."

Catherine sensed urgency in Magdalena's manner. Picking up her skirts she hurried after her, nearly running.

They reached the stable area, reeking with straw and afternoon heat, and in the shadows Catherine saw a black-cloaked figure sitting just inside a stall. Magdalena paused to let her rush ahead.

"Leonor?" asked Catherine uncertainly. Then she gasped as the figure rose and a loosened cape revealed her friend's face to her.

One of Leonor's eyes was blackened and a deep cut ran across her cheek. She tried to smile as Catherine came toward her.

"I have come to tax your friendship," she said, swaying as she spoke.

Catherine made a backward gesture to Magdalena.

"Bring a glass of Señor Valdivia's rum," she said. "Leonor, sit down. You are badly injured."

When Leonor did not comply, Catherine put a hand to her arm. Weak as a straw blown by the wind, Leonor sank backward onto the pile of hay where she had been sitting.

"You are so decisive, Catherine," Leonor mumbled. "I have decided to be likewise. I would rather face a certain death than take another beating from my husband. I have run away from him."

Magdalena returned with the rum. Catherine held it out to her.

"Drink this, Leonor. You are faint."

Leonor took a drink and choked, color coming back into her cheeks.

"Would you poison me, when I come seeking help?" she whispered.

Catherine felt her eyes mist at this humor from one so close to a swoon.

"You shall have my help," she said. "What do you need of me? I would gladly swear before the authorities how your husband mistreats you."

Leonor had forced down most of the rum. With effort she shook her head.

"You do not understand. I am running away. I have no faith in help from judges, I only want to escape. Rent me a horse—not from your stable, I would not involve my one true friend in this scandalous act. Here is the money. Go to another stable. Get me a horse."

She spoke with increasing difficulty. Her cloak had fallen away, and on her shoulders dark stains were spreading.

Catherine listened with racing heart, almost as shocked by what Leonor was proposing as by what she saw. It had never crossed her mind that a legally married woman would run away from her husband; she was not even sure such a thing was possible. To attempt it, to aid it—

"Leonor, you are not able to sit a horse," she said. In the tumult of her thoughts, that one alone was clear.

"I must," said Leonor, white-lipped.

Catherine sank onto the hay beside her. Pulses pounding she seized her friend's two hands between her own. If she helped Leonor and was caught, the wrath of the whole city would be upon her. Yet how could she call herself Leonor's friend and do nothing to end her suffering?

"I will rent a horse for you," she said. "But not now. You must rest. Your wounds need tending. When your household discovers you missing they will search for you. If you rode out now, you would certainly be overtaken."

Leonor watched her, fear in her eyes, expecting betrayal.

"What do you mean?" she asked.

"I mean it will be better in every way if you stay here tonight. We will hide you—tend you—and you may depart in the morning."

"But your husband. . . ." said Leonor, frowning, as if she could not grasp what Catherine was suggesting.

Catherine rose uneasily. "He must not know, of course."

Slowly Leonor gave voice to thoughts.

"It is too risky, Catherine, to hide me here. If your husband learned—if anyone learned—no, I cannot ask it of you."

"No one will learn," said Catherine. "Ana will keep her

silence if I ask it, and you will not betray us, will you, Magdalena?"

Magdalena stood quietly by. With lowered eyes she said, "It is a terrible thing when a man strikes his wife, señora. My people would have punished it."

"There, you see?" said Catherine. "You are safe here. We will help you. You must rest now, Leonor, and try to forget your worries."

Tears fell from Leonor's eyes, squeezing out where the blackened one was swelling shut.

"Dear Catherine, I never expected to have such a loyal friend."

Ana's hands were twisting nervously.

"But, señorita, surely they will look here. Where can we hide her?"

Catherine pressed her lips together.

"There is one place I can think of where they will not think to look. Ana, Magdalena, help Doña Leonor upstairs. We will dress her wounds and let her rest in my room. Then we are going to make her comfortable in Señor Valdivia's wardrobe."

Catherine gave a nervous twist to the hair cascading down her back. It was late afternoon, and while she had been alert for a long time for her husband's return, she knew now it was imminent. At least it had been possible for Leonor to sleep some hours on Catherine's bed. Now they dared chance her presence there no longer, and she sat in the cramped confines of Rodrigo's wardrobe.

How desperate she must be to endure the discomfort of that small, hot space, thought Catherine. She hoped that Leonor would not faint. She had given her friend one of her own gowns and urged her to eat soup and bread, and now she hoped her friend's strength would sustain her through this long ordeal.

Nervously she peered into the waters of the courtyard fountain, trying to catch a glimpse of her loosened curls. She never wore them thus except for bed. But Rodrigo could never refrain from touching her hair when it was free. She prayed it would prove enticing enough to keep him at her side through the evening ahead. It was courting disaster, she reminded herself, to let him do more than glance into the doorway of his room.

The sound of a stern command from the street made Catherine jump.

"Magdalena! Open the gate!" Rodrigo called.

Catherine swallowed apprehensively. She had expected him in neutral temper, but something appeared to have gone wrong. She watched in dismay as he rode in next to Leonor's husband. Behind them half a dozen more men dismounted.

"What—what is happening?" she faltered.

Rodrigo came toward her, his face forbidding.

"Señora de Silva has left her home and cannot be found. Her husband has searched the city for her. Is she here?"

"Why no," said Catherine, blinking innocence.

"Take care you speak the truth," Rodrigo said sharply.

Catherine squared her shoulders. "Why should I not? And what has Doña Leonor done? There seems to be more anger than concern at her disappearance."

Captain de Silva thumped his chest with a meaty hand.

"She took a good sum of my gold with her when she left. The woman is a thief. She has disgraced me and I mean to see her punished."

A cold dismay filled Catherine as she heard about the gold. Leonor had neglected to tell her that part.

"Ah," she said, more calmly than she felt. "You have often punished her, have you not, Captain de Silva? I have seen the whip marks on her back."

"We cannot moralize about the differences between Captain de Silva and his wife," Rodrigo said impatiently. "She is his property and his concern."

One of the men accompanying them made a short bow to Catherine.

"Your pardon, Señora de Valdivia. It is not right that we should force your husband to question you thus. Still, it is common knowledge that you are a freind of the lady we're hunting. A woman cannot be allowed to run from her husband when they have quarreled; still less can she be allowed to steal his gold. If Captain de Silva were to demand it, we would support his right to search your house."

Catherine saw Rodrigo stiffen, not quite willing to tolerate this treatment of her.

"There is no need for him to demand it," she said. "I invite him to do so if it will ease his mind."

Rodrigo looked relieved. His hand flew out to touch her arm.

"Forgive me, *preciosa*. Tempers are out of hand, as you can see. Come, de Silva, I will go with you."

With guarded breath Catherine watched the two men walk toward the stables. What if there should be some trace there of Leonor which she had not noticed? The men reappeared a few moments later and made their way to the kitchen area. The weight of her deceit lay heaviest on her as Leonor's husband and her own began to mount the stairs.

Their glances into the sala and dining room were no more than cursory. Who would hide a woman there? They made their way along the gallery. Passing Rodrigo's door they stopped at hers. They disappeared inside. Time crawled along. Suddenly Captain de Silva's grizzled head appeared in the doorway to Rodrigo's room. At a word from him which Catherine could not hear, Rodrigo reappeared from Catherine's room.

Her heart seemed to cease its beating altogether. De Silva had gone through the door connecting the two bedrooms while Rodrigo kept watch behind. Then, as they walked quickly on toward the *sala familiar* and the servants' quarters, she felt the weakness of relief.

"I apologize for the trouble I've put you to, Valdivia," said Leonor's husband in curt tones a few moments later. "I will be on my way."

Rodrigo took Catherine's arm as de Silva and his friends departed. When the gate had closed behind them he looked down into her face.

"I am sorry, *preciosa*," he said quietly. "I know you say de Silva whipped his wife. I share your sympathy for her if that is so. Still, it would run contrary to my civic duty if I permitted you to help her. She is his wife, after all."

The matter-of-factness of his position made her want to scream. And how could he say *if* it were so? Resolve grew in her. She gave a tentative smile.

"Have you been with Captain de Silva all afternoon, then? I wondered what kept you late."

Her husband's expression was one of mild surprise.

"I am no later returning than usual, I don't believe. Do you watch for me, then?"

She shrugged and turned a shoulder to him.

"Magdalena and I found some excellent grapes today. I thought you might like some while you were waiting dinner."

It was the first that he had noticed her hair. Through

lowered lashes she watched his teeth scrape over his lower lip.

"Your hair—"

Catherine put a hand to it.

"Oh! I forgot!"

As she turned as if to seek her dressing table, Rodrigo caught at her.

"No, leave it. It is lovely. Show me these magnificent grapes."

By dinnertime she had him talking amiably. They did not speak of Leonor, and she was glad. Afterward, in the sala, Catherine gave him her warmest smile.

"Shall we play dice tonight?" she suggested. "It has been months since we have done so, and I am weary of losing to you at chess."

She was not unaware of how his gaze had traveled to her hair throughout the evening. Eyes lingering on her now, he stroked his beard.

"I confess you made a better teacher than opponent. Very well, if it is dice you wish, we shall play dice."

When the third straight game in a row fell in her favor, Catherine laughed her delight. "This calls to mind the night we met," she said, in hopes the memory of that clash, and his later victory over her, would spark desire within him. She caught his eyes, teasing, tempting. "Will you not admit now that I am better than fair as a dice player?"

She heard the sharp intake of his breath, knew she was succeeding. But things must not proceed too quickly. Rodrigo's interest in her would be strongest if she first made him impatient. She was certain she would have him in her bed that night. What was important was that she insure his presence there until morning. Quickly she lowered her eyes.

"Ah, well, perhaps a game of cards would hold more interest anyway," she said.

Deliberately she made several plays which extended the game. Her husband did not seem to notice the carelessness, laughing instead with a faintly indulgent air as she pretended frustration.

"I believe you should stick to dice," he gloated when he at last won the game.

Catherine stretched daintily, making sure her hair fell back across her shoulders.

"Perhaps you are right," she agreed, getting up from the

table where they had sat. "Would you object if I played some music?"

He looked slightly surprised. Although the cittern they had borrowed for their party before the revolution had since been given to them, Catherine rarely played except in the afternoon. Heart pounding nervously, she picked the instrument up and drawing up a cushion settled herself on the floor, alert for his reaction.

On his handsome, open face a frown of puzzlement deepened.

"Since when do you sit on the floor?" he asked.

Catherine laughed and tossed back her curls.

"I can hardly do so when I am playing for guests. But since we are alone . . . if you do not object?" Dreamily she ran her fingers over the strings, producing a sweet hum of music. She smiled at him.

Rodrigo came to sit facing her with the easy posture of one accustomed to finding rest on open ground. His breathing had quickened.

"A strange whim," he said, "but you look most decorative."

She looked at him shyly.

"I have heard it is the pose always used by women in harems when they make music," she said. Again she let her fingers dance across the strings.

"What do you know of harems?" Rodrigo asked, voice low in his throat.

"Not so much as you, who have lived in Granada, I have no doubt."

She began strumming softly.

Eyes narrowing, Rodrigo stretched out an elbow, nearer her.

"Do you think that city would dare boast a single harem with the threat of the Inquisition ever present?"

"No? Ah, well." With a shrug of the shoulders Catherine began to play in earnest.

The blood in her veins ran more quickly when Rodrigo, after listening to her, at length rolled over on his back. Golden flames had kindled in his eyes. He reached a hand out and traced the faint line of her thighs.

Laughing she interrupted her song and pushed his hand away.

"That is not how one is supposed to listen to music, señor."

Everything was going just as she had planned.

Rodrigo gave a lazy smile.

"It is how one is supposed to enjoy a harem, I think."

He reached toward her again. This time his hand found her waist, urging her down toward him. Catherine resisted. Long enough to let him think that this was his own doing? Yes, she thought so. Slowly she relented and he pulled her down across him on the rug.

His lips brushed hers. "Let us go to bed," he said.

"But the evening is young," she protested, even though she knew the statement was untrue. "And it has been so long since I played—"

His arms tightened over her. His leg moved, imprisoning both of hers. He rubbed her against him.

"Supposing Ana were to find us like this?" he mocked. "I have no objection, *preciosa*, but I thought perhaps you might."

"You—you wouldn't," Catherine whispered. Her heart was fluttering wildly. How long dared she tease him? The more she aroused him, the more likely he was to stay with her the night, the more likely Leonor would be safe to ride away at dawn. Yet there was a limit, and she sensed he was dangerously close to it.

"Why should I not?" He pressed his lips to her neck. "My own wife . . . my own house. . . ."

She shuddered with the rippling desire which filled her, her urgent motive behind this encounter now half forgotten.

"I—will tell Ana we're retiring," she agreed. As she rose she moved against him, and his fingers flew out to imprison her. But she already was on her feet, hurrying toward the kitchen, breathless.

Her husband was watching her from the gallery when she appeared a moment later.

"By God, your hair could drive a man wild," he muttered as he seized her arm.

Catherine laughed breathlessly.

"You are in a strange mood tonight. So amorous! I shall have to be more careful when I play music."

His arm tightened almost painfully around her waist.

"It is not your music, it is your body. And you can no longer pretend you find my advances unwelcome, my prize."

They entered her room and Catherine turned to him, setting the candle in her hand on a nearby table.

"No, they are not unwelcome," she whispered. She ran one shining white nail down the front of his shirt, turning the back of her hand at his belt to move it back and forth against the flatness of his abdomen. It was for Leonor that she

219

behaved so brazenly, but some small part of her welcomed the opportunity with growing excitement.

Rodrigo caught her hand and pressed her hard against him. His kisses burned her mouth.

"So you have come to your senses at last," he said with labored breathing. Skillfully he unfastened the back of her dress. Holding his eyes with her own, Catherine removed the top part of her dress.

"I realize that I am fortunate to fulfill my wifely duties with someone whose body is lean and young."

She stepped free of her skirt and Rodrigo's hands slid around her.

"They are hardly duties in your case, are they, *preciosa?*"

Catherine smiled at him. "What do you think?"

"Damn you, Catherine!" He kissed her again, his free hand stroking her breast until a gasp escaped her.

Somehow, she found herself on the bed and him above her. Her body was taut, awaiting—desiring—their coupling. When he entered her she brought her palms up to stroke his buttocks, hearing his sound of surprise. A violent storm broke over them, its aftermath lasting for many minutes.

When Rodrigo at last rolled away, it was to look at her almost shyly.

"By my beard, *preciosa!* Show a little more restraint or we shall have no fun at all!"

Catherine tucked an arm behind her, filled with a strange sense of wonder at herself.

"Do you not like me to touch you?" she asked, lips curving. "You touch me."

"Yes, but that is different."

"How?"

Rodrigo scowled fiercely over the question.

"I am a man."

Laughter rose merrily from Catherine's lips. She sobered suddenly, remembering Leonor in the room next door. How angry Rodrigo would be if he ever learned how she had deceived him this evening. But no, she could not think of that. Safety for her bruised and weary friend now rested on how well she played the temptress, the seductress.

She reached lightly out to touch Rodrigo's chest with her finger tips.

"Surely, Lieutenant Valdivia, you are not afraid? Did you not tell me that women always demand your favors?"

He watched with dry amusement now. She ran her fingers

over the muscles of his chest, down his belly, finally to the sensitive skin beyond, stopping at the sound of his exclamation. Was it one of anger?

He caught her wrists.

"Catherine," he said with the effort of a man who had drunk too much wine. "Catherine."

Catherine had struggled to stay awake for the sound of Leonor departing. Indeed, as she lay wide-eyed beside her slumbering husband, she had expected the memory of her own wanton behavior to keep her sleepless. Even as she had lain thinking about it, marveling that she had dared the things which she had dared, her eyes had closed.

When gradually she awakened, alarm hit her as she realized the sheets beside her were empty. Rodrigo had left her. Then she saw the sun creeping in beneath her shutter and knew that day was established. Leonor was gone.

A knock at the door announced Ana. The maid slipped in with a tray bearing juice and eggs.

"Señor Valdivia has finished his breakfast and will come up shortly," she whispered. "He said you would soon be waking."

Catherine took the tray and realized that she was ravenous.

"And Leonor? What of her?" she whispered in return.

Ana's eyes shone brightly.

"Magdalena came and woke her, very softly. She ate well and seemed much the stronger for her rest. We gave her some food to carry, and I went with her to the place where the horse was waiting. Please God she is safely on her way."

With a feeling of relief Catherine swallowed her food. She did not know what life there could be for a woman who fled her husband, but she felt hopeful Leonor would find some happiness. Everything seemed wonderful about the day.

She heard the sound of Rodrigo climbing the stairs. The clothes which he had discarded the night before were no longer in her room, proof he had taken them to his own and found nothing wrong. She sighed in relief.

As she sat listening to Ana's chatter, the door connecting her room with her husband's slammed open. At the sight of his face she knew the enormity of her own crime had been discovered.

Rodrigo came toward them, his face almost as dark as his beard.

"Where is Leonor de Silva?" he asked sharply.

Neither woman spoke.

"I have asked a question," he said with growing menace. "What have you done with her? Where has she gone?"

Ana was trembling before the fierceness of his expression. Catherine saw the tears in her eyes as the maid was caught between loyalty to her mistress and fear of the man who now loomed over her.

"An answer!" thundered Rodrigo. "Do you think I do not know now where she spent the night? My wardrobe reeks of woman's perfume, and the scent is not my wife's."

Ana's mouth quavered. She shook her head in a desperate attempt at denial.

"I—I—"

"Yes, Leonor was here last night," said Catherine, relieving her. "Ana and Magdalena had no choice but to keep my secret. I threatened them with dismissal if they did not."

Her shoulder blades were pressed against the head of the bed. Her mouth felt dry and scarcely able to move. Never before had she seen such rage in her husband's face.

"You—you may go now, Ana," she said. "This need not concern you."

Ana fled for the door and Catherine faced Rodrigo with a defiance which denied the trembling inside her.

"Leonor was half dead when she came here. Her eye was blackened, her face was cut, her clothes were plastered to her back from the cuts which her husband had given her." Anger welled hotter inside her with every word, sustaining her. "What Leonor's husband did to her, he deserves returned in full measure. I hope he burns in the fires of hell. I helped Leonor, and I would do so again. She is well gone; no one will catch her now, please God. Whatever ill luck befalls her can only be better than what she has endured!"

Rodrigo's chest was rising and falling with his fury. His eyes were blazing.

"What have you done?" he hissed. "By God, I can understand de Silva's actions, for if I had a whip at hand, I would use it on you! Small wonder you acted the part of a whore last night. You were playing me for a fool! You have disgraced me in the eyes of the entire community!"

Catherine found her back no longer supported by the wooden bedstead. She leaned forward, shaking with emotion.

"Perhaps it is time you learned the taste of disgrace! I have fed on it long enough!"

She wanted to throw in his face the ugly whispers about the duels fought over her, and about his obvious interest in Francisca. She wanted to scream that in helping Leonor escape she had sent away her one true friend. The rapid drain of color from her husband's face checked her words.

"Does the fact of being a soldier's wife still stick in your craw, pretty doña? Very well, then I can free you to play the fine lady. Today is as good a day as any for riding. I can leave at once for Tumbez and wait for Pizarro there."

23

"I do not like the feel of this," whispered Ana. "It does not seem right for the Cabildo to summon you when you are alone."

They stood in the chambers of Luis de Alvarado. A messenger from the city council had come to the house that morning to order Catherine's appearance. He had refused to give a reason.

"It is not right," Catherine agreed. "I am sure Don Luis and the Cabildo know as much. But I will not let them think me a coward by refusing to appear before them."

She could not still the pounding of her heart. Pizarro, who had sworn protection of her husband's property, was but two days gone from the city, and already she was called to face Don Luis. Could this be another attempt to seize the *encomienda?* Surely, though there was sentiment against her, there would be no legal action over her help to Leonor. Yet she remembered how Valdéz had lost his stable because of Don Luis, and how Ramirez had said that the councilman fattened his pockets on the misery of others. And in that moment when she felt frightened and alone, Catherine suddenly remembered something else Ramirez had said about Don Luis.

She walked quickly to the room's single table. There was a strongbox near one corner, but the key lay beside it. Thrusting the key in the lock she opened the box and pulled out papers. Ana's gasp did not deter her. If she had been summoned before the Cabildo, her position could hardly be worsened by being caught examining Don Luis's papers. She unfolded one and glanced at it, discarded it and unfolded another. As she scanned the third paper, her eyebrows raised. the next drew from her also a nod of satisfaction.

Refolding the last two papers she thrust them at Ana.

"Take these to Señor Valdéz at the stable," she instructed in a rush. "Tell him he must hide them—hide them very well." As Ana hesitated, Catherine said in an impatient whisper, "These documents are proof of two sales by Don Luis of *encomiendas!* Such sales are illegal. Go, do you understand?"

"But—you will be alone," protested Ana, comprehending all with difficulty.

"Hurry!"

Backing a few steps Ana spun and obeyed. Catherine tossed the other papers back into the box. Several endless moments later the door swung open and she saw the scarred face of Don Luis.

He stood there looking at her, his fingers delicately exploring the point of his well-kept beard. Never, thought Catherine, had she seen eyes so unconnected to a soul. They seemed to belong to some animal, feral, vicious. They left her as Don Luis half turned to speak across his shoulder.

"This is the woman," he said.

The man he had spoken to came into the room, and Catherine recognized Cepeda, head of the Audencia. His thumbs were hooked into his belt. He strolled past Catherine, studying her as he might some piece of meat.

"So, Señora de Valdivia, you are rumored to have helped the de Silva woman escape her husband. Do you deny it?"

"I do not," said Catherine in ringing tones. Her heart was pounding wildly. So that was what had occasioned this interview.

"How regrettable," drawled Cepeda. "Your admission places you in a great deal of trouble."

Her brain was working feverishly. How could she be in trouble with the Audencia?

Cepeda strolled smugly toward the table. Don Luis made a sweeping gesture of welcome and the Audencia head sat down behind it.

"The Cabildo feels your actions are a dangerous influence on the city, señora. We cannot have every woman who is cross with her husband leaving him as if he had no claim on her. Nor is it in the interests of society if other women get the notion it is safe to help such ventures, as you did."

Catherine looked defiantly at Don Luis.

"I should like to know how many members of the Cabildo have such sentiments. It is curious, also, that the matter was never raised until General Pizarro had left the city."

A cold smile flickered across Luis de Alvarado's lips.

"There are enough who share the sentiments. Be certain of that."

"What I have done is no crime," she said, unable to give her voice the force she wished.

"Ah," said Don Luis. "But you forget the de Silva woman had taken her husband's gold. You aided in a theft."

Catherine felt her throat tighten. She hadn't thought about the gold, and surely the amount of it had not been great—Leonor's dowry, perhaps. Yet she could see how cunningly this was arranged.

"You will do well to think before attempting to charge me with such a crime," she said, struggling for breath. "You may have noted that I am alone. It is because I sent my maid away, Señor de Alvarado, with certain papers from your strongbox. Papers establishing the sale of *encomiendas*. I suspect they would arouse more outrage in the city than my helping Leonor de Silva."

Behind the table Cepeda gave a gasp. Don Luis's face flushed redder than his scar.

"You dare to steal from me!" he exclaimed, taking a step toward her.

Catherine stood her ground.

"Alvarado, you fool!" hissed Cepeda. "I will not be drawn into your quarrels when she has a weapon like that in her hands!"

"Leave us," said Don Luis shortly. With dangerous control he stroked his beard. As Cepeda left the room Don Luis came closer to Catherine.

"You had better return the papers, clever one. If you do not I will destroy you and your impudent soldier."

Catherine watched him with cool regard.

"I have no doubt you mean to do so anyway," she said.

He nodded slowly.

"But I can make it more unpleasant or less so. If you are wise you will return the papers. You would find no one to believe in their authenticity."

Catherine raised her eyebrows.

"Do you not think so? You have warned me, sir, and I will warn you. Do not attempt to harass me or my family again, or I will turn those papers over to fighting men who would gladly cut your throat!"

Surprised at the steel in her voice she swept around him and out of the room, half expecting him to make some move to detain her. When she reached the street she stopped and put a hand to her throat. A fine dew of fear covered every inch of her, chilling her until she shivered in the sun. She was not convinced she had won any sort of victory over Don Luis. Her threats had thrown him off balance, perhaps, but that was no guarantee he would drop the attempt to charge her with complicity in the theft of Captain de Silva's gold. She had challenged him openly, and now she began to be frightened of the consequences.

She could send word to her husband of what was happening. Surely he would come.

The thought flashed through her mind, followed by sharper grief than she had known before. There was nothing Rodrigo could do. And perhaps he would not come.

A horseman rode by at a gallop and his horse's hoof threw up a pebble which stung her cheek. Catherine's hand jerked up to cushion her smarting flesh, and suddenly she was overcome with the feeling that she could not go on alone, without advice. There was one still in the city who would not desert her. She would go to him.

"Catherine!" exclaimed Alonzo, hurrying toward her with hands outstretched. "Catherine, what are you doing here?"

She made no protest as he caught her hands between his own.

"I knew of nowhere else to go," she said. "I am in grave trouble, Alonzo. In need of advice. I did not think you would turn me away."

"You know I would never do that," he said, holding her hands more tightly. He looked beyond her. "Is Ana not with you?"

Catherine disengaged herself and shook her head wearily.

"No, I have come here alone like the wanton the whole town thinks me. I trust it will not reflect badly on you, Alonzo. Forgive me. I was too upset to think of doing otherwise."

She sat down in a chair he held for her, vaguely aware that his small sala was beautifully decorated. The deep green rug and the polished furnishings were decidedly masculine, but they reflected the same quiet sensitivity to beauty and proportion which was evident in his writing.

"I am pleased you have come to me, Catherine. What has upset you?"

Gratefully Catherine took the glass of wine which a Negro servant brought. She sipped at its ruby darkness before she spoke.

"I may be charged with theft for helping Leonor escape. I was called before Don Luis and Judge Cepeda this afternoon. Cepeda says I am a threat to the public welfare."

Made calmer by his quiet attention, she began to outline the encounter just concluded. As she spoke, however, she began to fear Alonzo's reaction should she tell how she had taken Don Luis's papers. It was theft; she could not deny it. What if Alonzo were as conscientious in his sense of public duty as Rodrigo had been? She decided to skirt all mention of the papers, concluding instead with Don Luis's threat to her and Rodrigo.

Alonzo sat on the edge of his chair leaning forward, his fine mouth even graver than usual.

"The man has no conscience, Catherine. I would it were in my power to see him in chains. I believe he would stop at nothing to ruin you."

With a deepening sense of defeat Catherine nodded.

Alonzo smiled suddenly. "You must not worry, Catherine. He cannot touch you with this ridiculous charge. De Silva himself would have to make it since he is the injured party, and I cannot believe he has done so. Too much time has passed, and besides I suspect they would have had him present this afternoon to add to their case if he had made the charges."

Catherine stared moodily down.

"They might yet persuade him to do so. He has not gone North yet. I saw him yesterday at Mass."

Alonzo reached out to cover her hand.

"You must not worry," he said urgently. "De Silva will not have the courage to charge you. You are a doña. It would make him look a fool in the judgment of others. No, Catherine, you must hold your head up, you must act bravely and shrug off any suggestion that what you did was wrong. Do that, and I believe de Silva will be too wary of your background to charge you and risk the label of ungallant."

"And if you are wrong?" asked Catherine. "If I am charged, by de Silva or by the Cabildo? Will they be content to jail me, or will they confiscate our property as well?"

"You will not be charged," Alonzo repeated. "If the impossible comes to pass and they should do so, they will never make the charges good. I will provide you with the finest legal help in Lima."

Catherine smiled sadly. "I hope you are right, Alonzo, and I am comforted by your support."

"Such as it is, you have it freely. But it is not sufficient, Catherine. You should not face this alone. Send word to Rodrigo and ask him to come."

Her eyes avoided his.

"I cannot," she said.

For six weeks Catherine lived on the edge of fear, wondering always if the charges Don Luis had promised would be brought against her. She made a brave show of following Alonzo's counsel, holding her head up, smiling brightly, trying to act as though no one could possibly censure her for her aid to Leonor. As she stood at an entertainment in the home of Alma de Palacios Rubios, she wondered if those efforts were worth it.

True, she had been invited to this gathering, and that surprised her. Surely Alma, newly arrived in Lima with her doctor husband, had heard gossip regarding the scandalous Catherine de Valdivia. This act of acceptance, however, could not blot out the fact that soldiers who once had bowed to her with admiring smiles now looked through her with disdain, or that women pointedly turned away when she came near. Or that a man from one of the finest families in Spain had moments ago propositioned her as bluntly as he might a tavern wench.

Catherine fanned to rid herself of the memory. Then hearing her name called, she stiffened. With swaying hips, and sly smile fixed on parted lips, Francisca Griega was coming toward her.

"What a lucky one, that husband of yours!" said Francisca in greeting. "To look death in the face and yet hardly be scratched—imagine!"

"What?" Catherine's voice was a frightened whisper. She was aware of the sharp and curious looks of those around her, but the importance of that seemed trifling as she heard Francisca's words.

Francisca raised an eyebrow. "Have you not heard? An arquebus which he was testing exploded in his face. Do not alarm yourself, he was not injured. Only a small cut on his forehead, which should add to his attractiveness, don't you agree?"

Catherine's voice had failed her. Elvira Berruguete, having taken in the exchange with eager ear, said sweetly, "How terrible that you must hear of your husband from someone else! Why, he has been away two months now. Doesn't he write you?"

Francisca regarded her with lazy satisfaction. Catherine knew the other woman had anticipated how this news from another source would strike her. By delivering it in front of an audience Francisca had given all within hearing much food for gossip.

"These modern weapons! Have I not always said they were not worth their mischief?" said the marquis with a furious clearing of throat.

"Yes," agreed Francisca. "The job of testing new-made guns is one better left to those who place no value on their lives. I wonder that Rodrigo would be so foolish."

Catherine turned blindly. Rodrigo had come near death and she had not known it. What scanty news came from the North had reassured her, for the viceroy's troops, young and inexperienced, were said to quake and retreat at the mere mention of Pizarro's name. Now Francisca told this story. Francisca had heard!

Alma de Palacios Rubios, a look of compassion on her face, reached out and slid an arm through Catherine's.

"I believe this whole country lives on the brink of madness," she said. "Revolts in the South, the eternal flight of the viceroy in the North—I grow so weary of it. You must too, surely? Come, let us divert ourselves for a while at least with the flute player I've engaged."

Catherine tried but could not concentrate on the music. From the Andalusians they had two perfect new foals, and the new mare was pregnant. The stable had turned such profit that the month before a stallion had been purchased for Valdéz to rent out as he had of old. In terms of business she could give a good accounting to her husband. Yet she knew it would do nothing to cancel the anger he bore her. She had betrayed him and she could not expect forgiveness. The admission caused an aching grief inside her.

She was stirred from her thoughts by the rising of her hostess from the bench where they both sat. Glancing up, Catherine felt the ice on her heart, as a moment she long had expected now came to pass. Luis de Alvarado and Cepeda were striding toward her.

Blood pounded in Catherine's ears causing the room around her to receed at every beat. Was she to be subjected to the final humiliation of being arrested here, in front of this gathering?

"Don Luis, President Cepeda," said Alma. "I am so glad you could make our little entertainment after all."

They were invited guests. Catherine felt relief spread through her.

"Ah, señora, I only regret that business prevented us from enjoying the entire evening," purred Don Luis.

His eyes, beneath the uneven brows, slid now to Catherine. She met them boldly, ignoring the clammy feeling which release from fear had left upon her skin. To her surprise his lips moved in a grin of satisfaction she could not fathom, and with exaggerated bow to her, he stepped aside to listen to the music.

Three more songs. She would force herself to sit through that many before departing, Catherine decided. She heard the first, the second, and then in the hall beyond there was a commotion. One of Alma's servants came hurrying toward her and spoke quickly. Alma turned toward Catherine.

"A messenger has come for you," she said. "He is waiting outside."

Icy with apprehension Catherine rose. As she neared the hall she saw the small figure of Mateo.

"Señora!" he cried at sight of her. "Señora, you must come! Valdéz sent word—your stable is burning!"

Buckets filled in the Rimac passed from hand to hand as men who lived in the streets surrounding the stable fought the blaze. Catherine watched the yellow flames move like a solid curtain billowing in the breeze. Her fingers were frozen in horror on the reins of Alonzo's horse, which had brought her here. Beside her Alonzo straddled another horse which he had borrowed from someone at Alma's. He had come with her over her objections, yet Catherine felt glad for his presence.

"They will never save it," she said, speaking what she knew was too apparent. Her eyes moved to the rear of the stable where fire was racing along the roof beams of adjacent shacks. "Dear God! That is Ramirez' house!" she cried in recognition as a young woman great with child appeared in one of the doorways dragging a table.

Alonzo sprang from the saddle to go to the pregnant woman, but another cry from the stable drew their attention back there.

"The stallion! The stallion!" yelled a figure racing toward the flames.

"Valdéz!" breathed Catherine. "Alonzo, stop him!"

She watched Alonzo run toward the stable man, who appeared half crazed at thought of the animal trapped inside. As soon as Valdéz had been dragged back to safety she flung herself from the saddle and made her way toward the burning homes.

"Leave the table!" she shouted in the ear of Ramirez' young wife. The heat from the fire seared her cheeks. In another minute the roof would fall.

"No! We shall have nothing!" screamed the distraught young woman as Catherine tried to pull her away.

Another woman appeared from the fringes of the fiery nightmare to aid Catherine in her efforts.

"It is the child inside her which crazes her!" she shouted, taking the pregnant woman's arm.

"Are you Sandoval's wife?" Catherine raised her voice to the breaking point to be heard above the fire. When a nod gave her the answer to her question, she asked, "Is everyone out?"

Señora Sandoval nodded again. Two young children held her tightly by the hand and two slightly older pressed near her. Tears were streaming down the woman's face.

Catherine cuffed the hysterical woman between them on the ears to stop her struggling.

"You will do as I tell you," she ordered sharply.

When they had retreated to safety, Señora Sandoval, gasping, said:

"Valdéz's youngest son ran to your house to tell you of this tragedy. Señora Valdéz, her daughter, and one of mine also went there. God willing, they are safe."

"They are safe," said Catherine grimly. Behind her she heard the groan of timber. As she turned, the roof of the stable over which her husband had labored so many hours fell in a shower of cinders.

Beside them Valdéz knelt, weeping. "The stallion you bought is gone, Doña Catherine. But a month we had him, and he's gone. Everything is gone!"

In a daze Catherine looked at the hungry flames which now were finding less to feed them. The enterprise for which she had urged Rodrigo to borrow money lay in ashes. The stable men who had depended on it for their livelihood had lost not only that, but their homes as well. She felt the sudden weight of being *la patrona,* Doña Catherine, the one to make decisions.

"Valdéz . . . Ramirez . . . Sandoval. Bring your families to my house tonight," she said, shouldering her authority. "Tomorrow, if you choose, you may go to the *encomienda.* I cannot pay you wages, but there is land there for growing food; there is game. You can build homes and own them. I will see that you have goods for clothing and seeds for planting."

There was a silence. Valdéz raised his careworn face.

"Doña Catherine, you are generous. You owe us nothing—"

"Then it is settled. Ramirez, your wife will not be able to make the trip, with a child so near. She will stay with me until it arrives. Valdéz, I shall need another pair of hands in my household. If your daughter wishes to train as a maid, I shall pay her."

Turning, she walked quickly toward her horse, afraid lest they see in her face the anxiety she was feeling. Alonzo overtook her, catching her horse's reins as Catherine swung into the saddle.

"Catherine, do you know what you are promising them?" he demanded. "You are making yourself responsible for them. Do you think it prudent?"

"How can I do otherwise? They have nothing left in the world."

She could not own to the thought which haunted her, the thought that Rodrigo's future and hers had also been seriously taxed by this disaster. All that stood between them and financial ruin were the two white foals at the *encomienda*. In the silent dawn she breathed a prayer for their safety—and Rodrigo.

24

Two days after the fire Ramirez' young wife died in child-birth. Once her hysteria had vanished she had remained an empty shell from which all hope had vanished. She did not touch the delicacies Catherine ordered prepared for her; she did not respond when cloth was brought for a new dress for her; she did not even speak until her birth screams started. When they fell silent, Catherine, who had held her hands through the whole of labor, rose grimly and went to the window.

"Wrap the child and fetch a wet nurse," she ordered Magdalena. "Señor Ramirez has lost much; he must not lose his daughter as well."

But a fortnight later the infant girl also lay dead.

Long after the Mass for the tiny soul, Catherine sat alone in the cathedral. There was no God to pray to, no Holy Mother, only this violent, brutal world wherein the innocent like the two she had so recently seen laid to rest, must suffer.

"The fire was no accident," she said aloud.

She knew the three men who tended the stable would not have been so careless as to carry in a lantern. The danger to their own homes would have prevented it, had habit not. And the weather had not been uncommonly dry of late. She recalled the strange smile of satisfaction on Don Luis's face that night when he encountered her. Having failed to persuade de Silva to bring charges against her, he had resorted to the fire instead. And in the fire her proof of Don Luis's dealings in *encomiendas* had perished.

Mid-June arrived. Catherine sat in the *sala familiar* one morning, the account book open before her. All at once she became aware of a commotion on the gallery. Alonzo Sanchez burst into the room, his expression alarming.

"Catherine, there is trouble," he said. "My manservant was in a wineshop, and while there he overheard conversation between another man and a clerk of the Audencia. The clerk said a warrant had been signed to claim the horses at your husband's *encomienda*."

Catherine gasped. "What? That cannot be! Surely they cannot take Rodrigo's horses because I helped Leonor!"

"No, no. The charge is that your husband failed to supply the missionary priest required, and that the *encomienda* itself is therefore forfeit."

Reeling beneath the news she stared at him. Each *encomendero* was required by law to supply a horse and arms for battle, a house in town where soldiers could be quartered, and a missionary priest to instruct the Indians on the lands in his control. She could not think of a single land holder who had met the last requirement.

Magdalena had left them. Alonzo stepped toward her. His hands reached out to encircle her shoulders and she did not resist.

"I am sorry," he said. "Oh, Catherine. Catherine, my darling!"

He pulled her against him with a force which in all her world just then was the only tangible thing. His lips met hers hungrily. Alonzo's arms were around her waist, desiring her, protecting her, and Catherine felt her own lift and cling tightly to his neck. She closed her mind to the voice which cried that this was wrong, feeling nothing but this blissful closeness.

"Catherine, my darling, I will go before the Audencia if you desire. I will take the warrant to court. But if you only knew how it pains me to see you forever harassed—forever denied the safe and certain future which you deserve. I swear it is driving me mad! I love you, Catherine, and I know you do not love Valdivia. Come away with me. Let me take care of you. Let me give you a life in which you will never be alone or frightened."

Catherine felt the force of his love surround her. She longed to respond. She had been lonely and frightened and now was not. But the memory of Rodrigo's hurt and angry face rose before her, and she extricated herself from Alonzo's arms.

"I have disgraced him before his friends, I have lost his stable. I cannot lose the horses too. You must not go before the Audencia on our account. It would likely do no good. The safer course is for me to ride to the *encomienda* and see that the men hide the horses."

She turned toward the door as she spoke. Alonzo caught her.

"I will go—not you. Draw me a map."

"A map would be little use. The *encomienda* is small. You could not find the way unless you had been there."

"Very well, then I will go with you."

"You cannot! Think of the scandal!"

"Have I not made it plain I do not give a damn about scandal? Take Ana. With or without your permission, Catherine, I will go with you. I will no longer stand by while you manage alone."

Catherine stepped lightly into the saddle. She saw the worried face of Magdalena. It was unthinkable to do as she was doing, but all that Rodrigo had worked for rested now on those horses. She must make the attempt to save them. Even if her husband never spoke a gentle word to her again. Even if all Lima saw her ride out with another man. Biting her lips, she smacked her horse on the flank and rode blindly toward the gate Mateo was opening.

They did not speak until they were free of the town, until they reined their horses to rest them in the narrow ribbon of grass which followed the Rimac River. On either side, within their view, the grass gave way to a dry, barren coast.

"How far?" asked Alonzo.

Catherine shook her head. "We might reach it by nightfall."

Even as she spoke she knew it was not possible. When she had made the trip with Rodrigo it had taken two good days. Even riding hard they could not make it in one. Not handicapped by Ana's slowness, not leaving when the sun was well established above the horizon. Her only comfort was her hope that whoever had been sent to take the horses would be well behind, traveling more slowly.

They set off with Catherine and Alonzo riding abreast, Ana trailing behind them. From time to time her mistress glanced back to find her clinging grimly to the saddle. Ana could keep her seat; their long-ago ride to Callao had taught Catherine that. But the maid's misery was evident in every line of her body. By mid-morning Catherine was ready to rest, and she knew Ana must be aching as she had done when she made the trip with Rodrigo. They climbed down to drink from the cold waters of the Rimac and then took to the horses again until the sun was high overhead when they stopped for lunch.

I have never seen such a wild, empty land, thought Catherine as she sat eating a slab of bread and cheese from the provisions Magdalena had so hurriedly assembled. They could sit here for weeks—months, perhaps—and no one would pass them. After the noise of Lima she welcomed the silence, and the sweet smell of the breeze which teased her hair.

She and Alonzo spoke to each other but awkwardly. They had come abruptly from those uncontrolled moments in the privacy of the *sala familiar* to duty, and she could feel the tension of having things unresolved between them. They avoided each other's eyes.

When they rose to continue their journey, Alonzo spoke to her.

"Catherine," he said, his voice kept low to avoid Ana's ears. "I promise to speak no more of the things I said this morning until your *encomienda* is once more secure. But will you think on what I have asked you? Say you will."

"I will think on it," she said with pounding heart. Rodrigo did not love her. Had he not told her so? And yet. . . . She closed her eyes. And yet she longed for the sight of him as she had never longed for anything else.

By the time the sun was low behind them, she reckoned them to be well over halfway on their journey. The desert which had lain beyond the valley margins so empty of vegetation was giving way to patches of grass and herbs and sometimes a tree. It was next to such a tree, no higher than her shoulder, where they eventually halted for the night.

"Oh, señorita, I do not think I will be able to go on another day," whimpered Ana, sliding stiffly to the ground.

"You are doing uncommonly well, Ana," reassured Alonzo. "It is rare to find a lady's maid who can ride for any distance, save for those serving royalty."

Ana's face brightened with the compliment, but her body indeed looked cramped with the unaccustomed ordeal.

"And you, Catherine, are you terribly weary?" Alonzo asked.

She smiled faintly.

"It has been no harder on me than on the horses. We've ridden them hard."

"In a moment you shall have a bit of shade to rest in," Alonzo promised, lifting down the bundle from behind her saddle.

It proved to be a small tent which he secured precariously against the tree. As the sky above them grew dark, Alonzo put dead wood together and built a fire over which he fried cured meat and slices of the native white tuber known as *batata* or potato. They ate in silence, a small, close group.

"You are most impressive in your camping skills," said

Catherine as Alonzo brought out a sheep's bladder filled with wine to finish the meal.

"I was trained in arms and the life outdoors. It was only the accident to my leg which made me an historian."

Catherine smiled at him. "Then that accident was most fortunate for all who would learn how this land was won. Have you had word of your manuscript? Will it find a sponsor at the court?"

"I have had a promising letter to that effect."

"I am glad of it."

Alonzo stirred the embers of the fire. "Every time a ship lands, every time I have news from Spain, or from Hispaniola, there is so much I long to share with you. . . ."

He stood abruptly, scattering the coals to safety with his boot.

"Sleep well," he said. "I will wake you at sunrise."

In mid-afternoon of the following day Catherine brought the sorrel gelding over a hill and knew with relief that she had found the *encomienda*. Two mud-brick houses, one of them larger than the other, squatted in the shade of a tree near a trickle of water. Next to them was the old corral for the Andalusians and a new addition which more than tripled its size. They rode toward the buildings and with joy her eyes picked out two graceful white foals beside their dams.

Sandoval saw them coming and shouted to the others. He came toward them, steps slackening with wonder as he recognized Catherine.

"Señora!" he exclaimed. "Doña Catherine!" His eyes traveled with unspoken question to Alonzo.

Behind them appeared his wife and their children and the rough-looking man originally hired as the *estanciero*. The latter had his arm around the waist of Sandoval's oldest daughter.

Catherine's hair was half loosened in a dozen places and blew untidily across her face.

"Sandoval, you must move the horses," she said, even as she slid from the saddle. "The Audencia has issued an order to take them, and perhaps this land as well. Señor Valdivia is still in the North, and that is why I bring the news myself."

Sandoval seemed to grasp all with a nod.

"There is a canyon with water where they can be left in safety," he said.

His wife held a wooden cup painted like some fearsome animal out to Catherine, and she drank gratefully from the

238

Indian vessel. Now for the first time she saw Ramirez. He had stood half hidden by the corral.

"It is Don Luis's doing," he said darkly. "This and the fire as well."

"Yes," said Catherine. "I believe you are right, Ramirez. We are his enemies. Perhaps it would be best for you if you decided to disassociate yourselves from us."

"Never!" declared Sandoval.

"We will die in the service of Señor Valdivia," said Ramirez.

Sandoval's wife spoke now. "Come into our poor house, señora. All that we own is yours. You must rest after such a long journey." As Catherine hesitated, looking from one house to the other, the woman indicated the larger one. "The other belongs to our oldest daughter and the *estanciero*," she said shyly. "They have married, and when a priest comes he will say words over them."

Alonzo, who had walked with them, touched Catherine's arm.

"I will go with the men," he said.

"Yes." Catherine turned and spoke to Sandoval. "This is Señor Sanchez, a trusted friend. These foals came from his stallion, and one will belong to him. Let him go with you."

There was no question of her authority. She entered the Sandoval cabin, where Señora Sandoval was pushing forward a crudely built stool. Ana, pressing hands to her rump, poised over another one. At sight of her mistress she hastily folded her hands in front of her and sat down.

"Where is Valdéz?" asked Catherine, collecting her thoughts now that she knew the horses were safe.

Sandoval's wife, with a great sigh, made the sign of the cross.

"He is gone, Doña Catherine. His wife died last week—her breathing had never been right since the fire—and he was greatly saddened. He was not a young man, señora. He grieved when he was forced to sell the stable, which he had labored so many years to own. Then, when it burned, why that was almost more than he could bear. His wife. . . ." She shook her head.

"But—did he come to Lima?" asked Catherine, shocked. "His daughter works for us. Surely he would have brought word."

"I think he did not know where he was going or why," said Señora Sandoval. "They tried to stop him, Ramirez and my husband, but all his sense seemed gone. He grieved."

"I am so sorry," said Catherine softly. Ramirez' wife and daughter . . . Valdéz' wife . . . it was too much tragedy for such loyal people to bear.

"It is the way of things," said Señora Sandoval. "Birth and death, and in between much misery." She paused for a minute before she added, with that recurrent shyness which overtook her when she seemed to recollect that Catherine was not just another stable man's wife, "Señora Valdéz spent her last days happy. It is peaceful here, a beautiful place."

"Yes," said Catherine, and mist seemed to blur her vision.

It was late afternoon when at last she freed herself on some excuse and climbed alone to the high ridge where she had stood long ago with Rodrigo. Down below her she could see the cottages of the Sandovals and the *estanciero* who had claimed their daughter as wife. Already the roots of life were going down here, spreading out. Marriages were being made, a single, solid unit was being forged, and she could only wonder: Would she ever be a part of it?

She put a hand to her cheek, remembering the feel of Rodrigo's touch when they had stood here together. How her heart ached for him, longed for him. Why was it only when she stood here, lonely and estranged from him by her own actions, that she could admit to herself she loved him?

The enormity of that admission shook her to the core. She sat down on a rock and locked her fingers together to stop their trembling. Down below she watched four riders come into view, Alonzo and the stable men returning. How ironic this dance of life was, she thought, that she should choose to love a man who would never return such a sentiment, who perhaps in his heart now bore an actual hate for her. And it had been a choice, she realized, completely voluntary. His arrogant pride, which so exasperated her, kept him unbowed; his mocking stripped the world of its pretenses. It would be easier to love a lesser man than Rodrigo de Valdivia, but she did not want to. The misery of their alienation permeated her like the growing chill from the snow-capped mountains at her back.

They left at dawn for the homeward trip.

"Christ's nails!" wailed Ana as her rump touched the saddle.

"Ana!" gasped Catherine in shock. "Wherever did you hear such an expression?"

"The *estanciero* used it often, and it seems quite meet," said Ana sullenly.

"Well, you'll have no supper for a week if I hear it again!"

They had ridden for several hours when ahead of them, coming toward them, two dots appeared. Men on horses.

"The Audencia's men?" asked Catherine, turning to Alonzo.

"Most probably. Other traffic through this valley seems unlikely."

They had halted at the sight of the other riders. Catherine looked at the rough terrain beyond the valley.

"Will they have seen us, do you think?"

"I would guess so. If we stray from the trail the going will be rough for us, impossible for Ana. I think we have no choice except to continue."

They rode in silence watching the unknown riders. The men coming toward them were riding with great speed, pushing their mounts as Catherine would not dare push her own even if she were confident Ana could match her pace. After twenty minutes an unspeakable terror began seeping into her. One of the horses ahead of them seemed unusually large. Her fingers grew icy as she stared into the distance. Suddenly she reined.

"That is Rodrigo on Boabdíl," she whispered, sick with certainty.

Alonzo looked at her. She knew he was sharing her own thoughts about the dangers of being discovered out here together. A man more even-tempered than Rodrigo would draw his sword over such a matter.

"There will be no trouble," Alonzo promised. "Come. Let's meet them."

The two of them put their horses to breakneck speed, while behind them Ana shrieked and attempted to hold her own horse in check. Catherine's gaze fixed on her husband's form. She had longed for his return, yearned for it, prayed for it, and now she felt nothing but fear. As they drew nearer, she saw with surprise that the rider with him was Diego Berruguète. In a hot stretch of grass with no trees to shade them, the four of them came together. But a few yards separated them. They regarded one another in silence.

Rodrigo's fist curled tightly on Boabdíl's reins. His face was hard. He did not look at Alonzo at all, but at his wife.

"I had been told that I would find you thus," he said. "I'd hoped it was not true."

Catherine drew a quivering breath.

"The Audencia had issued a warrant for our horses. I was determined we should not lose them. I came to tell the men to hide them, and Don Alonzo insisted Ana and I should not make the trip unaccompanied."

Diego Berruguete gave a disbelieving shake of the head.

"Upon my honor, Valdivia, there can be no such warrant. Surely I would have heard of it from my cousin Cepeda. If you care to inquire—"

"You lie," said Alonzo hotly.

"Alonzo! Please don't!" said Catherine, as he moved to urge his horse forward, his face livid with anger as he looked at Diego.

Alonzo jerked his reins and his horse reared slightly. With uncustomary bluntness he addressed himself now to Rodrigo.

"A clerk of the Audencia spoke of the warrant in a public wineshop. When you went North you left your wife without so much as a male servant to look after her. She had no one to protect her on such a trip as she proposed. We have been accompanied by her maid, Valdivia, and if you choose to see anything amiss in what we have done, you do your wife a grave injustice."

It seemed an eternity since Rodrigo had spoken, and it was his reaction which everyone awaited. Catherine watched the animosity deepen in his eyes as they played over Alonzo, assessing, studying. Alonzo sat straight, his countenance equally hostile.

"Ana's loyalty to her mistress is quite complete," Rodrigo said in scathing tones. "She would support my wife in anything she thought might bring her happiness."

Alonzo's mouth tightened dangerously.

"It pains me, Valdivia, to be the one responsible for bringing this to your attention," Diego Berruguete said with lofty politeness. "However I should have been less than a man had I not told you, with the whole city talking about it."

A sharp crack sounded in the morning air as Rodrigo's arm swept out to strike Diego across the face, throwing him from the saddle. Diego lay for a moment too stunned to move while Rodrigo, white lipped and shaking with the effort of control, looked down at him.

"Do you not suppose I can see how you've arranged this?" he growled. "You and Luis de Alvarado, most likely. How convenient that I was chosen to return and report Pizarro's progress to the Cabildo. What luck that you chanced to meet me as I rode into town, and with great reluctance implied I would not find my wife at home—leaving Magdalena to substantiate your story. Be glad I do not kill you for the way you have manipulated all of this with your lies."

In disgust he turned his horse away from all of them. Braced like some snarling animal about to spring, Diego Berruguete leaped to his feet, drawing his sword. As if catching the slight sound of movement which heralded danger, Rodrigo looked back. His boot flew out to send his attacker's weapon flying.

"Don't flatter yourself that I would cross swords with you," he said in scorn. "You're not worth my efforts."

He did not look at Alonzo or at Catherine.

"Ana," he said sharply. "You and your mistress will come with me."

25

Rodrigo looked in silence on the ashes and charred bits of timber which once had been his stable. His manner was rigid, closed, indifferent to Catherine's presence behind him. On his forehead, half covered by the black hair tumbling over it, a small pink scar gleamed fresh and new, reminder of the war which he had left.

Catherine watched the bitterness deepen in lines around his mouth. Three hundred *escudos,* one-third their annual income, had been wasted. His countless hours of labor had been wasted. There would be no fine new horse from Spain this year, no new investments. They would be lucky to have food and shelter.

She wanted to say, "I will stand beside you." But how would that seem now? He would take them for the words of an errant wife attempting to make amends, not the sheer outpouring of love which she intended.

"Two of the horses were saved," she said.

They had ridden together to Lima, making camp, riding again, all without speaking. She wanted to cry out to him, to tell him she had done no wrong, but her heart was heavy with the assurance he would not believe her. His words to Diego Berruguete suggested his realization that she had been tricked into her trip to the *encomienda,* yet he would not forgive her the company of Alonzo Sanchez, nor deem it innocent, she felt certain.

"Ramirez and Sandoval took the horse to the *encomienda,*" she added as his silence continued. "I told them they might take their families there to live. I told them they might build homes. There seemed nothing else to do. They had lost so much."

He barely glanced at her, neither approving nor condemning.

"There were no lives lost, then?"

"No—not then." Inside her something stretched close to breaking. She began to shake as she recounted the griefs and losses which she had shared in the weeks since the fire—griefs which she had been unable to confide in anyone. "Ramirez' wife died in childbirth not many days later. We worked to save her, Ana and I, but we could not." She forced back hysterical tears which wanted to come, shoved them deep inside her. With a breath she made her voice steady, though it was filled with the hollowness she now was feeling. "The baby died too. Valdéz lost his wife. Now his mind has snapped and the others do not know where he has gone. I shall have to break that news to his daughter when we return, for she works in our household now."

For a moment her husband's eyes were on her face. Then with unwonted sharpness he turned his horse.

Magdalena and her son stood back quiet and tense on their arrival. Young Belita Valdéz did not even venture out of the kitchen, hovering, instead, in the door beside the kitchen maid.

I shall have to tell her about her parents, Catherine thought again. But she was too weary now. Surely such unwelcome news could wait.

"Build up your fire, Magdalena," ordered Rodrigo. "Send up the tub and bring hot water. I want a bath." Without another word to anyone he led Boabdíl toward the stable.

From her room, as Ana undressed her, Catherine heard the sounds of the tub arriving and then the water. Mateo's voice raised in a question and his master answered shortly. Her eyes burned with unshed tears. Never had she longed so for Rodrigo's arms around her. She would welcome his anger, cruelty, anything but this awful silence.

When she had washed away the dust of travel and put on fresh clothes, the room beyond her own had fallen quiet. Señor Valdivia, Magdalena informed her, had ridden out. Catherine lunched alone and then in the sala settled down to watch the slow passage of hours. Would it have been better for her to risk the horses (believing them in danger, as she had) than to be discovered in another man's company, she asked herself.

At mid-afternoon Catherine sent for Belita Valdéz. The girl received the news of her mother's death with bowed head.

"And my father?" she asked in a whisper. "Why didn't he bring me this news?"

Catherine felt drained, unable to break the news of further tragedy and give the comfort which must go with it.

"He grieves too," she answered. "He needs time alone to reconcile himself to God's will. Be patient and I am sure he will come to you."

Dusk came, and with it the sound which for so many months had been absent from the household, the sound of its master returning. Catherine went onto the gallery and waited. She must speak about her ride with Alonzo, even if Rodrigo reviled and scorned her for it. She must end this terrible silence between them.

Rodrigo came from the stable and climbed the stairs. His eyes flicked over her without feeling. He went into the sala and she followed, but he had placed his back between them. He poured himself a cup of wine and went to stand looking out at the street.

"Tell Magdalena to send up dinner," he said. "I'm hungry."

His manner was so forbidding that Catherine didn't dare raise the subject of Alonzo. Disheartened, she ordered dinner.

Rodrigo ate with appetite, compensating, she supposed, for the dreary soldier's fare which had sustained him in the North. He drank often from his wine cup. His face was filled with dark thoughts. Catherine's thumb moved nervously up and down the stem of the silver goblet given them by Pizarro.

"Rodrigo," she said in low tones. "I must explain—"

"I have asked no explanations," he cut in with barely checked force.

"But you don't understand—"

"I understand all too well."

He made an impatient gesture and Belita Valdéz moved forward to refill his plate. Catherine was choked into silence.

After dinner, Rodrigo strode down the stairs and toward the stable. Time passed—enough for him to have brushed Boabdíl and seen him comfortable for the night. Still he did not return. At length Catherine went into the sala and stood, as he had done, at the *mirador*.

She did not hear him behind her until he spoke.

"Catherine."

She turned to find him standing in the doorway. The length of the room lay between them. His face looked tired. Set.

"What has happened was in part my fault," he said. "I rode off in anger . . . left you alone . . . made it impossible for you to notify me of your troubles. There is no undoing what has passed. We will never speak of it again."

Her heart twisted inside her. He was forgiving her, believing her guilty when she was not.

"But—"

He cut short her protest.

"Never again," he said.

He had a cape about his shoulders. He was going out. Swinging abruptly around, he left the room.

In misery Catherine sat at the tedious party, listening to the praise of her husband's report to the Cabildo. What a joke of fate, she thought, that when Rodrigo had almost certainly been brought back by the treachery of Don Luis he had distinguished himself at the task conceived as a ruse.

A week had passed since Rodrigo's return. He spoke to her rarely, and didn't come to her room. She had lost his trust, first by the way she had manipulated him to help Leonor, and then by being discovered in Alonzo's company. There in a roomful of music and candlelight and gaiety, she cursed herself even more bitterly.

A woman appeared in the door of the Palacios Rubios' sala and waved brightly to Alma, who rose to receive her. Catherine's heart sank even further, for it was Francisca.

"Ah, Catherine, I am relieved to see you have finally corraled this husband of yours for an evening," she sang, coming toward them. She wagged a finger at Rodrigo. "You, *hombre*, are a naughty one to risk such great sums playing at cards. This is a much more fitting place for a gentleman."

There were chuckles of admiration for Francisca's gay vivacity and she turned away for introductions. Catherine met her husband's eyes to find them hard and challenging.

There was much merriment after Francisca's arrival. Catherine strove to be a part of the general conversation and to answer questions. She had never expected Rodrigo to love her. Even now she couldn't complain that he mistreated her in any way. Yet she bled inside with Francisca's revelations.

Rodrigo, who seldom enjoyed parties, was late in signaling their departure. As they walked through the darkened streets, Catherine could not bring herself to mention the gambling. That Rodrigo would knowingly risk his home, the Andalusians he had bought so dearly, left her stricken. The knowledge that Francisca was intimate with him cut deeper still. And I have brought him to all of this, she thought. Her grief was blacker than the night around them.

They reached their own door and climbed the gallery steps together. Rodrigo turned away into the sala without speaking. From the darkness Catherine watched him, a lump in her throat, thinking how handsome he was even now, unsmiling. He took down a bottle of rum and poured liberally into a cup. She continued to her room.

After Ana had undressed her, as she lay sleepless staring at the velvet canopy above her, Catherine heard her door ease open. With loudly beating heart she saw Rodrigo. He stood for a moment looking at her, then moonlight shone silver on the back of his head as he turned away. The door beneath his hand crashed closed with a violence which echoed through the sleeping house.

"Señor Valdivia wishes to see you," announced Magdalena.

Catherine put down the new undersleeve she was embroidering. Apprehension filled her. No one in her household ever came to her room in the hour after lunch.

Rodrigo stood in the *sala familiar,* one arm atop the *vargueno.* His eyes were shaded. Catherine waited fearfully for him to speak.

"Why didn't you tell me that you had been called before Don Luis?" he asked. "That you were threatened with arrest?"

"I—didn't see what purpose it would serve," she answered with downcast eyes.

"You found it easier to go to Alonzo Sanchez?"

She winced. "You were far away," she said in a low voice. "And I did not know. . . ."

There was silence as her words trailed away.

"If I would care?" asked Rodrigo with sudden vehemence. "By God, Catherine, you are a fool!"

She looked up quickly to catch his expression, but he had crossed the room. The movement seemed inadequate to contain his anger.

"We are husband and wife, however much we may regret it," he said bitterly. "Our fortunes are one. Have no doubt I will come whenever you call on me." He paused. "Magdalena, who has told me all this, also says that Don Luis is responsible for the loss of our stable. Do you agree?"

"Yes—"

"And he is without a doubt the one who spread the rumor our *encomienda* would be seized."

"Yes. . . ."

In their past conversations she had fancied herself his equal. Now she felt herself swept aside.

"Well, he'll not have the chance to do so on even the smallest pretext. I will engage a missionary priest exactly as the law requires, even if I am the only one in a thousand leagues to do so."

"But we cannot afford a priest!" said Catherine, her voice finally breaking.

He spun around to face her. "But we can! I have made great profits from cards since my return. I will make more."

She choked back the protest which formed on her lips and faced him with tears in her eyes.

"What troubles you, doña?" He looked at her with cynical restraint. "Do you think it an unfitting way for a gentleman to earn money? I remind you I'm no gentleman. Or are you afraid that we will lose all and have to beg bread? Let me assure you, in that case, that I use the same plan which served me so well in the old days. Half of my winnings are saved; only the rest is risked in the making of more money."

Catherine looked away from him.

"The *encomienda* would not be in danger had I not challenged Don Luis," she said after a space. "When I was called before him I discovered proof that he was selling *encomiendas*. I told him I would publicize it if he bothered us further. All this in the end is my fault."

Rodrigo did not answer immediately.

"We both have opposed him," he said. "I should have killed him when I had the opportunity. Perhaps God will deliver me a second chance. In the meantime our only safety lies in becoming rich and powerful."

Catherine raised her eyes to his. How could he even dream of such a thing? Unless his winnings had been extraordinary, their household would barely survive if they took on the extra expense of a priest.

Rodrigo searched her face.

"Go and rest until dinner," he ordered. "You have grown too thin. If you were to carry a child now, it would kill you."

Catherine put a trembling hand to the *vargueno* as he walked from the room. Was he apprehensive that she carried Alonzo's child? Or had he begun to worry, as she had, that after a year and a half of marriage she had not conceived?

26

"Your husband must tire quickly of cards. When we are putting out our candles we see him walk almost nightly down our street toward Calle San Juan—out for a breath of air before returning home, no doubt."

Elvira Berruguete looked at her shyly outside the silk shop where they had met. Francisca's house was on Calle San Juan, and by the satisfied look on Elvira's face she suspected the other girl knew it. Was her tale the truth or a malicious lie?

Elvira's words gnawed at her heart as she and Ana made their way home through dusty streets. A man was expected to stray from his marriage bed; it was the way of things. And she had given Rodrigo more reason than most. Still it crushed her to think of him with Francisca. She had wanted—for so long—to touch his life, to be something more than proof of his rise from bastard stable boy to man of property, and she had failed.

Nearly three months had passed since Rodrigo returned, enough time to assure him she did not carry Alonzo's child. Yet neither did she carry his. In desperation she had gone to Doña Isabella and asked about the rumored Indian draught which could make a woman conceive. Perhaps if she gave Rodrigo an heir. . . .

But Doña Isabella's draught had little chance to prove its worth. Rodrigo rarely came to her, and then only when he'd been drinking rum.

Magdalena did not meet them at the gate when they came in. As Catherine looked around, puzzled, the housekeeper came from the kitchen wiping her hands. A faint frown of worry showed against the smoothness of her face.

"Señor de Valdivia bid me to tell you he will not be home for the rest of the day," she said. "He may, in fact, be gone until tomorrow. Word came from the León that Captain Rojo had ridden in quite crazy with a fever. Señor de Valdivia has gone to be with him."

Catherine caught her breath. Was there no end to troubles? Rojo was her husband's closest friend.

"Ana, fetch some squares of linen," she said. "I will get my chest of medicines. We must go at once and see if we can help."

Catherine had never set foot inside an inn before. It reeked of sour wine and onions, the odor of years undisturbed by ventilation. Many men sat around its long planked tables, for it was midday and time for lunch. She saw them look at her, and here and there, on the faces of travelers no doubt, a grin appeared. But they were quickly squelched. She was recognized as Rodrigo de Valdivia's wife, and none was eager to offend him.

The innkeeper, who had been brought out to meet them by an Indian boy in return for a piece of silver, ushered them up a dark stairway and down a hall. Catherine heard the whispered scurrying of rats on every side.

"Here is the room, señora," said the innkeeper, knocking at a door and then standing back. Catherine crossed the threshold.

The stench of the room was unbearable. Sickness, filth, and oppressive stuffiness seemed to press in on her. Her dancing senses were aware of Rodrigo's voice, and then his arm was encircling her shoulders.

"Open the window," she whispered. "How can you expect a man to recover in such a foul place?"

He led her to the room's single window and threw it open. She drew great breaths of the welcome air.

"You shouldn't be here," her husband said. "And Rojo is fevered. We must not chill him. Come, I'll see you outside."

His words sounded gentler than they had in months. Catherine put a hand out to his arm.

"You will not cure a fever by smothering him," she said. She looked about her now and saw Rojo's large form stretched on a matted bed of hay. His eyes were closed. On the floor beside him sat a bowl of greasy broth not fit for pigs. "Nor will you cure him with food such as that," she continued with greater firmness. "I had thought some of these medicines might strengthen him, but in a place like this I fear they would have little avail. We must move him to more favorable surroundings—to our own house."

Rodrigo stared at her a moment. His head moved back and forth.

"He was scarcely able to find his way to this inn. He hasn't spoken since I came. We cannot move him."

"We must!" She sought his eyes urgently. The red-bearded man who lay oblivious to their conversation had been kind to her. It appalled her to even think of leaving him here. "Rodrigo, I often nursed my father. I have been to tend the sick with the marquesa. I know what I am speaking of—the seeds of who-knows-what diseases are in this room. In a man of weakened condition they can easily take root."

Her husband's expression was bleak.

"But surely it would be injurious to him getting him on a horse."

"Indians can be found to carry him on a pallet."

Rodrigo looked a moment at his friend. "All right," he said with a sigh of relief. "Go ahead, then. I'll arrange it."

Within a few hours the unconscious Rojo was installed in a room in the servants' wing, as there was no guest room. The bed which had been hastily improvised was much thicker and cleaner than the one he had at the León, and cloths wrung out in water aromatic with Catherine's herbs lay on his forehead. With a spoon Magdalena trickled herb-infused wine known as Hippócrates into his half-open mouth.

"Let us hope he has only drunk some bad wine," said Catherine. "He is a strong man. He should recover."

In spite of the confident words she was worried. The cloths on Rojo's forehead grew rapidly dry. In her husband's eyes she saw an expression of helpless fear, and as she wrang out fresh cloths for the man beside her, she prayed.

When Magdalena left, it was as if she and her husband were alone. Catherine was uncomfortably aware of their confinement together in the quiet room. Rodrigo stood restlessly by the window, the vitality of his body availing nothing as he waited. The two of them had been suddenly allied by their concern for Rojo; they had spoken openly to each other. Now the situation was somehow awkward. Rodrigo's eyes met hers for an instant and then looked quickly away.

Catherine felt as she had on those now distant nights when Pizarro's courtiers had come for secret meetings. Her nerves were drawing together, awaiting calamity. From under lowered lashes she watched Rodrigo. The need to comfort him, to touch him, was almost overwhelming. Catherine ripped the linen beside her into squares—more than she would need to treat a dozen illnesses like Rojo's—anything to stop this trembling inside her, this longing.

By late afternoon the sick man was no better. Catherine rose and picked up the basin of water which she had used to cool his head. Immediately Rodrigo was beside her.

"What is it?" he demanded.

She smiled at him in reassurance.

"I am going to fetch fresh water, that is all. I didn't mean to alarm you."

She saw his shoulders relax.

"I will get the water," he said.

While he was gone she walked around the room's perimeter. She paused at the window. The spot where Rodrigo had stood seemed almost alive with his energy. Memories washed through her—memories of the feel of him, of the glistening darkness of his head beneath her fingers, of his lips against her flesh. The door behind her opened and she turned, caught unaware. She hurried to receive the basin.

As Rodrigo placed it in her hands their fingers met. His touch loosened reeling sensations and she jerked. The basin slipped. He steadied it, his hand coming up now to cover hers entirely. Her whole interior was filled with liquid fire.

Rodrigo's fingers pressed into her own. His eyes were filled with desire, and yet alongside it she saw anger too. They seemed welded to one another. Never had he looked so bitterly dejected.

"Perhaps this will help," she said, her voice small and dry.

She turned away with effort. After a moment's pause Rodrigo returned to the window. His back was toward her. Crossing his arms on the sill he bowed his head.

Neither of them touched the tray which Magdalena brought at dinnertime. By the light of the single taper brought in to banish darkness, Catherine saw the deepening lines of tension on her husband's face as he moved once again to stand looking down at the unconscious Rojo.

"Why don't you go to the cathedral?" Catherine asked somewhat tentatively. She had never ceased to marvel at the depth of her husband's piety. Perhaps in the darkened church he would find peace. At least he would have the comfort of knowing he had done all he could for Rojo.

Rodrigo hesitated. He shook his head.

"I would like to be here if there's any change."

"I cannot believe that God would claim him while you were away on such an errand," said Catherine.

He continued to look at the great, helpless form stretched out on a mattress of hay.

"Perhaps you are right," he said heavily. "I can do nothing here."

The night flowed on in an unbroken stream. Catherine sat alone with her thoughts. Twice she caught herself dozing, for the day had been a long one. The low stool on which she sat afforded little comfort. Yet she gladly accepted it as penance, if only Rojo's life would be spared.

Her husband's step was quiet when he returned. Catherine forced weary muscles into a smile.

"I believe he is somewhat cooler," she said.

Rodrigo did not answer. He drew up a stool across from her and watched as for a countless time she wrang out a fresh cloth for Rojo's head. Her delicate white hands were wrinkled from the water.

"I am very grateful for what you have done," he said.

Hot tears sprang to her eyes. Her hand shook and she was afraid to look at him. He thought ill of her, believed the worst of her a husband could believe of his wife, and she could not bear to have him see her love for fear he would despise it.

"Rojo has been a good friend to us both," she said, evenly.

For a moment, in the uncertain light of the candle, Rodrigo searched for something in her face. Then his own expression hardened.

"Yes," he said in leaden tones. "Now go and rest. I will watch the night with him."

At mid-morning of the following day, as Rodrigo dozed on a stool and Catherine bent over a piece of needlework, the man whom they had been watching opened his eyes. Catherine heard the rattle of breath in his throat and jumped up, dropping her sewing.

"By all the saints!" rumbled Rojo, blinking. "It's Doña Catherine, isn't it? And this is Doña Catherine's house!"

He looked around, bewildered.

Rodrigo, still half asleep, came to the bedside. Catherine put her hand to Rojo's forehead and gave a sigh.

"The fever has vanished. It is gone," she said.

Rojo, undeterred by Rodrigo's attempts to detain him, had pushed himself to a sitting position.

"But surely I remember riding into the León!" he growled.

"Doña Catherine thought such lodgings were beneath your dignity," Rodrigo told him, smiling in relief.

Rojo threw back his head and roared.

"I'll get you some broth," said Catherine, starting from the room.

"Broth!" her patient snorted with contempt. "Forgive me, Doña Catherine, but to a man like me such a diet promises more mischief than a fever. It is meat my belly wants—and bread!"

Catherine knew argument would be futile. A tray with pork and cheese and wine soon sat before the red-haired soldier.

Rojo ate voraciously. "Well, now, 'Rigo, it is well you sought me out," he said between mouthfuls. "The general sent me this cursed week's journey especially for the purpose of seeing you." He shoved a piece of bread into his mouth and winked at Catherine as he chewed. "What do you think of this husband of yours? In the midst of a war he sends word that matters detain him at home, and instead of reprimanding him, the general goes and names him a captain! He sends back orders for 'Rigo to raise a company of cavalry and train it. I swear, the general must be getting addled in the head."

Rojo belched and grinned, glad to be the bearer of this news.

Rodrigo received it in silence. The dark depths of his eyes were strangely clouded. Rojo, still grinning, reached out to thump the back of his open hand against Rodrigo's arm.

"Think on it, Captain Valdivia! You shall have a handsome share now of all we receive in the North."

"Yes," agreed Rodrigo slowly. "More than ever I am indebted to the general."

When Rojo had finished his meal Catherine ordered further rest for him. As he had drunk copiously of their wine, his protest was a weak one.

They left the room and bright, golden sunshine washed over them.

"I am glad for you," said Catherine. "Truly you deserve such an honor."

Her husband's shrug was impatient. "It will not take long to raise a company capable of defeating the unseasoned troops the viceroy has," he said. "I will begin at once to search for a manservant for you to rely on in my absence."

Catherine stood quietly, accepting the inevitable. They were as remote from one another now, by this gallery railing in the sunshine, as they would be when Rodrigo reined his horse in Quito, she thought with heavy heart.

"Perhaps . . . if Valdéz could be found. . . ." She let the suggestion go unspoken.

"His mind is gone," Rodrigo said.

"We don't know that for a fact. Even if it is, he still might serve us very well. He is a good man. He has suffered."

Rodrigo let his breath out noisily. She didn't know what it signaled. He crossed his arms and looked out over the court yard.

"Fray Ambrosio must be delighted with my promotion," he said, referring to one of the army chaplains. "He has been so certain that I should become a man of note that he was attempting to teach me to sign my name."

Lest voicing pleasure should make her seem too critical of his unlettered state, Catherine merely smiled at this infor mation. Rodrigo's face grew suddenly closed. Without another word he stalked down the stairs.

After three days Rojo left his bed. By the end of a week he was venturing into the courtyard, walking its length and cursing his lack of strength. Catherine welcomed his pres ence in the household, for it had made Rodrigo laugh again but that laughter was always quickly lost in brooding.

One evening the air felt especially hot and still after dinner. The two men played at cards in the sala while Catherine sewed. Each time she looked up she found her husband's gaze upon her. After a bit he got out a bottle of rum and poured liberally for himself and Rojo. Catherine's blood began to beat a question. Would he come to her tonight?

Without warning, after several games had passed, Rodrig tossed down his cards.

"It is too hot for this," he said shortly, "I am going out."

His retreating footsteps pierced the night like fatal swore thrusts. Rojo looked uncomfortably at Catherine as she tried to hide her own distress.

"That 'Rigo is such a restless one," said Rojo, recognizing the charged atmosphere in the household.

Catherine avoided his gaze. Anguish filled her. Dread Was it his belief in her betrayal which kept Rodrigo from her or was there more?

"It is warm," she said with forced calm. "I would desper ately like a breath of air myself. It is a fine night. Let us see how well your strength is mending by a walk."

Rojo's open face was flooded with relief.

"A fine idea," he said.

Catherine's feet seemed to turn down the streets of thei own accord. There was nothing to be accomplished by it bu further misery, she told herself. A street, a house reveale nothing.

She glanced up at Elvira Berruguete's darkened window as they passed. Calle San Juan was just a few yards away. Al at once Rojo seemed to comprehend her intentions. Catherine felt his steps slow. But he was a simple man, he couldn't think quickly enough to steer her another way, or perhaps he decided that any protest on his part would fuel her suspicions.

Francisca Griega's house sat halfway down the street. All its shutters were open, and one of the windows was lighted. Rojo cleared his throat noisily and started to speak. What he intended to say, Catherine never learned, for just then there came from the house a burst of deep male laughter, louder and heartier than any she had ever occasioned. Another followed it, and another. Francisca must be making Rodrigo quite merry tonight.

"Upon my word," blustered Rojo. "I had heard Francisca's husband was sick. Rodrigo must have looked in to see him."

"Yes," said Catherine, breaking at last the dazed paralysis which gripped her. She had wanted to be certain. Why, then, did the blow strike so deeply? "Forgive me, Rojo. I shouldn't have made you come with me. We can go now."

Rodrigo's laughter, almost lost in the night now, echoed again as they reached the end of the street.

"Believe me, Doña Catherine, you have nothing to fear from Francisca," said Rojo earnestly. "A man does not greatly value fruit from a tree where many eat. But you—Rodrigo prized you enough to make you his wife."

She was glad the rough Rojo could not see the tears cascading down her face.

"You are a good friend, Rojo," she said quietly.

In her own home Catherine drank a great draught of her husband's rum, but it produced in her none of the giddy thoughtlessness which it had on the night of the viceroy's overthrow. She still lay awake when the gate opened and she heard her husband's footsteps on the stairs. She tensed as they continued past his door, toward her own. Her nails dug into the sheets. She could not bear it if he came to her tonight.

The door opened. Catherine raised herself on trembling arm. She wanted to shout at him, to tell him to go back to Francisca; but more than anything she wanted him to come to her, that she might cling to the hope, however slim, that she might someday win him back.

Rodrigo came toward her with defiant step. His black curls tumbled in disarray across his forehead. There was a look of madness about him.

"Should I flatter myself that you were waiting for me?" he mocked.

Catching her by the chin he kissed her, tilting her head back so forcefully that a strangled cry escaped her.

"Well? Were you?" he insisted, his fingers tightening on her jaw as if they were about to break it. Recalling the night he had almost choked her, Catherine could only stare at him in frozen fear. His hand slipped to her throat and he shook her roughly. "By God, Catherine, there was a time you did! Admit it! Sanchez cannot have made you forget. Shall I show you again?"

He flung her back against the pillows. In the interval that her eyes were jarred shut and opened again, he was above her, breeches discarded. The thrusts of his thighs were bludgeon strokes, bruising her, violent.

"Say Sanchez could satisfy you as I do," he rasped. "Say it! God Himself would strike you down for such a lie. No woman has ever been indifferent to me, Catherine, not even you. I have made you love me because I won control of your body. Say it!"

She was sobbing, unable to speak. Soundlessly her lips shaped his name. Even now, when he was hurting her with body and words, she loved him. How could he come from Francisca's bed to hers?

His fingers writhed in her loosened curls.

"Confess that you love me, just as I have always said you would!" He shook her savagely. "Say it—or I swear I'll kill you!"

He gasped the words. Catherine, with a sudden calm, lay back and felt his seed flow into her. She was a fool. He cared nothing for her. He wanted only to destroy her pride. Her ears rang with the memory of his laughter at Francisca's house. Blinded by tears and anger she caught his shoulders and heaved with her whole body.

Rodrigo fell from her bed with a crash which shook the room. Catherine whipped onto her side, her hands forming fists.

"Then you had better kill me," she said, voice shaking. "How dare you even speak to me of love when you are fresh from the bed of that harlot! How dare you judge Alonzo and me when the whole town knows you go to her? Yes, kill me! That is the only way you know to measure victory!"

Her words fell in a torrent. Impressions piled one upon another. Rodrigo lay staring at her; she did not know if he would rise and strike her. There was a frantic knocking at the door.

"Señorita! Señorita, are you all right?"

The door flew open. Ana's eyes skipped from her mistress to the naked form of her master and she gasped. Rodrigo, cursing, fumbled for his breeches. Ana fled. He staggered to his room clutching his clothes.

Catherine sat upright, her chest pitching with erratic breathing. She could not undo the folly of falling in love with her husband, but never would she put such a weapon into his hands. Her tortured gaze fell on two items left behind in his haste. In an instant she was out of bed. She seized the boots and jerking wide the door to the gallery flung them savagely down into the darkness of the courtyard.

27

"I am told your husband drills his company until they are close to fainting," teased Alma de Palacios Rubios. "I am not sure that I can bear to watch."

She stood beside Catherine on a grassy field near the plaza. There, amid shouts and the rumble of hooves, Rodrigo was training the first of his recruits.

"Ah, but it is exactly that which is swelling his numbers," the marquis informed her grandly. "Captain Valdivia offers discipline—a far cry indeed from the motley armies usually raised in this land."

A sturdy Franciscan named Fray Isidoro laughed in merry voice. "Your pardon, my lord marquis, but I believe it is God who swells his numbers. Captain Valdivia gave a handsome sum to the church when his friend was delivered from illness, even though he is not a wealthy man. Seldom have I known a man more constant in his faith."

Catherine smiled faintly and looked at the other spectators. She hadn't expected such a crowd. In the days since she had met her husband's anger with her own, they had treated each other with strained politeness. She wasn't at all certain how he would look on her presence at the practice field, but Alma's invitation after Mass had been impossible to refuse. Alma's younger brother had enlisted in the company.

"I am amazed so many come to watch," said Catherine. "They've only been drilling a week."

"I'm amazed at the quality of his men," said the marquesa. "They are not rabble. Some come from the finest homes."

It was true. The company had lured volunteers exactly as some quest lured knights of old. Talk of it was heard in every public place, and clearly it had become a great entertainment. Catherine's throat tightened as she saw Rodrigo detach himself from a group of horsemen and ride toward her.

He wore the red sash of a captain across his cuirass. The polished armor caught the sun and Catherine put up a hand to shield her eyes.

"You have been to Mass?" he asked in greeting.

She nodded, spots of color rising to her cheeks. His manner in the last week had been one of extreme reserve. He was gone all day; returned and dressed in one of several fine new sets of clothes, inquired of her health, and then sat silently across the dinner table. Sometimes he stayed a while in the sala, but invariably he went out. The remedy furnished Catherine by Doña Isabella sat useless on a shelf.

"A fine-looking group of men," the marquis pronounced.

Rodrigo bowed to him. "Yes, my lord, but none of them experienced, I am afraid." He looked back toward Catherine. "There is shade at the other end," he said, indicating a tree. "If the marquis will escort you, we can easily move our exercises there."

She started to protest, but already he was gone. The marquis offered his arms to her and the marquesa. Alma and Doña Mercedes walked beside them and various maids came behind. Involuntarily Catherine's eyes swept through the crowd of merchants and working men standing near. There was no trace of Francisca.

"How handsome your husband is in his armor," said Alma gaily. "Are you not giddy to think the commander of all those men is yours alone?"

Catherine smiled grimly and rebuked the traitorous pain which sprang to her heart.

The men on the field before them used blunted weapons: swords made of wood and lances with flattened tips. Still Catherine felt certain that many would go home bruised and bleeding, as she watched Rodrigo divide them into two units which charged each other, hacking furiously. Alma gasped as her brother was all but unhorsed. On the edge of the field Rojo sat wagging his head. Catherine watched him wave some signal to Rodrigo and the skirmish ceased. Rojo trotted out to criticize one of the recruits.

Sometimes the members of the fledgling company struggled against each other. At other times Rodrigo formed them into even lines and led a unified charge, yelling out orders to wheel or fall back. The sun glittered on a sea of fluted helmets with upturned edges, for armor, too, was a tool of the soldier's trade and must be gotten used to. Juan Pizarro, an elder brother to the general, was said to have received his fatal wound because he had preferred a cool head to a head protected.

Catherine found herself staring in fascination as Rodrigo and Rojo rode out against each other to demonstrate some technique. This was her husband's business, his art. That he excelled at it was clear. The two men met with a jolt, and to her surprise she saw the much larger Rojo knocked sideways in the saddle by the contact.

"Now there is a soldier!" the marquis murmured, admiring the maneuver.

A few minutes later, amid a burst of laughter, Rodrigo's troops broke up and went their separate ways. Rodrigo and Rojo rode at a trot toward the little group beneath the tree. With the easy agility of one who had spent the morning resting, Rodrigo dismounted.

"Excellent! An excellent drill!" the marquis said.

Leading Boabdíl, Rodrigo fell into step with them as they walked back toward the plaza. He offered his arm to Catherine, and she steeled herself for the shock of physical contact, so long absent.

"Thank you, my lord marquis," said Rodrigo. "They weary quickly. Let us hope they will be refreshed by lunch." He addressed himself to Alma de Palacios Rubios. "Your brother has the makings of a very fine soldier, señora. He is a first-rate horseman and quick to learn."

He spoke from politeness more than from any natural enthusiasm, Catherine thought. More and more of late she noticed in his manner a labored courtesy. It sat on him as awkwardly as Ana sat a horse. Alma, however, brightened at the compliment.

"I confess your saying so reassures me. Seeing him on the field I cannot help but think how young he is."

Most of the spectators had dispersed, but here and there some stood in twos or threes still talking. As they walked along a silk-clad figure detached himself from one of the groups and Alonzo Sanchez came toward them. He wore a strained smile, and beneath his mild look lay the traces of determination which Catherine was beginning to recognize.

"I congratulate you on your training of a very fine company, Captain Valdivia," he said in greeting.

Rodrigo checked his stride and nodded stiffly.

"I will accept congratulations when they prove themselves in battle. A few men with experience in their ranks would make me easier."

The marquis and the others had halted a few steps ahead. Catherine, frozen to her husband's arm, watched Alonzo's eyes harden.

"Then perhaps you will not refuse me too quickly, Valdivia. I have come to enlist."

Rodrigo's mouth opened and then snapped shut on his intended comment.

"It is impossible."

Alonzo's gaze touched Catherine briefly and then met Rodrigo's.

"It would be wise for me to go, Valdivia," he said, voice lowered. "You can't deny that you feel the need of seasoned troops."

Catherine looked up at her husband. His eyes, beneath the scant shade of his helmet, were dark and troubled.

"You are a fine and spirited rider, Don Alonzo. I have no doubt your skill with weapons equals it. But I could not, in conscience, see you ride into battle—"

"You think my lameness a handicap?" Alonzo asked calmly.

Rodrigo flushed. "Your pardon for my bluntness, Don Alonzo, but it cannot be otherwise."

"Why do you not test me? Let us take to our horses before these impartial judges."

Catherine saw the marquis frown and watched Rojo scratch his beard. Rodrigo drew a breath.

"If that is what you wish," he said.

Catherine fell back with ambivalent thoughts and watched the two men take to the field. It was madness for Alonzo to return to war after all this time, with an unsound leg. Rodrigo was right to dissuade him. Yet she sensed Alonzo needed to prove himself. Not for me, she prayed. Not for me.

With the help of his Negro servant, Alonzo put on his armor. It was beautifully wrought and covered his arms to the elbow. The gleaming surface was smooth as a mirror, undented and unscratched. In comparison Rodrigo's sleeveless cuirass, though polished daily, looked shabby with use.

In the middle of the grassy field the two men conferred, then rode to opposite ends. Boabdíl charged forward at full gallop. Alonzo put his horse to a similar pace and met Rodrigo with wooden sword drawn. Their horses' hooves tore up chunks of turf as rider locked against rider. A dull metallic thud announced the long trough which now marred the surface of Alonzo's armor.

Catherine watched her husband's arm, aware now of the strength which drove his sword. She found no clue to his emotions in his face. It was intent and hard. He aimed a blow at Alonzo's neck and her breathing stopped for an instant. She realized that such a blow, even from a wooden sword, could be fatal. Did Rodrigo intend it to be? Was his hate of Alonzo deep enough to kill?

The brunt of the blow was deflected by Alonzo's swiftly moving weapon. The two men spun slowly around and around, their horses pushing against each other. Each of them now had landed blows.

"Don Alonzo makes an admirable argument for his abilities," said the marquis. "His arm is tiring, though. Rodrigo will soon force him to fall back."

Even as he spoke Alonzo wheeled his horse, dodged past Rodrigo's sword, and came charging at his adversary with lance in place. Rodrigo in a single movement sheathed his sword and urged Boabdíl to a gallop, grasping his own lance. With a cry of distress Ana hid her eyes.

Catherine could not. Hypnotized by fear she watched Rodrigo's lance take aim against Alonzo's shoulder. But as it struck, the long pole in Alonzo's hand also found its target on Rodrigo's breastplate. Both horses staggered backward at the impact. Rodrigo sat askew, half out of his saddle. The men reined quickly and climbed to the ground.

Alonzo stooped to retrieve the broken stirrup from Boabdíl's saddle. Too winded to speak, he handed it to Rodrigo.

"I cannot fault you on any count," said Rodrigo, breathing with difficulty. "You would be a welcome addition to any horse company."

Alonzo removed his helmet and wiped his forehead.

"May I have my captain's hand on it?" he inquired.

With obvious reluctance Rodrigo reached out and the two shook hands.

Catherine and her husband left the practice field as Alonzo received the compliments of all who had watched.

"You will need to order a new saddle quickly if it's to be finished before you go North," said Catherine in the strained silence about them.

Rodrigo looked down at the snapped leather holding the stirrup.

"There is no need for a new one. This one will mend."

"If one part has broken, another might break. It is not safe."

"The price of a saddle is also the price of another good mare," said Rodrigo grimly.

Catherine watched her husband's back as he stood in the *mirador*. This morning his shoulders had gleamed in yellow and crimson silk, resplendent as he drilled his men in uniforms of similar color. Pizarro had provided handsomely for this company, and in two more days they would be gone. The men in Lima would be allowed Christmas Day with their families and then ride North.

"Ana's suitor has not missed an evening this week," said Rodrigo without turning. "I swear, this must be getting serious."

Catherine looked up from the needle she was threading.

"A suitor! What are you talking about?"

A faint smile eased Rodrigo's mouth, long grown so serious, as he came to stand across from her.

"Señor Bocanegra, of course. Haven't you noticed?"

She sat staring at him, feeling entirely foolish.

"Ana is being courted? By our notary?" Suddenly she laughed. It was true that Ana had blossomed and become quite animated of late. Catherine had registered the fact yet she was so preoccupied with Rodrigo's departure, that she never questioned its cause.

Rodrigo smiled as he had not done in months. She laughed the harder.

"Come, come," he protested mildly. "The girl is attractive enough—when she is not sniveling."

They both laughed then. When the sound of their voices ceased, Catherine felt unaccountably shy. The labored politeness which they had shown one another since she threw Rodrigo from her bed had gradually relaxed. They treated each other with deference; but they did not share their thoughts as they had in this unguarded moment.

Rodrigo looked away quickly. "Let us go to Mass."

They received communion together, in the company of many men who soon would ride off with Rodrigo. The day had spent itself early, and when they returned home, it was golden with the glow of candles. Each moment was precious now, thought Catherine. Over dinner they spoke of business matters which would pass once again into Catherine's hands until her husband's return. Afterward they strolled into the sala, and she stood staring at the small fire burning on the hearth. The night was quiet, almost holy. She did not want Rodrigo to go to Francisca.

"You won't be here on Twelfthnight," she said, turning with a smile. "There is a gift for you. Let me get it now."

She went to a great footed cabinet, a handsome piece of furniture which Rojo had presented to them in gratitude for their hospitality during his illness. Her hands shook as she opened the door and reached inside. After spending hundreds of hours in the stitching of the tapestry intended for her husband, she had begun to fear his reaction to it if she made it seem a thing of great importance, so she had made it only the wrapping for a fine new sword of Toledo steel. She handed it to him without comment.

Rodrigo lay the cylinder on a table and unrolled it. The new sword gleamed in the candlelight. He nudged it aside. His fingers traced the pattern of the tapestry.

"The coat of arms of Granada," he said. His words came slowly as he looked down at it. He took her hand. "I can claim no family name, but I am glad to claim the city of my birth. It is lovely. You have labored long on it, and I am grateful." Raising her hand he kissed it lightly.

"Now here," he said, stooping for a bundle which he had retrieved from a trunk. He handed it to her and Catherine felt the fineness of the silk before she saw it. It was heavy, rich. "Open it and see if you like the color," Rodrigo instructed.

She placed it on the table which held his tapestry and unfolded it. As she did she gasped. Inside the silk lay a strand of milk white pearls.

"The price of a good mare," she said, looking up with tears in her eyes.

For a moment her husband was open and smiling as he had been of old. Then he seemed to change before her eyes.

He lifted the pearls and slipped them over her head.

"They become you," he said briskly. "Such jewels are fitting for a captain's wife. You shall have more of them."

Catherine heard with a pang of disappointment. The costly pearls were a gift to mark their status, then, not one which he had longed to give her. Even now he moved restlessly the length of the room.

"You—are not going out?" she asked as he neared the door.

He paused. "Do you wish me to stay?"

She struggled with the impulse to fly into his arms. He was making it plain the choice was hers, not his; that she meant nothing to him. With failing hope she clung still to a shred of pride.

"I wish that you might please yourself, of course. It occurred to me, however, that you might enjoy an evening of cards, though I confess I have grown rusty."

He stood for a long minute and she couldn't tell what he was thinking. At last he walked back toward her.

"Let us play cards, then," he said.

They played two hands and seldom spoke. When they had finished Rodrigo reached across the table and touched her fingers.

"We need stakes, Catherine," he said. "There is magic in our bodies, even if our hearts are bitterest enemies. I have acted the part of a gentleman these last months; I have not demanded a husband's rights. If I win now I will share your bed tonight and you will not resist. Do you agree?"

Wordlessly she nodded. Magic in their bodies? Yes. They were betrayed by their desires. Her heart was not his enemy, but she dared not tell him so. The cards before her blurred together.

Catherine called on the blessed Virgin and the Holy Father to let luck go against her. She played as badly as she could in stealth. When the game was finished Rodrigo uncertainly displayed three knaves.

"That beats two pairs," she said, and folded out of sight four queens.

Deep into the night she lay awake, her cheek pressed on her husband's shoulder. Her fingers touched the scar from the Indian spear. He stirred.

"Why did you ever link my love to a victory over me?" she whispered, knowing he did not hear. "Why, when I would yield you even that victory, do you go to Francisca? I am miserable with my pride, Rodrigo, but I would be more so without it."

"I do not understand a party such as this," Alma de Palacios Rubios confided as they strolled toward the marquesa and Doña Mercedes in the sala of the Berruguete house. All around them Christmas presents were being displayed. Rojo wore the red silk garters which Catherine and Ana had made him and Catherine wore her pearls. "Don Francisco isn't seeing his son off for the North tomorrow," Alma continued. "And from what I know of this family they are not great partisans of Pizarro's cause. What prompts this celebration?"

The mole on the marquesa's chin twitched with annoyance. "I suspect," she said as her eyes sought out Catherine's, "that the party honors Señor Sanchez."

Catherine looked quickly away. As if in confirmation of what the marquesa had said, she saw Cepeda, the Berruguetes' relative, stop and put a hand on Alonzo's shoulder. Cepeda. Don Luis's close associate. Alonzo. Soon a member of Rodrigo's company. Her stomach felt uncomfortable, as if Ana had laced her too tightly.

She was glad when Rodrigo returned to her side. Ever since their arrival his eyes had been on Don Luis. He started to speak, but just then the musicians who had been entertaining stopped playing. Don Francisco Berruguete stepped into the center of the floor, Elvira at his side.

"My friends," he said with aristocratic lift of the hands. "I trust you will join me tonight in wishing good fortune to the men who ride forth tomorrow in the service of General Pizarro."

Catherine saw Rojo grin roguishly at the flowery words.

"I ask you to wish the same," Don Francisco continued, "to my daughter Elvira and Don Alonzo. Their betrothal will be read tomorrow in the cathedral."

There was general jubilation in the room. Catherine, to her surprise, felt relief. She would have wished another bride for Alonzo, still she was glad for him. She turned to Rodrigo and found him looking at her.

"May I offer him our wishes for great happiness?" she asked. She saw his eyes darken. Impulsively she touched his arm, oblivious to people all around them. "I do not love him, Rodrigo," she said, her words too soft for any ears but his. "I have never loved him. I—I have never lain with him as you believe."

He searched her face slowly.

"Go and speak to him if you wish," he said at last. "I have never forbidden it."

Alonzo looked up from a group of well wishers at her approach. He had been watching her, Catherine thought, and tenderness spread through her. She valued Alonzo above all men save one, and yet it was true—she did not love him.

"Catherine," he said, seizing her hand. He turned quickly away from those who stood around him, his face bathed in a forbearing sadness which twisted Catherine's heart.

She pressed his fingers, then drew quickly away.

"I am glad for you, Alonzo. Truly glad."

He shook his head. "You asked me once to spare you congratulations on an unwanted match. I ask the same of you now. My heart is not in what I am about to do, but it is for the best. My father is growing old and has no sons but me. He is anxious to see a continuation of the Sanchez line."

"I shall pray love grows where you think there is none,"

said Catherine, moved to tears by his words. She started away.

"No, wait!" Alonzo glanced around, as aware of eyebrows ready to raise if they talked too long as she was. "I would have sought you out, had I not feared your husband's disapproval," he said, speaking rapidly. "I have come to admire him greatly, Catherine. I will serve him well. Whenever it is possible, I will send word to you to assure you of his safety."

"No! You must not!" They were whispering. Catherine saw Elvira look around, catch sight of them, and start in their direction with an angry look. "I thank you, Alonzo, from the bottom of my heart, but you must not write me. My husband is a proud man. What word he wishes to send me must come from him alone."

With a smile she left him. There warred inside her breast many feelings: a tenderness for Alonzo, a welling sadness that he would go and that he had not found happiness. Should she hold herself accountable for the latter? She had accepted his words of love; in a moment of despair and loneliness she had kissed him. She knew too well the wretchedness of giving love where it was not returned. Was there no means of offering solace to Alonzo?

Faintly melancholy, and scarcely aware of her own movements, Catherine drifted into the study which opened off the Berruguetes' sala. It was the same room in which Ana had overheard the treacherous alliance of Cepeda and Don Luis. Troubled by her thoughts she stood in the room's privacy, isolated from the merry crowd beyond. With a start she looked around as the door shut behind her.

Elvira Berruguete leaned against it, her small eyes as vicious as a tigress. Her breathing was rapid and angry beneath her yellow gown.

"So," she sneered, "you cannot bear to lose him, so you come here like some wounded animal to her cave!"

"What do you mean? You are talking nonsense!" Catherine spoke sharply, but warm color flooded her cheeks.

Elvira pushed suddenly free of the door, and for a moment it appeared the girl might launch herself toward Catherine.

"You know very well I speak of Alonzo! Well, you shall not have him! If ever again I see you talking to him, drawing him aside as you did just now, I will denounce you for the wanton that you are!"

"That would be most unwise for Alonzo's sake, don't you think?" asked Catherine, her words low with anger.

Elvira's lip curled.

"Who would fault me? Many would applaud me. A woman whose brother ran a gaming house . . . whose dueña left her . . . who wed a soldier! Then there is the matter of helping a woman escape her husband. You think you can live as you please, Catherine, but you cannot. Society is on my side. A woman who flaunts its laws deserves to be ruined. If ever you speak to Alonzo again outside my hearing, I swear I shall see it done!"

"It would seem you have little faith in Alonzo's devotion," Catherine said.

Elvira's voice rose in a screech.

"Harlot! He would never have you! You are lucky to have any husband at all, even one who cannot claim a father's name!"

Whirling she slammed out of the room. Catherine drew two furious breaths, then followed after her, her head held high.

She was shaking, blinded with her fury. She didn't care about Elvira's threats; but for the insults she yearned to slap the girl's smug face.

"Doña Catherine, will you honor me?" asked a voice at her side.

As her vision cleared, Catherine saw Alma de Palacios Rubios' younger brother. He was smiling, indicating the dance getting underway in the center of the room. Almost before she realized it, she was his partner.

The music moved quickly, and so did she, pride firing each turn. She saw eyes turn to her in admiration. As the dance progressed she wove her way down a line of men whose faces flashed in her memory: Don Pedro, the fat *encomendero* who once had bid on her; the marquis, whose dreams of gold and returning to Spain did not dim the fact he was ever a kindly friend; a lieutenant sent South with Pizarro's latest report to the Audencia, his face alive with pleasure and respect. And then a silken hand took her own, a pink scar met her eyes, and she looked up into the face of Luis de Alvarado.

For several beats of the music they merely looked at one another. Catherine, to her surprise, felt no fear, only loathing. She watched Don Luis's ruthless gaze travel over her.

"So you wear fine pearls now," he said with a movement of his always lifted eyebrow. "What success your husband has had for one of his background. But then," he said thoughtfully, "his background is mysterious, is it not? What a pity it would be if something were found there—if a man whose fortunes go so splendidly should be lacking in *limpieza.*"

Don Luis's disfigured face wore a look of contemplative satisfaction as the music parted them. Catherine, who but a moment earlier had thought herself immune to fear, felt a chill run over her.

In Spain the shadow of the Inquisition hung over anyone accused of lacking *limpieza*—cleanliness from any ancestral taint of Moorish or Jewish blood. A whisper was all it took . . . an accusation . . . and the charges and the identity of the accuser might never be known. Professing faith and living a christian life was no defense. A man lost his property if he was lucky, his life if he was not. His family and often the servants of his household were burned with him.

She shuddered again. In Spain a man like Don Luis could destroy Rodrigo with his malice. But not here. The country was still in the turmoil of settlement. Surely the church did not have time yet to transplant the dark seed of the Inquisition. Surely not here.

28.

The rider in the courtyard was young, little more than a boy. His horse was half starved and its hooves barely left the ground when it walked. Catherine received the letter the young man had brought with trembling hands and broke the seal while he drank thirstily of the water brought by Mateo. Her eyes skipped quickly, and with pounding fear, across the lines in front of her.

To my wife, Doña Catherine Bautista de Valdivia:
Fray Ambrosio, the chaplain, writes this letter for me. I do not know when it may be delivered as our men are near exhaustion and our horses are ill-fed. We have joined in battle with the viceroy and his excellency is dead. The general now is undisputed as the governor of Peru.

She bit her lip. All news which was already known. She hurried on, hearing Rodrigo's voice in the words penned by Fray Ambrosio.

We met the viceroy's forces but a quarter league outside of Quito late in the afternoon of January 18. Those under the general's banners numbered about 700, while those in the viceroy's service totaled little better than half of that. In cavalry we were evenly matched, each side having about 140. The general formed our army on a ridge outside the city, arquebusiers in the fore, pikemen at the center, and cavalry on each flank.

The viceroy fielded an admirable cavalry. They charged with such force that we at first fell back. My company performed as commendably as any other, and we soon rallied and the day was ours. Cabrera, a brave lieutenant from the North, fell in the viceroy's service. Alvarez, the Audencia judge who was sent with the viceroy to Spain and traitorously freed him, died in the battle. He fought surprisingly well for a lawyer, as did Cepeda, who will soon return to his duties as Audencia president.

In all, more than a third of the viceroy's troops gave up

their lives. We lost but seven, by the will of God, only one of them in my company. Rojo and I are well. I trust you are the same.

Below, in a hand quite different from the chaplain's neat script, sprawled a signature: *Valdivia*.

Catherine sighed. The letter, now three months old, might have been some battle report prepared for the Cabildo. There was no news of Rodrigo at all, save for that brief assurance he was well. Yet she was grateful for that, and he had written. She traced, with wonder, his signature.

"Were you in my husband's company?" she asked, looking up at the young man who now leaned against his horse.

He nodded. "Yes, señora."

"He—he is in good health?"

The young man's eyes shifted sideways. "In good health for a war, señora." Seeing her look of alarm he added quickly, "He is well, be certain. But oh, señora, how can I tell you what it is like up there! Four out of every five men the viceroy enlisted were dead before they even came to battle. When their horses dropped from exhaustion, they ate them from want of food. And we were little better. It is—"

He broke off, tears in his eyes. Catherine turned away, that he might not have the burden of composing himself before a woman.

"Ana, take him to the kitchen. Feed him," she said, and her voice was shaking.

April gave way to May and soldiers began to return. They brought many stories, one saying Rodrigo had saved the life of Alonzo Sanchez.

"It is true," Alma's brother insisted. "Don Alonzo was nearly unhorsed and your husband risked his own life to save him."

For her sake, Catherine wondered?

Day by day captains and foot soldiers came, but Rodrigo was not among them.

"Pizarro calls often on his opinion," Alma's brother assured her. "He is no doubt reluctant to let Captain Valdivia take his leave."

Catherine answered his kind words with a smile, but her heart lay heavy in her breast. Were her husband eager to return to Lima, she couldn't believe that a word from Pizarro would prevent him.

The time drew near for the birth of the two foals sired by Boabdíl. Valdéz, whom Rodrigo had found and at Catherine's request added to their household, left for the *encomienda* to await their arrival. Catherine watched him with fondness as he rode off. His mind had mended, he was as sane as any man. And he had taught all of them something of dignity.

It was in his absence, on a bright afternoon, that Catherine heard Mateo's voice rise in frenzied yelps. The boy burst into the house and raced up the stairs shouting her name.

"Señora! Señora!" He tumbled into the sala, panting. "He is home!" he gasped. "Captain Valdivia is home!"

Catherine's scissors fell to the floor as she sprang from her chair. She ran behind Mateo down the stairs. Outside in the street she could hear the clatter of hooves and excited voices.

As she reached the gate she could see them, Rodrigo and half a dozen men, their weary horses loping toward remembered homes. Words of welcome issued from every house they passed as citizens crowded into the street.

With blurring vision she looked on the disciplined countenance of her husband. A seasoned soldier, he betrayed no emotion. Perhaps he felt none. It did not matter as she reached out to him.

But as she moved toward him, she realized, dimly, that the men with him were stopping too, and that behind one of them rode a fat, brown-robed priest. Rodrigo caught her by the hands. He pressed a hurried kiss into her palms, holding her chastely at arm's length. Only as he held her finger tips for a moment against his lips and they looked at one another was she convinced that this restraint in greeting was as odious to him as it was to her.

"The inns are filled," he said, his eyes on her face. "Men have no place to go. I have offered hospitality to these, who have ridden with me."

"Of course," she said, voice choking with the words she longed to say. With wrenching effort she turned her attention to the men who sat silently by. "You are most welcome," she said. "There are not beds for all, but there is plenty of straw and you shall not go hungry."

"What you offer, Doña Catherine, is as great a luxury as we could dream of," one man said earnestly.

They swung down, dusty and looking not like victors but like weary slaves.

The priest caught Rodrigo's arm in a gesture of affection.

"I will leave you here, giving thanks you all are safe," he said. "Go with God, Rodrigo."

"And you likewise, Fray Jerónimo."

As they stepped through the gate to the courtyard, Rodrigo lowered his voice in uncertain apology.

"We will fill the house with lice. Our bodies are covered with them."

"It is to be expected. Valdéz is not here—the foals from Boabdíl were due and he has gone to the *encomienda* to attend their birth—but if you are willing to carry the tub up I will send Belita with water for a bath."

He nodded and she saw the lines of fatigue around his mouth and eyes. Boabdíl, in the courtyard, had grown so thin that the strong bones which gave him his size showed their outlines beneath his coat.

"Mateo and I can see to Boabdíl," she said as he lifted the wooden tub from its resting place in the kitchen. Magdalena and the kitchen maid were flying to and fro, bringing forth an odd assortment of food for an impromptu meal, while Ana and Belita carried a great plank into the courtyard to serve as a table. Catherine hesitated. "I am glad you have returned," she said softly.

Rodrigo's eyes skimmed over her, then lingered for a moment.

"Are you?" he inquired.

Before she could answer he swung the tub onto his shoulder and started for the stairs. Catherine stared after him. Had there been a deliberate edge to the question, or was it weariness?

Quickly she led Boabdíl into his old stall and gave him oats and water. When Mateo finished fetching his master's clothes and burning them, he could perhaps get the saddle off the horse and brush him. In the meantime, she suspected this treatment was as adequate as any Boabdíl had known in many a day.

She left the great charger munching oats with snorts of pleasure and went back to the kitchen. A kettle of water had been already heating for laundry when her husband arrived, and it had been carried up for his bath. But he would need rinse water. From the courtyard she could hear the soldiers falling hungrily upon the food set before them. Ana and Belita were struggling to carry a wine cask out. Magdalena was frying the thin corn cakes of the country which the

275

kitchen maid carried out as soon as they were finished. Her servants were busy with work which must be done. Catherine stripped off her jacket and pushed up her sleeves, looking around for the kettle, which she filled and set to heat herself.

Stepping out, she checked on the comfort of their guests. The men scarcely noticed her. Two days' supply of bread had already vanished. Returning to the kitchen she took out the duck intended for supper.

"You can send Mateo to the market for fish," she told Magdalena. "That will be our supper."

The rinse water now was hot, and Catherine called impatiently to the kitchen maid to carry it for her. Mateo was too small to carry a full pail, and she could hardly send one of the women in where her husband was bathing. She would take it to him herself.

She knocked at his door uncertainly. "I have brought you a towel and more water. Shall I come in?"

There was a pause. "Yes, come ahead."

The shutter at his window was flung wide. He sat in the wooden tub, body glistening. His hair and beard were lathered with strong-smelling soap. As she came in he ducked into the water to rid himself of the suds.

"Of all the discomforts of war, it is the filth which I hate most," he said viciously, his eyes closed against the draining lather.

Surprised by his vehemence, Catherine frowned. Did hunger and weariness trouble him less? The slaughter of the battlefield?

"Shall I—pour the water over you?" she asked. She recalled the time when he had performed a similar service for her.

"You cannot lift it," he said. "Hand it to me." He stood up dripping and she gazed at the solid form of him, scarcely able to believe his presence. He took the bucket from her and upended it. Wordlessly she handed him the towel.

"Boabdíl looks half starved," she said. "The rider who brought your letter to me said there were many deprivations."

He rubbed vigorously at his hair, glancing up as he passed the towel on down across him.

"Yes, many," he agreed. "Fewer for us than for the viceroy's men." The smile he attempted was nearer a grimace. "It works well for our personal interests. Many horses have been lost. There will be a great demand for replacements."

He tossed aside the towel and pulled on clean new breeches.

"The general gave six hundred *pesos de oro* to each captain who served him. That is worth a few weeks' hunger."

"It is a liberal sum," said Catherine.

Rodrigo tightened the waist of his breeches with a tug. They looked at one another. His shoulders seemed to block the light, yet every ridge of his flesh was visible with dazzling clarity. Catherine felt the tempo of her blood increase.

Rodrigo's hand fell away from the tie at his waist. Catherine saw movement beneath the tight cloth of his breeches. He came toward her slowly.

"There is no reason why I should refrain from embracing you now," he said as his hands encircled her waist.

She was aware of some subtle difference in him. He was in control of himself, the cavalry officer who could command his own emotions as easily as he commanded the men who followed him. Yet Catherine knew he wanted her at that moment as badly as she wanted him. She closed her eyes.

His mouth moved over hers slowly, tasting hers as he had not done since the episode with Leonor. Her fingers touched his smooth, bare skin. His hands pressed her breasts and his lips moved to her neck with soft kisses which caused moisture to flow from her.

For the first time he carried her to his own small bed. She was naked now, as he was. There was no time to repair to another room. She wrapped her thighs around his own.

"Wait. Wait," he whispered.

But a small cry escaped her and she shuddered, unable to wait. She thought herself spent until he began his exploration of her innermost recesses. Rodrigo was breathing with effort now. Poised above her he paused and fingered the rock-hard tips of her breasts. She moaned. He began to move again, and a cascade of sensation swept them both and her thoughts were only coherent enough to register a certain wonder.

Rodrigo lay on her heavily. He murmured her name.

"I must be getting old," he said drowsily. He turned over on his back and was immediately asleep.

Catherine watched the shadows on the wall beside them lengthen. The servants would wonder about their long disappearance, she thought, as would her husband's guests. Then her mouth gave a mocking twist. If they could not guess the behavior of a man and woman separated five months, then they were stupid.

She looked at the man beside her, and the intensity of her response made her cheeks flame. When embarrassment faded, impulse took its place. Deliberately she stirred. The arm he had flung across her tightened almost painfully. She moved again and Rodrigo opened his eyes.

"Strange," he said. "I seem to find myself in the same condition as when I brought you to bed."

When they had finished he rested comfortably on his back.

"Why is the army so long in returning home?" asked Catherine. "The war has been over for months."

Beneath the dark fringe of his lashes, she saw his eyes move in a calculating look at her. Slowly his lips formed a smile.

"There is much merriment in the North just now," he said. "The general has all but turned Quito into his capital."

She frowned. Was it because of merriment that he was so long in returning?

"I should think Pizarro would be impatient to take his place as head of government," she said. "And to see Doña Isabella."

His mood seemed to change. The amusement left him and he looked away.

"The general is changing," he said shortly.

By the following evening their visitors had departed. Two had found accommodations with certain women of the city, one had secured a room, and the others, refreshed in body and spirit, had turned their horses toward Cuzco. After dinner Rodrigo strolled into the sala and stood with one foot on a bench. He watched as Catherine settled in a chair, then spoke without warning.

"It occurs to me some discussion is needed of our life together," he said, as though the topic held little interest for him. "I see no point in delaying."

Fear swelled her throat and she could not swallow. His face, as he awaited her reaction, relaxed in a way she did not find altogether pleasant. It made her feel he was already the victor in some battle not yet waged.

"Come, my prize, do not look so concerned," he drawled. "I have merely been thinking these last months that it is fortunate neither of us has succumbed to love in this alliance." His eyebrows lifted, mocking both of them, and he

278

continued. "It allows us to work for our mutual good without the distraction of domestic squabbles, don't you agree?"

"Yes." She faltered before his calm and careless words. "Yes, of course."

"It may have come to your notice that I am a man of some ambition," he said, a twinge of amusement touching his lips at his own modest words. "You have suffered somewhat because of it," he acknowledged grandly, "though I think it likely you are the better for that if it has opened your lovely eyes to the hard realities of the world. Now you shall profit from that ambition as well as I. Let us have an understanding of what I will expect of you as my wife."

She sat frozen and cold as Rodrigo swung his foot down and began to pace.

"There is money now for you to dress in keeping with your background. I shall expect you to do so. You will also begin to reciprocate some of the many invitations which we have accepted in past years, and you will see to whatever further furnishings are needed to make this house suitable for such entertaining. You will be available to me whenever I wish your company at Mass. You will be available to me in bed when I desire that. I in turn will take great pains to see the latter demands upon you are not excessive. Well? It is little enough which I am asking, surely?"

Catherine did not answer. He completed the length of the room and pivoted, hands clasped behind him.

"A stable boy I may have been by birth, but I have now a wife of impeccable breeding and money enough to make handsome investments. Before I die I intend to see the name Valdivia known and respected throughout Peru. The blood which flows in the veins of our sons will be envied, and the dowries of our daughters will be fat."

She could scarcely speak.

"And—if there are no children?"

He paused a moment. His fingers flicked her chin.

"Your face alone is worth the price I paid for you," he said blandly. "Every man in Lima is jealous of me."

His hand dropped away.

"There, now. See to your dresses. I am going out."

He glanced back over his shoulder. A grin stole slowly across his face. He began to whistle as the door closed behind him.

Catherine sat in a stupor at this fresh arrogance in the man she had married. Gradually resentment rose in her.

A possession! He could not have made it clearer that she had been but the first acquisition to satisfy his ambition. A suit of silk which showed its owner's taste and wealth . . . the most richly carved sword . . . the horse with the finest mouth . . . an object prized not for itself but for the status it conveyed.

A silver goblet from Pizarro sat on the stool where her husband had stood. She picked it up and hurled it blindly against the fireplace.

Catherine smoothed absently at the gloves of soft white leather slashed to accommodate her emerald wedding ring. At the same grassy field where Rodrigo just six months before had drilled his troops a crowd had gathered to watch the auction of their first Andalusian yearling. Rodrigo was sure it would fetch a fine price, but Catherine was deaf to the excitement around her. Her ears rang with the words Señor Bocanegra had spoken to her just moments before.

Ana's suitor was a man of quick intelligence and he was clearly devoted to their household. Catherine had seen the uncertainty in his face when he asked to speak to her privately.

"I do not wish to distress you," he had said. "But as I hold you and your husband in great esteem, there is something I feel I should mention."

Then he had told how another notary of his acquaintance had witnessed an agreement between Don Luis de Alvarado and a man named Sotelo, and how as they were signing the agreement the name Valdivia had been mentioned. Sotelo, it seemed, was an unprincipled man well known among the lawyers of the city for his willingness to do anything for a price. In exchange for a good sum of gold he was going to Spain on some errand for Don Luis.

In the sunlight of the open field Catherine struggled now with fear. Her mouth felt dry. She remembered Don Luis's taunt the night she had danced with him:

What a pity if something should be found in your husband's background . . . if she should be lacking in limpieza. . . .

Should she mention it to Rodrigo? It would enrage him. His blood was pure. There was not a priest who knew him who would not swear to his soundness as a christian. Yet if this Sotelo would do anything for money, might he also be willing to fabricate if necessary?

The young stallion sold at a price well in excess of what

they had hoped for. Distracted by what Señor Bocanegra had told her, Catherine found her attention often on the crowd. One figure in particular drew her attention, so bizarre was his appearance. The man was old, white haired, and wore a violet burnoose like some Moorish chieftain, though she knew he could not be a Moor. He sat squarely on a russet-colored mule, observing the proceedings. A black silk hat was pulled low on his head, and from it there waved chicken feathers of various colors.

When a smiling Rodrigo joined her, thumped on the back in congratulations at every step, Catherine nodded toward the strange old man.

"Look," she said. "Is he not like a character from some tale of romance?"

As she spoke, the man in the purple burnoose kicked his mule and the animal came ambling toward them.

"Not from a romance," Rodrigo said grimly. "That is Carbajal."

Now Catherine found herself eyeing the man approaching them in sharp disgust. Once Rodrigo had said the man must be kin to the devil. This was Pizarro's ancient lieutenant, his adviser and ardent supporter, the one who had dragged men from their beds and hanged them to win the city of Lima's allegiance to his general.

"So, Valdivia, this is what lured you from your rightful duties as a soldier," he taunted in greeting. Eyes more piercing than those of many a man one-third his age gleamed out at Catherine from under snowy brows. It was a look of scorn.

"I have not been remiss in my duties. The war is over," Rodrigo answered, an edge to his voice.

Carbajal gathered his lips together and spit.

"In my mind a soldier does not forsake his general for a silken bed. Pizarro would do well to question a loyalty as shallow as yours appears to be."

Rodrigo shook his arm free of Catherine's hand.

"Are you accusing me of disloyalty, Carbajal?"

The old man spit again.

"That judgment is the general's to make," he said.

They watched him ride away in silence.

"You did not leave without Pizarro's permission?" asked Catherine anxiously.

Her husband shook his head. "He wasn't pleased, but he made none of the veiled suggestions which Carbajal makes."

The answer did little to comfort Catherine, for Pizarro was known to value Carbajal's counsel above all others. A messenger to Spain . . . an enemy in the army. In the blue sky over the port one low cloud chased another. She could not help but think it mirrored their own horizon.

29

Rodrigo stooped, picked up a rock and hurled it toward the River Rimac.

"More and more it appears you were right," he said. "The general may one day whistle Cepeda's tune."

Catherine turned to look at him, hearing the bitterness in his tone. They were headed for Pizarro's brightly lighted palace, and torchlight from it danced in the street ahead of them.

"Why? What makes you believe it?" she asked. "The more I have seen of the general, the more I have come to believe in his firmness and integrity."

"Cepeda has persuaded him to hold back the Royal Fifth," Rodrigo said, alluding to that part of the country's treasure which was to be shipped to the Spanish crown. "Cepeda argues it is the general's fair recompense for running this country. Last week, I am told, he even hinted to the general that he should throw off all allegiance to the crown and govern for himself."

"Surely he would not do so!" Catherine exclaimed.

"I do not know. The general is unpredictable."

For weeks there had been rumors that King Carlos would not name Pizarro governor, but instead had dispatched a royal president who was even now in Santa Marta. Were there new rumors, Catherine wondered?

The gate to Pizarro's palace stood wide before them. As they entered the room used for entertainments Pizarro himself came toward them.

"Rodrigo!" he said in a hearty voice as he clapped his hands around his captain's shoulders. As he talked with Rodrigo, Catherine studied him. Could a man so unaffected and forthright be manipulated by Cepeda? Always behind Cepeda, she thought, stood Don Luis.

Now she looked around for the man who was their sworn enemy. He stood in a corner with a pretty young woman named María Costella. Alma had told her, with great amusement, that Don Luis for months had endeavored to win the attention of the lady, despite the fact she was newly and happily married and displayed toward him only indifference.

"Well, Rodrigo, have you heard the news?" Pizarro was asking.

Catherine thought her husband stood straighter whenever Pizarro spoke to him. He clasped his hands behind his back.

"Yes, general."

"This Gasca, dispatched as president of a new Audencia, has landed in Panamá. It is not certain if he comes to confirm me in my position or to take power himself. If you were forced to choose between us, which one would you support?"

Catherine paled at Pizarro's bluntness. Rodrigo did not waver.

"I cannot believe you would make such a choice necessary," he said.

Pizarro looked thoughtful for a minute. One corner of his mouth rose in a grin, which seemed to be directed at himself.

"You are no man's fool, Rodrigo. That is why I esteem your opinion."

As they walked in to dinner Catherine leaned close to her husband.

"You were very courageous," she whispered.

He did not answer, and his eyes were troubled.

At dinner there was much talk about Pedro de la Gasca. It was said he was a cleric, a member of the council of the Inquisition who had examined certain cases of heresy in Valencia. He had then been appointed to investigate the courts of justice and of finance there.

"Just what we need, a money counter," snorted a voice from the long table facing the one where Catherine sat. "We do not need another priest to run the country. We need a soldier."

Catherine turned her gaze to the great main table on its dais where the marquis and marquesa, Don Luis, Cepeda and other high-ranking guests sat with Pizarro. If Gasca came to be president of a new Audencia, Cepeda would lose that position, she realized with a shock. He had every reason to urge Pizarro's resistance to the crown's authority. Her heartbeats seemed to trip over one another at the realization.

"They do not listen to us in Spain," a captain at her table was saying. "This Gasca will attempt to force the New Laws on us, as the viceroy did. Does the crown take no interest in the needs of its citizens? It is little enough we have to show for wearing that title!"

The atmosphere for resistance to Gasca was ripe. Catherine could feel hostility already growing among the people.

The decision for rebellion or peace rested squarely on the word of Gonzalo Pizarro. Surreptitiously she watched him, handsome in his suit of black and yellow silk. He laughed heartily with those around him. But once, as attention shifted from him to some jest further down the table, the smile slipped from his face and he looked sad and uneasy. For an instant Catherine felt compassion for the man who sat at the uncertain pinnacle of power.

It wasn't until the meal ended and jugglers had performed that she glimpsed Francisca. The saucy young woman sported a gown of crimson which caught the high color of her cheeks. She held to the arm of a middle-aged wheezing cavalier, no doubt her husband.

"You look melancholy, Doña Catherine," said a deep voice beside her.

Looking up, Catherine saw her host.

"If I do, it is not the fault of your hospitality," she smiled. "You are too lavish in the pleasures which you furnish for your guests. I have heard many ballads of late which call you generous, brave and daring. I confess I am bound to think them all true."

He looked pleased. Rodrigo had disappeared, and now Pizarro offered her his arm. As he did so, Don Luis crossed the room toward them.

"A word with you, general—"

Pizarro waved a hand with manifest disinterest and kept his course toward the adjoining room.

"Ballads!" he said to Catherine. "So they are sung else-where and not just in my presence! It is enough to flatter a man. But a lady as learned as you, Doña Catherine, is well aware they are little but fairy stories. Ah—here is your husband."

He linked his arm through Rodrigo's and stood with one of them on either side of him. "You know," he said with mellow thoughtfulness, "I count these two among my closest friends, Don Luis. Rodrigo once saved my life, and this lady once kept my neck from the *garrote* when the viceroy—and you were in his company—would have placed it there."

"And for your generous pardon of my brief alliance with the viceroy's party, I am most grateful," said Don Luis smoothly. "Those were difficult times for those who wished peace for our country and knew not in which quarter it lay."

The downward slant of his mustache betrayed his annoyance with the present situation. Rodrigo's mouth had tightened into a dangerous line. Pizarro, forgetful, it seemed, of the enmity which lay between them, continued in fine spirits.

"Were I to kill all who at one time had opposed me, I should have lacked some very fine soldiers in our latest battle," he said, chest puffing out with satisfaction. "And in you, Don Luis, I should have lost a fine adviser. Tell me, Rodrigo, what do you think of his latest suggestion? Is he not clever? He has proposed I take the *coya*, highest born of all the Indian women, for my wife."

"But what of Doña Isabella?" Catherine exclaimed.

Pizarro smiled. "Your pardon, Doña Catherine, but while I am fond of that lady, she is in no way legally bound to me."

Catherine stared at him, sharply disappointed. She had not thought him so eager for status. Would he so willingly put aside his loyal mistress simply to be linked with the female descendant of the Inca?

"To what purpose would you marry the *coya?*" Rodrigo asked bluntly.

Pizarro released their arms and stood with hands locked behind him, rocking on his heels.

"To unify the country," he answered without hesitation.

Rodrigo's stance was not so gentlemanly. He stood with legs spread and arms crossed.

"Unify it? For what?"

Pizarro, like a boy caught stealing wine, glanced at Don Luis and away.

"Well, it is an excellent piece of statecraft," he said, rubbing a hand across the back of his head. "By his suggestion of it, Don Luis shows himself to be a counselor worthy of any king."

"Perhaps what he aspires to," Rodrigo suggested.

The general's face darkened and he exploded.

"Enough!" he stormed. "How dare you presume to take issue with my counselor or with me? You forget yourself!" He reined himself suddenly and began to laugh. "Face it, Rodrigo, what do you or I either one know of politics? We are but ignorant men, though skilled in arms. If Don Luis advises I marry the *coya*, well, there are worse duties I could perform for the sake of my country."

He dug an elbow into Rodrigo's ribs in crude insinuation. Catherine averted her head. She was sickened by the way Don Luis's expression was easing.

"Just as you suggested long ago. The general has begun to

be his puppet," Rodrigo said as Pizarro and his adviser continued on their way.

Catherine shook her head in disbelief. "He seems a wise man in so many ways. How can he—"

"I don't know."

Her husband's manner had grown dark and restless.

"I am going for wine," he said.

Catherine stood in the sala, now crowded with people, and looked back toward the dining room. There was wine there, it was true; many men were lingering over it. But Francisca was also there. Her husband had disappeared. Catherine closed her eyes as Francisca's hand darted out to Rodrigo's chest and he caught it, folding his fingers around hers.

"Tell Rodrigo I have gone to fetch my cloak," she said to Rojo, who was coming toward her.

Unmindful of her agitation, he frowned.

"So soon? But it's early yet."

"Yes, and I don't want to spoil his evening. Perhaps you will see me home if he prefers to stay?"

She did not give the red-haired soldier a chance to answer. Nor did she go at once to the cloak room. She had tried countless times to purge herself of the jealousy she felt toward Francisca, and she had failed. Her husband did not love her; that she accepted. But the sight of another woman touching him hurt in a way she could not explain. For some time she stood at the balcony railing, her slim fingers strangling it, looking down at one of the inner courtyards of the palace as she tried to compose her thoughts.

When the darkness shifted she heard it. Then she saw him. Diego Berruguete. He wore the smile she once had mistaken as evidence of pleasing character.

"What, alone?" he mocked. "A terrible shame, in this moonlight. I would be glad to remedy your loneliness, Señora de Valdivia. In fact, I insist on it. I believe I owe your husband something of just that nature."

Catherine did not retreat before him, but regarded him with disdain. The cloakroom was only a few doors away. The palace was filled with people.

"My husband is on his way to join me," she said. "I do not think you are fool enough to risk a duel with him."

Diego's smile widened unpleasantly.

"How embarrassing to catch a lady in a lie. Your husband, when I last saw him, seemed quite engrossed in the charms of Señora Griega. It is amusing how you and your husband play the contented couple when all Lima knows you each are party to another liaison—or it would be amusing were it not my own sister who is aggrieved by yours."

Catherine struck him with such force that fire shot through her fingers.

"Make such a charge to your brother-in-law—if you dare!"

"Do you think he would own it? That mealy-mouthed scholar? His preoccupation with study suggests he has the vocation to be a monk, but I know he is not one—nor are you a nun!"

As the jeer left his lips he moved. Catherine, paralyzed by anger, saw and tried to escape. Her arms were pinned roughly up behind her and her mouth felt the pressure of rough, insulting kisses.

"Stop it!" she gasped. But a panic had seized her. If she screamed, if she were caught like this, would she be believed the innocent party? Not by a town which had come to associate her name with scandal. Not set against the powerful word of the Berruguetes.

"I have longed to part your legs since we first met," Diego panted, dragging her backward into shadow. "It will not take long. Here, where we will not be disturbed."

They were halfway up a small hall leading away from the gallery. A staircase to the third floor of the palace left a dark and sheltered corner, hidden from all who passed beyond. Diego's fingers squeezed her breasts. He did not repeat the mistake, this time, of allowing her any movement, but imprisoned both her hands in one of his, forcing her back, ever back, toward the wall. He crushed her spine against the dressed stone behind her, freeing his hand to hoist her outer skirt. His other hand was clamped tightly across her mouth. Her free hands swung now in cramped, ineffectual blows which he answered with laughter.

"It would be a shame to rush this," he said in guttural tones as he pressed against her.

She dared not cry out and she dared not submit. Unable to think rationally, Catherine moved by instinct. Her teeth ripped into the loose flesh between her assailant's thumb and index finger. As he jerked away she called out with all the strength of fear and anger.

"Hel—"

Pain shot through her, coloring her mind a lurid red, as a hard blow fell against her windpipe. The hand was across her mouth again, Diego's nails digging cruelly into her skin. She struck at him hopelessly, and suddenly he seemed to fall back before her.

As he fell to the floor she realized it was not her hand which had hurled him away from her. With mingled horror and relief she saw Rodrigo standing over him, and a few steps distant, Dr. Palacios Rubios, his hand on his sword. In a single movement Rodrigo seized Diego and flung him down the small hallway and onto the open gallery. There, Catherine realized, stood a dim group of faces. She heard a tongue click in disapproval, and knew with sinking heart it was the marquesa.

"This time I will kill you," Rodrigo said with heat.

Diego, elbows draped drunkenly across the railing, sneered up at him.

"For what? To defend the name of a woman who the whole city knows has long made you a cuckold?"

Dr. Palacios Rubios slipped a fortifying arm around Catherine. People were flocking to the gallery, crowding, whispering.

"Stop them!" a voice said sharply. Don Francisco Berruguete pushed forward, straight and commanding with his silver hair. "It is well known Valdivia stands unexcelled with a sword. He is using this ruse to settle an old grudge with my son, who he knows is no match. Those of you who are men of manners, throw the troublemaker out."

Rodrigo's head turned slightly.

"If you attempt to stop me, Don Francisco, I will fight you too."

There was an exclamation of anger from Elvira.

"Scum!" she cried. "Ill-bred upstart!"

Alonzo caught her by the arm and held her as she seemed about to fly forward. The crowd had given way to Gonzalo Pizarro, Don Luis, Cepeda. The latter turned hotly on the general.

"Surely you see the truth in what my cousin is saying! This captain of yours is known for his hot-headedness—"

"There is not room to draw our swords here," Rodrigo cut in, addressing himself to Diego.

Diego stood up with sullen agreement.

"The courtyard, then," he said, displaying contempt.

A glimmer of scarlet silk shone suddenly in the torchlit scene on the gallery. Francisca pushed her way to the front of the crowd. She caught Rodrigo's arm, detaining him, as he started down the stairs.

"You fool!" she said, her voice made clear by the passion in it. "Will you give all you have worked for—all you have risked your life for—to silence one man? Think, Rodrigo!"

Her face was earnest and pleading. Rodrigo looked at her for a moment but drew his arm away. He glanced—a pained, closed look—at Catherine. Then he went quickly down the stairs.

At a call from Pizarro, servants came running with extra torches to illumine the courtyard. The marquesa came to Catherine's side.

"Oh, my dear," she whispered, squeezing Catherine's hand.

"I must go down," said Catherine.

Dr. Palacios Rubios commenced to make some protest, then silenced it. The Berruguetes, the general and Rojo had already gone down. Catherine and her little group of supporters followed.

Already Rodrigo and Diego Berruguete faced each other. Diego's sword flashed out and met Rodrigo's in a high, metallic note. They did not separate enough to give full art to their execution, but aimed blows at each other in furious anger. There was a singing sound and Diego's sword flew from his hand.

"Pick it up," Rodrigo said coldly.

Catherine bit her lip. Perhaps if he humiliated Diego he wouldn't kill him. But did she want that? He had spared Don Luis, and it had proved a fatal mistake.

Diego retrieved his weapon and his movements seemed to grow more stealthy. His body tilted slightly forward, awaiting any opening. Suddenly he sprang. Rodrigo's sword turned his aside, but as Diego's sword plunged down with lightning speed, Catherine realized the strength of his first thrust had been counterfeit. The true blow was this.

Catherine didn't see the next move, she only guessed it. Rodrigo's sword pivoted on the blade of his opponent's, and before Diego's could accomplish his intended damage, Rodrigo's steel had found its way through Diego's throat.

Diego dropped to his knees on the tiled floor of the courtyard. His hands gripped his neck incredulously. Blood spurted like a pulsing fountain from his wound, and without a word or sound he fell.

Alonzo, the brother-in-law whom he had slandered, was the first to reach him. He bent over Diego's form, put an ear to the blood-soaked chest, and then sat back.

"He's dead," he said.

Across Diego's body, Catherine's eyes met his. They held an agony whose source she knew. There was no choice now but that Alonzo ally himself with his in-laws, becoming the bitterest enemy of her as well as Rodrigo, never speaking.

"Oh, I am sorry!" she whispered.

In the little group near the body Elvira was screaming. "You have killed him! Murderer! Butcher!"

Alonzo stood abruptly and wrapped his arms around her, turning her away from the sight.

"I call on you all to witness that this fight was not of my son's doing," cried a stricken Don Francisco, kneeling to touch the body. "And I swear I will not rest in my grave till I see you destroyed, Valdivia! You—who sprang of nothing—you act like a savage! You are not fit company for civilized men." He swung to face Pizarro. "I call on you, general, to purge your ranks of outlaws such as these. Or is it this, the violence of barbarians, which we must expect while you govern?"

Pizarro's voice was firm. "I offer you sympathy over the loss of your son, Don Francisco. But he insulted a lady—made scandalous accusations. Her husband would have been a poor man indeed had he not demanded this settlement."

Cepeda stood tight-lipped beside Pizarro. He turned on his heel and stalked away.

Rodrigo bent to retrieve the velvet coat he had discarded. His gaze fell on Catherine as she came uncertainly forward.

"What a fool I was to ever marry you," he said, voice taut with emotion. He slung the coat across his shoulder. "Rojo, take her home for me."

30

The duel seemed to revive all Rodrigo's old doubts. Catherine felt his gaze on her when he thought she didn't notice; but whenever she looked at him, he avoided her eyes. He was sorry he had married her. The knowledge was a dull knife sawing back and forth across her spirit.

She abandoned all hope now that she would ever carry a child in her womb. Even when Rodrigo had come to her nightly and she had drunk Doña Isabella's potion she had not conceived. Since the duel his visits had stopped. He went out every night.

If the episode with Diego Berruguete had widened the gulf between her and her husband, Catherine found to her surprise that it had also produced some subtle shift of public sentiment in her favor. Diego's slurs against her had outraged many and won her wide sympathy. Francisca's presumptuous behavior with Rodrigo had been noted too. Everywhere she went, Catherine was greeted with greater courtesy than ever before.

It was small consolation, she thought, as she and Ana, returning home one afternoon a few weeks after the party, smiled and returned the nods of several *encomenderos* and their wives. The hour was early. Of late she and Alma had begun to spend an afternoon together each week talking and doing needlework, much as she and Leonor and the others had done of old. Now Alma was in the early stages of her second pregnancy, and soon after taking up needle had fallen prey to a headache. It would be a great nuisance to carry a child, Catherine told herself. Yet her life seemed more useless than ever as she walked toward home.

Having someone who needed you—that was what mattered, she thought as they turned into their own pleasant street. Her father had relied upon her, and she had been happy then. She sighed. It was wrong to be consumed with self-pity. Perhaps she could devote her thoughts and energies to the church as the marquesa had done.

"Valdéz is slow in coming," she said with a frown as they stood waiting outside the gate.

Just then it opened and Catherine saw Magdalena hovering just beyond Valdéz, who was scratching his head.

"Ah, señora! You are early," the Indian woman said. "Is Señora de Palacios Rubios not well?"

"Not entirely," said Catherine. "She is with child."

Behind its smooth surface Magdalena's face showed signs of tension.

"Ah," she said. "Well, perhaps if you are not weary, then you might step into the kitchen. There are some matters on which I would like to have your advice."

"Has something happened?" asked Catherine with some surprise, for the household had, to her knowledge, been running very smoothly.

"Oh, no," said the housekeeper hastily. "But I have had some questions about the menus . . . about the marketing. . . ."

As her voice trailed off, another floated down from above, its tone merry. Catherine looked sharply up, her heart beating with such anger that it seemed to shake her body.

"Who is here?" she demanded, straightening.

Magdalena answered with lowered eyes and tight-pressed lips. "Señora Griega."

Catherine turned. Unconsciously she took a few steps toward the stairs, eyes fixed on the sala. Francisca. With Rodrigo. Here.

As she stood staring, the door to the sala opened and Rodrigo emerged, pulling the door closed behind him. He and Catherine looked at one another. He came down the steps with definite tread.

Catherine spoke without looking backward. "Ana! Go to the kitchen. Answer Magdalena's questions as best you can."

Her husband was near her now. Her words were low. She spoke with great calm which belied the turbulence inside her.

"Get that woman out of my house!"

Rodrigo's face colored. His mouth was hard. But when he spoke, it was lightly.

"I remind you the house is mine, not yours. Francisca has come on business. She wishes to join some money in one of our investments."

Catherine's head shook faintly. She could hardly see him for her rage.

"Spare me your lies—and do not put our servants to such distress again!"

A cruel smile curved his lips.

"Surely you are not jealous, my sweet doña?"

Catherine raised a firm chin in defiance of the hurt.

"Jealous? I do not care what you do. I ask only that you do it with some semblance of the tact expected of a gentleman, since that is what you now aspire to be. You may have your whore in her bed, in the street, wherever you like—but not here!"

His open hand caught her across the cheek. The sting of it in the first instant following seemed to have no reality. Her own fingers raised to nurse the burning spot, but she jerked them back, unwilling to betray so much of weakness. Lifting her head she caught up her skirt and swept past him.

"Catherine!"

She didn't stop although there was in his voice some pained note. Jerking open the heavy gate she returned to the street. She didn't slow her pace until she reached the plaza.

Out of breath, she stood looking at the long rows of merchants' and artisans' shops which crowded near. Her hands were curled into aching fists. She wanted to strike out at something, not because he had struck her, but because of the grief she could not express. She wanted solace, and there was none.

"I cannot endure this alone," she said aloud. She turned her steps toward the marquesa's.

"The marquesa is in her sitting room," said the housekeeper, who knew Catherine well. She glanced at Catherine a little curiously, but Catherine did not care. She followed the housekeeper.

A maid admitted them to the sitting room. Catherine stopped short. There, seated across from the marquesa, was Elvira Sanchez.

The girl's face filled with hate. She half rose from her chair. Even the marquesa's inborn equanimity slipped slightly as she looked at the two of them.

Battered by emotions which had taught her too well the hurt behind anger, Catherine spoke impulsively.

"Doña Elvira, I know you will not believe me when I tell you I deeply regret your brother's death, yet it is true. I would that it were in my power to change what has happened. I, too, have seen my brother die before me. I do not expect you to forgive me, ever, for the part I have played in this tragedy, but I offer you my sympathies—and my prayers."

Catherine put her hand back toward the door, but before she could turn, Elvira was on her feet.

"I do not want your sympathy, Señora de Valdivia. And I doubt that prayers from one like you are even heard!"

With haughty contempt, and careful her skirts should not touch Catherine's, Elvira marched with arched back from the room. Catherine spread her hands to the marquesa.

"My lady marquesa, I am truly sorry—"

"The error was Señora Nebrija's in showing you up unannounced, not yours, my dear." The white-haired marquesa possessed herself of a smile. "Your words were gracious when it is known by all that Doña Elvira's brother attempted to compromise you. The duel was unfortunate but necessary. Do not be overdistressed by Doña Elvira's reaction, for she can hardly be held accountable for her emotions now. It seems she is to be a mother."

The words, intended to console, rang in Catherine's ears like the judgment of God.

Her household had settled itself for the night. Sitting beneath the fig tree Catherine closed her eyes and tried to pray. Instead she felt the stir of wind across her face and heard the drowsy rustle of nesting birds. Two days had passed since Rodrigo struck her, and they had not spoken.

The stars were bright. Looking up at them she recalled the nights she had spent with Rodrigo at the *encomienda*. She had been hopeful then. But now. . . . Her thoughts blurred together and lost all form. She sat for many minutes losing herself in the night around her.

All at once the gate to the stable area opened and she jumped.

"Catherine?"

Rodrigo's voice was strained. She heard his footsteps stop.

"I—I didn't realize it was so late," she stammered rising. "I only meant to take some air."

"Forgive me if I frightened you."

"You did not. Only you—you are so often gone in the night. Ana has informed me she will marry and I was thinking. . . ."

She stopped, confused and dismayed by what she was saying.

"Marry!" Rodrigo took a step toward her. "What will you do if you lose Ana? You need her."

"I'll manage," she said tightly, even though the prospect of losing the girl she had come to love caused an ache inside her.

Rodrigo's voice became a purr deep in his throat. "And do you object to my absences?" he asked, seizing on her words.

"No!"

Catherine turned, intent on escape. She felt a hand catch her shoulder and she was forced around to face her husband. With infinite gentleness his finger touched her cheek.

"I'm sorry I struck you, Catherine. You don't deserve such treatment. But sometimes. . . . Damn! Why can't you be more like Francisca? Like any other woman?"

He strode to the bench where she had been sitting. Catherine watched in alarm. She could not comprehend his behavior, nor the meaning of his words. Was he saying he loved Francisca and did not choose to?

She looked up at him, so strong, so handsome. "There—there is something else which Ana told me. Perhaps you have heard. Sancho Costella and his family were arrested two days ago and charged with being Jews. They denied it, of course, but they offered no proof of their *limpieza*. All their property was seized. The men attempted to escape today. They were killed."

He frowned, clearly puzzled by her distress.

"Rodrigo, Don Luis sought the favors of María Costella, Sancho's daughter-in-law. She spurned him. Do you not see his hand in this?" She looked away. "The night before you rode North with the general I was briefly across from Don Luis in a dance, do you remember? He commented on our rising fortunes. He said it would be a pity if you were to be found lacking in *limpieza*. I believe he would fabricate proof if it suited him. I . . . I am afraid."

She could not bring herself to mention the messenger Don Luis had sent to Spain. She bit her lip. Rodrigo's hands came up to hold her tightly. There was a stunned expression in his eyes.

Slowly he shook his head. "No. Don Luis cannot touch us. You must believe it, *preciosa*."

But in his eyes Catherine saw briefly the shadow of fear.

Abruptly he released her. "There are things which will occupy this country more than the Inquisition in the days ahead, I fear. I have just seen a priest posting proclamations on various doors. Fray Jeronimo was with me and he read them. They have been smuggled in from Father Gasca and they announce his power and intent to repeal the New Laws and to grant full amnesty to all who fought against the viceroy. The general cannot have known the truth of Father Gasca's mission. Or the general has lied to us."

At once she saw what her husband was suggesting. Men

had less reason now to support Gonzalo Pizarro. They had feared Father Gasca because they believed he would enforce the laws which took from them their lands and Indians. Would the general yield graciously now, or jealously maintain his power?

"It will please you, Doña Catherine, to hear that I no longer think to wed the *coya*."

Gonzalo Pizarro smiled over her hand in the great hall of his palace where he had greeted them. There were many guests tonight and the general was striking in a fine new suit of scarlet velvet. The baldric crossing his chest and the sword case at his side were wrought of gold. He threw his shoulders back almost boastfully and continued.

"I have no need of such pretensions to further strength. I *am* strong. Does King Carlos' own representative not wait on me in Panamá, a virtual prisoner? Such carefully worded letters I get from him, and from the king himself, begging my recognition of this new president! They know my strength. They know this President Gasca will not come to take up his office unless I permit it."

A few steps away Cepeda and Don Luis stood watching. Monitoring his every word, thought Catherine angrily. How much control of his own decisions did the general now have?

"And will you permit it?" Rodrigo asked quietly.

In Pizarro's once open face Catherine now saw traces of cunning.

"When the king himself bends to write to me, I can demand concessions. This Gasca will have to yield to me certain things. He will have to name me governor."

There was a stir of excitement among those within hearing. Catherine saw Don Louis's eyes fix on Rodrigo.

"It is not for myself that I demand such powers," the general declared, warming to his audience. "The king and his Cortes insult every man who has fought for me—every one of you who raised your voices demanding my appointment as governor—when they send instead some priest who knows nothing of the affairs of the country. The rumors that he brings repeal of the New Laws and pardon for all are but feeble tricks to gain him power in a land where he has none!"

Warm applause met his comments. Flushed with pleasure Pizarro raised a hand in modest protest.

"A wise man, the general," said a cavalier named Aldana, strolling toward them.

297

Rodrigo made no reply.

Aldana was a temperate, well-mannered man, an *encomendero* and soldier who was universally liked by the other men. He had visited Catherine's house when it sheltered the rebel meetings against the viceroy, and he had been there in recent times. Now he touched the back of his fingers to Rodrigo's arm.

"I am glad you have come this evening," he said in confidential tones. "There is a matter in which your support will carry much weight."

As he spoke he drew a thick roll of paper from beneath his doublet. Catherine noted with some uneasiness that the lawyer Cepeda had followed them and watched closely. Aldana stopped at a table and unrolled the paper upon it, nodding to a handful of men who seemed to be waiting there for some scene to be played out before them.

"Tomorrow the archbishop and I myself, along with two other men of your acquaintance, will sail for Spain," Aldana said. "We propose to ask King Carlos for confirmation of the general in his present authority. When we reach Panamá we will deliver this letter you see before you to Father Gasca, that he might see the wisdom in returning with us since he is not needed here. Sixty-nine of us have already affixed our names indicating our support of Pizarro. Will you not be the seventieth?"

Catherine heard Alma de Palacios Rubios beside her, speaking her name. She ignored her friend. The men with Rodrigo had formed a little ring around the table, excluding her without a thought. She moved sideways, attempting to see between two sets of shoulders. The letter was visible now, and above the long list of names and X's which served for names, were sentences which shocked her.

It was true the opening words were polite enough, expressing pleasure that Father Gasca had landed safely and regretting in the most courteous terms that his services were not needed as the country was at peace. They quickly took a more ominous tone, however. Father Gasca was advised that his presence could only provoke trouble. It was even hinted blatantly that should he attempt to proceed to Lima, his life might be forfeit.

In desperation Catherine attempted to catch her husband's eye and warn him the letter's content had been misrepresented. He did not see her. He was looking at Aldana.

"Is the letter your idea, Aldana?" Rodrigo asked bluntly.

Aldana gave a fleeting glance at Cepeda.

"No . . . I acknowledge it was not . . . but I heartily support its contents. If we are to enjoy the fruits of peace we must take this action. If we stand united, men of property and elected officials, Father Gasca surely will see the folly of pressing his authority."

Rodrigo had caught the brief look at Cepeda. He knew as well as Catherine did whose guile lay behind the letter. She saw his lip curl.

"I fear my name does not belong in such illustrious company."

His words were barbed, and those listening knew it. Catherine heard murmurs of disapproval and there was concern in the watery eyes of the old marquis. Cepeda turned at once and started off at no slow pace.

Rodrigo offered no apology for his decision. Looking about he found her and held out his hand.

"I think we would do well to excuse ourselves without awaiting dinner," he said grimly.

"Yes, you are right," agreed Catherine with a nod to the bewildered Alma. As they moved through the room she was aware of heads turning to follow them, of a low and sibilant ripple like the sound of the sea going out. She pressed close to her husband. "The letter was outrageous!" she whispered. "You did well not to sign it. If one wanted proof of rebellion against the king, one would need look no further than that piece of paper!"

Rodrigo's eyes were fixed on the crowd ahead of them. She knew he was alert to the stir around them.

"There are those who will take my refusal to sign it as proof of rebellion against the general."

"Cepeda?"

"Yes. The scheming lawyer was behind that letter."

Catherine felt her voice fail in her throat.

"And—your decision? Does it mean you would support Father Gasca against the general?"

Rodrigo jerked his head to a gatekeeper and they left Pizarro's palace. His answer was long in coming. It merged with the rush of the River Rimac, bounced from the walls of the darkened cathedral and whispered back:

"I do not know."

31

In early November Ana married and moved her single trunk
into the rented rooms where she and her enterprising young
husband would make their first home. She came daily to
Catherine's household, arriving always in time to help her
mistress dress and begin the morning. Within a few weeks
the new routine had become a smooth one.

"I don't know when I shall find a girl to replace you,"
Catherine confided as Ana pinned up her hair. "There have
been no ships for an uncommonly long time. Rodrigo says
they may all be detained in Panamá."

Ana gave a delicate shudder.

"I have heard the climate is unhealthy there. Many sicken
and die."

Catherine nodded. She wasn't just concerned over a new
maid. Enough time had passed for the new mares ordered
from Spain to arrive. Horses too could sicken and die if held
in Panamá. She was anxious for them, as the whole city now
was growing anxious, with its stocks of sugar, wheat and
wine almost depleted. Some whispered that this was Pizarro's
fault, that he had ordered all ships held lest messengers from
Father Gasca slip aboard and, landing, do some mischief.

"Do not concern yourself in the matter of a maid, señorita,"
said Ana. "I am content to continue coming so long as you
need me."

Catherine gave a grateful smile. "You are loyal, Ana. But I
know you are anxious to be a free woman. And if you begin to
carry a child you won't be able to work."

Ana's eyes widened. "Oh, but surely that will not happen
for a time yet!" she protested in total innocence. "It hasn't
happened to you."

"No," said Catherine, rising abruptly so her face would not
be reflected back toward Ana. "No, it hasn't happened to me."

The day had been appointed for polishing floors. Catherine
went to the kitchen and found the brushes, rags and hot wax
ready to her satisfaction. She would supervise the kitchen
maid while Ana stood over Belita Valdéz, for Ana had assured her with a worldly wisdom that Belita was but an
ignorant young girl incapable of doing anything alone. Be-

tween them they soon saw the floors in the sala and dining room shine to perfection.

The cleaning operation had moved on to the *sala familiar* and Rodrigo's bedroom by the time Magdalena came home from market. Catherine, returning from the small latrine which was closeted in one corner of the gallery, saw the housekeeper thrust her basket into Mateo's arms and look anxiously up toward the source of the household's activity. She mounted the steps without undue haste, but Catherine could detect heightened alertness beneath Magdalena's calm.

"Ah, señora," she said in low tones. "There is much excitement in the streets. A rider last night brought news of grave occurrences in Panamá. Señor Aldana, selected by General Pizarro to represent him at the court of Spain, has instead sworn loyalty to Father Gasca. By his own hand he has sent a letter to the general urging him to do the same."

Catherine stared at her housekeeper, whose words for once outpaced her breath. She couldn't believe the report she was hearing. Aldana little more than a month ago had solicited signatures urging Gasca to leave. Did he now espouse the new president's cause?

But Magdalena, with more news to tell, hurried on.

"In addition, Admiral Hinojosa, governor of Panamá, has been swayed by the decision. He has placed the whole of his navy in the command of Father Gasca. Our city talks of war."

"Yes," said Catherine, aware of how ridiculously insignificant the business of washing floors was. "Yes, that is surely what it means."

Before Magdalena could speak again, there was a pounding at the gate. Valdéz hurried to open it, and Alma de Palacios Rubios came in. Her manner was plainly agitated. She glanced up and caught sight of Catherine.

"Have you heard?" she called up, drawing near.

Catherine leaned over the railing, all thoughts of decorum forgotten, as Alma's were.

"Yes, Magdalena brought the news to me just now," she said.

Alma's round face was earnest, bereft of its usual laughter.

"I'm so sick of war and the talk of war! There has been nothing else since we came here! And I didn't even see the great rebellion. How can you stand there so calmly at the thought of yet more fighting?"

"What good would it do if I were otherwise?" asked Catherine with a shaky laugh. She came down the stairs to join her friend.

"Yes, you are right, of course," said Alma bitterly. "What choice have we? It is the men who decide. Come, let us go to Mass."

By the time they reached the cathedral a large crowd had assembled outside. Their attention was fixed on a figure standing at the top of the steps, and as Catherine and Alma drew nearer they saw the man was Don Luis.

"Aldana has been bought," he declared to all who listened. His voice was smooth with authority yet carried clearly. "What manner of clergyman is this Gasca, that he would turn your governor's most trusted friend against him? And the traitor Hinojosa, placed in authority as admiral and governor of Panamá by the general's own goodness—is disloyalty such as his fair recompense to the man who has brought peace and prosperity to you all?"

In the crowd his harangue sparked ardent cries: "Pizarro! Pizarro! Death to all traitors!"

Don Luis's cold eyes flickered with the light of satisfaction. Alma's young brother saw his sister and Catherine at the edge of the crowd and came to join them.

"Don Luis has promised a meeting of the Cabildo to answer Aldana's arrogant letter," he whispered with great excitement. "Look how nobly the general bears all this. He speaks not one word of reproof toward those who betrayed him!"

Catherine looked beyond Don Luis to the spot where Pizarro stood listening, Cepeda beside him. The general's face was closed and wary.

On the other side of the crowd a veteran captain spoke up.

"Let us hear from the general! As for me, I will continue my loyalty until a priest lays oil upon my mouth. But does Aldana not address you as a friend? Does he not say that Father Gasca's offer of a pardon to us all for our late rebellion is genuine?"

Cepeda took an angry step forward. "You presume to know a great deal of the contents of the general's mail! Do you think a traitor like Aldana can be expected to tell the truth? This clergyman may have brought some offer of a pardon, but any man of reckoning can see by the time he sailed with it that full knowledge of events in this country had not yet reached Spain. The king and his Cortes did not know we had slain the viceroy when they authorized a pardon. Do you think they will hold to it knowing we have his blood on our hands? No! They will offer us our heads on pikes instead!"

"Your head, surely, lawyer, for you were sent to advise the viceroy, not turn against him," jeered a voice from the foot of the steps. Catherine saw it was the ancient Carbajal in his purple burnoose. "We would do well to pave this priest's way with silver and gold and hope for the truth of his promises," the old soldier said.

"Since when do you shrink from battle, Carbajal?" stormed Cepeda coming toward him.

Carbajal cocked a foot on the step above him and leaned forward with pretended intimacy, provoking laughter. He twitched a pendant of silver hanging at Cepeda's neck.

"Since when do you lead it—lawyer?"

Argument erupted everywhere and voices raised. Catherine felt a shoulder brush hers, and looking up she found Rodrigo beside her. His face was grim.

Alma's brother saw him too, and greeted him with unchecked enthusiasm.

"Well, captain, does this mean you will revive our company?" he asked cheerfully.

Rodrigo looked away from him, across the crowd.

"I have no doubt the company will be revived," he said.

Twelfthnight of 1547 dawned bleak. The port was blockaded and travel outside the city of Lima was forbidden. Soldiers in the showy livery of Pizarro watched every gate.

Rodrigo prowled the house, impatient for word from the *encomienda*. None came. New foals were long since due from the Andalusians, and the colts from Boabdíl as well as the first purebred from their own stallion were nearing sale age. He applied for a travel permit to check on them and was denied it. Catherine watched his tension mount daily.

"When will the fighting start?" she asked as they stood together in the sala at day's end. They were at the *mirador*. Groups of soldiers passed in the street, and even the lowliest pikemen wore doublets and breeches of silk. They were embroidered with the peculiar coat of arms King Carlos had bestowed upon the Pizarros, one quarter of it depicting the native Peruvian sheep, the llama.

"I do not know," Rodrigo said in heavy tones.

He had not put on Pizarro's livery. He wore no soldier's garb of late. Catherine hesitated, a question hovering on her lips which long had hovered in her mind.

"Will you slip away to join Father Gasca's forces?" she asked at last.

He turned on her savagely. "How can I? How can I fight the general, who is my benefactor and my friend? What do you take me for?"

"But you have not—"

"No." He interrupted her, anticipating the direction of her thoughts. "How can I support him when he's advised by Cepeda and Don Luis?"

She heard the torment behind his rage. Her hand touched his arm.

"I did not mean to anger you," she said.

Beneath her fingers she felt him tense and tremble like a frightened horse. His hand darted out to caress her cheek. For an instant he seemed to move toward her, and then he drew away.

"You do not anger me," he said, kissing her lightly on the hair. "I anger myself with my indecision. Now I must go. I had almost forgotten there is something I must attend to."

Bewildered, Catherine watched him retrieve his silk cloak from a chair where he had only moments earlier discarded it. He had said nothing about going out again. She could not understand . . . it had been so long since he kissed her . . . touched her . . . and his words had been so tender. . . . Had she imagined it?

"Where?" she asked, too puzzled by his behavior to refrain.

He flicked her chin with tolerant amusement.

"You forget your place too easily, *preciosa*, questioning me."

"No doubt," she said, throat aching with the hurt. "Especially when I know the answer."

He paused and cocked an eyebrow. "Do you?"

There was laughter in his eyes, and something else. Relief?

"My poor Catherine," he said beneath his breath. "Perhaps—" He shook his head as if with firm resolve. "Goodnight."

On the following day, Epiphany, Rojo joined them at midmorning. This year he brought no wine, for there was none to bring save that which local vines produced. Instead, with apologies, he presented Catherine with a small sack of sugar.

"Rojo! Where did you get it?" she exclaimed.

He grinned roguishly. "Ask me not on a holy day, Doña Catherine."

Their old friend wore a new silk uniform appropriate to his

rank. Silver ornaments gleamed along the length of the baldric holding his sword. He frowned at Rodrigo's civilian attire but said nothing.

Every soul in the city would attend the morning's Mass, for this was not only a holy day, but the anniversary of the city's founding. Great groups of people joined them as they neared the church. As they pressed inside to be met by the glow and scent of candles, Catherine saw Pizarro flanked by his two advisers, who now seldom left his side.

The attire of all of them was sumptuous beyond belief. Pizarro's sword case was made of gold and set with precious stones. His suit was of velvet brocade, slashed and showing cloth of gold. Don Luis was no more humbly dressed, and the band of the velvet toque upon his head flashed with three fiery diamonds. Cepeda had exchanged his lawyer's robes for the full breeches and plumed helmet of a military commander, leaving, Catherine thought, little doubt how he would answer any overtures of peace.

Pizarro marked their entry and his gaze lay thoughtfully on Rodrigo. He did not nod in recognition. Don Luis leaned near to murmur to him, and they turned away.

The city could not watch its archbishop in his high chair on this feast day, nor hear his words of hope and faith. The archbishop, too, had sworn allegiance to his fellow churchman, Father Gasca, and remained in Panamá. Was an army growing there, wondered Catherine? As bells tolled and they left the church, her breast was filled not with divine tranquility, but with a heavy premonition of onrushing events, of the future hurtling toward her.

On the steps of the church Pizarro waited, advisers beside him. Bodyguards and attendants spread out about him like a trailing cloak.

"Rodrigo," he called in clear tones.

Rodrigo bowed gravely. "General. I ask God's blessing on you this holy day."

Pizarro's face showed none of the easy warmth which Catherine remembered there. His eyes were unmoving. He came a few steps nearer, his retinue behind.

"It has come to my attention that you show little enthusiasm for my cause. You do not wear my uniform. Nor have you brought forth horses, though it's well known I've requested them from every man."

Catherine watched the uncomfortable shifting of Rojo's

shoulders. Her own heart was jerking erratically. Only Rodrigo seemed unconcerned by the blunt confrontation.

"Had I any horses to serve you, general, you should have them. I have but a few pregnant mares and some yearlings too young for the saddle."

Pizarro's look was cool and distant.

"You have a fine white stallion, and mares can drop their foals one place as well as another in times like these."

Rodrigo's face for an instant lost its color.

"Your pardon, general," he said, his voice held level with effort. "I would give you the horses if I were a rich man. I am not. The white horses are not livestock, they are our business. Our dearest investment. The source, we hope, of our livelihood."

His old commander stared at him for a minute. Catherine saw by the smoldering look in Rodrigo's eyes that he would not back down. Don Luis, touching his beard, gave a narrow smile.

Abruptly the general turned, twitching his short cape around him.

"Bring the horses to me," he snapped to Cepeda. "All of them."

Catherine heard the sharp outrush of Rojo's breath. Rodrigo, beside her, did not stir.

Vespers had rung when Rodrigo rode in. The afternoon sun burned low in the sky. Catherine knew by the slope of her husband's shoulders that his news was not good.

"No word—nothing but rumors," he said as she came down to meet him. "Through Fray Jeronimo I found a priest who had made his way from Tumbez and who had news from Panamá. He thought he might have heard that there was an Andalusian on a ship there, but he was not certain. Many of the ships which have crossed of late have run short of water and had to throw their horses overboard."

"And the spices?"

"Surely they're there too. They will rot and be of little value in any case."

He sank onto a bench and ran his hands through his hair in a rare gesture of despondency.

"God is judging me," he said.

Catherine came to his side. "This is not the work of God, it is politics!"

He looked at her but did not seem to hear.

306

"I have done many wrongs. I have not spoken openly in support of God's servant, Father Gasca, though my heart has long told me he is the legal representative of King Carlos and that the general will never be. It is little enough I could have offered his cause—a horse, a sword—but I have delayed too long, and now I cannot even offer that."

His humility filled her throat with words of love she could not speak. She put a hand against his arm.

"You have stood against Pizarro. You tried to deny him our horses. There is something in that."

He shook his head angrily, and as he rose Catherine saw the deep frustration in his face. At good risk to both men, Rodrigo had tried to smuggle Valdéz from the city so that the stable man might save their distant horses from Pizarro's requisition. The plan had failed. Rodrigo was a man who met difficulties with action, and now he could not move in any direction.

Blows, loud and threatening, sounded on the gate. Rodrigo looked warily up. Valdéz, who went to answer the summons, was almost run down by the horsemen galloping in.

There were four of them, wearing Pizarro's emblem on their breasts. They reined plunging horses and Catherine saw that the man in the lead was Alma's brother. With lines held high, in the manner of Rodrigo who had trained him, he spoke briskly.

"Captain Valdivia, you and the members of your household are hereby placed under arrest by order of General Pizarro. You are confined to this house until further notice. My men and I have orders to shoot anyone attempting to leave."

Rodrigo stood by the fig tree. His hands were planted on his hips. He did not stir.

"What a long wait you have had for me to return," he said, his head cocked in contempt. "You have the makings of an officer, Martín, to know I would be more easily trapped than taken. Under what charge are we arrested?"

Martín's gaze wavered.

"Under charge of mutiny, captain. A detachment sent by President Cepeda to fetch your horses returned this morning. They reported that your men fought them with clubs and pitchforks, and while they were so occupied, the priest whom you employ breeched the corral and drove the horses into hiding."

"The priest!" Catherine exclaimed.

From the side of the courtyard Valdéz stepped forward to raise a clenched fist.

"A just reward for a christian gentleman like the captain!" he proclaimed in hoarse tones. "God bless the priest! God bless our captain, who in all of Lima is the only one to stand against tyranny!"

Alma's brother moved uncomfortably to turn his horse away.

"Wait," Rodrigo ordered. "My wife's maid—you must allow her to return to her home."

Catherine glanced up and saw Ana's pale face, with tears squeezing out though she fought against them. The girl looked anxiously toward the soldiers.

"I cannot allow it," Martín said, squaring his shoulders almost desperately.

Rodrigo's hand flashed up to catch his bridle, staying him. His voice was low but uncompromising in its authority.

"Martín. Let her go. She has a husband."

The young man on the horse sat in awkward indecision. He looked at Rodrigo, then at the other soldiers who accompanied him.

"Very well, but she may not return," Martín snapped. He reeled his horse. A moment later the gate closed behind them and the street rang with his orders to surround the house.

32

Three days passed and they paced the house as captives. Silence filled the prison which once had been their home, for all impulse to speak and all lightness had fled with soldiers in the street.

"Will there be a trial? Will we be removed?" asked Catherine.

Rodrigo shook his head. "I don't know."

Their food supply was running low. The meat had not lasted beyond the day when they were arrested. Yesterday the cheese had given out, along with the eggs. Today there was nothing but dried beans and corn and a little fruit.

As afternoon waned, while Catherine and her husband sat playing cards in the courtyard, the sounds of commotion came to them from the street.

"Why, that is Rojo's voice," said Rodrigo, looking up in surprise.

They stood as one and hurried up to the *mirador* on the chance of seeing.

The carved balcony gave a view of the scene below. Rojo sat facing them on his gray horse, though he could not see them. He had put aside his showy new uniform and wore a patched shirt beneath his breastplate.

"I said, let me pass," he growled to the soldier guarding the front door to their house.

"I cannot, Captain Rojo. You know that this household is under arrest. The whole town knows it. The general would have my ears if they were allowed communication with anyone."

With a swiftness amazing for his size, Rojo bent down and swept the soldier aloft in one meaty hand.

"And I will tear them off myself if you try to stop me!" he said with his red beard touching that of the terrified soldier.

That young man dropped back to earth, his position lacking dignity. As Rojo rode forward, with a menacing scowl, the other soldiers at the gate fled from their posts. By the time Catherine and her husband reached the gallery stairs, Valdéz was already admitting him.

"Well, 'Rigo, this is a fine mess," he boomed with forced cheerfulness.

Rodrigo crossed his arms.

"Rojo, you should not have come here," he said severely. "You will find yourself among the enemies of Don Luis if it is learned how you forced your way in here."

"Don Luis. Bah!" Rojo spit. "Let Don Luis face me and I will pluck the hairs from his fine beard. When the general takes his counsel from roaches such as those, then I no longer will obey the general."

"You cannot mean that," Rodrigo said. He looked uneasily at Rojo's attire.

Rojo beamed broadly.

"You see? I do not wear his colors."

"You should. You have taken his money."

Rojo stuck the smallest of his fingers in his ear and scratched it, squinting.

"I have been thinking that perhaps it is His Majesty's money I have been taking. Perhaps my uniform was paid for from the Royal Fifth. If that is so, then it is to King Carlos I owe my allegiance."

Rodrigo smiled with affection.

"Truly, Rojo, you are more than a friend. You have shown it by coming here. But I did not propose to make a rebellion—"

"The seeds of one are planted," Rojo interrupted in low undertone. "Not by you, but by the act of your arrest. Men fear for their property now, not unlike they did when the viceroy first was forced upon us. They have seen the example made of you. They did not like it. No one dares speak aloud, for Don Luis's spies are everywhere, but when men piss together they whisper that Pizarro is a dictator."

Unconsciously Catherine slipped her hand beneath Rodrigo's arm. She was frightened for him. And out in the street she heard noise swell again, much shouting.

"Open!" barked a voice as a hand smote their gate.

Rodrigo signaled Valdéz to obey. He spoke quickly to Rojo.

"You have imperiled yourself by coming here, Rojo. Do no more."

He looked down at Catherine, his lips pursed to speak, but before he could do so a rider appeared. It was Pizarro himself.

Rodrigo crossed his arms again and spoke no word of welcome. The general advanced on a sleek dun horse accompanied by six bodyguards. He was alone, however, in the sense that neither Cepeda nor Don Luis rode beside him. Stopping a few lengths away he swung down from his saddle.

"I have come to ask your forgiveness," he said, looking squarely at Rodrigo. "I did not know of your arrest. It was not by my order."

"It was ordered in your name," Rodrigo said.

The general appeared unmoved. "And well it might have been," he countered. "Your men wronged me by denying me your horses when I sent for them. You wronged me likewise, Rodrigo. But I'll not have it said that I enlist men under my banners by terrorizing those who do not cooperate. The soldiers are gone from your doors. You are quite free."

In heavy silence Rodrigo regarded him. Pizarro turned his attention to Catherine.

"I apologize for the embarrassment to your household, Doña Catherine."

She nodded slightly. Impossible to keep from her mind the question of whether the general, by this gesture, hoped to win Rodrigo to his cause by displaying first his power and then his largess. Such would be a shabby trick, beneath the general. She hoped he was sincere.

He noted Rojo now, noted too the plain shirt and guessed at what it connoted, Catherine judged.

"It pains me not to have you call me comrade," said Pizarro softly, turning his attention back toward her husband. "I know you bear an old grudge against Don Luis. Is it that alone which keeps you from me?"

Rodrigo relaxed his pose. His eyes were welded to those of the man by whom he had come to his modest fortunes.

"No," he said at last.

He volunteered no more.

After a moment Pizarro nodded, slowly, as though all now were clear to him without the need of further words. He put a boot into the high stirrup of the dun and turned away.

Halfway to the gate he reined and twisted in the saddle.

"You are dangerous," he said to Rodrigo. "The youngest of all my captains—and yet there is many an eye that rests on you. Cepeda says I am a fool to free you, and that alone proves his wisdom. I wish that you were less honest, Rodrigo, and yet I would not have you any other way."

Rojo gave the puzzled, vaguely discomfited wag of the head which Catherine had come to know so well.

"I am not sure I like the smell of this wind," he said when they were alone. "What does it mean?"

"I don't know," said Rodrigo. From the street there came the sound of soldiers departing. He looked at his friend. "You must put your uniform back on, Rojo. If you do not, they will charge me next with raising followers and plotting rebellion."

The burly Rojo, half again Rodrigo's size and his senior by a decade, looked undecided.

"I will do whatever you ask me, 'Rigo. And there are many others who will do likewise."

The two men clasped hands. Standing beside her husband, Catherine watched their friend ride out.

"Will you?" she asked.

Neither of them had moved their gazes from the gate.

"Raise a rebellion?" Rodrigo questioned. "No. I understand war and little else. I would not ask others to follow me. I can speak and act for myself, and nothing more."

"And—for yourself?"

"I understand too well the general's reluctance to yield his power. All that we have, he and I, we have won by fighting. By fighting we can keep it. To sacrifice all for the sake of law—is that not madness?"

His smile was bitter. "By doing nothing I err twice, against the general and against the crown. And you—I exposed you to the criticism of society when I first supported the general against the viceroy. Now that every soldier in the city wears his colors but me, I expose you to it again. I forced you to bear much when I forced you to become my wife."

"I have no regrets," she said, looking earnestly up at him.

A mask settled over his features. He touched her hair.

"I thank you for your lies," he said, and walked toward the stables.

"Your husband does well to refuse his loyalty to General Pizarro," said the marquesa, drumming her fingers on the carved arms of a chair. "The city has succumbed to madness. Even Judge Cepeda himself has proved a traitor. Can they not see they are in open rebellion against King Carlos?"

"Ha! They are scoundrels, all of them," decreed the marquis, his old eyes snapping. "Some see the lay of the land, I'll warrant, but they are afraid to stretch their necks where those necks are so easily struck in two."

Catherine smiled wanly. All February had been, it seemed, the prelude to war. In the North and to the South, in Cuzco, rebellions against Pizarro had broken out. Small detachments had been dispatched to quell them. Now it was rumored Aldana had sailed from Panamá with four ships, intending to offer escape for any citizens of Lima who desired it.

"How he supposes we shall avail ourselves of it, I do not know," the marquesa pointed out with disgust. "All of us are virtual prisoners of General Pizarro. Sometimes it seems to me that men at war think with but half their brains."

Catherine stood reluctantly. It had been a rare treat to find the marquis and marquesa both at home. Her mood was jittery of late, compounded by Rodrigo's silence at home and the bellowing and galloping of soldiers in every street.

"I must leave now," she said. "You must ready yourself for the baptism."

The marquesa sniffed heartily.

"Let us hope Doña Elvira's mood will improve now that she's had her son. I fear I find her difficult to tolerate upon occasion."

Catherine busied herself with the strings of her handbag. It was hard to purge her heart of bitterness that after little more than nine months of marriage Alonzo and Elvira should be so blessed. She would rejoice in their good fortune for Alonzo's sake, she told herself.

When she arrived home, Magdalena met her with tight-set lips.

"You have a caller in the sala," she announced. "It is Señora Griega."

Catherine drew breath slowly.

"Señor de Valdivia is not at home?"

"No . . . it is you she asked for."

Catherine looked away from the housekeeper's angry embarrassment. In that moment she loved Magdalena for a loyalty which extended even to being offended when her mistress was offended.

"Very well, I will see her," she said crisply. "Ana, stay behind."

She climbed the stairs to the gallery quickly. At the door to the sala she hesitated. Then seizing the doorlatch, she entered with brisk determination.

Francisca lounged comfortably in a chair beside the fireplace, her feet on a stool. She did not even raise her mass of unbound curls as Catherine entered. For an instant it seemed to Catherine that the room belonged to the other woman, not to her.

"My husband is not at home," she said, and her words sounded harsh in her ears.

"I know," Francisca answered, lips parting in a lazy smile. "He goes out in the morning to hear the news, to attend to business. That is why I have chosen this time to come."

She sat up suddenly and patted the chair across from her.

"Come and sit here, Catherine. It is time we talked."

Catherine did not move. "We've nothing to talk about."

"Ah, but we do. I am a widow now, did you know? It is time we speak of Rodrigo."

Catherine shook with anger. She felt her chin go up.

"How dare you even presume to speak so brazenly! How dare you come to my house—"

"Yes, yes, I know you are a doña. You do not need to remind me with some grand display of temper," Francisca interrupted as if bored. "It is all the same to me whether you hear me out or fly into a rage, but if you are as wise as 'Rigo thinks, you will listen and spare yourself much grief."

Francisca rested one elbow on the arm of her chair in a teasing pose which now was challenging.

"You see," she said, "I love Rodrigo—and I know he does not love you. When Pizarro's army leaves Lima, I will be with them. So will Rodrigo. If you are wise you will return to Spain where you belong, for I promise you I will not return him to you for even this pretense of a marriage which you maintain."

Catherine's voice was cold.

"You are mistaken, Francisca. My husband will not ride with Pizarro. He has not enlisted."

"He will," said Francisca, twisting a curl around her finger with a knowing look. "He will, and I shall win him. Twice I have carried his child in my belly and flushed it from me with herbs. The next time I won't. What is a squalling brat if it gets me what I want, eh? If you go, you will make things easier for both of us, and for Rodrigo."

A heavy pain pushed at Catherine's breast. She couldn't breathe. She was sickened by the shamelessness, the power of Francisca's threat.

The other woman watched her intently, and when she did not speak, Francisca's face darkened. Her hands seized the arms of the chair where she sat, and rigid with anger she propelled herself to the edge of it.

"Why don't you answer?" she hissed. "Don't you understand? I'm tired of seeing Rodrigo only at night, with shutters drawn! I want to dance and laugh with him at parties. I want to walk through the streets with him and kneel with him in church!"

The words rushed out, and still Catherine couldn't speak. Francisca moved and seemed about to spring from her chair in attack when the door opened and Rodrigo entered.

Catherine looked bleakly to him, seeking some sign that he repudiated all which Francisca promised.

He frowned. "Francisca. . . ."

She hurried toward him and held out a hand which he took readily.

"I am so glad you've come, Rodrigo. I need advice. Who is the agent who can most quickly sell my house?"

"Sell it? Why?" Rodrigo asked.

Francisca's face was seductive in its sadness.

"When the army leaves I shall go along to nurse and cook. I have no need for a fancy house—and no taste for city life. It is so costly . . . so tedious. I wonder that you stand it, 'Rigo. Wouldn't you be happier on your *encomienda?* You could live without the pretense of manners there, watch your horses grow, build what you need with your own hands. Why, with the silver you saved—ah, but I forget! Your wife no doubt prefers surroundings such as these."

As she watched him, Catherine began to think her husband had forgotten she was in the room. He stood staring at Francisca as if bound fast by confusion. His puzzled expression was that of a man who tried to fathom something he could not understand. Unwilling to witness any more of their intimacy, she walked quickly to the *mirador,* her back toward them. As she did so she heard Rodrigo stir.

"Think on it another night before you sell your house, Francisca. If you find you still need an agent, I will get one for you. Now if you will excuse me, Catherine and I—"

"Yes, of course. Catherine has made her claims on you very clear," said Francisca in brittle tones.

Catherine heard the door close. She glanced across her shoulder.

"She shouldn't have come here. I have told her she isn't welcome," Rodrigo said. He smoothed his hair back with an awkward gesture. "Her husband died last week. She is. . . ."

"Consumed with grief," Catherine replied, culling the sarcasm from her words.

If Rodrigo knew it was intended, he took no issue.

"Yes, I suppose," he said, his voice a distant sound as she

looked again at the street. He came to stand behind her. "What is it, Catherine? I have respected your wishes. I did not deliberately bring Francisca under our roof."

Catherine dashed away the tears which hovered on her lashes.

"No." She turned, avoiding his eyes so he might not see the traces of tears. "The baptism should be over now. I am going to church."

"I will come with you," Rodrigo offered.

He spoke too eagerly. The offering of guilt, thought Catherine.

They walked to the cathedral in a world of uniforms and banners. An uneasy silence hung between them. Catherine agonized over Francisca's words, and anger filled her as she thought of the sly way Francisca had made her seem a barrier to the life Rodrigo desired.

There was whooping ahead of them as they returned home, and they were forced to stand aside as a trio of soldiers raced past. When they reached their own street, its usual peace was punctuated by the sharp crack of arquebuses firing in a field beyond. Rodrigo went to the *mirador* and stood looking out toward the sound.

"My God, I am weary of fighting," he said.

Catherine came to stand beside him.

"Then I am glad you will see no more of it. I am glad you have not joined either the general or Father Gasca."

Rodrigo straightened. His eyes held hers.

"But I have, my prize. I joined the general this morning. Tomorrow I will begin drilling my old company."

"What?" she gasped. Shock piled on shock, for as she saw the lines pressed in his face she began to realize he didn't love the life of a soldier. Perhaps he had never loved it. "But why?"

"It is the only trade I know. I cannot doctor like Señor Palacios Rubios or witness papers like Señor Bocanegra. I can only earn my living by fighting—on one side or another."

Never had they seemed so tightly bound. Everything between them begged to be settled now, before Ana called them to lunch or some other interruption ended this plunge into truth. Catherine's hands were surrounded by those of her husband. She pressed against their warmth.

"We don't need the money! Francisca spoke truly this morning. We could live at the *encomienda* and have no need

316

of this house. The income from spices would be sufficient for that."

A smile, much removed from the easy one which had won her heart, touched Rodrigo's mouth and made him seem almost old.

"You were not meant for a life of toil and deprivation, *preciosa*, any more than I was meant to sit by the fire and wear fine clothes. Our marriage, in retrospect, was a blunder, but let us make the best of it. We can prosper, given money to invest. But first we must have a country at peace. First we must have open ports so horses can reach us from Panamá."

"But—you have said the general is a rebel!"

He dropped her hands.

"Yes, the general is a rebel. Well, what of it?"

33

In a thin line the horses and carts came, followed by those on foot, winding slowly over land where there was no road on the plains outside of Lima. Catherine watched them from a gentle swelling of the earth. To her back were tents and livestock, scattered furniture. In front of her, between her and the approaching line, rode Pizarro's guards. When the line arrived, the evacuation of Lima would be complete. The circling guards insured no one would leave this forced encampment on the hill.

The rumors of February had all proved true. Four ships in the service of Father Gasca, and commanded by Aldana, lay now in the port of Callao awaiting any citizens who wished to flee. Pizarro had seen there would be no passengers. For four days now the residents of Lima had come in a steady flow to this spot, by his command. From here there would be no chance of communicating with the waiting ships.

"Oh, if your father could but see us now!" exclaimed Ana mournfully. "Who would ever have thought that members of his household should come to live like gypsies! Not that I am not grateful to have the shelter of your tent," she added with haste, for the ground was thick with men and women sleeping without the least pretense of shelter.

"These will surely be the last arrivals," sighed Catherine, turning away. "Let us go and see how Señora de Palacios Rubios is faring today."

The trip had proved too arduous for the pregnant Alma. Yesterday, the day of her arrival, she had given birth to a daughter, stillborn.

"I thank God her husband is a doctor," Ana murmured. "Oh, there is Captain Valdivia."

"What? Not drilling his company?" wondered Catherine, putting her hand up against the sun and looking in the direction Ana indicated. Rodrigo slept with his men, in the open, and on previous days had early made his voice heard on the practice field where several companies met. Now she saw his red and gold—clad form toiling at the center of a group of priests. In a moment she recognized what he was about.

"They are raising a cross for the chapel," she said, as a tree trunk crudely hacked in half came upright with crosspiece in place.

A priest apart from the group, a frail old man, took notice of them and came forward smiling.

"We should be lost except for your husband," he said. "His back is stronger than any of ours, and while he rests his horse, he takes for himself no such luxury. Yesterday he helped us raise our tent. Today we shall have a cross as well. Truly God is merciful to send us such a friend as him."

Threading their way through the camp they came to Alma's tent. Several women, Catherine included, had lent their pillows to her, and she lay against them looking pale but undaunted.

"It was worth it, losing a child, if it makes Martín see what a tyrant he serves," she whispered hoarsely. "He is so young—so impressed with himself as a soldier—and he has been blind. Now he isn't. But oh, what if the young fool now takes it into his head to escape? There was such an attempt last night, did you know? The guards shot the man down. Their arquebuses do not leave a clean wound like a sword. There was nothing my husband could do for him. I hate this country!"

"It is not the country," Catherine soothed. "The times are confusing."

And to me most of all, she thought later, when they left Alma resting. She did not understand how Rodrigo could fling himself so wholeheartedly into the service of Pizarro after hesitating so long. He pushed his men harder than any other captain and, she was told, they repaid him with a devotion which was almost adoration. He betrayed no doubt now of his decision to fight against Father Gasca. How could he show such zeal for the job before him, once unwanted?

Rodrigo was as confusing as the times. His bitterness when he spoke of the soldier's life thrust upon him still was fresh in her mind. Yet now that he had embraced it, his bearing was that of a man who loved no other quite so well. Always, among the men, among the other captains, he moved with energy and with laughter on his lips.

They neared the practice field and she could hear his voice.

"Higher! Higher! Aim for the face or the men you spear will pull your lances from you!"

She shuddered. How could he train men for the maximum slaughter of those he did not even want to fight? The sight and sounds of the camp around her filled her with rage. Even the soldiers who were resting played at war. In a narrow strip at the edge of the camp they rode at each other, two by two, high in the saddle in the game of canes.

"Catherine."

She heard Rodrigo's voice behind her. He had come from the practice field and he was sweaty, as was Boabdíl. He dismounted and fell into step beside her. Ana left them and hurried ahead alone.

"Have you slept well? Are you comfortable?" Rodrigo asked.

"Yes, more comfortable than most, I'm sure. You were generous to provide a tent for us."

"I am glad I heard of the move in advance. Tents were hard to come by once the word got out."

He made no move to turn back. His presence at her side when men were at work all around them impressed itself upon Catherine as unexpected, almost odd. In three days in camp she had seldom seen him, never in the middle of the day.

"And your friend Alma—will she regain her health?"

"Yes. She is worried for Martín. She is afraid he might be so rash as to try to escape and join Gasca's forces, he is so angered by her loss. Will you not speak to him?"

"Martín is a man now. I cannot tell him how to live."

He hesitated. She knew it was not Martín which was on his mind.

"There is a favor I must ask of you," he said.

She looked at him in surprise. Never before, in her memory, had he addressed that phrase to her. It suggested a trust between them.

"Of course," she said. "What is it?"

They were near the tent which he had set up for her and her female servants. He did not speak until he pulled the flap aside and they stepped in.

"Here is a pouch of silver," he said, thrusting it into her hands. "I do not have the time to find Valdéz and give it into his keeping so that you do not have the worry of it. Will you find him?"

"Yes. . . ." Catherine frowned. Her husband was behaving strangely.

"Next week . . . if I should not be here . . . will you seek out Fray Ambrosio and give him half of it? Tell him it is to mend his roof."

"If you are not here!" She searched his face. "Is the army about to move? Have you heard?"

His eyes told her nothing. They rested on her gently.

"The army can move at any time," he said.

An old ache filled her throat. For a moment more they lingered looking at one another.

"You are beautiful," he whispered. With a quick touch of his fingers to her chin he made his exit.

Catherine stood in the semidarkness of the tent feeling lost and alone. The pouch of silver weighed heavy in her fingers. So little claim she had to her husband, yet she could not bear to see him go.

A voice called from outside the tent. "God be with you, Rodrigo."

Slightly dazed she made her way to the opening and raised the flap. Outside stood a careworn Franciscan whose name she could not recall.

"My husband isn't here," she said.

The priest smiled apology.

"Ah. I am too late then. I saw him headed here in your company but a short time ago. I came. . . ." He seemed to falter. "I heard his confession this morning, Señora de Valdivia. I have come to give him this. It was blessed by the Bishop of Toledo."

As he spoke the smooth carved beads of a rosary slipped into her hand. Catherine looked down, not understanding. It made no sense to link a gift with her husband's confession.

"Because of his help in raising your cross?" she said slowly, feeling her way through the priest's apparent reluctance to speak.

He stared at her.

"Yes," he said. "Yes, because of the cross. Of course." Reaching out, he reclaimed the rosary. "Perhaps I should give it to him myself," he said in a voice strangely kind. "No doubt I will find him on the practice field."   .

When he had gone she stood for a moment in the sun. Then she shook herself to action. It was senseless, this foreboding. The product of nerves and the unfamiliar setting of the camp. She accomplished nothing by yielding to it. She set off to find Valdéz.

Late in the afternoon she went to stand at the edge of the practice field. As a soft breeze lifted her hair she watched the various companies. One was a haggard-looking group, arquebusiers by training, but in the extravagant outfitting of Pizarro's army, now mounted on horses. Ana showed more grace in the saddle than most of them. Catherine heard their captain, a veteran cavalryman, shout bitter insults as they struggled to maneuver both their horses and their clumsy weapons.

"They will be lucky if they do not kill each other," said Rodrigo darkly.

He had come up unobserved by her. She smiled at him, then followed his gaze as it moved back to the mounted arquebusiers. They fired a volley and half the horses beneath them plunged and wheeled in confusion. Rodrigo shook his head.

"That weapon will prove more a plague to war than an aid to it," he said of the smoking guns.

"Will you take supper with us tonight?" asked Catherine. "Magdalena is proving the most admired cook in camp."

"So I am told. Rojo returned from lunch singing her praises. Yes, I will come."

He stepped to the ground.

"Did the priest find you?" she asked.

"The priest?"

"With the rosary."

"Ah, yes."

He volunteered no more. In fact he seemed vexed by the subject. They walked in silence back toward the tents. Each company of soldiers in this lavishly appointed army had unfurled new standards, which fluttered on pikes throughout the camp. Some were emblazoned with their general's initials and some bore his coat of arms. On one of the latter Catherine noted there had been added a crown, the mark of a monarch. Her steps faltered. Quickly she resumed them, lest her husband notice. Then she saw his eyes were also fixed on the fluttering silk, and he was frowning.

From the distance there came an angry voice.

"Get back! Get back! How dare you set hand to my horses? I tell you to get back or I'll pin your ears together."

Catherine looked anxiously at her husband. "That is the marquis!" she said.

The marquis and marquesa had been among the last to leave the city. She had not seen them since their arrival that morning when members of their large household had struggled to set a pavilion of ancient vintage into place. Rodrigo moved at once toward the sound of the altercation, and she was at his side.

Four soldiers stood beside the marquis's sprawling tent, and two of them stood with halters in hand, attempting to slip them on horses. The marquis, brandishing his sword, kept them at bay.

"But we are ordered to take them," reasoned one of the four. "The army has need of them."

"You will not take them until I lie dead," the old man boasted. "Already I have given two to this army of rebels, and I tell you I did not give those willingly."

Catherine caught her breath. No one had dared speak so openly of their dissent with Pizarro's cause.

"Is it not enough that we are forced from our homes and made to live as thieves, our ladies with us?" the marquis continued.

The hand of one of the soldiers traveled to his sword.

"Move, old man."

Rodrigo pushed forward through a ring of timid spectators. "Stop it, I order you! Let the horses be."

The soldier with his hand to his sword looked uncertain.

"You are not our captain," he said. He looked to his companions for support. A crowd was growing.

"What is this?" demanded a new voice. "Can you not do the simple task of bringing horses when you are told?"

Cepeda, Audencia president turned rebel, rode into view. He was covered in showy armor from beard to knees and his manner was haughty.

"The Marquis de Zurbarán will not yield his horses, and Captain Valdivia forbid us to molest him."

The eyes of the lawyer flicked over Rodrigo with contempt. "Captain Valdivia forbid it? Captain Valdivia is deceived of his authority."

The marquis let his sword fall to his side. He drew himself up.

"You call yourself a gentleman, señor. I say you little deserve that title if you condone this outrage. We have given horses to your cause. We have none left but my charger and my saddle horse, the lady marquesa's palfrey and the horse which pulls her cart. Clearly those are animals of which we cannot be deprived."

Cepeda listened with bored expression.

"People of your age should not sit a saddle," he said incisively. "We will leave you the cart horse."

At a nod from him the soldiers moved. Two of them started for the horses, and the marquis, smarting from the insult, turned on them with a hoarse battle cry. A third soldier ducked behind him, catching him by the arms. The fourth seized the sword from his helpless hand and tossed it to Cepeda.

Rodrigo lunged forward swearing. A hand shot through the crowd and seized him by the neck of his armor.

"Do not be a fool!" panted Rojo, pushing his way past Catherine as his friend writhed in his grip. "Cepeda would gladly see you hung over just such a trifle as this. Do you think that will get the marquis his horses back?"

Ahead of them the marquis was howling his rage, calling his captors traitors and a good deal more. There was angry murmuring in the crowd.

"See—Cepeda does himself more harm than good by his act," Rojo insisted. Warily he loosed his hold on Rodrigo.

Cepeda wheeled his horse and rode away, the soldiers running behind him with the horses. The marquis stood like a man now broken. His shoulders sloped. He looked very old.

"My sword," he muttered. "They have taken my sword."

Then resolve returned to his watery eyes. He stood as straight as his years allowed.

"Bring me a chest!" he thundered to the servants hovering at his tent.

Rodrigo stepped forward.

"My lord marquis, I will go to the general at once. He will not approve this insult to your honor. I will try to see your horses returned to you."

"You are kind, captain," said the marquis with a bow of gallantry. "In you, at least, courtesy and bravery are not dead. But do not plead my case. I will plead it myself. I will teach this rabble the hopelessness of fighting Bernál, Marquis de Zurbarán, who fought the Moors and jousted with the finest knights of Italy!"

"Tempers are growing short throughout the camp," sighed Rojo as he fell into step with Catherine and Rodrigo and they started again toward Catherine's tent.

They had not gone a hundred yards when a clamor, punctuated by applause, erupted behind them. With a glance at each other the two men turned back, and Catherine was at their heels. Instead of dispersing, the crowd at the marquis's tent had grown. As they drew nearer, the reason was clear.

"Pizarro and all who follow his cause are traitors—rebels against our great and generous monarch, King Carlos!" the marquis proclaimed. He stood on the chest his servants had brought out for him, waving his arms in fiery oratory. "I exhort you, those who are true and loyal citizens, let us stand together! Let us demand our rights as citizens! Let us take up arms if necessary to effect our exit from this gypsy camp where we are held against our will!"

In the door to his tent the marquesa stood, hands raised to her lips in an attitude of prayer. She could not be other than fearful, Catherine thought, but her expression was as unmovable as that of her husband.

"Are we not men and women of Spain?" he continued. "Let us not be ruled by a tyrant who has no claim—"

His words were drowned out by the thunder of horses' hooves. A handful of soldiers burst through the crowd, provoking screams. They sprang from their saddles and two of them wrestled the marquis from his platform.

"Let us resist this lawlessness!" he cried, the words muffled as he struggled. "Let us die in honor rather than live in shame!"

One of the soldiers struck him in the stomach and the breath was driven from him. Rodrigo, eluding Rojo, fell on the man who had struck the marquis and sent him sprawling. He grabbed the neck of one of the soldiers who held the old man, and another of their number seized him in turn. Rodrigo heaved him to the ground and Catherine heard the sound of swords being drawn. She saw her husband dragged back toward her by two men.

"Enough," wheezed the priest who had come to her tent that morning. He held one of Rodrigo's arms while Rojo held the other. "You do not want blood on your soul at a time like this!" he said severely.

"He is an old man!" her husband shouted to the soldiers. "Have you no decency?"

Another horse and rider appeared on the fringe of the crowd.

"Here! Here! What is the trouble?" inquired Luis de Alvarado, riding forward. "My lord marquis! What has happened? Release him at once."

Sheepishly the soldiers obeyed. The marquis got to his feet. Luis de Alvarado, suited in black and riding a horse of the same color, raised his arching eyebrow.

"He was preaching rebellion," a soldier said. "You see, Don Luis, the size of the crowd he had gathered. And he was addressing them, urging resistance against the general."

"Yes, and I will urge it again, so long as I have voice in me," the marquis stormed, flicking dust from his clothes. "I am not afraid to speak out about that which all can see. I will

325

not live like a slave, denied my house and seeing my property taken from me!"

There were noises of sympathy from the crowd. Don Luis noted them with a glance.

"What property, my lord marquis?" he asked in earnest tones. "I pray you tell me what has happened."

"Your President Cepeda has caused my horses to be seized. He took my sword. I tell you I will not stand for it—"

"Your horses?" repeated Don Luis, making a fine display of being shocked. "My lord marquis, it distresses me to hear it. The army has gotten quite out of control these last weeks, and President Cepeda with them, I fear. I have spoken out time and again for the rights of our citizens, but I am but one. The word of the Cabildo is swept aside."

"Listen to how he would make himself sweet to the people!" Rojo exclaimed in disbelief.

"He will be left behind when the army rides," Rodrigo sneered. "He does not wish to see his neck stretched."

Catherine shared their disgust. Moreover she was angry with the crowd, the marquis among them, who could not see how Don Luis curried favor for himself from all sides.

"As to your sword. . . ." He paused dramatically. "Here, my lord marquis, take mine until your own is restored to you." He extended it with a flourish, bowing low. Sounds of approval were heard on the lips of the crowd.

Don Luis smiled smoothly. "I trust, my lord marquis, that you will make no more speeches if I give you my word to express the discontent of this citizenry to the general?" He lifted his head in recognition of the marquesa. "My lady, you can no doubt persuade your husband of the greater value of his wise counsel to the Cabildo than his blood to the battlefield where he has already distinguished himself so nobly."

The marquis seemed more than a little mollified by the words of praise. With satisfied hauteur he dropped the sword into his sword case and turned back toward his tent.

"The marquesa!" said Catherine bitterly. "Even the marquesa is duped by him."

This time Rojo did not come with them. As they walked along, the noise of the camp was deafening. It was nearing dusk and campfires had been lighted. The smoke from them choked her. The memory of seeing the gentle old marquis humiliated, struck and hurled into the dust was fresh and brutal in her mind. No sooner were they within view of the tent than she heard a sobbing shriek.

"Stop it! Stop it!"

A laughing group of soldiers moved on, and she saw Belita Valdéz, hands pressed to her offended backside, weeping.

No woman but a tavern wench was ever publicly embraced, but when Rodrigo's arm came up around her shoulders, Catherine leaned against it gratefully. He raised the flap to her tent and drew her inside, holding her while she shook with fear and hatred of the ugly, cruel world which now surrounded all of them.

"There, *preciosa*, all this will pass," he said softly. "Do not think on it. Soon you will be back in your own house. There will not be this clamor . . . this confusion."

As he spoke he covered her face with gentle kisses. At first she welcomed them, and this strange tenderness. But the kisses changed. He pulled her closer. Unexpectedly she felt herself filled with revulsion. How could he be amorous? How could he approach her like this, in the midst of men who prepared for killing, and expect her response?

Enraged by the senseless violence which surrounded them, she tried to push away.

"Stop it!" she gasped. "How can you—how can you stand here like this? You are part of this madness! All day you train men for slaughter. It is loathsome. Hideous. How can you take me in your arms?"

His head snapped back as though he had been struck. His face was white. The tent was nearly ripped from its moorings as he threw aside the flap and left.

Catherine cried his name but he did not stop. For an awesome eternity she stood stunned and bewildered, unable to move. What had she done? The words which had escaped her had been a sickness, spewing forth, uncontrollable. She started forward, tripped over a rope, righted herself.

"Which way did Captain Valdivia go?" she asked the kitchen maid, who was tending the fire.

The girl pointed and Catherine set off breathlessly, down a row of tents. She saw no sign of her husband's form ahead of her. As she reached the end of the row a dull realization began to dawn on her. When they had arrived and had walked about getting their bearings, Magdalena with curt word had pointed out Francisca Griega's tent. It was the second from the end. Catherine stopped in front of it and stood staring dully at the swaying of its sides in the breeze which heralded evening. Inside it, all was silence. Slowly she stepped forward and moved the flap a crack. Rodrigo stood

327

with his arm wrapped tightly around Francisca, his other hand wound in her flowing hair. He was kissing her with a violence which Catherine knew too well.

The tent flap dropped from her fingers. She saw nothing beyond the last of the tents, and nothing of her surroundings. With heavy feet she began to walk. She could not stand this camp with its smoke and yapping dogs and din of arquebuses and Rodrigo in Francisca's arms. The vision of Callao with its glaring beaches flashed into her mind, and then the memory of the blue-green sea beyond it, and suddenly she was walking on that sea, sliding lightly over the waves, dancing home toward Seville where the only sound was that of birdsong, and her father's fig trees grew.

She heard the shout of warning, but she did not heed its words, for she was headed for Seville. A flash of thunder broke above her.

"Hold your fire!" cried a voice which once had been familiar. "That is Señora de Valdivia!"

The thunder echoed again. It reminded her of rain. It reminded her that she was tired. She succumbed to the tiredness then, and she slipped toward the earth.

Catherine awoke in her tent. Ana hovered over her, weeping, and beside her, holding her hand, knelt Alonzo Sanchez.

"Catherine!" he exclaimed as her eyes turned toward him. "My God, I thought you had been wounded when I saw you fall. What possessed you out there? Why did you defy the guards? Are you quite mad?"

"Why," she asked, her words leaning together drunkenly, "did you take it on yourself to stop me?"

He squeezed her hand tightly and brought it to his lips.

"You know the answer to that."

She turned her head away, tears brimming in her eyes.

"Catherine, my darling, what is it?"

She did not look at him. "I saw—Rodrigo with that woman. I know it is foolish to expect fidelity in a husband, but—"

"Catherine." His voice was so urgent that she was compelled to meet his gaze. "I will ask you yet again—come away with me."

Above her she heard Ana gasp. The constancy of the man beside her moved her more deeply than mere words could say. She touched his cheek.

"Dear Alonzo. I would that in some other life we might.

But—do you not see? I—I love Rodrigo. I have loved him . . . very long."

Alonzo's blond head bent. She could not see his face.

"I envy him," he said slowly, "as I envy no other man. And I will pray henceforth for your happiness."

Sharp voices sounded outside.

"My wife—you are quite certain she was not injured, Magdalena?"

"Quite certain, for which you should thank your God!"

Rodrigo, face strained with anxiety, entered the tent. Having found him, Magdalena whisked ahead, open fury in her manner.

Alonzo rose to his feet.

"I beg you, Valdivia, do not be offended by my presence here. Your wife was in need of comfort, and you could not be found."

The reprimand was unmistakable. Rodrigo flushed.

Uncertain of his temper, Catherine held out her hand to him. "Please—do not quarrel," she said through parched lips. "I can bear no more fighting . . . no more killing."

He did not speak, nor did he take her hand, but stood looking down at her. His legs were spread, his broad shoulders blocked the single candle lighted in the tent. He looked invincible, and strong beyond all men, and yet there was pain in his face. Regret. His eyes rested on her face as if he were stamping precious gold into a fixed image for all time.

"When I held you, it was only to say goodby to you," he said, voice low. "I did not mean—I—but what does it matter? Thank God you are safe. Forgive me."

"Goodby!" cried Catherine, raising up on her arm. "But Rojo said the army was not leaving!"

"It isn't," said Rodrigo, kneeling at a trunk and inserting a key. "I am."

As he spoke, he took from the trunk a rectangle of red and yellow silk. The smooth material slipped free of its folds, and there in the candlelight were the castles and rampant lions of Spain.

Alonzo's breath came quick and sharp.

"Valdivia! Surely you do not hope to ride from this camp and join Gasca's forces. It is suicide!"

Rodrigo looked from Catherine to Alonzo.

"As you love my wife, Sanchez, I ask you to stay with her and not raise alarm against me. She has had no inkling of what I was about to do. She cannot be blamed."

"I will raise no alarm," said Alonzo quickly. "I wish God's every blessing on your purpose. If it should succeed, many will follow your example. But give me time to reach the other side of camp and I will create diversion for you."

Catherine struggled to rise as the two men left, one after the other. Magdalena held her firmly by the shoulders.

"No, señora. Stay here. It is better that you do not watch."

"He is mad!" choked Catherine. "I must stop him! His armor will not save him from the balls of the arquebuses."

She pushed aside her housekeeper and ran from the tent. Night had fallen and cookfires danced yellow and red, the colors in the flag her husband carried. He must have intended this action for some time, yet he had not spoken a word of it to her. It was this which he had confessed before the priest that morning. For this contemplated act of daring he had been given the rosary.

People stared at her as she ran past. She wore no cloak and her hair was disarrayed. At the center of the camp she drew up, gasping. Boabdíl would be with the other horses, at the corner of the camp where the soldiers quartered.

Even as she started in that direction, a cry rent the air. The beat of a horse's hooves shook the ground where she stood, and while she watched in dismay Boabdíl's large form appeared from the darkness and leaped a campfire, and for an instant she saw the moon strike silver from her husband's helmet.

"Stop him!" howled a voice, and arquebuses exploded.

Men and women ran from their tents. Soldiers caught horses and mounted.

"After him! After him! It is Valdivia!"

At that moment there came a cry from the opposite side of the camp.

"Rey Carlos y Gasca!"

Alonzo Sanchez put spurs to his long-limbed sorrel and broke from the shelter of tents, riding hard for Pizarro's sentry line. The arquebuses fired again and the riders who had been in pursuit of Rodrigo jerked their horses to a plunging halt in their confusion.

"Blessed Mother!" cried Catherine, clutching her throat. Alonzo had decoyed the camp by turning royalist himself!

"After them! Divide, you fools!" raged Cepeda, racing into the firelight with face contorted.

Pursuers now streamed after both men. Catherine felt a sob escape her.

"By my beard!" exclaimed the marquis behind her. "It is time. It is time."

He turned on his heel and went back toward his tent with autocratic stride.

The whole of the camp was assembling. Catherine withdrew her gaze from the distance and looked defiantly at all around her. Gonzalo Pizarro came galloping up on his horse.

"Is it true? Is it indeed your husband?" he asked sharply.

"It is."

"Where is he going, Señora de Valdivia?"

"I do not know."

"If he is caught, he will be hung."

Catherine was too stunned, even now, to acknowledge the words with more than the barest nod.

Then behind them there was the metallic clatter of armor. Turning, Catherine cried out. Mounted on his slow, stiff-jointed cart horse, the marquis came riding toward them like some knight of old. He was in full armor, his family arms emblazoned on his chest.

"*Santiago y Gasca!*" his cracking voice proclaimed. With sword drawn he charged straight ahead, so near that Gonzalo Pizarro was forced to jerk his horse around to avoid an impact.

For an instant those watching seemed too shocked to move. As the marquis on his sorry excuse for a war horse neared the sentry line, the arquebuses fired again. The gallant old gentleman fell from his saddle.

A screeching figure came racing from the crowd, and a pair of fists began to pound at Catherine as she raised a hand against the blows.

"You are to blame! You! You!" shrieked Elvira. "You have sent my husband off to be a traitor! He will be killed!"

Jewels flashed in the firelight as the marquesa's hand darted out to snatch Elvira back and slap her smartly across the mouth. A gasp went up from the spectators, now the entire camp.

"Your constant complaining disgraces Spanish womanhood!" the marquesa decreed in tones which all could hear. Tears were streaming down her cheeks, but she did not look toward her husband. "You should pray to be half so valiant as this woman whom you are so eager to blame. Go back to your gossip and simpering. It is all for which you are suited."

Elvira's mouth hung open, incredulous. The marquesa

turned her back and started to her husband. A priest was putting oil on his feet.

"My lady marquesa—" began Catherine, who had followed her and who, with her, looked down at a face sealed in a final triumph. The marquesa sank to her knees and Catherine did not finish.

The marquesa pressed the gold cross of her rosary to her husband's lips.

"Bernál," she said.

Never until that moment had Catherine heard her speak his name.

Pizarro rode slowly up to them and dismounted.

"Madam, I am truly sorry. He died as a soldier."

The marquesa rose, still looking at the quiet form in its old-fashioned armor.

"He did not want to make this trip," she said. "Now he must make it twice in as many days. We will take him in the morning to the cathedral."

The general ran uneasy fingers along his baldric.

"My lady marquesa, we will have to bury him here."

She did not allow him the dignity of looking at him.

"Bury him here? A man of his station? Preposterous!"

Pizarro's courtesy was genuine, Catherine thought, as he tried to reason.

"We have priests a-plenty. They will say a proper Mass for his soul. It can be no other way."

The marquesa stood unbending before him.

"No one of the Zurbarán line has ever been laid to rest outside a cathedral. I will not see my husband be the first. He will lie in Lima tomorrow if I carry him there myself."

The words were firm, but Catherine saw the lips which spoke them quaver. For the first time she realized that this woman who terrorized all Lima with her piety was frail and old. Catherine stepped quickly forward, including a handful of Pizarro's partisans in her glance though she addressed herself to him alone.

"General, you are known as a man of your word. Once, long ago, you said that any favor which I might ask of you, you would grant. I claim that favor now. Grant this woman's request."

The general looked amazed. He hooked his thumbs through his belt.

"You dare to ask me this, señora, when this very night your husband has turned against me and become my enemy?"

She stood quietly.

"Will you keep your word?"

He gave an angry exclamation. "It is not possible! Who should I send with you to insure your return? There appears to be no one I can trust."

She heard the bitterness of betrayal in his words.

"Surely you can trust yourself," she said.

He stared at her, then turned to his horse.

"Very well," he said from the saddle. "Let us cancel this debt between us, then. Choose a priest and have the body ready at sunrise. I will go with you."

34

Three months had passed since Catherine saw the marquis's body laid to rest in the cathedral. In the dining room of her own house she could hear Ana sobbing softly as she polished silver, for yesterday her notary husband had left to join Father Gasca's forces. No one knew for certain the size of that army, but after Rodrigo's example many a soldier had fled Pizarro's encampment. Now Father Gasca himself had landed.

The general, with the remnants of his army, had marched to Cuzco. Cepeda had gone with him, but Don Luis, after setting out with them, had doubled quickly back to be hailed by the citizens of Lima as a brave and prudent man. They lived now in a city where he held much sway.

Catherine ran restless fingers over the account book open before her. She knew what made it hard to concentrate this morning. Yesterday Don Luis had married María Costella, whose husband and his entire family had been destroyed—conveniently, it seemed—on a charge of lacking *limpieza*. The young bride who had spurned him had not escaped him, and Catherine couldn't forget his veiled threat to her, and the fact he had employed a treacherous man to go to Spain on some matter which pertained to them. Now Don Luis met every ship which docked.

She closed the book. There was no point to these thoughts. Better to try and comfort Ana.

At sight of her Ana whisked a handkerchief beneath her nose.

"It is terrible," Catherine said simply. "Not knowing when you will see a husband again, thinking of all the things you longed to say to him—"

Ana buried her face in her hand and began to sob.

"Oh, yes, señorita! That is exactly how it is! How do you stand it? You have seen Captain Valdivia leave so many times. I know my husband will not even be in the fighting. He will be in some tent writing, a mere secretary, but—"

Catherine wrapped her arms around the girl as emotion cut short her words.

"There, there," she soothed. "He will be safe. He will come

back to you. And think, Ana, how proud he will be that he had a wife who was able to say goodby with a smile and to keep herself busy in his absence. He must think very highly of your courage or he would not have asked you to bear this."

Ana hiccuped. "How could anyone think I have courage?" she asked crossly. "I disgust myself with my lack of it. But how could I let León know how miserable his decision made me? He was so eager to go—to do something for the country which has given him so much, he said."

"The silver will wait," said Catherine. "Let us walk into town and look at some linen. The least we can do for our husbands is to have some fine new shirts awaiting them on their return."

They did not start the shirts that day. As Catherine sat at lunch a messenger arrived to summon her to the home of the marquesa. Her friend was dying.

"It cannot be," Catherine whispered as she and Ana hurried through the streets. In the months since the marquis's death she had been increasingly aware of the marquesa's frailty. There was a weariness about her friend which discipline had held at bay before. Yet always the marquesa had rallied, embarking on some new project for the church and assessing the latest happenings with her usual shrewdness. If she had been melancholy, she had hidden it.

Next to Rodrigo, she is the most precious part of my world, thought Catherine. And I have no claim on either of them. How strange it is, that we can shape so much with our intellect and our hands, yet the things which really matter—friendship, love—these are beyond our control. Perhaps it is that which makes them so sweet.

The marquesa's great palace seemed hollow and empty, its grandeur faded. As she went to the marquesa's chamber, Catherine recalled the night Rodrigo first had brought her there, broken and disgraced. She remembered the way his eyes had marveled at the rich tiles and the gilded ceilings. She remembered their wedding banquet.

At the door to the marquesa's chamber she paused and wiped the tears from her cheeks. Her final gift to a lady who had supported her in so much would be a composure worthy of the marquesa herself.

Heavy velvet curtains had been drawn across the windows of the bedroom which she entered. Doña Mercedes, Marguerita, and other women of the household hovered in a corner. Two priests were there, and a doctor. Catherine's eyes skipped over all of them to the alcove draped in purple and the snowy head propped on pillows there. Bejeweled fingers rose from the sheets where they rested to beckon her.

"My dear, I am glad you have come," said her friend in a voice which had lost all strength.

Catherine fell to her knees and kissed the marquesa's hand.

"Dear lady marquesa—"

"Come, come, Catherine, will you always forget decorum?" chided the marquesa, but with affection. She gestured to a chair.

Catherine drew it close beside the bed.

"I did not even know you were ailing," she said.

For a lesser woman, the marquesa's posture might be called that of an invalid. But with a half a dozen pillows beneath her, she sat almost upright. Her face was composed, her eyes still sharp with authority.

"I didn't choose to spend much time in illness," that amazing woman said. "It is so without dignity. My husband died as befitted his station. I shall do likewise."

"But surely you are not dying," Catherine protested earnestly.

Again the jeweled fingers raised, this time to silence her.

"Do not begrudge my departure, Catherine. I have looked with joy to the day when I would stand before the throne of God. Now my only hope is that in my life I may have done some deeds of merit, and that my stay in purgatory need not be overlong."

"Your deeds will go before you like a host of angels," Catherine promised, for all her resolve dashing aside a tear. "I will pray daily for your soul."

A sigh escaped the marquesa. Such an alien sound made her seem fragile, a shell of fine porcelain strong until the end. Her eyes turned to the canopy of her bed, and Catherine saw in them the weariness of many years.

"I had hoped to die in Spain," she murmured. "Poor Bernál."

The vigor ebbing from her returned for a moment and she looked about the room.

"There are too many here," she said with familiar authority. "I am not some public spectacle. Catherine, remain where you are. Doña Mercedes may do likewise. The rest of you are near enough outside my door."

The doctor started to protest, but was silenced by the sharp look of his patient. All sound of footsteps was lost in the room's thick carpet. Only the rustle of skirts signaled the clearing of the room.

"I am honored to be at your side," said Catherine. "I cannot speak of the affection—"

"Yes, yes," said her friend. "It is not necessary to speak such things, for they are on the very air we breathe." Feebly her hand patted Catherine's. "I know the depth of your affection, child. I wish God's blessing on you and your soldier."

She paused and seemed to summon strength. Then she continued.

"Perhaps your marriage is not the misfortune it once appeared. He is a gallant man, your husband. The times are changing, and perhaps it is as well to judge a man by his deeds as by his lineage. What is a coat of arms after all? What is a title? It is a source of satisfaction when one is young and vain, but at the end, knowing one leaves no heir to pass it to weighs heavy on the soul."

Years of grief and loneliness clung to the words. Catherine gripped her hand tightly.

"If—there is ever a girl child—may we name it for you?"

A sad, pale smile softened the face of the woman before her. Even the marquesa's eyes had softened, looking toward another world.

"My dear child, do you even know my name?"

Catherine nodded, emotion choking her. "You are Doña Beatríz."

The marquesa's gaze was fixed upon her.

"Yes," she said softly. "Doña Beatríz." Her eyelids fluttered. "My rings," she whispered. "Take them from me. Not now, but when I die. It would be a senseless extravagance to bury them when they could serve some use. There are two horses left . . . some rugs . . . the marquis's ruby . . . I am Doña Beatríz of Salamanca. . . ."

Sinking back against her pillows, the Marquesa de Zurbarán opened neither eyes nor lips again. As vespers rang her faithful soul departed. Doña Mercedes, after her cousin's body had been anointed, drew the rings from her fingers and placed them in Catherine's hand. For the last time Catherine walked through the silent halls of the palace to which her life had been so intimately bound.

She walked to the plaza and turned her face to the breeze and with closed eyes listened to the soft rush of the River Rimac.

337

Her heart was swollen with sadness. What was it that made her feel as much a part of these surroundings as the distant river?

Rodrigo.

She cried to him silently, knowing he would not come. Was he in Cajamarca? Was he alive? Would she ever know?

With Pizarro's blockade of the coast now broken, ships arrived in rapid succession. One brought an Andalusian, thin and weak from the long confinement in Panamá.

"Good barley will soon make her fat," promised Valdéz stoutly.

Catherine smiled her gratitude. His confidence was more than a little welcome now that they knew the other new mare ordered from Spain lay dead beneath the sea. She was glad of his presence, too, as she saw the silk-clad form of Don Luis ride through the crowd which had met the ship. She knew why the councilman was there, for when a previous ship had docked, she had given Valdéz money to loosen the tongues of the sailors Don Luis had stopped to question. She had learned that Don Luis sought word of the man named Sotelo.

From the war, the news was bad. In late October the royalist army under Father Gasca had at last joined in battle against Gonzalo Pizarro. Far to the South, on the shores of a lake called Titicaca, the two armies had clashed and Pizarro, though but half of his men were left him, had won a victory which was undisputed, total and devastating to Gasca's cause. For two months since, disheartened royalists had streamed back into Lima.

"Look, señorita!" whispered Ana as they sat in the cathedral. "Señora Palacios Rubios' brother has come back! Lieutenant Orgoñez . . . Señor Avila . . . fully half the army has returned!"

Catherine bowed her head. Ana bethought herself and squeezed her mistress's hand.

"You must believe Captain Valdivia safe. Have we not heard at every report that Gasca's cavalry thoroughly routed that of the general? You know for a certainty that your husband left the field uninjured."

"I am not worried," said Catherine automatically.

Yet anxiety filled her. So long as Father Gasca kept to the field, Rodrigo would likely stay with him. And if Gasca had not yet admitted defeat, it could only mean he would fight again, no matter how diminished his forces.

After Mass she spoke to Martín.

"You must not think I have come here a coward and a traitor to your husband," he said in greeting. "I have come to lead men back with me. Father Gasca says we were too confident and that God chastised us for our pride. We will draw the general out of Cuzco, and this time we will defeat him!"

After a week Martín set out with a group of royalists for the valley of Jauja. Lieutenant Orgoñez did not go with him. Neither did Alonzo Sanchez, whom Catherine had seen several times since his return but with whom she had not spoken. There were many now who said Pizarro could never be vanquished. Two alternate fears tugged at her heart: Father Gasca's forces might be destroyed at the next encounter, or the war might drag on forever.

It was a bright, clear day between Christmas and Twelfthnight when Magdalena came into her presence with shaking voice and ashen skin.

"Doña Catherine," she said. "There is a *chasqui* in the courtyard—a runner with a message."

A great wave engulfed her at the housekeeper's words. Her feet slipped on the stairs as she hurried down. The Indian messengers who had moved news in relays along the Inca roads were little used now that their empire had been supplanted by another. The appearance of one was a strange and frightening occurrence. Magdalena, Ana, Belita Valdéz— the entire household stood staring with an air of sharp foreboding at the barrel-chested Indian in his short tunic.

He looked to Magdalena and she nodded. He held out a piece of paper sealed with red.

Trembling, Catherine broke the seal. Words leaped at her. The scent of citron and sweet orange filled her brain and made her dizzy.

> Your husband is gravely wounded and calls for you. If you leave at once, God willing, you may reach his side before he dies.
>> Yours faithfully,
>> Leonor García

No more. Nothing to cushion the words. She felt the impulse to retch and fought it back.

"It's Rodrigo," she said, dry mouthed. "He's dying. I must get a horse that is faster than my own."

The Indian man spoke quickly.

"He says the army is camped at Andahuaylas," Magdalena reported, tears running down her cheeks. "That is five or six days' hard riding for a man, señora."

"Then it will be the same for me. Ana, fix a bag. Doctor de Palacios Rubios has a horse of reasonable speed. I am going to fetch it. Valdéz, you will come with me and your horse will have to do. If it tires we will trade it for another."

She left with Ana running beside her and soon was knocking at Alma's door. She could not permit herself now to think about Rodrigo . . . to think she might be too late. Nothing but immediate action must be allowed in her consciousness.

"My husband is fatally wounded," she said to Alma. "I must go to him. May I have the loan of your husband's horse?"

Alma gasped and bit her lip.

"Oh, Catherine! The horse is not here. There was a duel in the Cabildo and my husband was summoned. He rode."

Catherine nodded, already planning. "Then I will go there."

In the street she saw an *encomendero* of her acquaintance ride past. She called to him.

"Please—I must get to the Cabildo at once. Will you take me?"

"Gladly, Señora de Valdivia, but I have no pillion—"

"It does not matter." She put up her hand and was swung up behind him. He put spurs to his horse and poor Ana was left standing in the dust behind them.

A few dozen men milled in front of the building where the Cabildo held its meetings. Catherine guessed the duel had been fought there. She slipped from her perch with a sense of disgust at such frivolous behavior from men who sat safe and secure in the city.

"Doctor Palacios Rubios. Where is he?" she said, catching the arm of the first man she saw.

At a gesture she saw the doctor, rolling his sleeves down as a man with a bandaged chest was carried off groaning on a litter.

"Doctor—" she said, and paused for breath.

"Why, Doña Catherine!" He looked up in surprise.

"Please, my husband is wounded in Andahuaylas. I need a fast horse to reach him before—before—" She stopped and pressed her lips together to stop their shaking.

"You could take mine, and gladly," the doctor said, understanding. "But alas, he will not wear a ladies' saddle. He does not like the feel."

"Then I will use the one which is on him, if you will but shorten the stirrups."

She was conscious of the crowd parting before them and sympathetic murmuring. Men followed to watch as Doctor Palacios Rubios led the way to a light roan horse with black forelegs. The doctor held a small stone bottle before her eyes.

"Here, if there is a fever this may be of some advantage. I am putting it into the saddlebag."

Valdéz, who had followed her trail, rode up on his own aging horse as she put a foot to the stirrup. Catherine threw a leg awkwardly across the saddle, aware of the clumsiness of her voluminous skirts.

As they were turning, a man with a yellow beard burst from the Cabildo building and ran down the steps.

"Catherine!" called Alonzo.

She did not quite rein the horse, who danced sideways, as anxious to take to the road as she was.

"Is it true you intend to ride to Andahuaylas?" he demanded, blocking her path.

She nodded. "Yes. Lend us your prayers."

Without answering he swung toward Valdéz.

"Valdéz, do you know the road? This is madness!"

Valdéz scratched his ear. "Doña Catherine is an excellent rider—"

"I do not question that, Valdéz. But if there were others here who are soldiers, they would tell you as I do that the road as far as Jauja is the cruelest in all Peru. You will die of the cold, both of you, dressed as you are. If you do not know the stopping places your horses will drop of exhaustion. If you persist in going, let me come to guide you."

"No." Catherine's voice was firm though her mind shrank from the picture being painted. Beyond the cold, beyond the mountains and hazards, lay Rodrigo.

Valdéz turned to her, hoarse with emotion.

"In the Savior's name, Doña Catherine, do not spurn his offer. It may be that we will save a day of riding if he comes with us!"

35

Catherine held her reins numbly, galloping along the road from Lima to Pachacamac. In five days, with luck, they could reach Andahuaylas. Indian runners, though no longer linked in the perfect network which had existed before their conquest by the Spanish, had nonetheless covered the distance in three.

Three days since Leonor had penned her note. Was Rodrigo already dead? And Leonor—to hear from her was almost to hear from the dead as well—from someone dead, buried, almost forgotten. How did she come to be with the army? The questions flew through Catherine's mind as miles of barren coastline went by in a blur.

By midday they reached Pachacamac, where a great pagan shrine had been raised before the time of the Incas.

"Eat—you will need all your strength," Alonzo ordered when Valdéz brought out cured pork and bread.

She ate the food without tasting. Five days. Five days. She had never told Rodrigo she loved him. She had not wanted to see him laugh with victory over her. How insignificant, now, that victory seemed.

At Pachacamac, the broad road built under Topa Inca turned eastward and followed the Lurin River. After resting their horses they crossed it. The road on one side fell sharply away and on the other was butted against a solid rock wall.

"We must make Huarochiri by nightfall," Alonzo called back as he squinted at the lowering sun.

They urged their horses to a faster pace. Already Catherine felt her thighs raw from the unfamiliar saddle. She did not speak. Grief wrapped around her like a rope, ever tighter, cutting her in two.

"Surely we must stop, Don Alonzo," said Valdéz when the sun sank low in the sky. "Doña Catherine cannot go on much longer."

Alonzo looked at her anxiously. "The ride from Huarochiri to Jauja is more difficult still. It were better if we continued."

"Then we will do so," said Catherine, grateful that the failing light hid the chattering of her teeth. The cloak in which she sweltered for propriety's sake in Lima was proving pitifully light against the chill which met them as they neared the mountains.

The moon was up when their weary horses loped into Huarochiri. A cry went up at the arrival of travelers, and at such an hour, and Catherine found them received like old friends into a stranger's house where they were fed and warmed by a fire. The wife of the *encomendero* who lived there showed Catherine to a finely furnished room where she fell quickly into a deep sleep.

Yet she was awakened, fear driving her heart and making her body damp, before the first cock crowed. Four days now. Would God be merciful? If only she had told Rodrigo of her love. In her pride she had denied him even the comfort of knowing that the old grudge of the rape and sale to him had long ago been forgiven.

She was supplied with substantial boots and a cloak lined with fur. They were not many hours in the saddle before she was glad of their warmth. Even with sun bright above them the air was chill. The road they followed climbed steeply and the land around them was rugged with many small rivers.

At mid-morning as they rested the horses, Alonzo fell back with her.

"Are you cold?" He took her hand, encased in a leather glove.

She shook her head. No word passed between them. He held her hand tightly and she gripped his. She could feel tears slipping down her cheeks.

By afternoon the wind sweeping down on them stung her skin. Mingled with her torment was a growing awe of her husband, the man who lay in some distant tent, the soldier who had crossed and recrossed this road and never spoken of it, never made complaint. She had known him strong, but she had never realized how undaunted he must have been by suffering and hardship.

They spent the night in a cave. Their breath made clouds in the air about them. The land outside was covered with snow.

"We would have perished without you, Don Alonzo," said Valdéz, stretching gnarled hands to the fire. In his eyes Catherine saw a terror, a disbelief at the ruggedness of the way ahead of them.

A second day they climbed through the snowy mountains, sometimes dismounting to pull their horses behind them. A second night they sheltered in a cave. Catherine's heart lay frozen inside her, as if she already presided at a wake. She wanted to believe she would find Rodrigo still alive, but she dared not hope it.

Toward the end of the fourth day the wind lost some of its sharpness. The road became more passable. Finally, ahead of them, they saw the town of Jauja where Father Gasca's army once had gathered.

"You have come from Huarochiri in only two days! And with no maid to tend you?" marveled the *encomendero*'s wife who was Catherine's hostess that evening. Evidently Alonzo had told her something of the reason for their ride, thought Catherine, for the woman looked on her with manifest compassion, and asking no questions urged her immediately to a warm and comfortable bed, sending dinner on a tray.

In the morning Valdéz and Alonzo looked like men much relaxed, the arduous part of their journey now behind them. Catherine, on the other hand, found herself shaking with apprehension. She could not eat. By nightfall they should reach Andahuaylas.

"I would never have asked Doctor Palacios Rubios for his horse, had I known the punishment I would put him to," she said, putting a grateful hand to the animal's neck as she stepped into the saddle. The roan flared his nostrils noisily, as though he too were apprehensive about this day. His steps were slower as they set off, and his neck did not maintain a graceful arch. Valdéz' horse, stumbling from the rigors of their previous days on the trail, had been traded for another.

After twenty miles of riding they descended at last into a river valley filled with fruit trees. On a plain near a lesser range of mountains than the one they had crossed sat the town of Huamanga. Its square was large and level and there were many great houses of stone, brick and tile. Beyond the town were wheat fields. Pigeons fluttered at the road's edge and llama herds grazed in the distance. A brisk ride brought them to the hamlet of Vilcas, and then to the *encomienda* of Diego Maldonado, nicknamed "the rich."

"I will leave you here," said Alonzo, reining his horse at last. Ahead of them a bridge made of twisted ropes stretched nearly eighty feet across a river.

Valdéz looked surprised. Alonzo spoke quickly.

"No one need know I accompanied you on this trip, Valdéz. If Captain Valdivia in fact is dying, such news would only distress him. If he recovers, which I pray to God he may, it would trouble him all the more. You know the love your mistress bears him, Valdéz, to have made this trip to reach him. Show her the loyalty of forgetting my presence on the way."

Understanding came quickly into Valdéz' eyes, and he nodded.

"So I will, Don Alonzo."

Alonzo smiled and clasped the stable man's hand. "God go with you, Valdéz. You will find the road to Andahuaylas an easy one."

He turned to Catherine. Tears filled her eyes as she held out her hand in turn.

"I do not know how to thank you, Alonzo."

"By hastening to your husband. By finding happiness."

By the time they had trotted their horses over the swaying bridge, Alonzo was but a dot on the road back to Vilcas.

In late afternoon they crossed a low ridge and saw the camp of Father Gasca's army. Tents were spread out for quarters and hospital sections, a cross had been raised, and on a small hill overlooking the road six cannon bespoke the defenses of the settlement. As they neared the hill with the cannon, two horsemen left its summit and came forward to challenge this approach by strangers.

When they were within shouting distance, one of the soldiers opened his mouth to speak with stern expression. He was interrupted by a cry from the other.

"María Santísima! It is Señora de Valdivia, as I am a christian!"

With Valdéz at her side, Catherine reined her borrowed horse. The ground was muddy from recent rains, and his hooves slipped a bit.

"My husband," she said, afraid to speak. "Is he alive?"

The soldier who had spoken to her shook his head.

"Alive, Señora, but little more. He sees and hears nothing. His hours are few."

Without need of asking, Catherine found herself escorted at full gallop toward the camp, down a row of tents, to a small tent which looked like all the others save that its flap was lowered.

As their horses drew up snorting, a low growl issued from inside.

"Who causes this racket? Have I not warned—"

Rojo's red head emerged from the tent, his expression

deadly. As he sighted Catherine, the threat fell silent on his lips.

"Doña Catherine!"

With a bound he reached her horse and his large hands raised to help her from the saddle. She fell into them sobbing like a child. He held her gently, enfolding her with his rough strength and the fiery odor of peppers.

After a moment she checked her tears and stood away from him. Her eyes turned up, full of pleading.

"We have done what we can for him," he said sadly, "but it is to no avail. Father Gasca himself has come to pray over him, and the surgeon burned out his wound, but still his fever rages. Come."

He lifted the tent flap and they stepped inside. Rodrigo's unconscious form lay on a small, rude bed. His hair and beard were matted and the tent smelled of waste. Beside the bed, a low trunk served as a table on which there rested a cup and a basin of water. A woman rose from a nearby stool as they entered. She stretched out her hands, and Catherine found herself embarced by Leonor García.

"We would have buried him a week ago, had it not been for Doña Leonor's constant care," said Rojo humbly.

Catherine squeezed her friend's hands, distracted and unable to speak. Leonor, with understanding, stepped aside.

"I knew you would come," she said as Catherine, with eyes for nothing else, approached the bed and sank to her knees beside it. "I have prayed night and day that I might keep him alive, a small repayment for the friendship you have shown me."

"Rodrigo?" whispered Catherine, touching the gray lips which she so longed to kiss. She did kiss them then, heedless of those who were watching. "Rodrigo?" She raised his hand to her lips. There was no flicker of response beneath his closed eyelids nor in the limp fingers which she held. Even his shallow breathing did not waver.

Leonor spoke with delicate kindness, close behind her.

"I fear, my dearest friend, that he does not hear you. When the men first brought him from the field, he spoke no word but your name, and now, for days, he has made no sound at all. Yet believe that somehow, in a way we cannot understand, he knows you are here and is comforted."

Catherine looked bleakly up. "How was he wounded? I do not understand. The battle with the general is long since past."

Rojo took charge of the conversation.

"Morale was low, Doña Catherine, and the men grew restless. 'Rigo took a small party to make reconnaissance of the general's movements in Cuzco. We were set upon by a rebel patrol."

She locked her slim eyebrows together, trying to understand, trying to stand against this thing which had split her world.

"And—Rodrigo was—"

"Shot, Doña Catherine. By one of our own arquebusiers, the clumsy fool." Rojo's face hardened with a grim rage. "He will not make that mistake again—or any other, may he burn in hell."

What little hope she had snuffed out at the report. She recalled Doctor Palacios Rubios saying that armies knew not what horrors they unleashed by their use of guns. Sword wounds could be treated, but not the ragged holes left by arquebuses.

Still she refused to accept the unmistakable writing of fate. Squaring her shoulders she laid Rodrigo's head back gently on the bed. She touched his forehead.

"He burns. No number of cool cloths has brought any change in it," said Leonor. "While we could force wine into his mouth, I entertained yet some small hope, but for two days now we have been unable to get anything past his lips."

Catherine stripped off her coat. "Rojo, fetch my saddlebag. Doctor Palacios Rubios sent a medicine which we must try."

"But Doña Catherine, he will only choke and drown," said Rojo sadly when he had returned and Catherine had unpacked the bottle.

"I have seen Valdéz help a colt swallow when it was too weak to nurse," she said with a quick glance to the stable man, who stood anxiously just inside the tent. "We must do the same for him."

"Gently! His shoulder!" cautioned Rojo as she slipped an arm beneath Rodrigo's head.

She nodded, feeling the frightening dead weight of the man she held. Leonor dribbled a swallow of the medicine into Rodrigo's slack mouth, and Catherine stroked her hand again and again down the front of her husband's throat. A choking sound escaped his lips, but his breathing continued. Catherine snapped her fingers.

"Wine," she ordered. A mouthful—pitifully small—followed the medicine in the same laborious manner.

When Rodrigo lay again against the sheets, she bit her lip, weighing the consequences of the next move, which she for some minutes had been contemplating.

"It is not enough to cool his head," she said. "We must bathe him. Valdéz, heat us water."

Protests burst from every mouth in the tent.

"If he takes a chill he will not last the night!" objected Leonor.

"We have no guarantee he will in any case," said Catherine. "He is fond of baths. He will be more comfortable. And I do not intend that he should be chilled. Rojo, can you not come by some braziers?"

The red-haired soldier stared at her uncertainly. "There are some few of them. They can be borrowed. But a bath, Doña Catherine? Whoever heard of such a thing for a sick man?"

Her voice shook with emotion.

"He is my husband, Rojo! I love him more than I have ever loved another human being. Do you think I would choose to do anything which might harm him?"

Rojo bowed his head. "I will bring braziers."

They set the iron firepots around the inside of the tent. The glowing charcoal in the braziers kept at bay the chill of the night which had fallen outside. A fire blazed in front of the tent. Rojo lashed lances together and plunged them in the earth near Rodrigo's bed, draping them over with blankets of alpaca wool as an added guard against drafts. Rolling up her sleeves Catherine plunged a cloth into a basin of warm, soapy water and washed her husband's arms, with Leonor drying each of them as soon as she had finished.

She washed his neck, his chest, his shoulders, avoiding the red and shining flesh where a hot iron had seared together the arquebus wound. She washed the surface, at least, of his hair and beard. She washed his legs and thighs. Each touch of the well-remembered body, now lying helpless, tore at her heart.

When there remained but the groin, hidden beneath a fold of sheet, her raw nerves snapped. She let the cloth fall back into the basin.

"Rojo . . . I cannot. . . ." She trembled with the strain.

Rojo took the basin from her.

"I love him like a younger brother," he said. "There is nothing I would not do for him."

Without another word the battle-hardened soldier performed the most intimate service which one man could perform for another.

The braziers were kept burning for a time, well after a clean shirt of light wool was pulled over Rodrigo's head and he was securely settled amid clean sheets and blankets.

"You must rest now, and eat," said Leonor as Catherine sank onto the stool at her husband's bedside. "You have not so much as paused since your arrival."

Catherine waved a hand at the dish of stew which Leonor offered.

"Please, Leonor, I am not hungry."

Leonor smiled. "Nor was I once, but you made me eat."

The affection in the words drew Catherine's attention momentarily from Rodrigo. She looked at Leonor. Her friend's face looked happier and healthier than ever she remembered seeing it. There were no fearful shadows under the eyes now. Only the small white scar riding high on one cheek gave testimony to the past.

"How did you come here, Leonor? I supposed you long returned to Spain."

Leonor clasped her hands, completely at ease.

"I met a man in Trujillo, a cavalryman. He was very kind to me. When he came South to join Father Gasca, I came with him."

"You knew your husband was dead?"

"I had heard rumors. There is no place left to me in good society, but the army has been kind to me. I am esteemed as a nurse, and known as a virtuous woman in the alliance I have chosen."

A companionable silence stretched for some moments between the two women.

"I can never thank you enough for what you have done," said Catherine.

Rojo came into the tent, puffing slightly.

"You have ridden far, Doña Catherine. How such a dainty, small body as yours has endured, I do not know. Go with Doña Leonor. Sleep. I will sit by Rodrigo till day."

She smiled at him.

"I cannot, Rojo. Sleep would elude me. I will rest more surely if I am here beside him."

"But Catherine—on a stool? You cannot even doze—"

Leonor broke off her objection as the tent flap raised again. A gray-haired man, his arms too long beneath a simple shirt and sleeveless armor, entered bearing in those arms a folding chair. With him was a soldier of some fifty years of age, two servants, and the archbishop of Lima.

"My lord archbishop!" Catherine exclaimed with a loneliness and relief she could not explain. Nearly two years had passed since last she saw him. She sank to her knees to receive his blessing.

He gave it gladly, resting his hand upon her head.

"It is not I whom you should honor, señora," he informed her. "You kneel in the presence of his excellency Father Gasca, president of the Royal Audencia."

The ill-proportioned man with the folding chair set it down and smiled at her. His straight hair was smoothed back from the plainest of faces. His attire was more humble than that of many a common soldier. Yet here was the man who had challenged the great Pizarro, and by his manner had raised the largest army ever seen in the New World.

"Get up, get up, you have ridden far," he said with gentle gesture.

Catherine rose, unable to check her mental comparison between this modest man and the handsome, magnetic Pizarro.

"I heard of your arrival," said Father Gasca. "There is little comfort, in any sense, which we can offer you, but I wished to make it known to you how highly I esteem your husband, both as a soldier and as a man of faith. His bravery in escaping Pizarro's camp led many a good man to the cause of Spain. I salute you for your loyalty in coming to him, and I pray this chair may ease your hours at his side."

"I thank you, father—your excellency," Catherine stammered.

When they had gone, Rojo drew the chair close to the bed and placed the stool in front of it.

"Sit here, Doña Catherine," he said. "Stretch your feet on the stool and I shall wrap these blankets around you. If you will not be comfortable, you will at least be warm."

He left, and Leonor with him. A single fat candle sputtered and soon would go out. Near the foot of Rodrigo's bed his sword had been plunged into the earth, the hilt of it thereby forming a shining cross in the manner so often used by the conquistadors. Should his eyes open for a final time, it would be his parting vision.

"Please do not die," whispered Catherine holding his hand to her lips. "You have fought so many battles, will you not wage this one for me?"

His closed eyes jerked in spasm as if to open. She held her breath. The shallow movement of his chest continued, unaltered, and her tears fell on his burning flesh. "Oh, Rodrigo, I love you. I love you."

In the night, with prayers and words of love still tumbling from her lips, she fell asleep. When the first thread of light penetrated the tent, she awoke.

She leaned forward, crushed by fear. She couldn't feel his breath. Her shaking hands searched beneath his shirt for his heart. It still was beating. Damp with the dew of her anxiety, she sat back in relief. Then flinging aside her blankets she went to the door of the tent.

"Rojo," she said to the swaddled form which rested against a tree.

His head came up at once. His face was filled with alarm.

"Find some broth," she said. "We must try to get it down him."

They forced a few spoonfuls down his throat before breakfast and again at mid-morning, mixing it with doses of the medicine from Doctor Palacios Rubios. Both times Rodrigo coughed and seemed to strangle on it, and Rojo shook his head.

"It pains him, Doña Catherine. Can we not spare him such agony? I do not wish to hurt you, but I cannot see how he will live."

Catherine was white and shaking as they eased her husband back against his pillow.

"If he is aware of discomfort, Rojo, then his mind, at least, still clings to life. Let us try again at noon."

Though twice more they gave him broth and medicine, what little hope she had slipped farther from her. He seemed no cooler than he had been on her arrival, and she knew for a fact that his breathing was fainter. He had grown restless too, rolling his head from side to side.

"I think it is your prsence alone which has sustained him even this long," Leonor comforted.

Catherine alternately paced the tent and sat stroking her husband's forehead.

"If only we could make him aware of our presence," she brooded. "If we could only break the hold of this stupor on him for a single minute!"

Rojo, who kept watch with her, rested a hand on her shoulder.

"He knows you are here, Doña Catherine. He will die in peace."

But she didn't believe Rodrigo was aware of her presence. He lay as senseless as when she had arrived. As darkness fell again she searched her brain for a means of reaching the distant recesses of his mind.

His arm lay lifelessly against her breast as she cradled his hand to her cheek. She thought of the many times that arm had encircled her. Those were the only times when she had been a part of his world, she thought sadly, when he chose to have her there because of simple physical appetite.

Her fingers halted midway through caressing his fevered hand. Dared she even contemplate such a thing?

For a long time she sat staring at the dark lashes closed so hopelessly. With sudden decision she rose and went to the door of the tent.

"Rojo," she said as he turned from the small fire he and Valdéz were kicking into ashes for the night. "No one is to come into this tent again until I summon you, do you understand? No one must enter. Not even you, Rojo."

He looked perplexed and frightened.

"What is it, Doña Catherine? Is—is he worse?"

"No. He is the same."

She lowered the flap. Beyond the flimsy walls of cloth which sheltered her, there were encamped two thousand men. Many a one was accustomed to looking hopefully in on Rodrigo, their comrade, and Rojo was in the habit of stepping inside several times through the night to assure himself all was well.

Catherine allowed herself one more breath, and then with cool precision began to unfasten her riding dress.

36

Once more doubts assailed her as Catherine slid into the narrow bed beside her husband. Life burned so low inside him. Was it insane to think he yet might be recalled by naked flesh?

Still, it was by the coupling of their bodies that they had reached out to one another and ceased being strangers. Cautiously, for fear of jarring his injured shoulder, she pressed her skin against his. She slid her thigh across his thigh and lay very still. He did not respond.

Slowly and with wonder she reached up to stroke his hair. Could he truly be so helpless, this man whose raw strength had dominated her from the very first? Her hand curled lovingly against his cheek.

"Oh, Rodrigo, you must live," she whispered. "You must live to know how much I love you. I ask nothing in return—but live!"

In the darkness she listened to his shallow breathing. She moved closer, fitting herself against his contours as she lay in the familiar circle of his arm.

It seemed to her that the arm which had lain so flaccid next to her stirred. She held her breath. Perhaps it had only been the movement of her own anxious heart.

Too involved to retreat now from this unorthodox attempt to rouse her husband, she raised his unresisting fingers to her breast and cupped them to her cool skin. Balancing her slender body on one elbow, she brushed the sensitive tip of his fingers against the sharpness of her nipple. Her other hand slid smoothly across the hot planes of his body.

A sound, faint and weak, escaped the man beside her. Her heart beat so violently that she could scarcely hold her pose beneath the scratchy blanket covering both of them.

"Rodrigo?"

His breathing had quickened. With tightening throat, Catherine moved her fingers down, down, to the firm flesh at his groin. She touched him gently. He moved, his head thrashing feebly to the side.

"Rodrigo!"

There was more command than ardor in her whisper. She

willed him to live. What did it matter if this was the onl
level at which they reached each other so long as it serve
her this time?

Instead of gentleness now, she gave him the soft scratch o
her nails. Her husband's head tossed restlessly to the othe
side. There rose in her simultaneously a growing hope—an
the quick fear that she might, by her rashness, kill him.

"My love, will you not look at me?" she begged. "I ar
here—here beside you, sharing your bed." Her body arche
white above him as she bent anxiously to scan his face.

Beneath his eyelids there was a flutter of movemen
Slowly they parted on blind, staring eyes.

Catherine brought her lips swiftly down to cover his, he
kisses pouring out the love overflowing inside her. Her singl
goal now became to rouse him to passion, and the grip on lif
from which it could not be severed. Her mouth sought his ha
wildly, and she was rewarded by the feeble quickening of hi
dry, parched lips. He moved. A fevered hand fell over the so
mound of her buttock.

She drew back laughing as the tears cascaded down he
cheeks. She showered light kisses on his mouth and hair. Th
hand which held her had lost its strength, but suddenly, t
her horror, he gathered himself in a strenuous effort a
movement, struggling to raise his bandaged shoulder. Th
stirring of his flesh beneath her thigh informed her of hi
intent, though she was certain it was habit which drove hi
and not any consciousness of the present moment. She pushe
him back hastily onto the sheets.

"No, my love, not while you are fevered. We have been to
near to losing you. Rest awhile here in my arms, and whe
you wake again. . . ."

The half promise held him. She brought the palm of hi
hand to her lips and kissed it.

"You must sleep, and you must take wine, Rodrigo," sh
said, becoming the firm nurse again instead of the sedu
tress. She reached to the table for a cup of wine mixed wit
water and held it to him, cushioning his head against he
arm. He drank, but already his eyes were closing. Only th
turning of his head toward her breast persuaded her that h
had wakened to her at all.

She was deeply asleep, succumbing at last to the exhau
tion of the long ride through the mountains, when she felt th

sudden, urgent pressure against her back. Waking drowsily she twisted, and looked into the black glint of her husband's eyes. They were glazed still, but there was a current in them whose force commanded her, and at sight of it every other impulse yielded to a raw hunger.

They did not speak. Her body moved up, avoiding his injury, and their mouths met with an impact which drew blood.

He was cooler, though the fever had not left him, thought Catherine, and then all was forgotten in the fire exploding inside her. Rodrigo's mouth slid greedily down her throat. She gasped and felt a warm stream spread in her. Hard and growing, his flesh stabbed at her thigh. He caught her roughly and made the effort to turn onto her.

"No, wait," she choked, trembling with her passion. "Lie still! Lie still."

There was no stopping this wild rush, for either of them. Kneeling she rose above him, her body gleaming like silver in the starlight which stole through a tear in the tent. The blanket had fallen away and the air was chill, but she did not feel it. With sensation so heightened that pleasure turned into pain, she impaled herself on the waiting shaft beneath her. Rodrigo groaned. His hand caught clumsily at her waist. She leaned over him and his mouth sought the swaying globes of flesh which teased him. She felt him swell inside her until she almost cried out at the pressure. Then flesh seemed to burst and there was nothing but the present moment, growing, spinning, freeing them of all except each other.

Catherine lay weakly beside her husband, stunned and frightened by what she had done.

"Rodrigo?" she said. "Rodrigo, can you hear me?"

Small waves still broke inside her as she reached for the cup and brought it again to his lips. He took three deep swallows.

"Dreaming," he muttered, looking directly at her. Then he lay back, fast asleep.

For a long time she lay watching him, counting each breath. Then a smile curved her lips. Dawn had arrived. His forehead felt almost normal to her touch. She rose, a song bursting silently from her lips, and drew on her riding dress, laughing with chagrin at her shortsightedness as she tried to fasten it behind her and found she could not.

She went to the flap of the tent and peeked out. Valdéz still slept by the coals of the fire. Rojo's head was up, alert.

"Rojo." She motioned to him. When he came to the door, alarm in his eyes, she stepped aside and turned her unbuttoned back toward him, lifting her hair. She heard his sharply indrawn breath.

"Fasten me, Rojo, and if you forget your manners, Rodrigo will likely kill you. He is going to live."

Glancing across her shoulder, she saw the bearish man's slow look toward the bed, and then the dawning of his understanding grin, which set her blushing.

"I doubt he would have the chance to kill me, Doña Catherine. I expect you would beat him to it."

Beaming with relief, the red-haired soldier began to play his role as lady's maid.

Rodrigo slept the next day through, but his slumber now was a natural one in which he sometimes sighed and shifted. When the campfires were lighted his eyes finally opened and rested with wonder on Catherine, seated beside him.

"Preciosa?" he questioned hoarsely. His eyes moved slowly around the tent as if to establish his surroundings. Rojo, standing by the door, threw back his head and roared.

"How soundly you sleep, Rodrigo. I swear Doña Catherine has wasted her nursing skills on you."

Catherine felt her cheeks blaze as Rodrigo looked in bewilderment from one of them to the other.

"I have been dreaming—such dreams," he said, raising a hand to brush his eyes. His gaze returned again to Catherine. "How did you get here?"

"I brought her," spoke up Valdéz. "And I tell you, captain, never has a woman been a better rider."

Catherine waited uneasily for the question of how they found their way, but her husband sighed and closed his eyes.

"I'm thirsty," he said.

Throughout the weeks which followed, Rodrigo's recovery was slow but certain. He was visited by Father Gasca and the archbishop, as well as the bishops of Quito and Cuzco. Catherine felt a growing awe for the authority arrayed behind the humble Father Gasca.

When her husband took his first steps she was on his arm, and as their daily walks grew longer she struggled to find a way to speak the words of love which had come so easily when he lay unconscious.

They eluded her. Sometimes she asked herself if Rodrigo

could not see the depth of her feelings when they lay together at night in the silent tent. He could not yet support himself on his injured shoulder, but his appetite for her raged hotter than the fever which once had held him. Turning her away from him, he rolled onto his side and entered her. She did not object, though the act so performed was almost certainly unchristian, and despite the fact it caused a blinding pain against the wall of her womb.

The day arrived when Rodrigo, his face paling with the effort, was able to heave himself onto Boabdíl. They rode to a spot not far from the camp where water ran in a sparkling stream down an outcrop of rocks and filled a pool waist high. Many such a bathing spot had been constructed by the Indians in days gone by.

"Ah, if only summer were here, *preciosa,*" murmured Rodrigo, pulling her toward him. "How I should love to see you standing there like some pagan goddess!"

His lips brushed across her mouth and Catherine felt the quick response which his touch never failed to arouse in her.

"I am—so grateful we are together," she said as tears glossed her eyes.

He turned Boabdíl back toward the camp.

"Tell me," he said, almost too casually, "did I say anything while I lay senseless? Did I—speak any name?"

Uneasiness was evident in the question.

"No, none," said Catherine. After an interval she could not help asking, lightly, "And Francisca? Is she well? Did she not join Father Gasca?"

They did not look at each other now. They were as awkward as children.

"She joined Father Gasca," said Rodrigo, "but she did not stay. Her health was not good, nor her humor either. She returned to Lima."

An awful pressure descended on Catherine's stomach. "Was she—with child?" she asked.

Rodrigo turned his head to look at her reflectively.

"Yes," he said slowly. "Yes, perhaps that was it."

There was such a studied indifference to his tone that she could not believe it genuine. They finished their ride in silence, seeking refuge in the bustle of the camp.

Catherine had come to feel at home amid the tents and rough jests of the soldiers. She was treated everywhere with courtesy, and it had not escaped her notice that she was regarded with a certain awe for the ride she had made. Spring was approaching. Rodrigo's shoulder was healing into a satin scar. Soon, she knew, she must be leaving.

Often, when she was alone, her mind moved with sick uncertainty to thoughts of Francisca. Then she hurried to Rodrigo. Never had he spoken to her one word of affection. He seemed glad enough now for her company, but when the war was over, would he return to her?

"I hear the English fry their eggs in butter instead of oil," said Leonor one noon as they sat around the cook fire.

The four of them laughed—Rodrigo, Catherine, Leonor and her cavalryman—laughed at the thought of such a barbarism. Catherine liked the cavalryman. He was clear eyed, tall and gentle. His hand rested often on Leonor's shoulder. They talked now of marriage, and of staying in Cuzco, a city which would surely be kinder to Leonor, Catherine thought.

Rojo stretched lazily in the sunshine and Valdéz grinned. It was a lovely day.

"Eh, Valdéz, we scarcely see you these days," teased Rodrigo. "There must not be a horse in camp you have not put shoes on."

"Or there will not be, if Father Gasca has his way," chimed in Rojo. "I have heard the good priest say you can do the job in half the time of any other man in camp."

"We shall have to make you part of the army," said Rodrigo with a wink.

Valdéz, grinning above his scruffy beard, gave a shake of the head.

"The army is not for men of my ilk," he said. "My knees grow weak at the very thought of battle. Why, even the mere thought of being in these mountains made my beard turn gray when Señor Sanchez left us on our own at Vilcas."

Silence crashed into the little group like a boulder from the mountains above. Catherine felt the arm around her grow rigid. Leonor's face had paled and Valdéz, aware of what he had said, was ashen.

His jaw locked in a dreadful clench, Rodrigo rose. Without a word he started back toward the tent, his steps long and hard. Catherine ran after him, heart thudding against her throat.

"Rodrigo, wait!" she cried.

In a flash she recalled running after him in the camp outside of Lima. She had been too late then, and he had ridden off to this place and almost to his death. She called again and he whirled at her.

"Why did you not tell me Sanchez was with you?" he snarled, eyes blazing.

She was angry and frightened at once.

"Because I knew this is how you would receive the news!" she answered, flinging a hand out in despair. "I knew you would think us guilty of—of—"

"What am I to think?" he interrupted harshly. "What, when you took such pains to keep the matter secret?"

They were at the tent. He caught her by the arm.

"You have had the best of both worlds, have you not, my fine doña? Here in the camp you are applauded as a courageous and devoted wife. There on the trail you could bed with a gentleman, which you have always desired in preference to the lot which fate cast on you."

"I did not—"

"Do you think I care? I own you and Sanchez does not. That is all I care about. As for pleasure, I have had more from the rump of many a tavern whore. They, at least, do not traffic in lies!"

Catherine's slim body shook with rage, and with the terrible wounds left by his words.

"Go to hell!" she whispered.

Jerking aside the tent flap she stepped inside. Blood pounded at her temples. She did not even hear her husband's footsteps leaving. For many minutes she could think of nothing rational, only of what he had said.

Tears wet her cheeks. She drew her sleeve roughly across them. He did not own her. She would show him that. And to think how near she had come to confessing her love for him!

She snatched up the fur-lined cape which lay on a chest in the tent. With quick, precise movements she fastened it and collected her purse. She flung back the tent flap, chin set against any opposition which she might encounter, and finding the way was clear she began to walk with swift steps toward the rope enclosure which held the horses.

Doctor Palacios Rubios' roan came at once to her call. There were no men about, and she went unobstructed to the lean-to where the saddles were stored, finding the one she wanted. The effort to swing it aloft required her entire strength, but it took her mind from the tent, from Rodrigo. The roan, though of restless disposition, did not pull away, and the saddle settled onto him. Catherine, in what seemed to her an act of violence, brought her knee up sharply against his belly, jerking the saddle girth with both her hands. The horse gave a grunt. She tested the saddle and found it secure.

"Catherine! Catherine!"

Looking around she saw Leonor in the distance, running toward her. If Leonor came, then others might follow. She gathered the reins of the roan, berating him as she attempted to put a foot to the stirrup unassisted. The horse moved and she struck him smartly on the flank. He stood still, and she, with another effort, gained her seat just as Leonor caught up with her.

"Catherine, what are you doing? Where are you going?" gasped her friend. Leonor snatched at the reins and held them when she would have turned away.

"Please do not delay me, Leonor. I am going back where I belong—to Lima!"

Leonor's eyes were wide with concern.

"Alone? Oh, Catherine, be sensible! Whatever has happened just now between you and Rodrigo is passing—a husband's anger."

"I have had enough of his anger," said Catherine, white lipped. "Now stand aside."

A moment more Leonor hesitated.

"Oh, Catherine . . . my dearest friend," she said in broken tones, and then her fingers fell free of the reins.

Consumed by a violence she did not know was in her, Catherine kicked the roan and kicked him again. He leaped to a full gallop, leaving the camp behind. There was a shout and then another, but Catherine did not slack her pace. She did not look back toward the place where she had been, and she could not see the road ahead for the tears which ran from her eyes.

Images formed in her mind of the horse beneath her hurtling from some mountain trail, or stumbling at this breakneck speed in the flat road ahead of them, bringing her to a welcome end. She gave the roan his head. Her heels urged him to yet a faster pace. It would have been a simple matter to fling herself from the saddle, but the instincts of a skillful rider held her in place, though her muscles as the miles passed began to cry out at the punishment she was giving them.

Even then she slowed only to spare the horse. She was

fleeing not only her husband, but a life now grown intolerable. She longed to die there in the desolate mountains, but a cynical wisdom told her fate did not grant such favors.

Wearily she leaned her head against the horse's neck to clear it. They started on again. The sun was a great ball of orange when they reached the swaying bridge where Alonzo had left them.

At thought of his gentle devotion, Catherine passed a hand across her eyes. She remembered the moment when she had reached Rodrigo and thought him dying, and the desperate fear which had gripped her then was once again her companion. Her lips quivered with a grief which was deeper than anger, but no tears were left her. She was dry inside, empty. Rodrigo had said that he owned her—that that was all which mattered. Dusk was falling as she crossed the bridge. She could not see the road. She did not care.

The movement of the horse beneath her hypnotized her. She swayed untidily in the saddle, and a warm and welcome numbness began stealing over her, making thought unnecessary.

When the roan horse neighed and stopped abruptly of his own accord it startled her. At first she did not understand. Then she was aware of the two men staring at her and a voice was speaking.

"A lady on this road at night? Alone? Why, it must be the one we have heard about who rode to join her husband! She is pale. She is ill. Go quickly and tell my wife to prepare a bed for her."

It seemed to be some other woman who was received, and fed beside a great fire, and put to bed. But when she awoke next morning, Catherine found herself immediately in the cruel grip of reality. Day was well established. The *encomendero*'s wife who had received her stood looking down at her, frowning.

"Your husband arrived before the stars had faded, hunting you," she said.

Catherine felt her lips tremble.

"Rodrigo?" she let herself hope for a moment that he regretted his words . . . that he had not meant them. "Is he—is he downstairs?"

Her hostess wore the expression of one caught between disapproval and pity. She shook her head.

"He would not stay," she said. "He would not even take

wine. He asked if you were safe, then turned away. He left no message."

Catherine's blue-green eyes turned to the window. There had been a message. Rodrigo had left her there alone. That was his message.

37

Conceived in a tent, in unorthodox coupling, Rodrigo's child was growing inside her. Catherine still could not believe the miracle. But for every breath of joy, she drew ten of despair. What if Rodrigo did not rejoice on learning he would have an heir? What if he only sneered at any child her body produced? She could not bear for this child to mean as little in Rodrigo's life as she did. While Ana and Magdalena fluttered around her in a state of constant happiness, her heart was sore.

"Does the tale not interest you?" asked Ana, putting aside the book from which she had been reading aloud in this hour before bedtime.

"No—that is, yes. It is most agreeable. Please continue."

Ana's light voice filled the *sala familiar* and Catherine returned to her thoughts. March was waning. Had Father Gasca not yet led his men to battle?

The door popped open and Magdalena entered, her dark eyes pools of hate.

"Señora—" she said hoarsely. "Señora, Don Luis is here."

Catherine's heart beat like a horse's hooves on rocky road.

"Here. . . ." she said slowly. "Here in this house?"

The housekeeper's head bobbed.

"Yes. Outside. He demands to see you. He—says he brings an interesting tale from Granada, and that you will not turn him away."

Catherine felt the blood drain from her. That messenger sent to Spain so long ago . . . what had he learned?

Ana had listened with perplexity. Her voice, when she spoke, however, gave evidence she knew she must protect her mistress.

"Doña Catherine is not dressed for receiving guests," she said with a quick look at Catherine's unadorned lawn underblouse.

"It—it is no matter," Catherine faltered. "I must see him."

The maid stared at her, and Catherine saw her fear increasing. She gave an impatient gesture. Magdalena moved, turning slowly toward the door.

Catherine did not deign to take her feet from the stool on

which they rested. She let her posture speak her contempt as the door swung open and Don Luis stepped into the room.

Contempt alone was not sufficient to still the panic breaking in her as she met the cold and gleaming triumph of his eyes.

"Señora de Valdivia, you are so kind to receive me," said her old enemy with a mocking flourish of his cape.

"Indeed? I was led to believe I had no choice," said Catherine, determined to keep her fingers from drumming nervously on the arms of her chair as they were inclined to. "Please state your business briefly, Don Luis."

His raised eyebrow moved higher still. His gaze bored into her, divesting her of any shield, of decency itself.

"Ah, but it is a matter deserving of privacy, madam—for your ears alone," he purred.

He hoped to torture her, to see her writhe, completely in his power, Catherine thought. Whatever damning information he now possessed, he surely did not intend to keep it from the public ear. He sought privacy only to see her suffer more, cut off and entirely alone.

Her soft lips drew together with exquisite dignity. Was she not the daughter of Don Pedro Bautista? He had never bowed to anyone save his monarch and neither would she.

"I think, Don Luis, that your fine concern for privacy is but a pretense," she said coldly. "Do not attempt to frighten me. Anything which you wish to say to me may be said before these members of my household."

His long fingers lightly touched the point of his beard. To Catherine's dismay a cruel amusement flickered in his face.

"I think you will do well, Doña Catherine, this time to do as I advise. If your ladies had knowledge of certain facts contained in this document—" He drew a folded square of parchment from beneath his doublet. "It would place them in a very unpleasant position in the eyes of the church."

The parchment swayed before her eyes like a fat white serpent. She was held mute by her fear.

Don Luis spoke in silken tones. "Dismiss your servants."

She knew what the paper must contain: Some proof of Rodrigo's lack of *limpieza,* of pure christian blood. Suddenly, in defeat, she nodded.

"I—I will stay no matter what the penalty," quavered Ana.

"No—please leave us," Catherine instructed. Her tongue felt flat and dry. "Go to the kitchen. Do not come again until I call for you."

As Ana and Magdalena, with heavy steps and reluctant faces, withdrew, she left her chair and went to stand by the *vargueno*. She put a hand up to the top of it to steady herself. It was Rodrigo's pose, and it occurred to her that by assuming it she sought to imbue herself with some small part of his strength. Whatever had passed between them, she knew she must defend him against this man. The means of dealing with Don Luis flew frantically through her mind. Bribery? No, there would be others to pay as well. Reliance on public opinion to defend Rodrigo's name? Such defense never came in questions of *limpieza*. She must win enough time to plan her strategy, she told herself as the door closed and Don Luis turned.

He came to stand before her, nodding twice before he spoke.

"Well, Doña Catherine." The title was a jeer. "I have waited long enough for my revenge. You will rue the day when you spurned my attentions."

As he spoke he stretched an insolent finger out to twirl the curl at her temple. She struck his hand away angrily.

"I am well aware you sent Sotelo to Spain in hopes of finding some hint of scandal involving my husband. I am also assured by various men of this city that he would not hesitate to fabricate such information, and that his word is regarded as next to worthless. Speak if you wish, but you will find me little moved by whatever you say."

The man in the black brocade suit seemed momentarily taken aback by her assessment of Sotelo's credibility. Self-sureness returned to him almost at once.

"You make an admirable show of courage, but alas, poor Sotelo is not here to have his honesty questioned. He died in Panamá. But not before arranging to have this paper he witnessed delivered to me. Forgive me, but I would not entrust it to your white hands, Doña Catherine. Shall I tell you its contents?"

"Please do," she answered, stiff lipped.

He made a half circle around her, and Catherine was forced to relinquish her hold on the open *vargueno* to keep her face toward him.

"It is the statement of an aged hag of Granada attesting to a birth with which she assisted, not of your husband, but of a certain woman of the lower class who was his mother. The youngest of seven children she was, all born of a pretty little

365

slave girl who was purchased when Granada fell to their Catholic Majesties—and who was half Moorish!"

Catherine heard without flinching, though inwardly she shrank. It was not Rodrigo and this taint of a heathen faith which she rejected, for she felt a fierce and quickening love for the man who had been forced to carry this secret in the darkest recesses of his heart. It was rather the destruction which it promised for all his dreams. A senseless destruction which would ignore Rodrigo's valor, his loyalty to Spain, his deep devotion to the church—all which he was—and condemn him for his ancestry, which he could not control.

"Unfortunately, the hag too has died and cannot recant her statement, should any court of the Inquisition ever wish to question her," said Don Luis.

"No doubt your messenger saw to such precautions," said Catherine with disgust.

He gave a small bow of agreement.

Catherine's fists were clenched at her side. She couldn't think of any way to stop the coming disaster. She could only resist.

"And when shall I expect them to arrest me, Don Luis? Are there soldiers of the church already downstairs? Does a council wait?"

"Ah, no." He took a step toward her. "It is absurd the number of times that you have slipped between my fingers, you and your upstart of a husband both, when by every right I should have ruined you. The night the viceroy came here . . . the fire at the stable . . . surely you can see such luck was not to last forever. And now, when I have waited so long to see you separated from your pride, I could not bear to have the moment snatched from me before I drained it of its sweetness. I will go directly to Father José with this evidence, which I have collected as a public service. Perhaps in the morning, perhaps tonight still. But first there is one small matter of business to finish between the two of us."

His hand fell insultingly into the valley between her breasts and moved to one side, crushing her painfully. In his other hand she saw the glimmer of a dagger.

"If your servants intrude upon us, dear lady, they shall have their throats slit," he warned with false pleasantness.

A vision of him plunging his blade through her weakwilled brother sprang to her memory as if Juan's blood had flowed but yesterday. Darkness clouded the back of her brain, threatening her senses, but she pushed it back. The point of the dagger slit through layers of lawn, exposing her breasts. It moved to the heavy blue silk of her skirt and she smothered a cry, not for what was befalling her, but for its nearness to the baby in her belly, scarcely an inch removed from the gleaming steel.

A calm born of desperation flowed through her. She must protect Rodrigo's baby. And she knew what she must do.

The sight of her body had aroused her attacker. His cold gaze ravaged her nakedness. With vicious glee he squeezed one breast as if to burst the nipple at its tip. Grinding a knot of expectant flesh into her thighs, he fumbled with the fastenings of his breeches.

Catherine gave a low moan and sank back against the *vargueno,* ceasing her struggles. The tactic gave her the momentary advantage she desired, and as he grunted satisfaction she slipped sideways, around to the open front of the writing desk. He caught at her with a curse. Seizing the arm she had raised against him, he twisted it up behind her while her other hand, pinned behind her, flailed helplessly amid the papers on the desk.

But the hand which thrashed and fumbled was hunting something. Somewhere under the papers lay the dagger which she had once attempted to turn against Rodrigo. It had long ago been replaced and resigned to no further use than opening letters. Perhaps it still was sharp enough to kill a man.

Too late, too late. Don Luis tossed his own weapon onto the floor and opened his breeches. His flesh came up against her, pressing, nudging. In another instant he would enter.

Catherine's desperate fingers swept sideways in a great arc and she felt the sudden cold of metal. Groping, shaking, she found the hilt of the dagger.

Don Luis drew back the little space required to complete her humiliation, and as he did, Catherine poised her arm. This time she knew where to strike. The steel blade sank in below the heavy leather of the corset protecting his chest. With all the strength of her body she drove it up, up, twisting it, for if she could not reach the heart, she could perhaps disable him so that he could not stagger from the room.

His hands came down heavily, gripping her arm to wrench it away. But even as they struggled she felt his strength abandon him. With a final effort of determination and contempt she shoved him from her, off the carpet, that it might not give evidence of his blood.

He did not die quickly. Clutching her torn clothes about her Catherine watched him writhe before her, snarling and spewing. It was not only blood which oozed from the hole in his belly, but yellow innards. Dazed, she looked down to see the gory dagger hanging from her fingers. She let it clatter to the floor. Did anyone know he had come here? If not, Rodrigo's secret, his half-Moorish grandmother, was safe.

And I have avenged you, Juan, she thought. She had made good her vow.

When Don Luis lay still, his eyes fixed on some vision of welcoming hell, she tied her clothes crudely together and went onto the gallery.

"Ana. Magdalena," she called tonelessly.

Their ears had been straining for any sound, for they came at once. They were on the gallery, quite near her, before the weak light of torches revealed her disheveled state to them. Magdalena gasped.

Wordlessly Catherine turned from them toward the railing and leaned against it, staring down at the courtyard. Behind her she heard muted voices, exclamations, as the women entered the room where the body lay. There was a light tread and she knew Magdalena stood behind her. Straightening, she turned.

"You must go and lie down, Doña Catherine," said the housekeeper with worried frown. "You must let us care for you."

"No." In the starlight Catherine was slim and pale, and for all the women serving her knew, not shaken in the least. "No, I have killed a man, and by morning I intend to have buried him. It—it is the only way my husband and I will ever be safe."

Ana stepped forward. "Then we will help you—and our lips will be forever sealed."

Catherine looked anxiously to Magdalena and saw on her face the affirmation of Ana's words. She could not afford, now, the emotion which such loyalty produced. There was much to be done.

"Belita Valdéz and the kitchen maid," she asked briskly, "where are they?"

"Asleep, Doña Catherine," answered her housekeeper promptly. "The kitchen maid in her corner and Belita in her room."

"See that they stay there."

"Oh yes, Doña Catherine. The kitchen maid will not stir

while it is dark, and I will go to Belita's room and order her not to leave."

"First help Ana drag the—the body downstairs. Blood will wash easier from the tiles of the courtyard than from the floor where he lies now." For the first time it sank into the depths of her mind that she was a murderess. She pushed the thought aside and continued, planning as she spoke. "Wake Mateo. Tell him to take Don Luis's horse to the plaza and turn it loose. Tell him he must not be seen. . . ."

As they moved to obey and the body of Don Luis was dragged past her, she recalled the paper in his doublet. With her bloodstained fingers she removed the statement of Rodrigo's impurity. Walking swiftly to her room she lighted a candle and fed the document to its hungry flame.

The door opened behind her. Ana came in with water and Catherine freed herself of the traces of the man who had so long been her enemy.

"Lay out but a skirt and bodice for me," she instructed. "Then go and burn these clothes."

Ana's face showed signs of stress, but she did as instructed. When Catherine reached the courtyard she found Magdalena standing with hands on hips and shaking her head. Two torches set in pots of sand illuminated a circle just large enough to include the two of them. The body lay beyond it in the darkness.

"There is no place to bury him, Doña Catherine," said the housekeeper, her face revealed in strange, moving planes of light and shadow. "Every place there is not tile there is grass. If we dig, and someone should look for him, the digging will show."

"But we can fit tile back," said Catherine rolling up her sleeves. "We will take up the stones and then dig."

"But where?" asked Magdalena.

Her mistress looked around the darkness. "There," she said with quick decision. "Beneath the fig tree."

Moving one torch she sank to her knees and began to pry up paving tiles.

"Señorita, you will ruin your hands!" objected Ana, kneeling across from her. "They are so soft and fine! They were not meant for work like this."

"The night is passing," said Catherine. "If we are to hide Don Luis before he is even missed, we must all work."

Ana, with no other argument, began to wrestle with tiles. Magdalena hurried to the stable and returned with a shovel. As soon as sufficient tiles had been removed, she began the difficult task of digging. There was a small sound from the stable.

"Mateo," said Catherine looking up. She sat back on her heels. "Magdalena, ask him to go on yet another errand. Ask him to bring a set of clothing like a man of your own people might wear, not a christian Indian but a—a heathen."

As Magdalena left them, Ana drew an absent hand across her nose and left a trail of dirt. Her eyes were quick with conjecture.

"A set of Indian clothes, señorita? Do you mean to dress Don Luis as an Indian, then?"

Catherine put her hands again to the tile. "I do, Ana. Houses are sometimes sold. Gardens are dug up. It would not do to find the body of a Spanish gentleman beneath this house when it is common knowledge there was ill feeling between Don Luis and us. But the body of an Indian, that might in a little time be laid to the previous occupants of this place. Even the out-and-out murder of such an individual would provoke little interest."

"I will help, then," said Ana.

With a sniff which spoke her scorn she took hold of Don Luis's body and began to strip away its doublet

Magdalena returned and again took up her shovel, but after a time it sank into the earth with less and less force.

"That is enough tile, surely," said Catherine rising. "Here, let me take a turn at this now."

"Doña Catherine, you must not," argued Magdalena, still holding the shovel though unaccustomed to any show of defiance. "If you do lifting, you will risk the child inside you."

If they did not finish their digging, they risked Rodrigo. Catherine held her hand out, knowing that ultimately not one of them dared oppose her. Reluctantly Magdalena passed the heavy tool to her.

It seemed to Catherine that her progress with the dirt was pitifully slow. Her hands, not used to the abuse of heavy work, were quickly raw.

"No more, señorita. We will finish," insisted Ana at last. She plunged the shovel into the hole appearing at their feet, and though she staggered with the effort, she quickly steadied herself and swung it again.

By the time Mateo returned with the clothes, a shallow grave was ready. Magdalena met her son in the stables and ushered him around the darkened margins of the courtyard to their room, careful that his young eyes had no chance to detect what was underway there in the darkness.

"Now," the housekeeper said when Ana had pulled the clothes onto the stiffening corpse. "There is one thing more."

Reaching into her pocket she drew out a pair of scissors and, kneeling, she began to cut away handfuls of the beard which Don Luis had kept so finely trimmed. When she had finished she brought a sharp knife from the kitchen and scraped his face clean.

I have no qualms about what I have done, thought Catherine with shock, looking down at him. She had hated the man who lay dead. She felt no guilt. She had wondered how Rodrigo could kill without remorse in battles, in duels, and now she understood.

Above them in the sky the stars began to fade. By shovel and by hand the three women filled in the grave and covered over the beardless body in Indian clothes.

"I will set the tiles back," promised Magdalena stooping to the task. "Now go and sleep."

But first Catherine made her way back slowly to the room with the *vargueno*, looking for signs of the night's events which must be obliterated.

"There is blood on the stairs yet," she said, pointing.

Ana nodded. "I will scrub them."

At the door to the *sala familiar* Catherine paused and looked around. Such an ordered room. It gave little evidence of what had happened there.

Suddenly her eyes fell on the dagger, covered with blood, which she had dropped. A wave of nausea rose in her, and leaning against the frame of the doorway she succumbed. When she had finished she cleared her throat and spit.

"Get rid of the knife," she said. "And see that every floor in the house is scrubbed clean by morning."

At her usual hour Catherine prepared to go to Mass. Sooner or later Don Luis would be discovered missing. Sooner or later there would be questions directed at her. It remained to be seen how closely those questions were pressed.

As she was drawing on her gloves, her ear caught a knock at the gate. She stood there waiting in the middle of her room for Magdalena's summons.

"Who is it?" she asked when the housekeeper knocked.

"The mayor," said Magdalena. "And two members of the Cabildo are with him. He asks to see you."

She nodded. Fleetingly she touched her waist, its increasing girth as yet scarcely discernible. She walked the length of the gallery and descended the stairs.

"My lord mayor," she said in greeting.

The mayor, a round little man, shifted uncomfortably from foot to foot.

"Señora de Valdivia, forgive our intrusion. I see you are going out. But you see, señora, Don Luis de Alvarado has disappeared."

The courtyard sparkled fresh and clean. Water splashed in the fountain and the sweet orange and the fig tree nodded branches in the breeze. Catherine's voice was softer than the sounds about her.

"Has he?"

Again the mayor shifted. He peered at her intently.

"It has been suggested that you might know something about it, señora. His horse was seen near here last night."

Catherine smoothed her gloves. Beneath the leather a tender blister broke and ran.

"No, I'm afraid I know nothing," she said.

A moment more the mayor peered at her. He sighed.

"Thank you, señora," he said, his plump face bunching in relief.

38

In late afternoon, in the middle of April, all the bells of the city began to toll, not the prayerful notes of vespers, but a wild, unceasing din.

"What is it?" demanded Catherine. There was something frightening about the bells, something savage.

"Perhaps we are finally at war," said Doctor Palacios Rubios.

He and Alma sat in Catherine's sala, along with Don Pedro Molina and his wife and two other couples. A poet from Panamá had been brought in to recite, and afterward there would be supper. Catherine looked uneasily toward the *mirador*.

"I will go into the street and see," said Juan de Vargas, newly elected to the Cabildo. He left the room.

The ringing of the bells continued. Another sound reached Catherine's ears, faint at first and then growing louder, a hum which she could not identify. Finally she recognized it as human voices, so many of them, speaking out of doors, that they blended into a single whole.

"A crowd is forming," she said to Alma. "I am uneasy."

"Do not worry," soothed her friend. "It will be no time at all until Señor de Vargas returns. Then we shall know what is happening."

But Juan de Vargas did not return, and the sky outside the *mirador* was darkening. Her guests were restless. Catherine bid the poet to begin.

While he was reciting there at last came the noise of hurried footsteps. Juan de Vargas came back into the room. He was out of breath and his hat had been knocked askew.

"It is over," he said. "The general is dead. There was no war, no fighting."

Excited voices filled the room, all talking at once.

"No fighting! But how can that be?" cried Alma.

De Vargas drew a breath. "The army of Father Gasca met that of the general near Cuzco. The lawyer Cepeda, relative to the Berruguetes, was to lead the general's infantry, but he turned traitor. When the armies were formed to battle each other, lawyer Cepeda galloped at full speed over to Father Gasca's lines. Other cavaliers followed—a column of arquebusiers—a squadron of cavalry—Pizarro's whole army deserted him, save for a handful of faithful."

Ana, in gratitude, made the sign of the cross and, falling to her knees, began to weep.

"Thanks be to God," whispered Catherine. Yet she could not but feel sorry for Gonzalo Pizarro, whose daring and vigor once had merited better loyalty. She jerked her thoughts back and asked, "How did the general die, then? Did he fall on his sword?"

"He surrendered, Doña Catherine. He was beheaded by the order of the new Audencia, and the old soldier Carbajal was drawn and quartered."

Laughter filled the room, and gaiety. Magdalena, without need of instruction, brought out wine. Catherine felt Alma embrace her.

"How fine that we are already together to celebrate!" said Señora de Vargas in high spirits. "Now, Doña Catherine, bid your poet begin his lines again!"

Catherine made a gesture and settled herself on a stool, but the noise outside was filling her with tension. She did not want to hear poems now. She did not feel like celebrating, for a sadness she could not explain was creeping over her. The war was so remote from these people who were her guests. She felt estranged from them.

Glancing around she saw Magdalena in the doorway, and the housekeeper's naturally dark face was as pale as her own. She got up quickly and crossed the room.

"What is it, Magdalena? Have you heard something? My husband—"

"No, surely he is safe, Doña Catherine," the woman assured her quickly. "It is . . . the city. The crowd. I—I went out too. There are soldiers returning, the ones who brought the news. They have also brought. . . ." She paused and steeled herself. "They have brought the general's head and set it on a pike. I saw it."

Catherine pressed a hand to her throat.

"I have never seen anything like it," said Magdalena sadly. "They are looting the general's palace. Soon they will burn it." She shook her head.

Catherine looked toward the distant street. Gonzalo Pizarro was dead. Beheaded. Father Gasca would rule. As she digested the facts, a yellow glow began to spread against the night sky, verifying Magdalena's prophecy.

All at once Catherine's mouth flew open. The ugly thought

374

which leaped at her held back all sound. When at last she was able to speak she whirled about.

"Doña Isabella!" she gasped. "The mob will kill Doña Isabella if she tries to escape!"

Then she was moving, giving orders, while Magdalena tried to stop her.

"Go into the street and fetch the first man you see. Tell him to saddle my horse and the marquis's gelding. The gelding will get Doña Isabella a few miles outside the city, at least, before his wind gives out."

Magdalena caught her arm and held it.

"Doña Catherine, you are mad! You cannot go out in that crowd, and you cannot ride!"

"I must. She is my friend."

"But your guests—"

"You must not tell them where I have gone. Give them wine. Delay them. Give them dinner."

Quietly she slipped from the room, beckoning to Ana. The poet was still reciting. She put on her riding dress.

"My cape," she snapped, hurrying toward the gallery.

She did not pause to ask who had saddled the horses, or even to look at them. With the reins of the spare horse in her hand she flung herself at the saddle. Shouting to Mateo to open the gate she kicked her horse in the ribs. She reached the street at a gallop, her black cape billowing behind.

The streets reminded her of the night of the viceroy's overthrow. She dodged past men on horseback and milling pedestrians, pressing toward the plaza. At the end of her own street she drew up abruptly, looking with a sick despair at the throngs of people moving in that direction. It would be impossible to make her way through the crowd at anything more than a walk, and at that pace she might be stopped. Turning her horse she thundered back past her own house and up a side street, heading for the perimeter of the city.

There was wisdom in approaching the palace from the rear in any case, she reasoned as she raced along beneath glittering stars. The mob would be in front of the palace. Perhaps she could reach the rear gate unchallenged.

But as she once again neared the plaza, from the opposite side, she found the streets were crowded there as well. Here and there she saw the glint of armor. Returning soldiers. Would Rodrigo be among them? Would he ever come back to her?

She could not pause to think about it, for she was now in

the middle of coarse shouts and revelry. Another horse brushed her own as she tried to squeeze past. From somewhere in the crowd she caught a murmur: "Look, a woman!"

Her nostrils recoiled from the smell of smoke. Looking up she saw the dark back of Pizarro's palace just ahead of her, and from the roof of it, curling orange, were tongues of flame.

There were men everywhere, mounted and afoot, soldiers, laborers, and ruffians from the streets. They were rolling out wine barrels, carrying off chairs and saddles. Their wild, elated cries were the sounds of ravening animals, not creatures of reason. In dismay Catherine watched them spill forth. She could not hope to make her way through their number.

As she sat looking for another way into the palace, a section of wall some distance from the rear gate began to move. An opening appeared there, and almost at once a cloaked figure on a horse slipped through.

It was a woman. With a glance at the looters, Catherine hurried toward her.

"Doña Isabella?" she called uncertainly.

Muffled in black, a face turned toward her. The eyes of the Indian woman were dazed and frightened. She did not speak.

"I didn't know if you would have a horse," said Catherine, drawing near. "Take this one if you need another."

"You came to me," said Doña Isabella in wonderment.

Catherine's smile came slowly.

"To say goodby to you," she said. "I doubt we shall ever see each other again. Now hurry. I will show you the way."

Together they started for the outskirts of the city. When they reached an open stretch of road Catherine halted and pointed. "There, that way will take you past our *encomienda* and into the mountains. You will not encounter soldiers as you might on the road to Pachacamac."

Doña Isabella's hand flew out and met her own in the darkness in a strong and silent clasp.

"Go quickly," Catherine urged.

"Wait." Pizarro's mistress put a hand to her neck and drew off the wealth of gold chains hanging there. "I will have no need of these among my people. Take them, and remember our friendship as I will remember it."

Catherine bowed her head to receive the gift.

"I will remember," she promised.

Long after Doña Isabella had disappeared, Catherine sat

looking after her. Behind her all was din and confusion. She did not want to turn again toward the crowded streets. A great weariness settled over her as she thought of the toll which war had taken. The marquis . . . the marquesa . . . Gonzalo Pizarro.

Reluctantly she turned her horse back toward the city. As she neared her own house, her heartbeat quickened. The gate stood wide and the red-gold glow of torches filled the courtyard. There were voices, too—voices speaking with a loud heartiness not known to the guests she had abandoned. Slowly she guided her piebald mare through the open gate.

The courtyard was a scene of chaos and revelry. A plank table had been spread and it was groaning with food. There were soldiers everywhere. The young rider who had brought her husband's letter to her long ago. A man with short beard whom she recognized from the encampment. Rojo, large and grinning. And Rodrigo.

He stood apart from the others, in the distance, near the stables. He looked at her. His cuirass had been discarded and his white linen shirt billowed softly in the night air. What was he thinking?

She reined, then slowly rode toward him. A hundred memories from their life together rose in her mind: The touch of his fingers on her hair, his laughter drifting from Francisca's house, that moment when they had stood overlooking the wilderness of the *encomienda,* his repudiation of her in Father Gasca's camp. The torchlight crested gold and garnet on his hair. Never had he looked so vigorous and handsome, Catherine thought—or so completely closed to her.

He came a few steps forward and caught her horse's reins. They faced each other without speaking. Her tongue felt wooden, and nailed against the roof of her mouth, unable to move.

Rodrigo's stance was rigid. It was the same one he had assumed in the general's presence. He glanced uneasily toward his companions.

"I'm sorry we have disrupted things," he said. "You are entertaining guests this evening, I am told."

She had forgotten the people upstairs. Her heart shook so she could hardly speak.

"It—it doesn't matter. I give thanks you have returned."

He stood looking up at her. A long interval passed and there was silence.

Abruptly her husband reached beneath his shirt. He shoved a folded piece of paper up into her hands.

"I am going to an inn," he said, and turned away.

In shock she stared at his retreating figure. Her reactions seemed paralyzed. Almost in a stupor she looked down at the paper he had given her, and then unfolded it.

The letters which crossed it were uneven in size and difficult to decipher. But suddenly she knew whose hand had written them, and her heart read where her eyes could not.

My precious Catherine,

I love you, but I dare not stay with you. I have come too near to harming you, trying to force an admission of love from you which was not in your heart.

Forgive me, my dearest Catherine, for the things I have done, and said. I know that if you had ever been unfaithful to me, you would not have chosen to stay beneath my roof, for your loyalty and integrity equal those of any man I've ever fought beside.

But it is not your loyalty which I desire. It is your love. I do not fault you for the lack of it. With my anger and my clumsiness, I little merit such a gift.

So I will leave you in peace. I will provide for this household and all your needs. And if ever, in anything, you need me, I will come.

Rodrigo

She swallowed, shaking with emotion. The humility of the sprawling words had brought the tears to her eyes. She knew, without reflection, the long hours of thought which had preceded this letter and the labor which it had taken for an unsteady hand to write it.

Looking up she saw her husband's back about to disappear into the darkness of the stable.

"Rodrigo!"

She did not know what she would say to him, but she knew that if she lost him now, it would be forever. He turned, reluctantly, it seemed, and the quick trot of her horse as she rode toward him added another sound to the laughter of the soldiers in the courtyard.

Those soldiers seemed a world removed from them. She put a hand out to her husband.

"Help me down."

She saw his dark eyes flash, angry and hurt by what he must perceive as deliberate cruelty. Strained of face, he reached up to her.

Her feet touched earth, and for an instant they stood very close. She opened trembling lips.

"I need you now, Rodrigo. I love you."

A bitter disbelief rose in his eyes. He thought she was being the loyal wife, saying only what he longed to hear. How could she convince him otherwise? As he tried to put her away from him, her slender fingers dug into the folds of his shirt.

"No!" She spoke with force. "You will hear me out this time! I love you, Rodrigo. Even if you leave me now, I shall love you. I would have spoken of it long ago, but I—I thought you wanted only a final victory over me."

He wavered, but still his face was bathed in wary uncertainty. Words alone would not persuade this man of action.

Desperate now, and winding her fingers still more tightly in his shirt, she shook him.

"Listen to me! I have killed Luis de Alvarado!"

Her words were but a whisper. A stunned expression gripped him.

"You— What?"

Her head was thrown back to look at him. She could feel the hard beat of his heart against her own. From the sala there came a cascade of laughter, lighter and briefer than that of the men below. Catherine's eyes, as luminous and unwavering as the stars above them, held her husband's.

"He knew about your grandmother, Rodrigo—and I killed him."

All defenses had abandoned him for a moment. She saw his slow understanding, and his wonder.

"You killed a man? To keep my secret? You could have denounced me publicly. You could have rid yourself of me forever."

She did not stir. His hands still gripped her arms as if to keep her from him.

"But why?" he asked.

"Have I not just told you? I love you, Rodrigo—whatever your blood, whatever your birth."

He frowned, unable to believe what he was hearing. She could not bear the torment in his face. Her hands loosed their hold on his shirt and raised to touch his cheeks, and as they

379

did his dark curls bowed into them. The hands on her arms slid behind her to fold her against him.

"Oh, Catherine . . . Catherine, my precious one," he murmured through his kisses.

His lips touched her eyes, her temples, her hair. The hand which could hold a sword so steadily lay trembling against her cheek.

Sunshine seemed to break over her, and all the birds of Seville sang in her breast as she stood pressed against the strong and regular beating of his heart.

"Tell me that you do not love Francisca, then," she whispered.

He shifted just enough to stare at her.

"Francisca! Francisca means nothing to me and never has. Though she has made offers enough, I have not lain with her since the night you threw me from your bed. Even then—" He stopped and appeared to search for words which would explain. "Even then I went to her only to mend my pride—to prove to myself I still held attraction for other women, if not for you."

Catherine bit her lip, afraid to jeopardize the declaration of love which he had given. Yet what was that declaration worth without assurance?

"But—the nights you were gone—"

"Did that wound so deeply?" His smile was faint and anxious. "Forgive me, then. I had failed to win you—I thought—with kisses and honesty. When the war with the viceroy was done I resolved to treat you with indifference, in hopes that might bring you to me. You assumed I was seeing Francisca, and I thought it would serve you well to endure pangs of jealousy such as I had known. In truth I was with Fray Jeronimo, learning my letters."

His face was so earnest that she knew he spoke the truth. And Francisca's brazen visit had been . . . but the ploy, perhaps, of a desperate woman.

"Francisca is only a woman," said Rodrigo, his eyes caressing her upturned face. "You are something fine and priceless which I should never hope to touch—yet have."

Catherine smiled, and heedless of the men at the other end of the courtyard, raised her lips.

He kissed them only briefly before he drew back laughing.

"But here, my lovely doña—you have endured so much— hear what the bastard Valdivia now is able to lay before your feet! Father Gasca called me to him before I left and gave me

380

a promise. Because I was the first to flee the general's camp, and because I served King Carlos well, the lands entrusted to us are to be increased tenfold. Think on it, Catherine, what lands and herds we shall have!"

Catherine knew, as he spoke, that she was not just a possession, not just a wife, but an integral part of his life, present in every thought and plan. She leaned back in the circle of his arms. Tomorrow she would tell him of the child she carried. But tonight was for the two of them, and the savoring of this newfound bond more precious than lands or gold or even life itself.

Her palms slipped over his chest with wonder, and now, within her, she felt the sharp call of her flesh to his. Rodrigo's breath caught. She saw his eyes grow dark and emberlike with his reply. Beneath her cloak his hands slid upward from her waist.

From the gallery there came the call of Ana's voice:

"Señorita! Your guests! They are growing anxious for dinner."

Rodrigo's head jerked in acknowledgment of the intrusion. Never had desire's spell been so impossible to break, thought Catherine, as now, when it was strengthened by this union running so much deeper. Her eyes were closed and she felt nothing—cared for nothing—but the slow movement back and forth of Rodrigo's thumbs on the soft swelling over her ribs.

"I . . . could dress as a gentleman ought and join you," he said in labored voice.

"Yes."

She could not stand to be apart from him for even that brief time. The prospect of being in a room with him and not touching seemed harsher than a hundred years of purgatory. Her nails dug through his shirt to nudge the slight tips of his breasts.

Her husband groaned. He caught at her hands and imprisoned them, and she could feel the tautness of his body. A strange look crossed his face.

"When I lay sick and senseless in my tent—that was no dream!"

Her eyes had narrowed as the hunger within her grew.

"No," she confirmed.

There was no chance of separating. If they were to couple now, all would be over in a matter of seconds.

"We—cannot remain like this," Rodrigo said hoarsely.

Ana was waiting. A silence had fallen among the soldiers who shared the courtyard with them. Catherine knew they were watching. They could have no inkling, though, of what was passing between Captain Valdivia, disciplined commander, and Doña Catherine Bautista, bred to manners and restraint.

Delight curved her lips as she thought of the solution. Glancing over her shoulder she found Rojo in his armor and a patched shirt, watching, grinning.

"Rojo, will you go up and entertain my guests for me?" she asked.

With a knowing chuckle Rojo bowed.

"Certainly, Doña Catherine. But how shall I explain your absence?"

"Tell them—" She slid her arm around Rodrigo's waist and started with him toward the stairs and the velvet-canopied bed which waited in her room. "Tell them that my husband has come home."

GREAT ADVENTURES IN READING

A NEW DECADE OF CREST BESTSELLERS

☐	KANE & ABEL *Jeffrey Archer*	24376	$3.75
☐	PRIVATE SECTOR *Jeff Millar*	24368	$2.95
☐	DONAHUE *Phil Donahue & Co.*	24358	$2.95
☐	DOMINO *Phyllis A. Whitney*	24350	$2.75
☐	TO CATCH A KING *Harry Patterson*	24323	$2.95
☐	AUNT ERMA'S COPE BOOK		
	Erma Bombeck	24334	$2.75
☐	THE GLOW *Brooks Stanwood*	24333	$2.75
☐	RESTORING THE AMERICAN DREAM		
	Robert J. Ringer	24314	$2.95
☐	THE LAST ENCHANTMENT		
	Mary Stewart	24207	$2.95
☐	CENTENNIAL *James A. Michener*	23494	$2.95
☐	THE COUP *John Updike*	24259	$2.95
☐	THURSDAY THE RABBI WALKED OUT		
	Harry Kemelman	24070	$2.25
☐	IN MY FATHER'S COURT		
	Isaac Bashevis Singer	24074	$2.50
☐	A WALK ACROSS AMERICA		
	Peter Jenkins	24277	$2.75
☐	WANDERINGS *Chaim Potok*	24270	$3.95
☐	DRESS GRAY *Lucian K. Truscott IV*	24158	$2.75
☐	THE STORRINGTON PAPERS		
	Dorothy Eden	24239	$2.50

Buy them at your local bookstore or use this handy coupon for ordering.

COLUMBIA BOOK SERVICE (a CBS Publications Co.)
32275 Mally Road, P.O. Box FB, Madison Heights, MI 48071

Please send me the books I have checked above. Orders for less than 5 books must include 75¢ for the first book and 25¢ for each additional book to cover postage and handling. Orders for 5 books or more postage is FREE. Send check or money order only.

Cost $_____   Name _____

Sales tax*_____   Address _____

Postage_____   City _____

Total $_____   State _____ Zip _____

* The government requires us to collect sales tax in all states except AK, DE, MT, NH and OR.

This offer expires 1 January 82   8158